PENGUIN BOOKS

Prayer for the Dead

Prayer for the Dead

A Detective Inspector McLean Mystery

JAMES OSWALD

PENGUIN BOOKS

PENGUIN BOOKS

UK | USA | Canada | Ireland | Australia
India | New Zealand | South Africa

Penguin Books is part of the Penguin Random House group of companies
whose addresses can be found at global.penguinrandomhouse.com.

First published by Michael Joseph, 2015
First published in Penguin Books, 2015
001

Set in 12.55/15.04 pt Garamond MT Std
Typeset by Jouve (UK), Milton Keynes
Printed in Great Britain by Clays Ltd, St Ives plc

A CIP catalogue record for this book is available from the British Library

ISBN: 978–1–405–91711–7

www.greenpenguin.co.uk

For the Ashprington Crew

Peter, Alice, Jo, Lyle and Io

I

He kneels before me like a penitent, face to the stone wall. The bag over his head means he can't see the indentations in the rock face, the last marks made by those ancient masons so long ago. Their chisels built these caves, a million million strikes chipping away at the slow sandstone, revealing the secrets of their innermost thoughts in the patterns that stretch all around us. There is history here for anyone who takes the time to read it, prophecy too.

'This is the dark place, the warm and the wet. We are here unborn. Waiting.' I pitch my voice higher than normal, occupying the character I've created for this little game. He doesn't answer. Can't answer. His mouth is taped shut. I used the same roll on his wrists, tying them together behind his back. And the funny thing is he let me.

'We await our birth here. Bound and gagged by our previous lives.' I push his head forward, firmly but not roughly. He resists for a moment, but soon bends low to the gritty floor. A channel cut in the rock dribbles a stream of water, leached in from the city up above us. The men who built it knew the secrets of the earth, planned this place so that it would never flood. There are channels throughout, all carefully worked to drain into a sump. From there, the water goes straight down to hell.

'Are you ready to be reborn? Are you ready for the mysteries to be revealed?'

The faintest twitch by way of a nod, felt through my hand rather than seen in this almost total darkness. We brought candles, my new friend and I, but they are over on the far side of this carved room. I look briefly back at them. See mine still burning straight and true, his almost out as it devours the last of the wax, burns out the cotton wick. Not much time left.

'Come, stand, and begin your journey of rebirth.'

I help him to his feet, steady him as he sways a little. He's been kneeling a long time on the cold stone, legs weak. The rope around his neck is too thin for a proper hanging, and too short. A symbol like the many others in this ceremony. I take it up, pull him around.

'The way is dark. The way is not easy. Trust is the only way. Trust in your friends. Trust in your brother.'

The words are nonsense, of course, but they are what he wants to hear. This whole ceremony is for him and no one else. I lead him down the narrow carved passageways, taking care to avoid the lowest parts of the ceiling. Most of them, at least. It's important he suffer a bit, here at the last.

There is a narrow path around the pool, so I can stay dry. For him, the experience is less pleasant. One moment he is shuffling forward, slowly gaining in confidence, the next he is up to his armpits in cold water, struggling to stop himself from going under.

'Do not falter here, at the last.' I tug on the rope and he flounders for a moment before getting his footing, surges up and out of the pool like a performing dolphin in expectation of a fish. His mouth is taped, so he cannot shout, but I can hear his breath forcing its way out of his nose in terrified snorts. He moves his head from side to side as if trying to see where he is. I pull him forward a couple of steps until we are back where we started.

'Come, brother.' The knife is as sharp as I can make it, blade thin and pointed. I slide it out of its sheath and slice the tape holding his wrists together. His hands go immediately to the sack over his head, whipping it off to reveal wide, staring eyes. A glance over to the carved stone table, and I see his candle gutter once, then expire with a little flicker of blue light. It is the sign I have been waiting for.

'Welcome to the brotherhood,' I say as he reaches up and starts to peel the tape from his mouth. In that instant I know that he is ready, his soul shriven and pure. Only corruption awaits, or salvation. Before he can free himself, I run the blade swiftly across his exposed neck, just above the rope. Hard through skin and artery and the crunchy cartilage of throat. Blood wells as he opens his mouth to speak, finds himself unable even to ask why. I can see it in his eyes though, that question writ large. It is not for me to answer him as he sinks slowly to the floor, his life force mingling with the water in the carved stone channel. He goes swiftly to a far better place and all I can do is watch, hope, pray that my time will come again. And when it does that I will be found as worthy as he.

2

'You got a minute, Inspector?'

Detective Inspector McLean slowed his stride more in surprise than from any desire to talk to the person who had appeared, as if by magic, beside him. He'd been hoping to have a chance to clear his head of work-related thoughts before his meeting. Fate would appear to have had other ideas.

'Ms Dalgliesh. Thought you'd be down at the Parliament. Isn't there supposed to be some new angle on the independence vote today?'

'Today and every day. Doesn't sell papers, so my editor's no' interested.' Dalgliesh wore her trademark long leather coat despite the muggy afternoon heat. An unlit cigarette dangled from her mouth, which meant she wanted something from him. Had it been lit, then chances were she was just paying a courtesy call before digging the knife in.

'Heard you'd caught that gang of scallies pickpocketing all them tourists come for the Festival.'

'That more interesting to you than politics?'

'Anything's more interesting to me than politics. Word is they was mostly Eastern Europeans. People love it when you throw in a bit of racial tension. No' just over here stealin' our jobs, but plain stealin' our cash and all.'

'Sorry to disabuse you of your casual racism, but the gang we lifted were all home-grown. There'll be a press

conference tomorrow, maybe Thursday.' McLean quick-
ened his pace, hoping to get to his destination before the
rain came on. And before Ms Dalgliesh could pester him
any more.

'Truth is, Inspector, that's not really what I'm after.
Can't abide all that nonsense myself, but you've gotta do
what the editor says or no bylines and no cash.' Dalgliesh
sped up, keeping time with him, though every third or
fourth step was a skip.

'What do you want then?'

'A favour.'

McLean stopped so suddenly, Dalgliesh was a few paces
on before she realised. She wheeled around and trotted
back as he stared at her, incredulous.

'A favour? Are you serious? Why would I even think of—?'

'Well, I'd owe you, for one thing.'

McLean studied the reporter, looking for any sign that
she was taking the piss. Hard to tell when her perpetual
expression was of someone who'd been pulling a face
when the wind changed. It was true he despised almost
everything she did and stood for, but on the other hand
the goodwill of a journalist, particularly an investigative
journalist with questionable ethics, was not something to
be passed up idly.

'I'm listening,' he said, and was rewarded by a lengthy
pause. Whatever it was that Dalgliesh wanted, she was finding it hard to ask, which had to mean it was important.

'Ben Stevenson. You know him?'

McLean nodded. 'Another one of your lot, isn't he?'

'Aye. You don't need to be so sniffy about it. Ben's all
right.'

'I'm not sure everyone would agree with you. Seem to recall he's not been all that nice about my boss in the past.'

'Dagwood? There's nothing worth digging up on him. Might be a buffoon, but he's one of the straightest coppers I've met.'

'I was thinking more about Jayne McIntyre, actually. She might've been Assistant Chief Constable if your friend Ben hadn't run that piece about her family life.'

'Aye, well, there is that.' Dalgliesh had the decency to look embarrassed, for all of two seconds. 'Still, she'd've bin wasted up there at the top. Some folk're just meant to be detectives.'

'You're all heart, Ms Dalgliesh. And so's your ghoul of a friend. Goodbye.' McLean turned down East Preston Street, heading towards the remains of his old tenement block and his meeting with the developers trying to renovate the site.

'He's gone missing,' Dalgliesh called out after him. 'Ben. He's disappeared.'

McLean stopped. Hardly surprising that a journalist might go off the radar for a while; it was the nature of their job, after all. That Dalgliesh was concerned enough to come to him made it far more serious.

'What do you mean, disappeared? He gone on holiday and forgotten to tell anyone?'

'Ben's not had more than a couple of days off at a time in five years. He lives the job, can't stand sitting around doing nothing.'

'So he's chasing a story.' McLean knew he was only saying it because he didn't want to get drawn in. He also knew that it was too late for that.

'Chasing a story, aye. But it was here. In the city. Told me it was going to be big, too.'

'He say what it was about?'

Dalgliesh leaned against the wall as she lit her cigarette. Took a deep drag and held on to the smoke for a few seconds before letting it go. 'And let someone like me pinch it? Don't be daft.'

'So how do you know what he was up to?' McLean glanced across the road, where a shiny black car had just double-parked. No doubt his developer arriving for their meeting.

'I'm a journalist, aren't I?' Dalgliesh said. 'Sticking my nose in other people's business is what I do.'

'So you reckon Mr Stevenson's got himself into trouble, then?'

'Well, he's no' bin seen at work for almost a month. He's no' answerin' his phones. He's no' bin home and his ex hasn't heard from him in six weeks.'

'His ex? Why would she care?'

'Coz he's meant to have custody of their wee girls alternate weekends. No' like him to miss that, apparently.'

The car had disgorged two suited businessmen who were even now donning hard hats and being shown in through the front door.

'I'll look into it as soon as I can, OK?' McLean dug out his phone, jabbed at the screen until it brought up the notebook function and tapped out a badly misspelled note to remind himself. 'Right now I need to be somewhere else.'

Dalgliesh smiled, a sight so alarming McLean thought for a moment her head was going to crack open and reveal something rotten inside. 'You're a star, Inspector. I'll send over all the stuff I've got already.'

Visions of his desk, legs already buckling under the weight of unattended paperwork. He really didn't need more piling up.

'I'm not promising anything, mind,' he said. 'And if this friend of yours turns up with a tan and a new girlfriend, you'll owe me double.'

He'd been avoiding the place. Hiding from the emotional turmoil it represented; that's what Matt Hilton would say. Perhaps he'd be right, but mostly it was just that his old flat in Newington was a long way down the ever-growing list of priorities. Of course, that didn't explain why he'd not done anything about the letters from his solicitors or from the developers trying to acquire the site, why he'd been ignoring calls about the matter for weeks now.

It was a simple problem. He owned a share of the site because he'd owned one of the tenement flats that had been destroyed by the fire. A sharp development company had managed to buy out most of the other shares, but they couldn't do anything without his say. They'd offered him money, quite a lot of money, for a quick sale. There really wasn't any reason why he shouldn't have taken up the offer and walked away from the place. But he couldn't bring himself to do that.

The senior partner from his solicitors had come to the station in person, waited for an hour in the reception area with the drunks and the vagrants and the just lonely, until McLean had come back from a crime scene. That more than anything else had finally persuaded him of the serious nature of the matter. It wasn't something that would go away if he just ignored it long enough, and other people were being inconvenienced by his inaction. His grand-mother would have been appalled at his rudeness.

And so he was here, back in Newington for an on-site meeting to discuss the redevelopment. Perhaps the build-ers thought seeing what they had planned would sway his mind. Certainly seeing the facade still there, shored up with scaffolding, its windows empty eyes on to the sky behind, brought everything into focus. The front door was the same, too. The paint faded a bit, the number gone, but it was even propped open with a half-brick, just like the students downstairs had always done in times past.

'Detective Inspector McLean?' A voice behind him. McLean turned to see a man in a dark suit, black shoes polished until it was almost painful to look at them. He was wearing a hard hat, but otherwise could easily have been mistaken for a banker or accountant.

'That's me. Mr . . . ?'

'McClymont. Joe McClymont.' The dark suit held out a hand to be shaken. McLean took it, surprised at how firm the man's grip was. His skin was rough to the touch, too. Hands that did more work than pushing a pen around.

'Sorry I've been a bit difficult to pin down. Only so many hours in the day.'

'Well, you're here now. Why don't we go in and have a look at the plans.' McClymont didn't try to pretend it was no big deal his project being delayed months, McLean noticed. He just headed into the building, assuming he would be followed.

Apart from the lack of roof, the entrance hall was remarkably similar to how he remembered it, possibly a bit cleaner. Rain had washed the large flagstones, and the extra ventilation had managed to remove almost all trace of a hundred and fifty years of cat piss. At the back of the hall, the staircase only climbed a dozen or so steps now, the rest of the building having been cleared away beyond the top of the ground floor walls. McClymont stepped through an opening that would have been Mrs McCutcheon's front door, then down a set of new steps where the back wall had been and into the communal garden. A couple of Portakabins had been craned in to form a site office, but McLean took a moment to turn and look up at the back of what had once been his home. All he could see was the inside of the front wall, held aloft by massive steel pillars and braces. Individual flats were marked out by the different coloured walls, and there at the top on the right, the bay window of his front room still with a bit of skirting board hanging on like a drowning man. He'd stripped paint off that board, sanded it until it was smooth, and varnished it. He'd spent hours, days, years in that room, staring out the window or just sitting on the sofa, listening to music, reading a book, sharing pizza and wine with friends, cuddling up with one in particular. The rush of memories made him dizzy.

'We have to keep the original frontage. That's part of the deal with the council. Much easier if we could knock it down and start again, but it wouldn't be the same, aye?'

McLean turned back, seeing another dark-suited man, this one without a hard hat. He was older, grey-haired and thick-set, eyes cracked with lines set deep in leathery skin.

'Joe told me you were here. Come on in the hut and I'll show you what we want to do to the place.'

3

'The front stays the same, but we're going to extend out here into the back by three metres on the first four floors. Fifth will have a balcony looking out towards Salisbury Crags and the top two storeys will be twin-level apartments.'

Joe McClymont had A1-sized plans splayed out on a large table in the Portakabin, and a scale model of the development stood in one corner. The old man had turned out to be his father, Jock. Whilst he let the youngster talk, he was quite obviously in charge. McLean couldn't say that he took much to either of them. Despite their outwardly professional appearance, the well-polished shoes, the suits and the expensive car, these two screamed dodgy to him. A third person hovered in the back of the office, a middle-aged lady McLean hadn't been introduced to. She was working at a slim laptop computer, but every so often would look up and eye him with ill-disguised hostility.

'Hang on. Balcony on the fifth and two storeys at the top?' McLean counted on his fingers. He'd not really been paying too much attention, but that detail suddenly hit home. 'You're building a six-storey block here?'

'That's right. Six storeys, aye. Three flats each on the first four, two big apartments spread over the top two floors.'

'How's that going to work? The building's only four storeys high.' McLean glanced over at the model in the corner, then studied it a bit harder. From the front it looked just like the building he knew of old, but then of course it would have to. No way the council would let anyone demolish it if they could make life difficult by insisting it be preserved. No matter that half of the street didn't match anyway.

'See those steps you came down from the ground floor?' Joe McClymont jerked a thumb over his shoulder towards the remains of Mrs McCutcheon's flat. 'We had to underpin all the old walls, front and side. Meant digging down the best part of three metres. You've no idea how much that lot cost, by the way. But it means we've space for a couple of basement flats below the original. They won't get much light from the front, but the backs'll open out on to the gardens. Be great for kids.'

'They'll still be communal, though? The gardens?'

McLean didn't need to be a detective to see the shifty look that passed between the two developers. 'Something like that, aye,' Joe eventually said.

McLean looked back at the plans, paying a bit more attention now. It certainly looked impressive, but he couldn't help thinking the rooms were rather small, the ceilings low. He turned fully and studied the model a bit more carefully this time. The frontage was as it ever had been, but the floors didn't line up with it any more. The facade was just that, and a much more compressed living experience was being created behind it.

'Seems to me you've already done quite a bit of work.'

'Site like this doesn't come up often,' Jock McClymont said. 'You can't sit still in this game.'

'Which brings us to the point of the meeting, really.' This time it was Joe McClymont who spoke, but it was obvious that the two of them had rehearsed their pitch.

'You want me to sell you my share in the site. I know.' McLean paused for a moment, watching the expressions on the faces of the two men. Now that he knew, he could see that they were father and son, but where old Jock had an avuncular look, his face filling out with the years, Joe was thin and hungry. Of the two, he looked the most dangerous, but McLean had been around long enough to know that if he had any trouble it would come from the old man. Behind them, the woman was muttering strange words under her breath as if on the phone to a foreigner. They made his head ache slightly, so he tuned her out as best he could.

'What if I don't want to?'

A distant siren underlined the long moments of silence that followed. Even the woman stopped speaking.

'I don't understand.' Joe's face was creased with genuine bewilderment, as if no one had ever refused to be bought before. 'Why wouldn't you? I mean, what's the alternative?'

'I was rather hoping you might be able to tell me. I mean, it seems a bit presumptuous starting work when you don't actually own the site, doesn't it?'

'We own a controlling share, laddie.' Jock McClymont's gruff but cheerful voice changed to a low growl. 'We've been playing nice so far, what with this being your home an' all. But there's only so much slack we can cut you.'

Interesting choice of words. He didn't really need the hassle all this was going to create, but he also knew better than to fight his own nature. 'What if I just want my flat back?'

Jock's eyes narrowed. 'You want one of the apartments.'

'No. I want my apartment. Top floor left. Shiny blue door. Three bedrooms, proper bathroom and a box room a hard-up student would be happy to live in. I want a kitchen where I can look out over the garden and see Arthur's Seat if I crane my neck a bit. I'll pass on the rusty bicycle frame chained to the railings on the stairs outside, and if there's no lingering smell of cat piss in the entrance that would be a plus.'

Both McClymonts stared at him, their expressions nearly identical. Joe was the first to speak again.

'But the plans—'

'Are a bit rubbish, aren't they?' McLean cut him off. 'Six storeys? Really? How the hell did you get that past planning? All you're doing is leaving the front wall and building a crappy modern box behind it. You really think that's what the city needs?'

'What the city needs is unimportant.' Jock McClymont's growl was even more menacing now. 'We've a lot of cash tied up in this place. More besides. We're not going to let it go just because of you. Top-floor flats are going to cost way more than your share's worth. If you'll no' take the money we've offered . . .'

'I think you misunderstand me, gentlemen. I appreciate the time and effort you've put into all this.' McLean swept an arm around the general area of the Portakabin. 'But what you're proposing . . . I can't begin . . .' He picked up the top sheet of plans, spun it around on the table. 'You need to come up with something a lot better than this if you want me to help make it happen. Now if you don't mind, I've important work I need to get back to.'

McLean stood outside the front door, took a deep breath and looked around the street. It was as familiar to him as his skin, a place he had lived for fifteen years and more before that terrible fire. But that was then and this was now. He had a house, far too big but just as difficult to part with. It wasn't that he needed a place nearer to work, he could have bought one if he wanted. No, it was something much less rational, a feeling that the people who'd lived and died in that tenement block somehow deserved better. More than that, was a growing dislike of McClymonts senior and junior. And finally, the nub of it. He'd been taken for granted. They wanted him to sell up, thought that throwing a little more money at the problem would make it go away. They should probably have made the effort to get to know him a bit better first.

Head down to avoid making eye contact with passers-by, he set off on the walk back to the station, hoping for a chance to get his thoughts together. When his phone started to buzz in his pocket, it wasn't one of the ring tones DC MacBride had programmed into it that he knew he had to answer, and yet something about the trilling gave it an urgency he couldn't ignore. Fishing it out of his pocket, McLean stared at the screen. An international number. No doubt someone trying to sell him some scam financial scheme or get him to part with sensitive passwords for his computer. Intrigued, he thumbed the accept call icon and held the slim handset up to his ear.

'Hello?'

'That's not Gordon. Shit, have I dialled the wrong number?' McLean recognised the voice even though it was far too long since last he had heard it, and couldn't help the smile that turned up the corners of his mouth.

'Seems so, Phil. How's things?'

'Wait . . . What? Tony? Jesus mate. How are you doing?'

'Oh, same old same old. Busy. You know how it is.'

'Tell me about it. Place is running me ragged. American students. They're so . . . what's the word?'

'Committed?'

'Yeah, that's it.' Phil laughed. 'Either that, or they should be.'

'How's Rae? You two not going to be asking me to be godfather any time soon, I hope.'

'Rae's . . .' Phil paused a little too long, out of practice at talking to his old friend the detective. 'Rae's fine.'

'Not taking to California then?' McLean slowed his pace, eking out the time before he reached the station and had to end the call. Then he realised he was in the wrong street, stopped, looked around. He'd started walking home without realising it.

'Damn. Forgot who I was talking to. Yeah. She's not really enjoying it all that much. And truth be told, she does want kids. Just not sure this is where I'd want to raise them, you know.'

McLean didn't say 'and you think over here's any better?', even though he wanted to. It surprised him that Phil would even consider having children, but then it had surprised him when his old flatmate had got married too. People change.

'Might be better off coming home. Who knows? Could be an independent nation in a month or two.'

'Don't joke about it, Phil. The whole thing's a bloody nuisance.'

'You don't think Scotland could go it alone?'

'Could? Aye, course it could. Should? Well that's a question for a long evening of beer and pizza. Probably a bottle of whisky to round it all off.'

'Sounds like a date. Next time I'm over. Listen Tony, it's been great chatting but—'

'You still need to phone Gordon. Whoever he is. Yeah, it's good to hear your voice, Phil. Should call more often. And you know you can, any time, right?'

'Yeah. I will. Maybe see you soon, too.' And with that the phone went dead.

McLean stood at the edge of the Meadows, watched the afternoon walkers, the students lazing on the grass or playing kick-about football. A couple walked past, their young daughter holding one hand each. She swung crazily with every third or fourth step, totally trusting in their grip, certain she could come to no danger. Such innocence was both touching and troubling. Bitter experience had made a cynic of him, but that didn't mean it had to be the same for everyone. He shook his head at the strange thought and the even stranger circumstance that had brought it. A glance at the clock on the corner of the old Dick Vet building told him it was late enough to consider not going back to the station, heading home for a well-deserved evening off.

But that was never going to happen, was it.

4

They always pick on the little ones.

They'd pick on me, only I know the teachers have been talking. Telling everyone about mum and dad. I can see it in their eyes, the way they won't look at me, or speak to me. They want to bait me like they did last term, but something stops them. They still talk about me behind my back, though, just quiet enough that I can't really hear. Johnson and Bain and Cartwright, they know they can't be mean to me, and that just makes them want to do it more.

So they take it out on the little ones.

This boy's new. His folks live in the big house around the corner from mine. Just moved back from overseas, wherever that is. The bullies have been working at him for a week now, and he just won't rise to their bait. That's not good. I learned the hard way. Ignoring them doesn't make them go away, just makes them crueller. He'll learn, but how long will it take? And how badly will they hurt him?

He's in the corner now, surrounded by them. Johnson's maybe a year older than me, Bain and Cartwright my age. They're all big, and stupid. The new boy's tiny. Like he's only four or something. He doesn't really stand a chance. And he lives just around the corner from Gran's house, which is maybe why I step in.

'Leave him be, aye?' My voice wavers as the words come

out. As I realise what I've done. Never draw attention to yourself, that's the first rule.

Johnson turns slowly, his piggy little eyes searching to see who's interrupted him. At first I think he's going to hit me. Won't be the first time, won't be the last. But then he sees who it is, and his face changes. A hint of uncertainty in his frown, a hint of fear?

'What's he to you, McLean?'

'Nothin'.'

'Aye, right. Nothin'.' Johnson pauses for a moment, then slaps Bain on the shoulder, his frown breaking into a grin, making him look like the idiot he is. 'Hey everyone, McLean's a homo. He's got a new boyfriend.'

Bain and Cartwright laugh like it's the funniest thing they've ever heard. 'Homo! Homo!' And they run off down the corridor in search of someone else to pick on.

'You OK?' I ask the boy. He says nothing. Just nods. Eyes still wide.

'Best keep away from them. You're Bale, right?'

He nods again. 'N . . . Norman.'

'I'm Tony. I live just round the corner from your place. You know the old lady who used to live in your house died in her bed? They didn't find her for months.'

It's not true. Well, not entirely. Mrs Leslie did die in her bed, but my Gran was there with her when it happened, and they buried her in the churchyard a week later. 'Hey. I wonder if that's your room now?'

Norman's eyes widen even further, the colour draining from his face.

'Y . . . You think it might be?'

I'm about to answer, tell him it's unlikely, but the bell cuts me off. 'Gotta run. Maths next.'

It's only when I'm in the classroom and opening up my exercise book that I realise I've probably been just as cruel to him as Johnson, Bain and Cartwright.

5

'Hurry up, Constable. I haven't got all day.'

McLean held open the back door to the station, waiting for Detective Constable MacBride to come in. Heavy rain spattered off the tarmac of the car park, bouncing up as high as the constable's knees as he ran from the squad car he'd just vacated. It didn't matter; by the time he reached the door, he was just as soaked as if he'd walked. Or maybe fallen into a swimming pool.

'Bloody hell. Where'd that come from?' MacBride shook himself like a dog as McLean let the door swing closed. Water sprayed liberally around the entranceway, soaking the already slippery floor tiles, the grubby walls and the detective inspector.

'Cheers. That's just what I needed.' McLean slapped his damp folder against his legs, trying to wipe the worst of the rain off it. He'd missed the downpour by seconds, counting himself lucky that seniority meant MacBride had been driving and had to lock up.

'Sorry, sir.' MacBride dipped his head like a serf before a nobleman, then ran a damp hand through wetter hair. It was long, McLean couldn't help noticing. Perhaps a bit too long for regulations, though he wasn't about to say anything. Things were a bit more lax in plain clothes anyway, and there was that other matter . . .

'They still giving you grief about your scar?'

MacBride's hand stopped mid-run, a familiar red tinge blushing his cheeks. McLean could see the mark quite clearly, despite the long fringe of thin ginger hair. If anything the attempt to hide it just brought it more to everyone's attention.

'You know what policemen are like. Bunch of wankers the lot of them.' MacBride patted down his fringe, not quite managing to hide the livid red scar on his forehead. The result of a near miss from a piece of glass blown out of the window of an exploding mental hospital, it formed a perfect lightning-flash mark. Even more so now the tiny dots where the stitches had been had faded.

'Still calling you Constable Potter, I take it?'

'And worse. Like bloody children.'

McLean tried not to laugh. DC MacBride looked like he wasn't long out of school himself.

'They put a cloak in my locker. Must've nicked it from some university professor or something.'

'Could be worse. Knowing this lot they'd probably have hidden a black cat in there if they could find one.'

MacBride looked at him like he was mad. 'A black cat?'

'You know. Witchcraft, covens, that sort of thing.'

'You've not actually read the Harry Potter books, have you, sir?'

McLean shook his head. 'I think I caught some of the film on the telly a while back. Might have fallen asleep before it finished.'

'There were eight films, sir. Not sure even you could've slept through all of them.'

'Is that so?' He tapped the folder against his leg again. 'Well, at least they've got something harmless to focus on.

Pete Robertson gets called all manner of nasty things and he broke his back, poor bugger.'

McLean didn't add that both accidents had taken place on his watch. He knew all too well what the junior detectives and uniforms called him behind his back. Couldn't really say he didn't deserve it half of the time.

'Aye, well. If they put half as much effort into the job as they do taking the piss . . .'

This time McLean did laugh. 'You've been hanging out with Grumpy Bob too long. Beginning to sound just like him.'

'Did I hear my name being taken in vain?'

Both McLean and MacBride turned to see Detective Sergeant Laird approaching from the direction of the station canteen. He had his paper under one arm, a large Styrofoam cup of coffee in his hand and looked like a man in search of an empty incident room in which to snooze.

'All the time, Bob.' McLean held out the folder for the sergeant to take. 'Here. Make a start on collating this lot, will you? I've got to go see Dagwood.'

Grumpy Bob looked nonplussed for a moment, then managed to shift his coffee into the other hand and take the folder. 'Done something wrong, have you?'

'Christ, I hope not. Mind you, with Dagwood you never know.'

'Hear you caught those pickpockets working the Old Town.'

McLean stood in the familiar position, the wrong side of Detective Superintendent Duguid's desk, in the large office on the third floor that had once belonged to Jayne McIntyre. That Dagwood hadn't torn him off a strip as soon as he'd entered put him on edge. It was unusual to be called before the boss for anything other than a dressing down. Mostly he was ignored if he did things well, abused only when he cocked up.

'I'd hardly take credit for it myself, sir. DC MacBride coordinated the operation along with DS Laird. And if anyone deserves praise it's DC Gregg. If she ever gets tired of working here, she'll make a fine actress.'

Duguid stared up at him as if the names only vaguely meant anything at all. It hadn't been that momentous an operation as these things went. Gangs of thieves appeared every year as the city swelled with tourists come to see the Festival and the Fringe. This lot hadn't even been all that well organised; stupid enough to all be staying in the same squat, interested only in the cash and smartphones they nabbed. A tiny tracker beacon in the detective constable's bag had led a team of uniforms right to their door. McLean's total involvement had been approval of the plan and allocation of the budget.

'You'll not get far with that attitude, you know.' Duguid slumped back into his chair, its springs squeaking in protest.

'Far how, sir? In case you hadn't noticed, I've not really been pursuing promotion. I'm happy where I am.'

That brought a ghost of a smile to Duguid's thin lips. 'Happy?'

'Poor choice of words, perhaps. Put it this way. I don't fancy a chief inspector's post, let alone anything higher. Don't suppose I'd get very far even if I did.'

'Aye, well. At least you know your mind.' Duguid fell silent for a moment. McLean was about to ask him what he wanted when he finally spoke again.

'You know I'm retiring. End of the year.' Neither sentence was voiced as a question.

'Yes, sir. You told me back in the winter. At the hospital. When—'

'When those buggers stole my car. Still not found them now, have you?'

It was true. Far more man-hours had been sunk into that investigation than it could possibly justify, and yet no single clue had emerged. It was as if whoever had boxed the detective superintendent in, hauled him out of his beloved Range Rover, given him a swift, sharp kicking and then stolen the car had never existed. Given the other events that had happened that fateful night, DC Mac-Bride's wizard scar the least of them, McLean couldn't help thinking that might well be the case.

'I'm sorry. We tried. Chances are it's in the Middle East now, or Africa. China maybe. Sad to say, but high-end motors get nicked the whole time. Hardly anyone smashes windows to steal a purse or rip out a stereo for the drug money any more, but you park something worth a hundred grand in the street . . .'

'Do I need to remind you it wasn't parked?' Duguid's voice dropped an octave.

'No sir. You don't. But we did what we could, and I've passed what little we found on to the NCA. Something like this is nationwide, not local. We have to let them deal with it.'

Duguid did something that might have been the bastard child of a shrug and a nod, and let out a noncommittal grunt at the same time.

'Was that all you wanted to see me about, sir? Only—'

A knock at the open door interrupted McLean, and he turned to see DC MacBride.

'Constable?' Duguid asked.

'Erm, sorry to disturb you sir. Only I thought you'd want to know. There's been a body found. Out at Gilmerton. Suspicious circumstances.'

As if on cue, McLean's phone chimed. He pulled it out of his pocket to see a text from the control centre at Bilston Glen.

'Looks like they want my unique expertise on the matter, whatever that is.' He held the phone up, angling the screen so Duguid could see it. The detective superintendent shook his head as if he didn't want to know. Or didn't care.

'Go on then. Get out there and see what all the fuss is about.'

McLean said nothing, just turned and headed for the door. He expected Duguid to say something right at the last minute, just to make him stop, but for once he was quiet. As DC MacBride fell in alongside him and they both walked down the corridor in silence, he couldn't help wondering what Duguid had really wanted to tell him. Not about the stolen Range Rover for sure, which meant it had probably been about his retirement, his replacement. Well, there'd been speculation enough, and it wasn't as if he had a say in the matter. Whoever it was, McLean would have to work with them as best he could. It was either that, or a job at Vice.

6

With its commanding position on the hills to the south of the city, overlooking the Castle Rock, Arthur's Seat and the Firth of Forth, Gilmerton ought to have been a fine place to live. No doubt in the past, when the big estates at Burdiehouse and the Drum had been built, the rolling countryside would have lent itself to long walks and summer picnics, at least for the gentry. Now it was a busy intersection on the Old Dalkeith Road, funnelling commuters into the city, or out towards Midlothian and the Borders. Rows of grey-brown houses blocked the best of the views, and a brutal 1970s prefab block housed a couple of boarded-up shops and a library. The only place with any life in it was the betting shop.

DC MacBride hadn't said much all the way out, piloting the car with a grim determination that suggested he was still angry about his scar. Coppers could be as stupidly cruel as kids, McLean knew all too well. Chances were the detective constable had been the brunt of bullying at school as well.

'Park up round the back there.' He pointed to a small opening at the end of the block, and MacBride turned swiftly, gaining himself an angry blare of the horn from a car coming towards them. A couple of squad cars were already hogging the space at the far end of the car park, behind the library.

'Someone said something about a body?' McLean spoke to one of two uniform officers who were leaning against a nearby brick wall. The smell of cigarette smoke still lingered in the air around the one who pushed himself upright, then came over to the car.

'Aye sir. Round the corner past the bookies.' He made a half-hearted attempt to point, a motion that made him look like a one-armed man doing the breaststroke, only without any water to swim in.

'It's a bit casual, isn't it?' McLean asked. 'Shouldn't you be setting up a perimeter? Keeping the public away?'

The constable shrugged. 'It's no' as if anyone can see him, sir. I'll take you there.'

MacBride parked, then the two of them followed the constable back out of the car park and around the corner. Another constable stood by a nondescript black door that McLean might have taken for someone's home. He nodded once, then stepped aside to let them in.

Inside was a dark room with posters hanging on the walls, a small shop counter just past the door. It took McLean a moment to realise that this wasn't a house or a shop, but some kind of visitor attraction.

'What is this place?'

'Gilmerton Cove, sir,' the uniform constable answered. 'You telling me you've never heard of it?'

'Can't say as I have.' McLean peered at the posters on the walls. They were like those in many modern visitor attractions, a series of historical pieces explaining what the place was all about. He had just started reading about the Covenanters when a familiar voice came from the back of the room.

'Had a feeling this would get punted your way, Tony. You do seem to get all the odd cases.'

Angus Cadwallader, city pathologist, stood in an open doorway dressed in his white overalls and, rather incongruously, a hard hat and green wellies.

'I could say the same for you, Angus.' McLean knew better than to shake Cadwallader's hand, especially at a crime scene.

'Ah, but I get to choose my cases. Not have them handed to me by some dispatcher in Bilston Glen.' Cadwallader paused a moment, looked down at his feet. 'Not sure whether that's better or worse.'

'Maybe I should have a look-see and make up my own mind.' McLean peered past the pathologist, seeing an even smaller room than the first. 'No forensics team yet?'

'Oh, they're here. It's just there's not a lot of room. Or air for that matter.' Cadwallader must have seen the bemusement on McLean's face. 'You've really no idea what this place is, have you?'

McLean shook his head. 'Nope.'

'Well, come with me and discover the mysteries of Gilmerton Cove.' Cadwallader stood aside to let McLean step into the small room. 'Might be best if we leave young MacBride behind, though.'

Gilmerton Cove, it turned out, was a series of caves and underground passages, just beneath the pavements and crossroads. For all that Cadwallader had said there wasn't much space, it was surprisingly large. Even more so when McLean was told that it was all man-made.

'No one's quite sure who first carved it all out. Some say

Covenanters, some the Hellfire Club. There's similar caverns up Roslin Glen way, underneath Hawthornden Castle. Probably loads more still waiting to be found.'

McLean listened to the potted history as he climbed into a pair of standard-issue white overalls and slipped paper covers over his shoes. They had descended some steep steps carved into the rock and were now in an arched cavern, piled high with battered aluminium cases filled with forensic equipment. Further on, along a narrow passageway, bright arc lights flooded what would normally be a dark and claustrophobic space. No doubt that way lay the victim, as well.

'Who found the body?' He asked the question before realising that his tour guide for the day was Cadwallader, and not the first officer on the scene. 'Sorry. Habit.'

'I've just been studying it, Tony. Why don't we both go and have a look, eh?'

Cadwallader led the way down a confusing collection of passageways, through strangely hewn rooms, rough rock tables and benches carved from floor and wall. The ground was littered in fine gravel except where water channels had been carved in the bedrock, leading to a sump that drained down to God knows where. Or maybe the Devil. A heavy cast-iron grille covered up the hole, four channels dropping into it from four points, like the points of a compass. Water ran through all of them, fed no doubt by the recent rain. A distinct dampness in the air lent a chill, unpleasant note to the caves. Three of the water channels were uncovered, little rivulets of murky water trickling along them and into the well. The fourth was mostly hidden by a temporary raised walkway installed by the forensics team.

Given the walkway, McLean was sure they must be close to the body, but Cadwallader carried on, through a metal doorway that wouldn't have looked out of place in a submarine, then stooped as the passageway they were following became lower and lower. There were rocks to either side too, as if this area had only just been opened up. Or the ceiling had fallen in recently. McLean had to crouch right down for the last bit, the weight of the rock crushing in on him as if he were Atlas, bringing with it a deep-seated fear that was hard to suppress. Stepping out into the final cavern was a relief. At least for a moment.

The body lay close to the far wall from where he and Cadwallader had emerged. McLean could see that it was a man, a bloody gash ripped from the front of his neck. Another floor channel led from his prone form to a nearby sinkhole, filled with dark, still water. In the half-light, it looked like blood, but no one body could have produced such a volume.

'I'll say this much, it would have been quick.' Cadwallader stepped carefully over to the body and knelt down with an uncomfortable popping of knees. Two white-suited forensic scientists had been carefully examining what looked like another entranceway, piled up with rubble and rocks, nearby. They had stopped what they were doing as soon as McLean had entered and were even now watching him, waiting for him to put a foot wrong so they could tell him off. Even behind their face masks and paper hairnets he could see their scowls. As if anyone as lowly as a detective could hope to glean anything from a crime scene.

'We got an ID yet?'

'Again a question best put to the first officer on the scene. Unfortunately he had to be taken off to hospital.'

'Hospital?' McLean moved closer, keeping his feet firmly on the temporary walkway. There was something horribly familiar about the white face, half mashed into the fine grit of the cavern floor.

'Yes. He threw up, fainted and banged his head on the rock over there.' Cadwallader pointed back towards the door, and as he did so, McLean saw the blood.

It was smeared all over the back wall of the cavern in great swirls and patterns. Sticky black whorls, glistening under the harsh spotlights like the trails of demonic slugs. Stepping backwards to get a better look, McLean let one foot slip off the raised walkway, then caught himself as a harsh intake of breath reminded him he was being watched.

'Are those words?' He tilted his head, trying to make sense of it, failing.

'Best you let us photograph it all. We can use some trick filters to bring it all out nice and sharp.' One of the SOCOs lifted up the camera slung around her neck, just in case he wasn't sure how it was done.

'Good point. Sorry.' McLean bobbed his head, walked carefully back to the body and hunkered down beside Cadwallader.

'Want to hazard a cause of death?' the pathologist asked.

'Thought that was your job. But I'm guessing this.' McLean pointed at the mess that had once been the man's throat.

'Judging by how far the blood's gone, there's probably not a lot left in him. Unless it's been mixed with something to make it run. We'll get a sample for analysis.'

'Killed here though.'

'Best guess, yes. And quite a while ago. Days, maybe weeks. Difficult to judge when the conditions for preservation are so good. I'll know better after the post-mortem. Any idea who he is?'

McLean leaned back, twisted his head around until he could take in the face. Scrunched into the gravel, almost white skin. One eye was obscured, but the other one stared ahead unseeing, glazed over. Fair hair cropped short, light build, difficult to gauge height whilst he was lying crumpled on the ground. He could have been anyone, really, but there was something about the face. He'd seen it recently. No he'd been reminded of it recently. Hadn't seen the man for a while.

'I wish I didn't, but I think I do.'

7

'Nobody's been in there. It was all locked up.'

They'd commandeered the library just around the corner from the little house that hid the entrance to the caves. Soon everything would be moved down to the station, where DC MacBride and Grumpy Bob were busy setting up a major incident room. For now, McLean wanted to get the few witnesses interviewed as soon as possible.

'Locked up? What do you mean?' He was sitting in a small alcove formed by the bookshelves. Across a wobbly table from him, the tour guide from the visitor centre looked nervous and pale, picking at her fingernails and occasionally sliding her spectacles up her nose.

'Do you know anything about the cove?' she asked. McLean shook his head. 'Well, it's an old site, goes back at least a couple of hundred years, probably a lot more. There's passages leading off in all directions from the main complex, but they're all collapsed, or filled with rubble. We'd love to excavate them all, only, well, money's not exactly free-flowing for something like that. And being off the beaten tourist track, we don't make as much as we'd like. There's the problem that some of them go underneath the main crossroads, too. The engineers get nervous.'

'But you did open up that cavern. The one where we found the body.'

'There's a team from the University Archaeology Department. They've been coming out for a while. Using the place to test kit, that sort of thing. They got some money together and were going to do a survey of the blocked tunnels. They opened up that cavern a couple of months back, put the metal door in to keep it sealed off from the public until we could work out if it was safe or not.'

'So no one could get in there?'

'Not unless they had the key. And they'd have needed other keys to get into the caves in the first place.'

'So who has the keys?'

The tour guide pushed her spectacles up her nose again. 'I have a set for the visitor centre and the caves. My son's got one too, and there's a spare set at home. I don't know which of the archaeology team had their keys, but I've never had one. They couldn't get to the door without me or my son letting them in first.'

McLean glanced over to where the archaeology students were sitting. They didn't look old enough to be at university. But then when he'd been that age he'd not looked old enough to be at university either.

'I'll be speaking to them next,' he said. 'But I'm trying to put together a timeline. When were you last open?'

'Us? It's the peak season. We've been open every day over the summer.'

'What about that cavern, then?'

'No, that's been locked, and the archaeology team's been off for a couple of months. Don't think anyone's been in there since June. Well, apart from . . .' The tour guide swallowed hard, her face going pale.

'Could someone have come down on a tour, hidden and

stayed in after you locked up for the night?' It was a long shot, McLean knew, but he had to ask.

'I don't think so. We do a head count, same number in and out. And I always take a walk around the caves last thing, before we lock up and go home. There's nowhere down here you could hide, really.'

'Except that locked cavern. If you had a key.'

'I guess so. Was he there long, do you know?'

The question brought McLean up short. It was the nub of the investigation, after all. Rigor mortis had been and gone, and the core body temperature was the same as the cave, which meant the death hadn't occurred in the last few hours, but beyond that Angus had only offered the vaguest of guesses. Given the conditions in the cave the poor bastard could have been lying there weeks.

'We'll find out soon enough. In the meantime, I'm afraid we're going to have to shut you down for a while. At least until forensics have processed the scene.'

'I guessed as much, soon as I heard what they'd found when they opened up the door.' The tour guide's face told the story eloquently. It was a small tourist attraction and this was peak season. The loss of income would hit them hard.

'I'll try to get them to go as quickly as possible,' McLean said, although he knew he wouldn't. 'Just one last thing. You were first in this morning, right? Before the archae-ologists turned up?'

A simple nod by way of answer.

'Did you notice any blood on the floor? Any sign that anyone had been there since you left last night?'

'Blood?' The tour guide's face turned pale. 'No. I don't

remember any blood. Just the poor wee lad running out down the passageway. He was sick in the well, you know.'

It didn't take McLean long to work out which of the archaeology team had thrown up down the well. His name was Eric and he still had a stain of vomit down the front of his T-shirt. Should really have been sent home to clean himself up. His pale face had a sheen of sweat on it that made him look only slightly more healthy than the dead body even now being carefully removed from the cavern somewhere beneath their feet.

'You were the first into the cave, am I right?'

The student swallowed, his Adam's apple bobbing like some alien life-form trying to escape through his neck. Had anyone thought to offer this lot a mug of tea? McLean looked around the library for a constable to send off in search of something suitable, but could see no one close by.

'Was dark in there. Smelled bad.'

McLean's attention was drawn back to the young man. 'Stale? Like it hadn't been disturbed for a while?'

'No. It was like bin bags. Rotting. Something else, too.'

'There were no lights in there?'

'No. We only opened the cave up recently. Hadn't had time to survey it properly. Got some temporary arc lights in there, but we took them away with us for the summer. I was rolling out the extension cable so we could set them back up again.'

'When did you see the body?'

'The body. Yes.' The young man's eyes went out of focus for a moment, the alien trying to burst out of his neck again. McLean thought he was about to be sick, readied himself to get out of the way. It wasn't necessary.

'Couldn't work out what it was at first. I mean, there wasn't meant to be anything in there. Wasn't when we left it. If it'd been a new cave I might've expected a skeleton, maybe. There's a story about old man Paterson being buried somewhere in there.'

'Paterson?' McLean wrote the name down in his notebook.

'Oh yeah. That's right. You've never been to the cove before.' Eric seemed to recover some of his composure once he had a task to concentrate on. 'Tradition was it was built by a blacksmith, name of George Paterson, back in the early eighteenth century. He lived in it, for sure. Used it as an illegal drinking den for a while and claimed he dug it all out himself. But it's much older than that. He probably found it, cleared it out and used it. No way he actually built it, though.'

'So who did?'

'Well that's the mystery, innit? No one knows right enough. There's all manner of weird conspiracy theories. Why we were digging out that tunnel, wasn't it. Trying to put a bit of science behind it all.'

'So, the body.' McLean nudged the interview back on track.

'Yeah. It was weird. And the light wasn't good. Thought it was a rock formation or something. Anyway, Ali was coming up the tunnel behind me with the big lamp, so I had to go in properly.'

McLean wondered whether that was correct protocol when exploring caves just a few feet beneath houses and a busy street, but kept it to himself.

'He plugged in the lamp. Shone it up at the ceiling like I'd done, then over to the body. I'd got a bit closer to it by then, and when the light hit it I could . . . oh God . . . his throat.'

McLean was on his feet quickly, but not quickly enough. Someone obviously had given the archaeology team tea, and biscuits too. Second time around they didn't look anything like as appetising. Even less so spattered over his shoes.

8

'His name's Ben Stevenson. He's a reporter with the *Tribune*. Sometime colleague of our old friend Jo Dalgliesh.'

McLean stood in Detective Superintendent Duguid's office, and not for the first time wished there were more chairs in the place. The afternoon sun shone through the long glass window wall, making everything uncomfortably warm and humid. Duguid had his jacket off, draped over the back of his expensive leather executive's chair, shirt-sleeves rolled up. McLean had just walked from the car park at the back of the station, up several flights of stairs. He was short of breath, and sweat was beginning to trickle down his back.

'And someone cut his throat open, eh? Going to be hard narrowing down the list of suspects for that one.'

McLean ignored the attempt at humour. Duguid's mood had lightened considerably since he'd announced his retirement, but it was still hit and miss. 'The thing is, Dalgliesh approached me just a couple of days ago. Wanted to know if I could look into his disappearance. Seems he was on to some big story, then just disappeared.'

'Dalgliesh asked you for a favour?' Duguid grinned in an oddly simian manner. 'Which part of her anatomy did you tell her to shove that into?'

'Actually I said I'd see what I could do. Was on my way to an important meeting, so anything to get rid of her, really.'

'Well it's not going to be so easy next time. You'll need to speak to her, get as much detail as you can about what this Stevenson fellow was working on. Trace his movements over the past few weeks.'

McLean suppressed the urge to remind Duguid that he knew how to carry out an investigation.

'You want me to work with her, sir?' Just asking the question was enough to send a shudder down his spine.

'Makes sense. She came to you, after all. And you've got history.'

'If you mean by history she wrote a book about the man who killed my fiancée and I've hated her ever since, then I guess you've got a point.'

'Don't be such a drama queen, McLean. She's a useful asset for the investigation or she's a pain in the arse making life difficult for us. Which would you rather have?'

Put like that McLean had to admit that the detective superintendent had a point; that old saw about keeping your friends close and your enemies closer. It didn't make it any easier to accept, though. Still, if Duguid was going to make life awkward for him, he could just as easily do the same.

'You going to be Gold on this one, sir?'

'Christ. You think it's that important?'

As excuses went, it was a bit rubbish. So Stevenson was a reporter, and one who'd gone for one of their own when he'd exposed lurid details of Chief Superintendent McIntyre's private life that were, as far as McLean could see, none of anyone else's business. But even so, he'd died violently. There was no denying it was murder, and there was nothing domestic about it either. Protocol dictated that it be classed as a major incident.

'You're right, of course. It's got Cat A murder written all over it. I'll have to take charge, I guess.' Duguid ran an over-large hand through his sparse hair. 'Still, keep it as low-key as possible for now. Not that it's going to be easy, him being a journalist and everything.'

'Grumpy Bob and MacBride are setting up the incident room.' McLean turned to leave, was almost at the door before Duguid spoke again.

'You're going to make it complicated again, aren't you McLean?'

'A body with its throat cut, hidden in a secret cavern underground and no obvious idea how it got in there?' McLean stood in the doorway, enjoying the faint breeze wafting in from the corridor outside. 'I don't think even I could make it any more complicated than that.'

It was always cool in the city mortuary, but that was about all it had going for it on the positive side. Cool and dry. Summer had been warm, but the past three weeks had seen almost endless, miserable rain. McLean thought he might have been starting to grow gills, and he couldn't remember a time when his feet hadn't been damp. Of course that was mostly his own fault for insisting on walking everywhere.

The silence in the mortuary was a plus, too. He had to admit that as the doors swung closed behind him, cutting off the splashing roar of traffic from outside. There was only the gentle swish of air through the ductwork, the occasional far-off clatter of a dropped specimen tray or the squeak-squeak-squeak of an un-oiled trolley wheel as another departed soul was taken from the cold store to the place where all their most intimate secrets would be revealed.

He took his time walking to the examination theatre. The journey from the station had been leisurely, too. McLean liked to think while he walked, helped by the rhythm of his feet on the pavement, but this time it had been difficult to focus. A man had been murdered, of that there was no doubt. He needed justice, deserved it as much as anyone. And yet this man had been a thorn in the side of many a police officer over the course of his journalistic career. He was part of a pack more interested in salacious detail than important fact, favouring spectacle and hype over solid investigative journalism. He was a hack and proud of it – or rather, had been a hack and proud of it. It was hard then to drum up any great enthusiasm for catching his killer.

McLean had seen it in the eyes of the junior officers at that morning's briefing, and in the eyes of some of the more senior officers during informal meetings the night before. It annoyed him that they could be so childish, these professional grown men. And it annoyed him that he got annoyed at what he'd known he would face, as soon as the identity of the dead man was confirmed. So the thoughts had gone around in his head, always bringing him back to the wrong questions, stopping him from focusing on the killer rather than the victim.

'Ah, Tony. You made it then.'

McLean looked up, surprised to find he was already at the examination theatre. Angus Cadwallader stood on one side of the table, his ever-present assistant Tracy on the other. Between them lay the mortal remains of Ben

Stevenson, already well into the post-mortem examination process.

'I wasn't sure if I really wanted to.'

'Well, you don't have to attend, you know. Dr MacPhail's here to verify my findings and it'll all be in the report.'

Cadwallader sounded almost hurt as he spoke. McLean wondered if he, too, was upset at the imposition this man's murder had put upon him. Then he realised just how stupid that sounded, shook his head to try to rid himself of the malaise he'd picked up at the station. It helped, a bit, although it got him a strange look from the pathologist.

'You know I prefer to get the news first-hand, Angus.' McLean stepped a little closer to the examination table, saw that Stevenson was already open, stopped before he could see what was inside.

'Well, we'd better get stuck in then.' Cadwallader grinned at his pun, then added to it by reaching into the dead man's torso and carefully lifting out something slippery. Tracy was ready with a plastic container that looked suspiciously like it might once have contained ice cream. Newly filled, she placed it on a nearby set of scales and noted something down.

'You've done the exterior examination already, I see,' McLean said. 'Any clues you might want to share?'

'All in good time, Tony.' Cadwallader pulled out something else and handed it to Tracy to weigh. 'I need to finish this. Then we can discuss what happened to the poor fellow.'

McLean opened his mouth to reply, then shut it again. Cadwallader was right, of course. If he'd arrived on time, then he could have listened as the pathologist detailed his examination for the microphone hanging above the table. Coming in late and expecting his old friend to stop, switch off, talk about what he'd already just talked about and then start all over again was really a bit much to ask. And besides, if he was busy pulling stuff out of the poor man, there couldn't be all that much longer to go.

'Cause of death was almost certainly the cut to the throat. It's very deep. Almost took the poor man's head off. He'd have lost consciousness very quickly, bled out in a matter of minutes.'

Half an hour later and they were sitting in the shared office that opened on to the examination theatre. Cadwallader had taken off his gore-smeared scrubs and was even now climbing into a new, clean set, ready for the next body to be wheeled in. Outside, Tracy was busy putting the removed organs back into Ben Stevenson's torso and sewing him up with her large, neat stitches. Dr MacPhail had wandered off in search of some lunch.

'What about ligatures? Was he tied up?'

'There's marks around his wrists, but they're very light. He never fought against them. And there's nothing around his ankles, so he wasn't tied up. He could walk.'

'Forced at gunpoint, maybe?'

'It's possible, I suppose. That's your department, though. I'm more interested in what I could find on him.'

McLean said nothing, just leaned against the desk and waited for Cadwallader to decide his audience was ready.

'First off, his knees were marked where he'd been kneeling on the ground for a while. He was wearing trousers, but the rough surface had puckered his skin before death. There were similar marks on his forehead.'

'So he knelt right down, put his head to the ground. Praying?'

'That sort of posture, at least. But he'd have had to have knelt that way for some time. Ten, fifteen minutes. Maybe more.'

'There was blood on the cave wall. Do we know if it was his?'

'It was, yes.' Cadwallader reached for a sheet of paper on his desk, picked it up and waved it around as if that made everything clear.

'So that would have been done by the killer. After Stevenson was dead.'

'If not by the killer, then by someone with him.'

'Let's not complicate things any further, shall we?' McLean said. 'Bad enough we've got a body in a cave and the only way in is through a locked door with only one set of keys.'

'Yes, well. You'll have to puzzle that one out, I guess. There's one thing you might find interesting though.'

'There is? What?'

'He was wet.'

'Wet?'

'Soaked right through. His hair's quite short, but it was damp at the roots. It was damp in the cave, of course. The whole bloody city feels like it's underwater. But damp air wouldn't soak him through.' Cadwallader paused a moment as if trying to remember. 'No, it was Tracy who noticed it first. When she was taking off his clothes and bagging them up for the forensics people. They were damp as well, you see. His trousers were almost dry, but his underpants were still wet. Like he'd been starting to dry out. His body heat would have driven most of the moisture off eventually, but of course he started cooling down the moment his throat was cut.'

'How long was he down there? Can you hazard a time of death?'

Cadwallader smiled, that evil glint in his eye that McLean knew meant nothing but trouble.

'Difficult case, you know. The temperature down there was cool, and very stable. No rodent damage either, and very little insect life on him.'

'So it was recent?'

'That's what I thought at first. Oh, a few days, of course. Rigor mortis had been and gone, and what little blood he had left had settled on the side where he was lying. But there's a few other tests we can do, and they all suggested he'd been there longer.'

'Longer?' McLean felt the familiar unpleasant cold sensation in his stomach that always came when things were about to get weird.

'Best guess is about three weeks,' Cadwallader said. 'Could be four, but certainly not less than eighteen days.'

9

It's remarkably easy to pose as a doctor. Hospitals are so busy, their staff turnover so rapid, all you really need is a white coat, a stethoscope, a smattering of medical jargon and you're there.

The hard part is keeping it up for any length of time. Sooner or later someone's going to ask you to do something you don't know how to do, or ask you a question you can't answer. That's when you need a quick-exit strategy.

I don't really like hospitals. I died in one not so different from this. And yet here I am. Drawn to this place like a moth to a flame. Goodness flourishes here, amongst the wickedness and despair. It is a place where ordinary people do extraordinary things, a place where souls are redeemed. That's why I keep on coming back. God's work, my sacred duty demands it of me. It is my refuge and my hunting ground both.

Everyone needs to eat. Watch them eating and you'll see more of them than they'll ever tell you themselves. I start with the staff canteen. Check out the late lunch crowd. It's easy to spot the groups, the med students who've been in it together since first year, the trainee nurses who'll probably head into the private sector as soon as they graduate. These are not special people. They shine with a dull light at best. Given time and effort I might coax the goodness out of them, but time is a luxury I have never had. No, somewhere in here there is one who is almost pure. I can feel him like an angler feels the gentlest of tugs on his baited line. It is not sight or smell or touch that brings me to him; I do not taste the air like a snake, or listen to the voices clamouring all around. Instead this is a different sense, a knowing that guides me away from the crowd, off towards the edges of the room. God's hand.

And there he is, alone by the window, playing idly with a plate of congealed spaghetti bolognese, drinking occasionally from a stained white mug of cold coffee. His obsession oozes from him like a disease. Maybe that's why his colleagues shun him. Whatever the reason, he is perfect. I can see his secrets writ large across his face. I know he is the one.

'You mind?' I ask as I sit down opposite him, slide my tray on to the table until it neatly lines up with his own. His look is startled, wary, but I can see the interest there as well. He doesn't know me, but that means he hasn't been scorned by me yet.

'New here, aren't you?'

'Aye. First week. Crazy place.'

'A and E?'

I shake my head. 'Geriatric care.'

'Lots of that here. I'm in oncology. Specialise in terminal cases, lucky me.' He holds out his hand. 'Jim,' he says.

I wipe my own hand on my purloined white coat hurriedly before taking his. The touch is warm and dry, the grip firm. I sense the aura of near-perfection about him and know he will be saved. 'Ben,' I say. 'Ben Stevenson.'

10

'You seen Dan Hwei about?'

McLean looked across the incident room, hoping to spot the press liaison officer at one of the media desks. They were all empty, as was much of the rest of the room. Only Detective Constables Gregg and MacBride were in attendance, along with a half-dozen support staff. So much for a major investigation.

'Think he went off to DCI Brooks' briefing.' MacBride dragged his eyes away from his computer screen, and scanned the room as if only just realising there was almost nobody there.

'He does realise this is a murder investigation?' McLean asked. 'What's he briefing about, anyway?'

'Some big drugs operation, I think. Been working with Serious and Organised, or the NCA or whatever it's calling itself this week.' DC Gregg didn't even look up as she spoke, just continued jabbing at her keyboard with two fingers. Obviously not happy at being left out of the action. Either that or she really was rubbish at typing.

'Ah yes, I remember now. Thought we were getting a busload of detectives over from Strathclyde to work on that.'

'Chance'd be a fine thing.' Gregg abandoned her typing and finally turned to look at him. 'They keep dragging us over there to fill numbers. Not saying they don't need the help, mind. But we're not exactly overstaffed as it is.'

McLean held his hands up in mock surrender. Sandy Gregg wasn't someone to mess with at the best of times. 'You'll not find me arguing with you, Constable. Not much I can do about it, either. I was just looking for Dan.'

'Anything specific you needed him for, sir?' MacBride asked.

'A phone number for Jo Dalgliesh, actually. Words I never thought I'd hear myself say.'

MacBride grabbed his mouse, clicked a couple of times, then scribbled a string of digits down on a Post-it note and handed it over. 'It'll be on your phone anyway, sir. She's always calling you, after all.'

McLean retreated to the quiet of his own office before placing the call. Not that the incident room was exactly overcrowded, but something about the act of talking to the press made him feel strangely guilty. Using his office phone meant that he could at least pretend he wasn't giving Dalgliesh his mobile number, too. MacBride was right though; he'd changed it once before and she'd still managed to get hold of the new number in a matter of days. Hours, possibly.

'Aye?' Dalgliesh's telephone manner was in keeping with her general demeanour. McLean imagined her sitting at a cluttered desk, unlit cigarette dangling from her lip, leather coat still on despite being indoors.

'Ms Dalgliesh?' McLean asked.

'Aye. Who is this?'

'Detective Inspector McLean.' He almost added 'Lothian and Borders' but managed to stop himself at the last minute.

'So it is. Well, well. What an unexpected surprise.' Dalgliesh paused for a moment, the line crackling with gentle static. When she spoke again, her voice was flat. 'You found Ben.'

'Is it that obvious?'

'Can't think of any other reason why you'd phone me. He dead?'

'I think it'd be better if I spoke to you in person. It's . . . complicated.'

'Shit. No' that body you found up at Gilmerton Cove?' Dalgliesh muffled the receiver at her end, but McLean could still hear a string of colourful words. It stopped him asking her how she knew about the body long enough for him to realise it would be a wasted question. Guarding her sources, particularly within the ranks of the police, was second nature to the journalist.

'You want me to come round the station?' she asked after the air had cleared. 'Only I've a meeting set up for this afternoon's taken me months to arrange. Really don't want to cancel it.'

McLean glanced at his watch. Almost noon. 'No. I'll come round to your office. I could do with stretching my legs a bit. Give me fifteen minutes.'

Never having been a fan of the press, McLean hadn't spent much time in the offices of the *Edinburgh Tribune*. He knew where they were though, just a short walk from the station, down towards Holyrood and the parliament building. A hot sun and humid air meant he was sweating by the time he got there, but the reception area was well air-conditioned, bright and surprisingly modern. He gave his name to the receptionist, then waited while she phoned up to the floor where all the hacks lived. Sooner than he was expecting the lift pinged and Jo Dalgliesh bustled out.

'Fifteen minutes on the nose, Inspector. I'm impressed.'

McLean didn't know what to say. He was taken aback by Dalgliesh's appearance more than anything; couldn't recall a time he'd seen her not wearing her trademark battered leather coat. Even more unsettling was seeing her in a skirt, cut just below the knees, calf-length suede boots and a blouse that looked like it might have been fashionable in the 1980s. She even had a red silk scarf tied loosely around her neck. The only thing suggesting she might be a journalist with questionable ethics and not some well-to-do middle-aged lady off to tea at Jenners was the fact that she was carrying a battered notebook. That and the severe crop to her greying hair.

'Going to a party?' McLean asked.

Dalgliesh paused a moment. 'What? This?' She half-gestured at her blouse. 'Important meeting later this afternoon. Got to look my best.'

McLean let the obvious comment slide; scoring points off Jo Dalgliesh wasn't why he was here, after all. 'There somewhere we can go and talk?'

'Sure. This way.' She led him through a security door that took them into a large, open-plan office. This was more the type of thing McLean had been expecting to see – a busy, barely organised chaos as dozens of journalists clattered away at keyboards or clustered around large screens discussing how best to frame their more lurid stories. He recognised a few of the faces and some even smiled at him, warily, as he followed Dalgliesh through to a small meeting room.

'So, Ben,' she said once she'd closed the door behind him and wound down the blinds covering the window that looked out on to the main office. 'He's dead.'

'Yes. He's dead. I'm sorry.'

Dalgliesh cocked her head to one side like a confused puppy. 'You really mean that, don't you? I'm sorry too. He could be a pain in the arse at times, but he was . . .' She broke off as if unsure what he was.

'Do you know what he was working on?'

'Not a Scooby, Inspector. Ben's . . . Ben was very secretive when he had a project on.'

'OK. What sort of things interested him? What might he have been working on that would take him out to Gilmerton Cove?'

Dalgliesh leaned back against the conference table that dominated the room, ran a scrawny hand over her face, frowned as if the effort of thinking needed to be shown on the outside. McLean was fairly sure it was all an act, the pauses just a little too dramatic.

'He loved a good conspiracy theory, did Ben,' she said eventually. 'Secret societies were his thing. Last time I saw him he was babbling on about the Beggar's Benison and the Hellfire Club. But I got the impression his project was something different. How did he die?'

Always the journalist. Well, she'd find out sooner or later. 'He had his throat cut. Ear to ear. Deep, too.'

If she was shocked, Dalgliesh didn't show it. But neither did she immediately scribble down notes in her book.

'And you found him in a cavern behind a locked door. Least that's what I heard.'

'One of these days I'll find out which constable is talking to you and he'll be spending the rest of his life directing traffic on the Gogar Roundabout.'

'What makes you think it's a he? Or just the one?' Dalgliesh gave him a shark's smile.

'True enough. And you're right. Yes, we found him in a cave behind a locked door. How he got in there is one question, but perhaps more pertinent is the fact that he appears to have gone there of his own volition, and died without a struggle. And his killer left behind a little message for us, too.'

'He did? Are you going to tell me what?'

'That depends on whether you're just going to print it all, or help us with our enquiries. If it's the former, we're done here. The latter and you'll get an exclusive.'

Dalgliesh tried to look casually uninterested, but McLean could see that he had her attention now. Her back was straighter, her eyes bright, even though they were narrowed in a suspicious frown. 'What's the catch?'

'You don't publish anything until we let it out.' McLean saw the protest coming before Dalgliesh could even open her mouth to voice it. He raised a hand for her to wait. 'I don't mean you can't write anything at all. You'll get a story, and before anyone else out there. I just need to control how the details are released. Don't want our killer getting tipped off as to how close we are. Or how far-off.'

Dalgliesh considered for all of ten seconds. 'OK. What do you want me to do?'

'I want you to try to find out what he was investigating, who he was talking to, where he's been the last few weeks.'

Dalgliesh stood, crossed the room to where McLean was standing. 'Deal,' she said, and stuck out her hand to be shaken. For an irrational moment, he thought of refusing to take it. She was someone he would have happily seen hung upside down in chains in a dungeon, after all. But she was also as close to an answer to this case as he was going to find. Swallowing his pride, he took her hand, finding it both warm and surprisingly small.

'You hold anything back, I'll find out,' she said.

'Likewise, Ms Dalgliesh.' McLean let go of her hand, resisted the urge to wipe his own on his trouser leg. 'Enjoy your meeting. Good luck with the promotion.'

'How did you . . .?'

'All dolled up like that? And the man who owns this paper's in town for a couple of days. First visit he's paid to Scotland in a decade?' McLean shook his head to suppress the smirk that wanted to spread across his face. 'You're not the only one good at finding out things, you know.'

'How are we getting on down there?'

McLean stood in the entrance hall of the tiny cottage that served as a visitor centre. The posters telling the history of the place still hung on the walls, but all available floor space had been taken over by the forensics services and their endless piles of aluminium cases. There were more downstairs, with a steady stream being brought back up from below.

'Almost done in the caves. And no, I'm not going to tell you what we've found so far because I don't want to be rude.' Jemima Cairns stood with a clipboard, noting down the numbers on the battered cases, checking them all before they were taken outside and loaded into the big van. It was somewhat menial work for a forensic scientist of her experience, skill and pay grade, but someone had told McLean in passing that she wasn't overly fond of enclosed spaces. She'd been down once, apparently, then taken an uncharacteristic interest in the paperwork.

'That little, is it?' McLean asked.

'Might have got more if the scene hadn't been disturbed by a herd of elephants.' Dr Cairns' normal expression was a scowl, but it wasn't often this deep. 'Don't know what they're teaching archaeologists these days. I thought they were meant to be all about preserving evidence. The way they tramped around that cave and scuffed up all the ground . . .'

'I don't think they were expecting to find a body in there,' McLean said. 'Well, at least not one quite so fresh.'

'Still makes our job almost impossible. Nothing but the body, and the blood on the cave wall. Can't even tell how he got in there. No sign the lock's been tampered with, so whoever did it must have had a key.'

'OK if I go down and have a look?' McLean asked.

'Knock yourself out. We're pretty much done. You can even skip wearing the bunny suit. Unless, you know, that's your thing?'

McLean smiled at the joke, left Dr Cairns ticking off boxes. He was about to tell Grumpy Bob to join him, but the old sergeant was busy reading one of the wall-mounted display panels and seemed happy enough.

'I'll see you down there,' he said and headed for the narrow stairs that descended into the cave complex.

On a second viewing, it seemed somehow smaller, and yet also more impressive. Whereas before he had been led straight to the scene, this time he was able to take a moment to look at the way the sandstone had been carved, the many alcoves and rooms leading off the passageways. It was cool down here, a welcome relief from the humid heat of the day outside, but it was also damp and smelled like a small army of SOCOs had been working in it for days.

Lit up with arc lights, the cavern where Stevenson's body had been found was an impressive sight. Almost perfectly round, the walls rose vertically for about ten feet, before curving elegantly into a dome. There was nothing else in the place except for the markers where the body had lain, the channel dug into the rock floor to divert water to the sinkhole, and the sinkhole itself.

McLean walked over to the spot where Ben Stevenson had met his end, noting the soft, gritty floor as he did so. Dr Cairns was right; it looked like a herd of elephants had been practising dressage on it. No chance of finding a footprint that could be matched to a potential killer. Of course, forensics weren't as careful in leaving as when they arrived, so the state of the place might have had something to do with them. It didn't matter, there were no answers here.

Looking up at the wall, he squinted to try and see any pattern to the blood smearings. Like the other caves, this one had been hewn from the rock with sharp-pointed chisels, leaving a rough surface. The arc lights cast shadows that seemed to leap and writhe as he tilted his head this way and that. It made his eyes ache just looking at it, not helped by the rivulets of water seeping through the rock and smearing the blood as they travelled slowly to the floor. He gave up and turned his attention to the site where the body had lain.

Ben Stevenson had bled out into the drainage channel, his blood mingling with the rainwater and flowing unimpeded to the sinkhole. The channel was smooth and clean, curving almost perfectly with the arc of the walls. McLean followed it around until he was standing at the edge of the sinkhole.

It was about four feet in diameter, oval-shaped and cut into the floor with a slightly raised edge all around except where the channel met it. The water inside reflected the arc lights, perfectly still and mysterious. He wondered how deep it was, whether the water was stagnant or connected to an underground stream somewhere. He knelt against the low stone lip, peering into the blackness as if that was a good way to find the answers.

Which was when the lights went out.

'Oi! I'm in here.' McLean shouted the words over his shoulder, slipping as he did so. He shot a hand out to steady himself, missed the edge and plunged it into the water. He was fully expecting to follow it, wondering how he was going to live down the inevitable jokes, but after a couple of inches, his hand hit solid rock.

Relieved at not having an impromptu swim, it took him a while to realise that it wasn't a very shallow well, but a step carved into the side, perhaps a foot wide. He rolled up his dripping sleeve a bit before feeling further. Another step. After that it was too deep. In the gloom, with very little illumination spilling from the entrance at the other side of the cavern, he thought he could see beyond the reflective surface of the water, down to where something white reflected in the darkness. He pulled out his torch, flicked it on and pointed it straight down. Sure enough, maybe ten feet below at the bottom of the well there was something pale and foreign. Out of place.

'Still in here,' McLean shouted, his voice echoing in the darkness. A couple of seconds later the lights came back on again. He squinted, surprised at how quickly his eyes had become accustomed to the darkness.

'I'm sorry sir. Thought everyone had left.' A young SOCO shuffled through the opening, then stood up tall. He was the complete opposite of his boss, Dr Cairns. Wiry-thin and at least six foot four. Completely the wrong build to be down here in the tunnels.

'It's no matter.' McLean stood up, rolling his jacket

sleeve back down and feeling the dampness in it. Soaked right through. 'Has anyone checked out the well?'

'How do you mean? We took a sample of it, but . . .' The young SOCO looked puzzled.

'We'll need to get a remote underwater camera. There's something down there.'

'You know, I don't think it's a well at all. Think it might be another passage.'

All the arc lights in the cave had been gathered around the well. Pointing downwards, their glare reflected off the surface of the water, but enough penetrated into the depths to show a series of steps spiralling to the bottom. With the extra light, McLean could tell that the white object wasn't a fallen rock or something old. It looked like a discarded shopping bag, moving back and forth ever so slightly as if tugged by an invisible current.

'Could be. We're heading in a downhill direction so it'd make sense to go deeper if you were digging tunnels further.'

The unusually tall SOCO's name was Karl. He had managed to find a telescopic pole with a hook on the end, but it wasn't quite long enough to reach all the way to the bottom. McLean watched from the other side as he leaned over the short parapet, arm up to his elbow in the water. A couple of shorter forensic experts looked on, one with a camera on a strap around his neck, the other holding a clipboard that, as far as McLean could tell, had no paper attached. He got the impression they were there more out of idle curiosity than any kind of professional pride. Only Grumpy Bob was paying no attention to the well. The old sergeant seemed to find the cavern walls far more interesting, peering up at the vaulted ceiling as he wandered around muttering to himself.

'How far do you think they go?'

'Ah, now that's a question for the archaeology boys. I've heard there's caves like these up Roslin Glen way, and the city centre's full of hidden passages and stuff. Could be it all links up.'

From where he was standing, McLean couldn't tell whether Karl was being serious or not. He knew about the caves at Hawthornden Castle though, and there was the small matter of the subterranean world underneath Rosskettle Hospital that had come to light recently. Mine workings and tunnels lay undiscovered all over Midlothian, dating back to Roman times and earlier. It wasn't so far-fetched to think that these mysterious caverns might spread further than anyone realised.

'If it's not a well, then why's it full of water?'

'Looks like it's blocked at the bottom. There's a jumble of rocks and stuff. All the rain we've had the past few weeks, wouldn't surprise me if it just got flooded out. Ah, here we go.' Karl leaned even further into the water, his chin just a fraction of an inch above the surface as he extended his considerable reach. He'd stripped off to the waist, and McLean couldn't help but shiver at the thought of how cold he must be.

'Got it?' he asked.

'Yup.' And slowly Karl pushed himself away from the low stone parapet surrounding the hole, with first his shoulder, then his arm and finally the long telescopic pole emerging from the water like Excalibur.

'Get some plastic sheeting down, can you? And turn that floodlight round.'

The SOCO with the clipboard frowned at McLean, but did as he was told. Soon Karl was pulling the end of the pole out of the water, a sodden mess of something fabric drooping from its hooked end. He manoeuvred it, dripping, over the stone parapet and on to the freshly laid sheet, rivulets of water flowing away from it as it took on a more recognisable shape. A pale white jacket.

McLean slipped on a pair of latex gloves as he approached the newly fetched plastic sheeting where Karl was laying out the coat as if he were the best man setting out the groom's suit before the big day. The SOCO with the camera was busy taking photos, the flash making it hard to focus on any detail.

'Doesn't look all that old to me. Craghoppers. You can buy them in pretty much any outdoor clothing shop. Got one myself.' Karl opened up the front of the coat, fingers working slowly down the line of the zip, checking the pockets. McLean wondered if he was going to get dressed any time soon, felt it best not to say anything.

'Sort of thing a journalist might wear?' he asked.

'Sort of thing anyone might wear. Ah, here's something.' The SOCO put his hand carefully into one of the pockets and pulled out a damp notebook and pen. 'Bag, please.'

His colleague bustled over with an evidence bag, sealing up the notebook before it could disintegrate any further.

'Can I see that?' McLean put his hand out.

'We need to get it to the lab. We can dry it out properly there.'

'I'm not going to open it. Just want to look at the cover.'

A short pause, then with obvious reluctance, the SOCO handed his bounty over. McLean turned the notebook around very carefully. He could feel how sodden it was, and the water pooling in the bag was grey with pulped paper. It was cheap, spiral bound, the sort of thing you picked up in packs of six for a pound from the local supermarket. There was nothing written on it, no useful name or address, but there was a crude symbol, etched in biro across the cover.

'That what I think it is?' Grumpy Bob loomed over his shoulder, blocking out the best of the light. 'Aye, it is. Isn't it?'

'Yup.' McLean handed the notebook carefully back to the SOCO, taking one last look at the compass and set-square. 'Bloody Masons. Dagwood's going to be happy as a clam.'

12

If I were a kind man, I'd tell him to improve his home security. I'm not though, at least not like that. So I won't.

It takes thirty seconds to get in through the front door, and I don't even have to try all the entry buttons until someone buzzes me in without asking who it is. The lock is old, the electro-mechanical release mechanism worn enough that a couple of well-timed shoves spring it open. Inside, the city noise drops away, leaving me with a smell of foreign bodies, bin bags left out too long, cat piss. Upstairs the only way of knowing I've got the right place is a torn-off strip of paper with a name written on it in biro, taped underneath a bell-push that has long since been painted solid. Security here is no better, just a Yale lock that yields to a supermarket loyalty card, and I'm in.

I know these tenement flats are small; I posed as a buyer for the one being sold next door so I could get a look at the layout of the place. Even so, the sense of being in a cave is almost overwhelming. A narrow skylight darkened with many years of city grime is the only source of illumination for the tiny hallway, filtering down from high above and setting me at ease. I take a moment to gather my wits about me, listen for any sound that the flat is occupied even though I know it won't be. He has no family, no life beyond his work. This is his lair, but it is no more than a place to sleep, occasionally to eat. And to feed his obsession.

The kitchen is barely more than a cupboard; the cooker, sink, fridge and cupboards squeezed in with commendable ingenuity. An empty bowl and mug sit by the sink, waiting to be washed. From the smell of sour milk it's been a day or two since last he had breakfast. Black grounds in the bottom of a one-person cafetière are the only sign of sophistication. I move on.

The shower room – no bath here – is at least tidy, although limescale pastes the glass enclosure and black mould is feasting on the grouting between cracked white tiles. The medicine cabinet over the basin holds no surprises. He may be a doctor, but he doesn't self-medicate. Not that desperate. Not yet. It's the pile of reading material beside the toilet that interests me most. Some medical texts, printouts from the teaching hospital library, slipped between copies of *Scientific American*, *New Scientist* and a couple of more obscure medical research titles. They are well thumbed, the pages stained with toothpaste and saliva where he's read them whilst brushing his teeth. The articles are about new techniques in stem-cell therapy, off-licence drug treatments, alternative medicines of a kind far removed from the homeopathic. I begin to see a picture of the man emerging.

The bedroom is tidy, which surprises me. I expected more scientific papers, clothes thrown across the bed, signs of the hunger that gnaws at him, that has honed his soul to such a fine edge. I find them instead in the living room to the front, overlooking the street, and the depths of his obsession become apparent.

This is where he lives when he's not at the hospital. The other rooms have functions that can more or less be circumvented; who needs to sleep in a bed when there's a couch? There are no pictures in the whole flat, that's one of the first things I noticed. The decor looks as if it was left behind by the previous owner. But the walls in the living room are covered in papers torn from medical journals, printouts of emails from research scientists across the globe, newspaper cuttings and other snippets of information. This is what I was looking for, what I saw in him the first time we met in the hospital canteen. This is what drives him to the exclusion of all earthly temptations, what shrives him.

This will be the key that opens him up.

13

McLean stared at the pile of reports, folders and other general detritus strewn across his desk and stacked precariously alongside it. Just looking at the mess made him weary; the thought of tackling it, doubly so. He'd managed to grab a bite to eat once he and Grumpy Bob had returned from Gilmerton Cove, but had completely failed to find either Detective Superintendent Duguid or DCI Brooks. There were other officers in the station who were Freemasons, but those two, and Duguid in particular, held senior enough positions to be of use. Not that he really thought the Masonic link was anything other than a hoax, a diversion maybe, but it was a lead that would have to be followed. He rubbed at tired eyes, not looking forward to having that conversation with either man.

When the phone rang, at first he couldn't work out what it was. The handset on his desk normally lit up when a call came through. Then McLean realised it was his mobile, hidden under a folder containing transcripts of the interviews with all the archaeology students. Yet another dead end in the investigation. He snatched up the phone and managed to hit the right button on the screen before it switched to answerphone.

'McLean?'

'Aye, so it is. Thought I'd get you on this number rather than go through the station.'

McLean took a moment to recognise the voice. The short, round, senior forensic scientist. 'Dr Cairns?'

'The very same. We've processed the crime scene photographs from the cave. Thought you might like to see them.'

McLean looked around his office again, disappointed to see that it was just as full of unnecessary paperwork as it had been five minutes ago. His laptop was folded up and buried under the mound somewhere. 'You want to ping them over in an email?'

'Aye, well, I could do that. But then you'd only see what you wanted to see. Better if you come over and I show you what we've got.'

He didn't really need an excuse, even if the paperwork would still be waiting for him when he got back.

'I'll be right over.'

'You said you had something to show me?'

It had only taken him half an hour to get from his stuffy little office to the fresher, air-conditioned labs of the forensic services across town. Dr Cairns had been passing the reception desk when he'd arrived. She had taken him straight through to the room with all the computers in it, where the photographic image manipulation was done. He couldn't help looking over at the desk where Emma had worked, pleased to see that no one else seemed to be using it. The last he had heard, she was somewhere in North Africa, but he hoped that she would come home soon. Seemingly the forensic service hoped so too.

'You wanted to see the photos from the cave.' Dr Cairns broke through McLean's distraction. He dragged his gaze from the empty desk back to her, catching the merest hint of a grin on her normally taciturn face.

'I did, yes.'

'Well Benny's been running them through the image analysis software. Reckon we've got something that makes a bit of sense now.'

Dr Cairns led McLean across the room, past a half-dozen casually dressed technicians hunched over computer stations, each of which probably cost more than the entire IT budget for his station. They all had enormous flat screens, two or three per operator, and he couldn't help but feel a twitch of jealousy even though he had no real need for anything more sophisticated than a laptop that actually talked to the network.

'You got the Gilmerton Cove file up, Benny?' Dr Cairns pitched her words loud to the scruffy fellow sitting in front of the largest screen in the whole room. Earphone cables snaked away from his long, ginger and slightly greasy hair, and he peered through spectacles so thick McLean had to consider that they'd given him the big monitor because he couldn't see anything smaller. His ears must have worked though, as he reached up, unplugged his earphones and turned to his boss, eyes flicking a quick glance in McLean's direction without any hint of alarm.

'Just finished it now.' Benny tucked his earphones carefully into the top pocket of his shirt before reaching for the mouse and clicking up a screen full of thumbnail images. 'You want me to print it out?'

'And waste our budget on ink? No, you can email the whole file over to the incident room. Let them pick up the tab. Come on, shoo.' Dr Cairns flicked her hands at the technician until he slid, reluctantly, off his stool. Standing, McLean could see that he was at least as tall as Karl, shoulders and back hunched in the habitual pose of a man who doesn't really enjoy standing out in a crowd. Dr Cairns scrabbled up on to the vacated stool, and grabbed at the mouse in a lunge that nearly saw her topple to the floor.

'Bloody hell. D'you no' get altitude sickness up here, Benny?' she said, before clicking through a series of images too quickly for McLean to see. Finally she stopped and he peered close, trying to make something out through the pixellation. The overall impression was blue. Early Impressionist.

'What am I supposed to be looking at?'

'This is your cave wall. Blood reflects a narrow band of the light spectrum, so we've run a filter to cut out everything else. See?' Dr Cairns clicked once more and the scene changed. It was a bit like one of those old parlour magic tricks McLean remembered from when he was a boy. The blue deepened, but a series of lines, letters and words leapt out at him in glowing yellow.

'Is this the pattern, then? What was written in Stevenson's blood?'

'Written?' Dr Cairns turned on the stool, lifting a single eyebrow in his direction. 'You ever tried to write in blood on a sandstone wall?'

'Not recently, no.'

'Well, it's not easy. Let me tell you that. Our man here's tried to write some words. You can see them here.' Dr Cairns highlighted an area of the screen, then zoomed in on it. The lines looped around each other in a way that at a casual glance might look like letters, but the more McLean stared, the less he could see.

'I don't . . .' he began.

'Perhaps it'll make more sense if I do this.' A couple more clicks and the image shifted, widened out, stretched. 'See?'

McLean tilted his head, just about seeing the letters now. 'Does that . . .?'

'"Seek not Baphomet and the Brotherhood, for all are brothers in death." Isn't it charming how misogynous these secret societies are?'

'The Brotherhood? Never heard of it. Baphomet sounds familiar. Can't think where, though.'

'Me neither.' Dr Cairns shrugged, then clicked the mouse a couple of times to bring up a new image. 'Might have something to do with this, though.'

McLean peered again at the large screen, unsure what he was looking at for a moment. And then he saw it. Not words any more, now the lines formed a pattern, a drawing, roughly sketched out over ten feet or more of cave wall.

'You managed to do anything with that notebook we found?' McLean asked. In response, Dr Cairns turned and gave him a teacher's best smile.

'Top marks for the detective. And before you ask, no, it's still drying out. We won't be able to do anything with it for at least a week.' She clicked the mouse again and the screen split into two images. One side showed what had been there before, the other a photograph of a very soggy note-book in an evidence bag. The pattern drawn on the wall with Ben Stevenson's blood was hard to make out – impossible without the aid of many thousands of pounds' worth of computing and image processing equipment – but it was undeniably the same as that scrawled in biro on the front of the notebook. The Masonic compass and set-square.

A pile of empty boxes stood outside the office on the top floor, waiting to be filled with the detritus of Detective Superintendent Duguid's mercifully brief stint in charge. No one manned the desk beside the open door, so McLean rapped on the jamb, peered inside.

'Hello?'

There was no reply, so he stepped inside, looked around. The desk was strewn with reports and folders piled almost as haphazardly as in his own office. The large executive chair on the other side was empty, though. He was about to turn and leave – the old schoolboy fear of being caught in the master's study alone never really left you after the first thrashing – when a cough behind him suggested it was already too late.

'What do you want, McLean?' Duguid pushed past him on his way to the chair, trailing a waft of stale tobacco. A lot of the hardened smokers were using e-cigarettes these days, at least until someone in HQ found out and put a stop to them vaping indoors, but Duguid had always been a high-tar, twenty-a-day man. Nothing was going to stop him now, least of all technology.

'About the Ben Stevenson investigation, sir. Something's come up that . . . well . . . you have a greater knowledge of these things than I do.'

Duguid slumped down into his chair, slapping his hands against the desk to keep from tipping over backwards. 'What on earth are you talking about?'

'This, sir. Was hoping you might be able to have a look at it.' McLean reached forward with the slim folder he'd been partially concealing behind his back, held it up for Duguid to take. The detective superintendent eyed it suspiciously before finally conceding. He opened it up as he slumped back once more into his treacherous chair, pulled out the photographs nestling within.

'This some kind of joke again?' The growl was back, McLean noticed. That almost always happened when the subject came up.

'Far from it. We found that mark on Stevenson's notebook, and daubed on the cavern wall in his blood. I believe it's the Masonic compass and set-square.'

'Of course it's the bloody Masonic compass and set-square. Any idiot could tell you that. Same as any idiot could have drawn it. Doesn't mean the Masons are out there cutting people's throats.'

McLean took a step back to avoid being burnt by Duguid's sudden rage. It was always thus when his beloved Freemasons came up.

'Did you ever write your name on the wall when you were a boy?' McLean asked, then added, 'Sir?' The effect was as he'd hoped, calming the detective superintendent's anger with bafflement.

'What the fuck are you talking about?'

'I didn't. Wrote other boys' names a few times, to see if I could get them into trouble though. Never worked.'

'No. You've lost me completely.' Duguid shuffled the photographs back into their folder.

'Would someone involved in Freemasonry paint the

74

most recognisable symbol of their organisation in the blood of their victim at the crime scene?'

Duguid looked a little embarrassed. 'Oh, I see.'

'Exactly. This isn't about the Masons. It's about someone pretending to be something to do with them, or someone deliberately trying to send us off in the wrong direction. There's plenty of you on the force, sir, but not many senior detectives, and not many at your level within the organisation. I'd appreciate your input on that.' McLean nodded at the folder and its photographs.

'DCI Brooks would have been able to help you with this. If you'd asked him.'

'I know, sir. But I chose to ask you. Thought I might actually get somewhere that way.'

Duguid took the compliment, he had at least that much sense. 'I'll ask around, show it to some people. Looks phoney to me, but if your man Stevenson was a Lodge member I'll find out.'

'Thank you, sir. There was some writing on the wall, too. A mention of something called the Brotherhood. Capital B. Does that mean anything to you?'

McLean studied the detective superintendent's face as he flicked through the photographs and came to the enhanced image of the writing. He was looking for any telltale flicker of recognition. There was nothing for a moment, then a weary shake of the head.

'Sounds like utter bollocks to me. I mean it's a male institution, no women in the order, but I've never heard of something referring to itself as "The Brotherhood".'

'Well, if you could ask around I'd be grateful. Not sure

this will go anywhere, but we've precious few leads to work on.'

'That bad?'

McLean looked past Duguid, through the window and out into the darkening city beyond. Another day gone, the trail to the killer that little bit colder. Who was he kidding? It had been stone cold the day they discovered the body.

'Worse,' he said, then turned and left.

'Detective Inspector McLean?'

He had thought the street empty. It was certainly late enough as he walked out through the gates to the parking lot at the back of the station. He'd looked in vain for a squad car to cadge a lift from and was resigning himself to a long walk home, perhaps via a pub and a curry. Looking around, he saw a woman standing just a few feet away, no obvious shadows to explain how he'd missed her before.

'Can I help you?' As he asked the question, he realised he'd seen her somewhere before. It took a moment, then he placed her. Tapping away at a laptop computer in the site office around the back of his tenement building. She was short, slim, and with her severe, grey hair might have been thought frail were it not for the way she carried herself. Back straight, eyes clear as they fixed their gaze on him without the aid of spectacles, she exuded an inner strength quite at odds with her appearance.

'Violet Grainger. I work with Joe and Jock McClymont.' She held out a hand. McLean wasn't surprised to find her grip firm, was surprised at how cold it was. She fixed him with the stare of someone who has heard about being friendly but hasn't yet mastered the skill. 'Wondered if I might have a word. About the development in East Preston Street.'

'Not sure if there's much more I can say.' McLean released his grip, but Ms Grainger still clasped his hand, enveloping it with both of hers.

'It means such a lot to them, you know. That site. They've put everything into it.'

'Isn't that a bit presumptuous? I mean, they don't even own it all.'

Ms Grainger stared straight at him, her pale grey eyes unnerving in the half-light. It felt like he was trapped. A small animal in the headlights as the truck came bearing down on him. For an instant he knew the old fear, from his childhood. The monsters lurking under the bed, the troll in the attic, the ugly, half-formed creatures that roamed the graveyard beyond his garden in the hours of darkness. He knew them then, and would have done anything to escape them, escape that feeling.

'Not yet, no. But they own most of it. You could sell them your share, you know. Take the money and walk away. Then everyone would be happy.'

McLean tugged his hand away from the old woman's cold grasp. Something about her words, particularly that last one, rang hollow. Only one person would be happy in this arrangement and it wasn't him. Neither was it Joe or Jock McClymont. He knew that as clearly as if it had been written across Ms Grainger's face. Instead, a fleeting confusion filled her eyes, then she pulled herself together. Drew down a mask of blankness over her face, pursed her lips before speaking again.

'But I can see you're not a kindly man.'

Her petulance burst the surreal bubble that had surrounded the whole meeting. 'I've made my position clear on the matter,' McLean said. 'My old flat, or as close to it as modern building regulations will allow. You can have the rest of the building for all I care, but that's my price. Now if you'll excuse me, Ms Grainger, it's been a long day and I'd quite like to get home before it ends.'

He walked back towards the station. He'd call for a taxi if there were no squad cars heading out. Turning at the entrance, McLean looked back to where the old woman had been standing. The street was clear, straight in both directions for a hundred yards or more. But she was nowhere to be seen.

14

Mrs McCutcheon's cat stared up at him from its favoured place in the middle of the kitchen table as McLean let himself in through the back door. Another long, frustrating day and all he really wanted to do was crack open a beer, order a pizza and put his feet up.

'You and I need to have a chat about hygiene sometime soon.' He dumped his folder down on the table, getting nothing more than a suspicious stare from the cat in return. He couldn't bring himself to shoo it out of the way. It wasn't as if he spent a lot of time preparing food at the table. Or eating at it, for that matter. It was nice just to have someone to talk to when he got home, really. And Mrs McCutcheon's cat was a good listener.

The heat of the day was dissipating quickly, evening fading to night, but the air in the hall was still and humid, cooked by a long day under the sun. He would have liked to have left windows open, let the place ventilate properly during the day, but with just the cat to keep an eye on things, McLean knew that was a bad idea. If the local community support team found out how lax his security was, they'd give him hell. Or worse, use him as an example to all the other officers. There was an alarm system, of course, but the house had been built at a time when there was always someone at home, and burglary was very much a minority sport. It wasn't an easy place to make totally secure.

A little pile of flyers, catalogues and brown envelopes lay on the mat. He scanned them from a distance, hoping to see the slim form of a cheap postcard. McLean couldn't help it, every day was the same. It was over a year now since Emma had left, gone off on her mad quest. At first the postcards had been fairly regular, the places she sent them from at least vaguely familiar. More recently though, they had become sporadic, sometimes two in a week or even on the same day, then months of nothing at all. The last one had shown a picture of a stone fort in Ethiopia, and had travelled to Edinburgh through at least six different countries if the blurred franking marks obscuring most of her words were anything to go by. He'd pinned it up with all the others, on a large map of the world taped to the dining room wall, charting her progress in the hope that she might head back towards home soon. But if anything she was getting further and further away, and as the months rolled past, so his memory of her shifted from something urgent and vital to yet another sad loss. One of so many it was hard to care about any of them any more.

Crouching, he scooped up the pile of mail, flicking through it swiftly as he stood up again. Nothing immediately of interest, he was turning back to the hall and the kitchen, thoughts of that beer and pizza at the forefront of his mind, when the doorbell rang.

It wasn't a foreign sound, but he heard it so infrequently these days that it took McLean a moment to realise what it was. He shoved the post down on the old wooden chest to one side of the porch, then set about the task of unbolting and unlocking the door. Finally it swung open, let in a waft of cooling evening air and revealed a large figure on the doorstep. He couldn't have said who he was expecting to see, since he'd not been expecting anyone and hadn't received any visitors in weeks. Of all the possibilities though, this was quite a long way down the list.

'Madame Rose?' McLean looked up into the large face of the transvestite medium, esoteric antiquarian bookseller and part-time fortune teller. 'Umm . . . Hello.'

'Oh, Inspector.' Madame Rose clutched a large hand to her bosom in a gesture of well-timed theatricality. 'I'm so sorry to bother you. But I couldn't think who else to turn to.'

'It's been a nightmare. You just wouldn't believe the trouble I've had.'

Back in the kitchen and McLean was busying himself with the making of tea. Madame Rose had settled into a chair at the kitchen table and almost immediately Mrs McCutcheon's cat had leapt into her lap. The medium looked haggard, there was no other way McLean could describe her. Normally tweedy to the point of ridiculousness, done up like the most old-fashioned of Morningside grandes dames, now she clasped a slightly tatty old overcoat around her as if the summer heat were no more than a memory. Her hair was a mess, grey the dominant colour, but it was her face that was the most shocking.

'Trouble?' McLean asked, trying hard not to stare. How long had it been since last he'd seen her? Around about the time Emma had left, at Jenny Nairn's funeral. She'd been sombre then, but larger than life. Now for all her great size, she seemed small. She'd lost weight, noticeably, and where once her skin had been a flawless mask of foundation and rouge, now she wore barely any make-up at all. She even sported a dark hint of stubble around her chin.

'I've always tried hard not to be judgemental.' Madame Rose scratched at the side of her nose with a fingernail rimmed with dark grime. She let out a little laugh. 'Could hardly be, could I? Not the way I am. Live and let live, that's always been my motto. Shame I can't say the same about other people.'

'Who's been giving you grief?' McLean fished teabags out of the two mugs, poured in milk and carried them over to the table. It was perhaps more telling than anything that Madame Rose didn't make any comment about the lack of teapot, loose-leaf tea, proper cups with saucers. She just cupped the mug between both hands and lifted it to her mouth.

'Who hasn't?' she said after taking a long sip. 'I had to close the shop, you know. Regular customers who'd been coming for years. They were getting shouted at in the street. Old Mr Jeffries was shaking with fear the last time he came for a reading. Took him almost an hour to calm down. I offered to walk him out, but he didn't want to be seen with me in public. He's been coming to the shop for twenty years.'

McLean leaned back against the Aga, cradling his own mug of tea un-drunk. Any minute now he expected Madame Rose to break down in tears.

'You've still not told me who they are. I take it they've a problem with what you do, who you are?'

'I really don't know what their problem is. If I'm being honest, I'm not really sure who they are, either. That's a large part of the problem. Oh the people doing it are Neds, mostly, I guess. I'm no stranger to a half-brick through the window. Worse shoved through the letterbox sometimes. Do you know how long I've lived in that house, Inspector?'

McLean recalled a room, larger than he'd expected to find at the back of a Leith Walk shop front, filled from floor to ceiling with antiquarian books, esoteric objects, things that could only really be described as 'things', and cats. Lots of cats. Curiously he didn't recall it smelling much of anything. 'I've no idea.'

'Before you were born, that's for certain.' Madame Rose took another long drink of tea.

'I'm really not sure—'

'What I'm saying, Inspector, is that I've lived in this city, in that particular part of this city, for a very long time. By and large people have been at the very least civil. Not much outward hostility, even given my . . . condition. Oh, there's been the odd person who'd have a go. There's always bullies, wherever you are. But mostly I've been left to live my life the way I chose.'

'So what's changed?'

Madame Rose looked at him for a moment before answering. McLean could see the lines around her eyes and mouth, the skeletal nature of her neck. He'd never really considered her age, but it was possible she could be in her sixties, he supposed. Older, even. Still, to have lived in the city so long?

'Everything, Inspector. And nothing. Things have been getting steadily worse since the eighties. But now it's like the bullies are being organised. Like there's an invisible hand behind their actions. They're hounding me out of my house and home. Driving away my livelihood. They even killed one of my cats.'

At these words, Mrs McCutcheon's cat, which had been curled up in Madame Rose's lap, purring gently, stood up and nudged the medium's hand. Without thinking, she began to scratch its ears.

'Have you been to the police?' McLean asked.

'Of course. But what can they do? It's never the same faces I see outside the window. That's if I see anyone at all.'

'But you said you thought they were being organised. I'm not saying you're wrong, but if you've not seen them, how do you know?'

Something of Madame Rose's former slightly imperious self came to the fore as she drew herself upright and stuck out her faux bosom so that Mrs McCutcheon's cat was almost trapped beneath it. 'I'd have thought of all people you would have understood. The likes of you and I, we deal in intangibles, gut feelings.' She swirled her mug, put it down on the table with a solid thunk. 'The portent in the tea leaves.'

'But you must have some idea—'

'If I knew who it was, I'd put an end to it. I am not without resources, my protections. This isn't the first time my place in the city has been challenged, though I have to admit I've not seen such a sophisticated attack in many a year.' Madame Rose stared back at him with some of her old vigour returning. Despite appearing less like a dowdy spinster and more like a man dressed badly in drag, McLean found himself referring to the medium as 'her', thinking of her as the gender she so obviously felt happiest being. She'd helped him, possibly helped Emma too, though that seemed to be a work in progress. And now something had upset her so much she had to come to him in return.

'I'll look into it. Can't promise anything, but if someone's organising a hate campaign, well, we have laws against that these days.'

Madame Rose's smile almost split her head in two. 'Thank you, Inspector. Tony. You have no idea how much that means to me.' She lifted Mrs McCutcheon's cat off her lap, placed it carefully on the table in front of her, stroked it once, left her ample hand resting on its head. 'There was one other thing.'

'Go on.'

'I'm not looking for a place to stay. They'll not drive me out of my home that easily.'

'But?' McLean held Madame Rose's gaze, almost certain he knew what he was going to be asked next.

'Just for a little while, maybe a month until I've dealt with this . . . delicate situation . . . I was wondering if you might have space in this lovely home of yours for one or two more cats?'

15

It never ceases to amaze and amuse me how easy it is to fool people. They hear what they want to hear, see what they want to see, and if you know what that is then the rest is child's play.

Child's play. I allow myself a small smirk of amusement at the realisation of just how appropriate that is. I am in the Royal Hospital for Sick Children, after all. The Sick Kids, as it's universally known. Not as easy to get into as you might think, which is a good thing, I suppose. No problem if you know how. If you've spent as much time here as I have.

He's here, though. Jim. He consults in the oncology ward two days a week, often more if he allows himself to get too attached to a case. I've been watching him a few weeks now, noting the simple patterns to his life, working out where his strings are and how to pull them. Today is a special day. Today I bring him one step closer to apotheosis.

'Ben?' His voice is hesitant. I have my back to him, head slightly turned so he can recognise me as I converse with one of the nurses on reception. He's three minutes late, which is annoying. The nurse was beginning to bore me.

'Jim?' I turn, let a second pass before smiling. 'What on earth are you doing here?'

'Could say the same about you, Ben.' He crosses the hall

with a weary step, the gait of a man who doesn't see his bed often enough. To my side, the nurse looks at him with an expression that suggests she wants to mother him, if only he'll let her get close. He hands her the clipboard he's been carrying, exchanges a familiar greeting before turning back to me. 'So what brings you to this neck of the woods?'

'Not in front of everyone.' I tap the side of my nose in a conspiratorial manner, lead him away from the nurse who is so obviously looking for some gossip to spread around the hospital. Across the hall it is quieter. I can lower my voice. This is serious business that should not be overheard.

'We're hoping to set up a trial for a new leukaemia therapy. All very hush hush at the moment. You know what people are like if they get a whiff of a possible cure.'

'I . . . how don't I know about this? Are you using differentiated stem cells? Nucleic refactoring?' His eyes go from tired to ablaze in an instant, the questions coming thick and fast. I never realised it would be this easy. Takes away a lot of the challenge, really.

'Please, keep it quiet.' I lay a hand on his arm, squeeze gently until he stops. 'It's early days. Might not even get approval.'

'I want to show you something. Someone.' He pulls away from my hold, starts to walk back across the hall. I don't move, and when he turns to see why, I mime looking at my watch.

'I can't. Already late for the meeting. Maybe another time?'

His impatience is a beautiful thing to see. Such a mind

that can heal the sick and not know what is wrong with itself. He is so close, if he could just see the simple step he needs to take.

'Tomorrow,' he says eventually. 'Meet me here at eight, OK?'

I nod, say nothing, move another piece on the game board.

16

'Thank you for coming in. I know this must be a very difficult time. For you and your daughters.'

Interview room three had been redecorated recently, which meant that it didn't look too shabby or intimidating. There was a powerful odour of paint though, and the window didn't open. On a warm August morning that made for a somewhat uncomfortable meeting. McLean had taken off his jacket and hung it over the back of his chair. Beside him, Grumpy Bob slumped like a man half asleep. Across from them the object of their interview looked fresh and well by comparison.

'It's not easy explaining to a child that daddy's not coming back ever again. But in some ways it's better they deal with it at such an early age. The young mind is so plastic. So malleable.' Charlie Stevenson wasn't exactly wearing widow's weeds. She was dressed for summer in a flowing floral dress that was so thin it revealed rather more than it hid. She was perhaps early thirties, well tanned and even better toned. A fashionably large pair of sunglasses was pushed up into her long straw-blonde hair, itself piled up in a loose knot on the top of her head. She had piercing grey eyes that fixed on McLean as he spoke and wouldn't let go.

'You and Mr Stevenson were recently divorced, I understand.'

'Yes. The papers finally came through about six months ago. Of course we'd been apart for a couple of years by then.'

'How long were you married before that?'

'Ten years.' The ex-Mrs Stevenson gave a little theatrical frown. 'No, I tell a lie. It was eleven. Give or take a month.'

'And you had two girls.'

'Lucy and Clare, yes. Lucy's five, Clare's seven. Is this relevant, Inspector?'

McLean paused before answering, holding that grey-eyed stare. She was undeniably good-looking, but something about the way she carried herself put him on edge.

'I'm trying to get a picture of Mr Stevenson's mental state over the last few months. You are . . . were closest to him.'

'That's debatable. Not since Lucy was born, at least.'

'Mr Stevenson had custody of the girls at weekends, I think.'

'Twice a month, yes. And he'd take them for longer if I needed to get away. He wasn't a bad father, Inspector. Ben doted on the girls.'

'What is it you do, Mrs Stevenson?'

'As I said, the papers came through six months ago. I've not been Mrs Stevenson in a very long time. I'm Miss Christie again now.'

'Of course, I'm sorry. What do you do, Miss Christie?'

'Do?'

'Work. What's your business that you occasionally have to get away for, for longer than a weekend?'

An angry scowl flitted across Miss Christie's face at the question. 'Again, I'm not sure how relevant that is. I'm not a suspect, am I? Only I've not got a lawyer or anything.'

'No, Miss Christie. You're not a suspect.' McLean clasped his hands together to keep from fidgeting, leaned his elbows on the table. Miss Christie uncrossed her legs, then crossed them over the other way, leaning forward herself.

'I'm trying to get some idea of Mr Stevenson's state of mind leading up to his death. You say you've been separated a couple of years, but you probably saw him as often as his colleagues at work, and you've known him longer than anyone. So tell me, when was the last time he had the girls for more than a weekend? When was the last time he had them at all?'

Miss Christie didn't answer straight away. It might have been that she was genuinely trying to remember, but McLean got the impression she was acting. She uncrossed and crossed her legs again, like a little girl desperate to be excused. He gave her all the time she needed, confident that Grumpy Bob wouldn't butt in. The silence was probably only twenty or thirty seconds, but it felt like a small ice age.

'He hasn't had the girls over in eight weeks. Maybe three months.' This was obviously a source of great annoyance to Miss Christie.

'But he saw them? Every so often?'

'He'd drop by my house sometimes. Pick them up from school and bring them home, maybe. But he'd never stay long.'

'Did he say why?' This from Grumpy Bob, the first he'd contributed to the conversation so far.

'He was working on something big. I know that much. It was like when he had that scoop a few years back. You remember, the corruption scandal in the council? Back-handers and nepotism and God only knows what else. That was Ben's last big story. I kind of got the impression he was on to something similar. As big, anyway.'

'But he didn't discuss it with you.'

'Not even when we were married. Ben was always very protective of his work, his sources. He often said he'd rather the story didn't get published than he betray a confidence. Took that very seriously. Too bloody seriously if you ask me. Like these narks, whatever they were, were more important than his wife and children.'

'So this new thing. It started about three months ago, then?'

'I reckon so, Inspector. That's when the girls started complaining, anyway. They love going to stay with their daddy. Kids are so innocent that way. Can't see the faults in us adults.'

McLean leaned back into his chair, as much to get away from the eye-catching view of Miss Christie's décolletage as anything. He'd scribbled a few notes down, but the main questions Mrs Stevenson – Miss Christie, he corrected himself – could answer, she had done.

'I think that's all for now. Thank you. Detective Sergeant Laird will see you get home OK.'

They all stood, Miss Christie gathering up the large canvas bag she'd brought with her, as Grumpy Bob went to open the door. She was about to leave when McLean thought of one last thing.

'You have a key, to Mr Stevenson's flat?' he asked.

'Of course. It was my home once.' Miss Christie hefted her bag as if to fetch something out of it.

'I'd be grateful if we could have it. Just until we've finished with the forensic investigation. I'm sure you'll keep away if we ask you to, but I'd hate for it to fall into someone else's hands.'

McLean held out his hand, maintaining eye contact all the while. There was a pause, and then Miss Christie shrugged, reached into the bag and pulled out a key ring. 'Fair enough,' she said as she handed it over. 'But I'll be wanting a receipt.'

The CID room was quiet, with most of what little action there was taking place in the major incident room up the stairs. McLean had gone there in search of DC MacBride, or at a pinch DC Gregg. He needed someone to come along with him when he visited Ben Stevenson's flat, and Grumpy Bob had disappeared after escorting the late journalist's ex-wife away from her interview. He didn't expect the pale, freckled face topped with an unruly mop of straggly red hair that stared up at him from a desk that had been empty for a couple of months now.

'Didn't think you were back until next week,' he said, then realised how rude that sounded. 'Sorry. It's good to see you, Kirsty.'

Detective Sergeant Ritchie's initial frown turned to a smile. 'I was going stir-crazy, sir. Cooped up in that wee basement flat.'

'You could have gone out, you know. Enjoyed the Festival, taken a holiday, rested.'

'Oh, I did plenty of that, but it gets a bit dull after a while. There's only so many books you can read before your brain starts to go all mushy.'

'That a fact?' McLean wished he had the time to put that theory to the test. He'd love the opportunity to lose himself in a good book for a change. Instead he had overtime rosters and reports so dry they made his eyeballs shrivel.

'Thought I'd do a bit of background reading. Bring myself up to speed before I start back proper on Monday.' Ritchie pointed at the computer screen in front of her, just in case he didn't know how she might do such a thing.

'I've got a better idea. Fancy a stroll up to Marchmont?'

'What's up there?' Ritchie was already out of her seat and lifting a lightweight fleece jacket off the back of her chair.

'A journalist's flat. Come on. I'll tell you all about it on the way.'

It took rather longer to walk there than he'd anticipated. DS Ritchie might have been declared fit for work by the doctors, but a fortnight in a hospital bed followed by a couple of months recuperating had left her frail. Walking more than a few hundred yards made her short of breath, and she couldn't match his normal pace at all. Not for the first time McLean was reminded of just how close to death she'd come, and all because of a kiss.

Ben Stevenson's address was a surprisingly large tenement flat in Marchmont. As McLean and Ritchie walked up the street towards it, he couldn't help thinking either that journalists were paid far more than their whining and complaints might suggest, or that Stevenson had a sideline in bank robbery. Then again, maybe the man had inherited money. It wasn't unheard of, after all.

''Bout bloody time. What took you so long?' As they

approached the front door, McLean noticed a figure standing by the door. It didn't take long for him to recognise Jo Dalgliesh, and he was relieved to see that she was back in her normal gear – scruffy jeans, Doc Martens, tattered leather coat and a canvas bag big enough for a fortnight's holiday. The pavement around her feet was littered with dog ends. Clearly she'd been waiting a while.

'What's she doing here?' DS Ritchie asked.

'Should have told you. She's working with us on this one. Sorry.' McLean had phoned the journalist before he'd gone in search of a constable to accompany him to Stevenson's flat. He'd been so surprised to find Ritchie in, he'd quite forgotten about it.

'Thought I'd have a quick fag.' Dalgliesh checked her watch. 'Didn't think I'd get through the whole packet.'

McLean ignored the jibe, unlocked the door with the key Charlie Christie had given him and entered the hallway. He remembered these tenements from his student days. Not Stevenson's block, but one or two along. They were bigger than the Newington flats, the communal stairs more opulent. This one was well kept, too. No students living here now, if the lack of broken bicycles and discarded pizza boxes was anything to go by. No half-brick to prop open the front door, either. And a complete absence of the stench of cat.

'You been here before?' McLean asked.

'No' fer a wee whiley. Used to come round a lot when Ben and Charlie were still together.'

'Charlie being the ex-wife?' Ritchie asked. She'd been eyeing the journalist suspiciously from the moment she'd first appeared.

'Aye. Never really liked her, if I'm being honest. Ben must've though. They stuck together long enough.'

'And they had two children.' McLean started the climb up to the top floor, glancing out of the window on to a neat communal garden behind the building.

'Two wee girls. Ben dotes on them. Doted, I guess. Poor wee things are going to miss their daddy.'

He stopped mid-step. The concept of empathy from the likes of Dalgliesh was so alien to him that he simply couldn't walk for a moment. This was the woman who, after all, had written a book dissecting in minute detail the final hours and violent, terrifying deaths of ten young women, without a thought for what the sharing of such information would do to the relatives of the dead.

'Top floor, Inspector.' Dalgliesh pushed past him on to the next landing. McLean stared at her back for a moment, realised that his mouth was hanging open. He shut it with an audible click, then followed her up the stairs.

17

From what little he recalled of the man whilst he was alive, McLean had been expecting Ben Stevenson's flat to be an untidy place, piled high with bric-a-brac, probably smelling faintly of carry-out and unwashed plates. The reality was a stark contrast to the slightly scruffy reporter's work persona.

They stood in the open doorway, looking over a large, wide hall. Doors led off to various rooms yet unrevealed, and an iron spiral staircase wound its way up into the attic. Everything was tidy, the furniture he could see a mixture of antique pieces and a more modern sideboard.

'Best you put some of these on before you touch anything.' McLean took a pair of latex gloves out of his pocket and handed them to Dalgliesh. 'And don't touch anything without asking me first, OK?'

She nodded, pulling the gloves on with far too much dexterity to suggest it was something she hadn't done many times before. McLean forced his hands into another pair, snapping them tight around his fingers. Behind them, Ritchie reached the top of the stairs and the front door with an audible sigh of relief.

'You want to take the back of the flat to start with, Sergeant?' McLean asked.

'Just give us a minute to catch my breath, aye?' Ritchie leaned heavily on the railing. Her normally pale face was almost white now, just the beige spread of freckles to give her any colour.

'Take your time. Not meant to be working today, anyway, are you?'

Dalgliesh raised an eyebrow, but said nothing, shadowing McLean like an obedient spaniel as he stepped into the hall. He didn't go far, just turned slowly on the spot, trying to get a feel for the place and the man who had lived here. Even from this viewpoint he could tell the tenement was huge and airy. Christ only knew what it was worth, especially if there was a second storey.

'We looking for anything in particular?' Dalgliesh asked.

'Anything that points to what he was working on, I guess. Did he have a study?'

'This way.' The reporter led him down the wide hall and through the living room. McLean noticed a familiar-looking Linn turntable, nestling in front of a wall filled with shelves of vinyl LPs. He thought he'd amassed quite a collection himself before the fire in his Newington tenement had turned them all into puddles of black liquid, but Stevenson made his efforts seem positively amateur.

'If I'd known journalism paid this well I might've gone into it myself.'

Dalgliesh let out a snort of laughter. 'Ben came from old money. He was good, but no' that good.'

Through a door at one end of the living room was what might once have been a maid's room. It was relatively small, but still big enough to hold a large desk dominated by an enormous computer screen. Bookshelves and filing cabinets lined three walls. The fourth, facing the main road, was mostly taken up with a sash window.

'Behold, the inner sanctum.' Dalgliesh lifted up both arms and turned on the spot. 'This is where Ben worked, when he wasn't at the paper.'

McLean walked around the desk, casting his eyes over the books on the shelves. Stevenson's reading tastes seemed eclectic and his filing system was haphazard. Autobiographies of famous footballers nestled cheek by jowl with crime fiction; political diaries snuggled up to scientific and economic textbooks. There were quite a few conspiracy theory books, too, but they covered a broad range of subjects.

'You worked with Stevenson on a few big stories. Seem to recall your byline on that piece about the independence referendum a few months back.'

'Oh aye, Ben 'n' me were thick as thieves, Inspector.' Dalgliesh didn't try to hide the sarcasm in her voice.

'But you worked with him. You came here? Discussed stories you were writing?'

'Sat just there.' Dalgliesh pointed at an armchair in the corner by the window. 'Me with my laptop, Ben on his Mac. Get the right story and we could be quite the team.'

'The right story?'

'Aye, well. There's times when collaborating's fine. Other times you just don't want another journo snooping around what you're doing.'

'And Stevenson's latest story was one of those times.'

'I asked him, sure. You could always tell with Ben when he had something on the go. But this one was personal. He wasn't going to share.'

McLean pulled out the chair and sat down at Stevenson's desk. It was uncannily tidy, just the computer, keyboard, touchpad instead of a mouse. A couple of hard-bound notebooks sat to one side, but when he opened the first, it was blank. The desk itself was a thick sheet of smoked black glass on a couple of chrome trestles. No drawers in which to hide things. To his right, a low, wheeled cabinet stood just within reach. The sort of thing artists used to store paints and brushes in the studio, it had a few small drawers and a big hinged flap on the top. Opening them revealed an assortment of pens and pencils, a couple more notebooks with nothing much written in them and a bar of expensive dark chocolate from Valvona & Crolla.

Swinging round in the chair, McLean put his hand out to the nearest bookshelf, just within reach of a long-armed man. The books here were the same haphazard mix of novels, biographies and historical texts, but there seemed to be something of a pattern. Two thick hardbacks were histories of the Freemasons. Alongside them, a couple of thinner paperbacks claimed to reveal the mysteries of the Knights Templar. A third was simply called *Head*, but when he pulled it from the shelf and looked at the front he could see that it had a subtitle: 'Baphomet, the Brotherhood and the Temple'. He frowned at the word 'Brotherhood'. Too much of a coincidence for his tired old cynicism to accept. McLean had never heard of the author, but when he flicked open the cover he saw that it had been signed and dedicated 'for Ben, a true believer'.

'You know anything about this?' He held the book up for Dalgliesh to see, wondered if she knew about the words daubed in Stevenson's blood on the cavern wall. She leaned over the desk, took it from him, peered at it myopically.

'Oh aye. I remember this one.' She laughed, then handed the book back. 'Dougie Ballantyne. Wee nutter that he is. Got this theory about the Templars and the Masons and Rosslyn Chapel and all that stuff. How they worship this severed head or something. Supposed to be the secret society to end them all, you know. Batshit stuff.'

'Seems Stevenson took it seriously enough.' McLean opened up the book again, looking at the signature. He flicked through the pages briefly, saw that the text had been marked in places. Damn, that meant he was going to have to read the bloody thing.

'That might well be it, then. What he was working on,' Dalgliesh said. 'That's his current project shelf, after all.'

McLean leaned back in the chair, hefted the book a couple of times. It wasn't a thick volume, but he reckoned the contents were going to make his head hurt more than the whisky it would take to read them. 'You want to help find who killed him, right?' he asked Dalgliesh.

'Aye, anything I can do.' She nodded.

'I'll get this computer to our IT bods. No point me messing with it here. But if you really want to be helpful, you can find out all there is to know about this.' McLean held up the book. 'See where he was going with it, and maybe we'll get a clue as to why someone wanted him stopped.'

They were heading for the door, McLean with the book clasped in one hand, when DS Ritchie's voice broke the quiet.

'Sir? I really think you ought to see this.'

McLean turned on the spot, almost knocking Dalgliesh

flying. He looked around for the detective sergeant, unable to see where she had called from.

'Up here.' Ritchie appeared at the top of the spiral staircase, crooking her head so she could see them without taking too many steps down. McLean started towards her, then realised Dalgliesh was following him.

'Stay here, OK?'

She scowled at him, but hung back as he climbed the stairs. They opened on to a surprisingly spacious attic, neatly converted into a master bedroom suite.

'I thought these places usually had communal lofts,' Ritchie said as she stepped out of McLean's way.

'Usually. Depends how the titles were drawn up when the place was built. Dalgliesh said Stevenson came from old money. Chances are this place has been in the family since the start.'

'Well, it's been done up recently if that's the case. Here, look.'

Ritchie headed off across the room, leaving McLean to follow. It was difficult to get a sense of the size of the apartment below, where the party walls were. The bedroom was magnificent though, under the pitched roof, with the ceiling rising to a high point maybe fifteen feet overhead. Facing the road, there were two small skylights designed to look like the original fittings, but at the back much larger dormer windows opened on to a narrow balcony and a view out across the Meadows to the Old Town that made him stop and stare.

'Through here, sir.' Ritchie stood beside what looked like a built-in wardrobe that surrounded the bed and filled the end wall of the building. McLean dragged himself away from the view.

'What is it?'

By way of an answer, Ritchie slid open the door. Instead of a row of suits hanging over drawers of socks and shirts, there was a narrow doorway that led into a small, hidden dressing room.

'Think this might have been where he was doing most of his work recently.' Ritchie nodded at an old dressing table pushed up against one wall. It had been cleared of the usual contents and was now piled up with books, notepads and maps. The notepads were the same type as the one they'd found in Stevenson's jacket, only dry. The mirror that would have been attached to the dressing table had been carefully removed from its frame and placed in the corner a few feet away. The wall behind it was covered in newspaper cuttings, pages torn from books, photographs and all manner of other papers, pinned up and with coloured strings running across everything as if a drug-addled giant spider had taken up residence.

'Aye, Ben could get a bit obsessive like that sometimes.'

McLean and Ritchie both turned to see Jo Dalgliesh standing just outside the dressing room, looking in.

'Thought I told you to stay downstairs.'

'What, and miss all the fun? No way Jose.' The reporter crossed into the room, peering up at the wall and its seemingly random collection of images. She pointed to one close to the centre, an elderly man with a massive, bushy white beard. 'See him. Is that no' the chappie wrote that book?'

McLean still clasped it in his hand. He looked at the cover, then turned it over to see the back. Sure enough, there was a tiny photograph of the author. It was possible there might be two people with such a distinctive beard. At the right time of year there would likely be hundreds in department stores and shopping malls all across the land. Only one Santa Claus lookalike was on Ben Stevenson's wall, though.

'Douglas Ballantyne the third.' He read out the name on the book, then followed a long thread of red woollen string across the wall to a page torn out of a magazine, an interview with the very same man. 'Think we might have to have a word with him.' He tapped a finger against the thin card of the book cover. 'If he's still alive, that is.'

18

'Heard you took that reporter off to Stevenson's flat. What the hell were you thinking doing that?'

McLean stopped mid-stride, not so much because of what Detective Chief Inspector Brooks had said as because of the podgy hand that had grabbed his arm. He'd been hoping to slip from the back door of the station up to his office without being noticed, but today it would seem he was out of luck.

'I'd have thought that would've been obvious, sir.' He shook his arm free of Brooks' hold, then perhaps a little over-ostentatiously adjusted his jacket. The DCI rewarded him with a scowl, same as ever.

'It's a potential crime scene and you go marching in there with a civilian. I don't see anything obvious about it at all. Bloody irregular if you ask me.'

McLean tried not to shake his head, but may have failed a little. 'Ben Stevenson died in the cavern where we found him. His flat was never a crime scene, but it could yield clues. Dalgliesh went there regularly; she knew the place better than anyone. Knew Stevenson better than anyone. Without her I'd never have picked up what he was working on when he died.'

'That still doesn't answer my question though. Since when did you start hobnobbing with the press?'

'I can think of many people I'd rather hobnob with

than Jo bloody Dalgliesh. She came to me in the first place, before her colleague turned up dead.'

'And you don't think that's suspicious? You think it's a good idea bringing her in on the investigation when she might be a suspect? Christ, it's no wonder they turned you down for the DCI job. Surprised you even made it to inspector.'

'If you really think Dalgliesh is a suspect in the violent, ritual murder of her colleague, then I'm not sure there's anything I can do to help you, sir. As you're well aware, I have less reason to like her than many people in this station, after that book she wrote all about how my fiancée was abducted and murdered. Remember that?'

McLean paused a fraction of a second, just enough for Brooks to start his reply, then cut in. 'As it happens, I'd rather work the case without her getting in the way, but she knows Stevenson, knows his work and more importantly she's agreed not to publish anything we haven't cleared.'

'Chance'd be a fine thing. She'll be making shit up about how useless we are and spreading it around like she always does. She's a menace, and you of all people should know that. I want her cut out of this investigation. You understand?'

McLean studied Brooks' face. He was a fat man; there was no charitable way of putting it. He liked his food and was less keen on exercise. He wasn't a bad detective when he put his mind to it, but lately most of his effort seemed to have been going into pushing for promotion. If the rumour mill was anything to go by, he would be scrabbling up the greasy pole into Detective Superintendent Duguid's office just as soon as the man himself had retired. The prospect filled McLean with weary gloom. True, he'd be rid of Dagwood, but he'd learned over the years how to deal with him. Brooks was a different matter altogether.

'As SIO for this case, I think that's my decision to make actually, sir. And the suggestion to work with her came from the superintendent, so it's not something I've done without consultation anyway.'

Brooks reddened, his jowls wobbling as his anger rose. It was usually possible to gauge when he was going to explode, as sweat would shine his forehead. That hadn't happened yet, but it was only a matter of time.

'Fine,' he said after perhaps ten seconds of escalating tension. 'Use her. Or try to. She'll stab you in the back though. It's the story with her kind. Nothing else matters. You mark my words.'

He turned away, marching off with a sideways rolling motion like a sailor not long off the sea. McLean watched him go, trying hard not to admit that, annoying idiot though he was, the man was probably right. Well, Dalgliesh had kept her end of the bargain so far. Only time would tell how long that could last. Shaking his head with weary resignation, he began the long climb up the stairs to the major incident room.

'My office. Now.'

McLean glanced up from the report he'd been checking with DC Gregg to see Detective Superintendent Duguid standing in the doorway. As far as he could remember, this was the first time Duguid had visited the major incident room since the first briefing on the case, days ago.

'Get that over to forensics. See if they've got anything

from the notebook yet.' He sent Gregg off before addressing Duguid.

'Is it important, sir? Only I've got a mountain of actions to get through.'

'Of course it's bloody important. You think I'd come down here looking for you if it wasn't?' Duguid turned away from the door, forcing McLean to follow. He said nothing all the way up the stairs and along the corridor to his office, waiting until he was seated and the door was closed before finally speaking.

'You asked me if Ben Stevenson was a member of any Masonic Lodge. Well the simple answer is no. He wasn't.'

McLean stood in his usual position in front of the desk, hands clasped behind his back. He bobbed slightly on his feet, waiting for the detective superintendent to get to the point. Unless that was the point and Duguid had dragged him all the way up here for no good reason.

'The simple answer?' he asked after a moment's silence.

'You're not a Freemason, McLean. Can't expect you to understand. There's a lot of nonsense written about us. Lurid speculation by the gutter press, disdain from the broadsheets. You'd be surprised to know how much good we do. How much money we raise for charity.'

'I'm sure it's all a bit of harmless fun, sir. But someone cut Ben Stevenson's throat open and then daubed your most recognisable image on the wall in his blood. I know whoever did that isn't a Freemason, or if he is he wasn't doing it for anything other than his own sick reasons, but this is a legitimate line of enquiry, don't you think?'

Duguid glowered at him for a moment, and McLean

wondered if he'd pushed a little too far. The detective superintendent was notoriously prickly about his precious Lodge, and secretive too. Not one of the reformers who wanted to drag the whole organisation kicking and screaming into the nineteenth century.

'If you'd let me finish. I asked around and Stevenson wasn't a member of the order. His father was, but Stevenson was considered—' Duguid paused a moment as if choosing the right word. 'Unreliable.'

'You thought he'd spill the beans as soon as he knew anything important.'

'Oh, we fully expected that. It happens far more often than you'd think. No, we weren't worried about that so much as the damage he'd do digging around for secrets that didn't actually exist. Like your reference to the Brotherhood, capital B, and Baphomet, the talking head.'

'You know about these things?'

'I know of them. Stupid conspiracy theories with no basis in fact. One of the more idiotic accusations made against the Knights Templar was that they worshipped a demon in the form of a disembodied head. That was Baphomet, apparently. Truth is there was no Baphomet, no conspiracy. The Templars were rich and the king of France owed them a lot of money. He persuaded the pope to accuse them of witchcraft and demon worship. It was a power grab, simple enough, and it happened seven hundred years ago. The Freemasons have been about for less than three hundred. You do the maths.'

'So why does it keep coming up? Why the reference to Baphomet in the cave?'

'Search me. It's like a bad penny. Always there when you least need it. But I can tell you this much. That gobbledegook that went on down in that cave's got fuck all to do with Freemasonry.'

'An elaborate hoax then.' McLean remembered the book he'd found in Stevenson's flat. 'Or maybe a trap.'

It was Duguid's turn to look surprised. 'A trap?'

'Do you know a chap called Douglas Ballantyne?' McLean didn't have to wait for the answer; Duguid's face said it loud. 'Stevenson had his book. It was inscribed "to Ben, a true believer".'

'Ballantyne's a nutter. Grade A conspiracy theorist. Take anything he says with a bucketload of salt.'

'Oh, I intend to. Don't worry about that. But if Stevenson really did believe him, what if he were looking into his claims? Maybe kidding himself he could bring a journalist's open mind to them?'

'Don't tell me you think he might have found something and been killed for it. I already told you there's not a shred of truth in that nonsense.'

'No, I don't think that. But someone may have used that to lure him in. You can't tell me this murder wasn't planned meticulously, after all. The killer's put a lot of effort into it. They had to have a reason even if it wasn't anything to do with Freemasonry or this non-existent Brotherhood.'

Duguid said nothing for a moment, as the implications percolated through his brain. McLean could see their progress written on the detective superintendent's face.

'Who would want Stevenson dead?' he asked eventually.

'That's the wrong question. Chasing down his enemies isn't going to solve this case.'

'How no?' Duguid ran long fingers through straggly greying hair.

'Because it's too elaborate. Too contrived. No, it's not who wanted him dead we should be asking, but why.'

19

The squad car had dropped him half a mile from home before executing a tyre-burning U-turn and disappearing at speed to an urgent call-out. McLean didn't mind, really. It was late, but there was still plenty of light left in the day. That was the great thing about the summer so far north. You paid for it in the winter, of course.

Walking up the street to his house, he noticed something odd about the silhouette of the church, and paused to work out what it was. Somewhere in the back of his mind he'd noticed the arrival of piles of scaffolding, portable site huts and building machinery in the street. He'd made a donation to the roof restoration fund a while back, and the minister had told him they were only waiting for the good weather before starting. Judging by the steel fingers reaching up into the evening sky, the good weather was here. It looked like a massive hand, clawing its way out of the ground in a bid to grab the church and drag it down to hell.

Shaking his head at the strange image, McLean was about to set off again when a voice broke the rumbling silence.

'Inspector. Tony. What a pleasant surprise.'

He turned to see the slender form of the minister emerge from the shadows in the graveyard, like some hapless spirit bound by the iron railings that stopped the dead from escaping. She was wearing her usual black, just the white smile of her dog collar underlining her pale face and grey shoulder-length hair, so that she was for a moment just a floating, disembodied head.

'Minister, I—'

'Mary, please.' She emerged fully into the light, and McLean could see that she was wearing gardening gloves, a pair of secateurs in one hand. A clump of what looked like dead brambles hung limply from the other.

'Doing a spot of weeding?'

'It's never-ending at this time of the year. So much nutrition in the soil.'

McLean glanced around the graveyard. None of the headstones looked to be less than a hundred years old. Not much in the way of nutrition left, surely. Then he noticed the smile crinkling the edges of the minister's eyes.

'I see they've started on the roof.' He changed the subject before it turned to the recently interred.

'They have indeed. I know you're not a praying man, Tony, but if you felt like asking for a nice dry fortnight or so . . .'

'I could always ask my boss. He seems to think he's got a direct line to the Almighty.'

'Probably best you don't.' The minister rolled her eyes, looking upwards. 'We don't want to piss him off, after all.'

'Good point.' McLean shifted on his feet. It had been a long day and he was hungry, anxious to get home. On the other hand, he didn't want to appear rude.

'I've been running a series of evening meetings. If you're interested.'

He started to protest, but the minister interrupted him.

'Oh, don't worry. They're not prayer meetings or anything. Just informal discussions over a cup of tea or a beer. They're quite popular, you know. There's a surprising number of single folk around here, too. Young professionals like yourself. Too busy at work to make friends. Not enough hours in the day.'

It seemed an odd thing for the minister to say. McLean knew that he wasn't the most sociable of people, but that suited him just fine. He had friends, could always go out for a drink or a meal if he wanted. True, they all tended to be fellow police officers or closely linked to his work, but that wasn't so unhealthy really, was it? So much easier to make conversation if you weren't constantly having to second-guess whether the other person was going to be horrified by something you might say.

'We also have poker evenings once a month. With a face like yours I'd love to play a few games. Might even raise enough to finish the whole roof.'

'I'm sorry. I know you mean well, but it's really not my thing. And card games leave me cold.'

'Fair enough. But bear us in mind if you find yourself rattling around in that big old house. Can't be easy all alone there. Especially after . . . well.' The minister dropped her gaze to her hands, fiddling with the dead brambles. It was a good act, McLean had to admit. She'd have been great at interrogating suspects. On the other hand, it was hardly a year since the house had been full of life. Bizarre, unpredictable life, but life all the same. Now it was just him and the cat. The cats, he corrected himself. He had to admit there were times when a little human company might have been nice.

'I'll think about it,' he said, knowing that he wouldn't.

'Speak to your colleague. Kirsty. She'll tell you what we get up to. There's no happy clappy stuff. Just a chance to chat. Or listen.'

'Ritchie?' McLean couldn't help looking up at the scaffold-clad church. The sky was darkening now, orange sunset fading to the deep blue-black of night. 'She's been coming here?'

'Oh yes. About two months now. Didn't she tell you?' The minister looked a little worried, as if she'd betrayed a confidence.

'No. She's only just come back to work. She was off sick. I'll ask her about it though. Tomorrow.'

'You do that, Tony. And mention me to her, won't you?' She nodded a quick goodbye, turned and walked back into the gloom.

He was so wrapped up in his thoughts that he almost walked straight past his entrance gate. On the face of it, there was no logical reason why Ritchie would have gone to that particular church and that particular group; she lived halfway across the city. He was surprised to find that she was religious-minded at all, if he was being honest with himself. It wasn't something that had come up in conversation, and she wasn't the sort of person to disappear on a Sunday morning when there was work to be done.

But there was the illogical thought that wouldn't go away. She had been touched by evil in the form of the enigmatic Mrs Saifre, saved by a blessing from the font of that church. That was a connection he really didn't like to think about; the ramifications were too much.

'What the—?' Something twined itself around his feet as he crunched up the gravel driveway. He'd not left any lights on in the house, and under the trees it was as dark as night, branches whipping at his arms as he tried to stop himself from falling over. 'Bloody cats!'

The offender skittered off into the bushes, then stopped and turned to watch him. Its eyes glowed faintly in the dying light and he could just about make out enough of its shape to see that it wasn't Mrs McCutcheon's cat. She was smooth-coated and this was a great shaggy beast of a thing. One of Madame Rose's perhaps, or the local pride that seemed to have decided he needed protection.

'I can look after myself, you know.' McLean stalked off to the back door and let himself in. Through to the kitchen and he flicked on the lights. At least a dozen pairs of eyes looked up at him from well-chosen positions about the room. It had been like this every evening since his visit from the old medium. In the main he didn't really mind. They were all house-trained, as far as he could smell. Mostly they kept to the kitchen and the garden, too, with only Mrs McCutcheon's cat venturing into the rest of the house. How long that would last, he had no idea. Same as he had no idea how long the cats would be staying. He'd try and remember to ask Grumpy Bob to have a look into it. The old sergeant had friends at Leith nick who might do him a favour.

'Don't get up on my account,' he said as he passed through the room. Mrs McCutcheon's cat was the only one to ignore his command, stretching from her favoured spot in the middle of the kitchen table before leaping down and following him out into the hall.

A small pile of uninteresting mail waited on the mat by the front door. Some bills, some junk, and a letter from his solicitors. He slid a finger under the seal, tore it open as he headed to the library. The typing was dense, its content a bit too dry for his frazzled brain to take in. Something to do with the tenement block in Newington. An offer from the McClymonts that would probably be easier to understand with a dram of the Scottish Malt Whisky Society's finest.

McLean dropped all the letters on the side table, then fetched his prize. He considered putting some music on, but found he wasn't in the mood. Looking over at his turntable and the meagre collection of LPs he'd managed to amass since the fire just reminded him of Ben Stevenson's collection. What would happen to that?

Mrs McCutcheon's cat leapt into his lap as soon as he sat down, nuzzled at his free hand until he scratched her behind the ears. She had taken the arrival of Madame Rose's cats well, but seemed determined to remind him at every opportunity that she was the first.

He took a long sip of whisky, feeling the burn on his tongue, then reached for the pile of letters. Sooner or later he was going to have to make a decision about the flat. Logic argued he should just take the money and run, but there were always more important things to do.

As he lifted the letters towards him, a slim card slipped out of the pile, landing picture side up in his lap. The cat sniffed at it, then batted it with a paw before he managed to pick it up. The photograph showed a slightly out-of-focus image of the Taj Mahal, and when McLean turned the card over he recognised the untidy scrawl of Emma's handwriting.

Not many of us left now, but it's getting harder to follow the trail. Heading east again soon. Missing you. E. XOX

McLean stared at the words, turned the card over and peered at the picture again, studied the smudged postmark as if it might give him some clues. He sniffed the card, and imagined he could catch the faintest hint of her scent even though he knew that was impossible. Mrs McCutcheon's cat nudged at his hand once, then curled up in his lap and began to purr. He took another sip of the whisky, placed the glass down on top of the letter from his lawyers, and just sat in the quiet, staring at the postcard.

20

'It's for your own good, Anthony. That school's just holding you back.'

The library is Gran's serious room. I don't normally go in there. The books are older even than she is, dusty and dry and covered in cracked leather. Some of them are written in foreign languages like French and Spanish and Auld Scots. It's where she has her writing desk, and the hidden cupboard with the whisky in it that she thinks I don't know about. And it's where I am summoned when I've done something wrong.

'But all my friends are there.'

'You'll make new friends. There'll be plenty of other new boys. The Grove is a fine prep school. Good enough for your grandfather and father both.'

The sun is shining outside. It's been a long hot summer so far and I'd really rather be out there playing than in this stuffy old room.

'Dad went there?' It's been two years now since they left and never came back, mum and dad. I can still remember them as clearly as the moment they waved goodbye with promises they'd be home soon. It's hard to imagine my father as a boy my age.

'He did. And he made lifelong friends there.' Gran has been sitting in one of the high-backed armchairs, but now she comes across and sits next to me on the sofa. 'Oh, Tony. You're so like him. You'll do well there, believe me.'

'But my friends—'

'Will still be here when you come home for the holidays. And there's plenty of those left. Term doesn't start for another month yet.'

A month seems a very long time. Too far in the future to really worry about. And I'll be going to a place where my dad went. That has to be pretty cool.

'Go. Play outside a while. It's far too nice a day to be cooped up indoors.'

I don't need to be told twice. It's only when I'm at the door that I think to ask, 'Can I go round to Norman's?'

'Norman Bale?' Gran frowns in that way she has. 'Yes. I suppose so. It's not far. Just be careful going up the road.'

I nod my understanding and rush out the door before she can change her mind.

21

A terrifying scream woke McLean from dreams of his childhood. He tried to sit upright, then realised he already was, wedged into the high-backed armchair in the library. Mrs McCutcheon's cat was long gone, Emma's postcard fallen to the floor where his sleepy arm had dropped it. The windows were dark, just the light from the table lamp casting a small glow around him like a protective shield. The echo of that scream unsettled him, even if it was just in his mind. He strained to hear anything but the low, constant hum of the city and the occasional creak and groan of the old house settling around him.

Then it came again, different now that it wasn't being warped by sleep. A wailing, hissing noise from outside. Caterwauling, there was no other word for it. With a heavy sigh, McLean hauled himself out of the chair and went to see who was fighting whom.

A glance at the old clock in the hallway showed that it was ten to four in the morning. He'd not thought himself so tired, but he must have been asleep in the armchair almost five hours. It didn't bear thinking about that his alarm was going to go off in another two.

The kitchen was empty as he walked through it, then out the back door. The night was warm, a gentle breeze ruffling the leaves all around him as he let his eyes adjust to the darkness. Whatever had been screaming had stopped for now, but as the night noises began to filter in, McLean could hear something unusual from the end of the drive-way, where it opened out on to the street.

Gravel crunched under his feet like explosions in a quarry as he tried to walk as quietly as possible in the direction of the noise. It sounded like someone was cursing under their breath, or having an argument with themselves, and for a moment McLean wondered if a tramp had decided his gateway was a nice warm spot to kip for the night. He wished he'd brought a torch, then remembered he was still wearing his work suit. It wasn't brilliant, but he always carried a pen light in his jacket pocket.

Green light reflected back off the dark, rubbery rhodo-dendron leaves, the occasional flash of blue eye reminding him that wherever he went in his own home, he was never far from a cat these days. McLean played the torch around the end of the driveway, trying to see into the shadows cast by the far-spaced street lamps in the road beyond. Something much larger than a cat let out a muffled 'fuck' and then a dark figure burst out of the bushes. For an instant it stood in the gateway, facing him, and McLean could see a pair of startled eyes peering out from a black balaclava. Then the man turned and ran. McLean made a half-hearted pursuit out into the road, but he knew when he was outclassed. Whoever had been hiding in his bushes would have given a professional sprinter a run for his money. In no time at all he was at the road end, not stop-ping or looking back before he disappeared around the corner.

McLean stood in the gateway for a moment, staring at the empty spot where the running man had last been. His hand went to his pocket of its own accord, pulling out his phone. He had brought up the speed dial screen and was about to call the station when he was distracted by something rubbing against his leg. Mrs McCutcheon's cat was standing beside him, looking pleased with itself. It looked up at him, blinked slowly, then sauntered off into the bushes. Well, he could take a hint.

The rhododendron leaves were thick around the outside of the bush, but they soon gave way to a cave-like interior. McLean remembered it well from his childhood, the best of dens for a lonely child thrown out of the house to get some fresh air. Under the meagre light from his torch, it seemed smaller than his memory, and there was a pungent odour of human excrement that he wasn't expecting. Careful where he put his feet, he swept the torch back and forth until he located the source.

'Seriously? Some drunkard took a dump in your garden and you think it's important enough to get forensics involved?'

There hadn't been much point in trying to get to sleep after the incident. McLean had made himself a large pot of coffee and sat in the kitchen until the forensic expert had turned up somewhere near six. She was new; he'd not met her at a crime scene before. But obviously someone higher up the chain had warned her about him. Still, she'd understood the importance of the task, collected up the stool and promised him it would be analysed for DNA. Amazing how much information you could get from shit, had been her exact words as she left.

Getting into the station early, McLean had hoped he'd be able to immerse himself in the Ben Stevenson case, plough through the mountain of useless actions the investigation had thrown up so far. Unfortunately DCI Brooks was also an early riser, and he appeared to have daily updates from the forensic service fed directly to his brain. There was no other way he could have known, surely.

'Half-three in the morning, dressed completely in black, with a balaclava over his head?' McLean shook his own; this man was going to be in charge soon. Things never change.

'If you thought there'd been a crime, McLean, you should have reported it. Not used your personal hotline to the forensic services to get you ahead of the queue.'

Pinching the bridge of his nose didn't usually help relieve the stress of dealing with superior officers, but McLean found it did at least stop him from resorting to violence. That rarely went well, and besides, Brooks had a reputation as well as bulk on his side.

'I did call control, sir, and I also told them it was low priority. I've spoken to my neighbours, no one's been burgled recently. If someone was casing the area, they've had a nasty surprise. Will probably try their luck somewhere a bit more downmarket. Grange or the likes.'

Brooks' nostrils flared at the insult. McLean knew perfectly well where the DCI lived and how it fitted into the complicated hierarchy of the city's social-climbing classes.

'And just how does a forensic analysis of this crap help, then?'

'Believe it or not, sir, they can get a good DNA sample from human excrement. Especially if it's fresh, and I can assure you this one was very fresh. If this man's on the database, we'll know who he is.'

'And then what? You going to try and do him for damage to your property because he shat in your bushes?'

'No, sir. But I will make a note of it on file. Should he come to our notice again. Besides, I don't think the crap was meant for my bushes.'

Brooks stared at him as if he were mad. 'What on earth are you talking about, man?'

'I'd have thought it would be obvious. You want to shove shit through someone's letterbox, you don't really want to be carrying it around for too long. Well, not in a bag anyway.'

'Letterbox?' Brooks lumbered to a slow realisation. 'You mean this was meant to be a warning? What the fuck for?'

The idea had come to McLean in the wee small hours, and he'd turned it over and over ever since, unable to let it go. 'That's what bothers me. I don't know.'

'Well you've pissed off enough people, I guess. Policemen tend to be a bit less direct, mind.'

'Yes, I've found that. Was thinking of someone else who had shit shoved through their letterbox recently.'

'Oh yes? Anyone I know?'

McLean hesitated. He'd not had time to ask Grumpy Bob to speak to Leith station about Madame Rose, and the more he thought about it, the less keen he was on sharing anything about the medium with DCI Brooks. 'It's probably nothing, sir. I'll let you know if anything comes of it.'

Brooks narrowed his eyes until they almost disappeared in the folds of flesh that made up his round face. Perhaps he thought doing so would help him to read McLean's mind, or maybe he was just trying to squeeze out a reluctant fart. Either way he seemed to fail.

'You do that, McLean,' he said after a while. 'And don't go blowing the departmental budget on petty vandals. Bad enough chasing whoever did this.' He waved a pudgy hand at the major incident room.

McLean thought of Ben Stevenson's daughters and how pleased they would be to hear that the police were doing their utmost to bring their father's killer to justice. He bit back the retort he wanted to give, just nodded an acceptance of his superior's crassness. Sometimes that was all you could do.

'You got a moment, Bob?'

It was a stupid question, really. McLean had spent ten minutes searching the empty offices and unused incident rooms until he'd found the detective sergeant. Grumpy Bob was sitting in the corner of the CID room, feet up on his desk, head wedged against the wall and giving his newspaper very close attention indeed. He slowly lifted it off his face, folded it and placed it on the desk before answering.

'I could probably find some space in my hectic schedule, sir. What did you have in mind?'

McLean cast an eye over the rest of the CID room, looking for other officers lurking in the corners. It was empty, but this early in the morning that was hardly a surprise. Even so, he felt uncomfortable letting too many people in on this particular piece of business.

'You still on speaking terms with the duty sergeants down in Leith station?'

'Some of them, aye. You looking for something in particular.'

'Madame Rose. You remember her?'

'Him, if I'm not mistaken. But yes. Has that shop down the Walk. Peddles fortunes and deals in old books.'

'That's the one. She helped out with Emma last year. Came to me yesterday asking if I could look into a little local problem she's been having.' McLean told Grumpy Bob the whole story, noting as he did that the old sergeant took his feet off his desk, sat upright and started to pay attention.

'They killed a cat?'

'Left the poor thing just inside the front door. Gave one of her regular customers a terrible fright when he turned up for his weekly tarot.'

'So what do you want me to do?'

'Well, I know she's spoken to someone at Leith a couple of times, but whoever's doing this is being very cunning about it. Seems it's never the same faces twice. Difficult for us to take it seriously.'

'You sure he's not just being paranoid. I mean, he's not exactly dealing from a full deck, right?'

McLean slumped against the wall, the weariness of too little sleep fighting with his patience.

'She, Bob. You've been on the equality and diversity training, right? Madame Rose might've been born a man, but she's happier being a woman. She wants to be a she, who am I to tell her she can't?'

Grumpy Bob paused a moment before answering. 'Aye, you're right. I was meaning more about the whole fortune-telling thing, mind. Unless you're telling me you believe in all that stuff too, now?'

'You know me and belief, Bob. But this isn't about me. It's about Rose. She's helped me more than once now, the least I can do is return the favour.'

'You mean the least I can do?' Grumpy Bob grinned. 'You want me to have a word with someone at Leith?'

'My guess is no one takes her seriously because of what she does, how she dresses. Sure they'll have taken down her complaint, it'll be in someone's PDA. But no one will have done anything about it. See if you can't change that, will you?'

'Consider it done.' Grumpy Bob picked up his paper, and for a moment McLean thought he was going to drape it over his face and go back to sleep. 'Tomorrow soon enough? I'll be seeing old Tam Sykes then anyway.'

'Tam's still working? Surely they put him out to pasture years ago.'

'Aye, they did. But you know what us old coppers are like. He's been helping out with some cold case reviews. Tam'll have a word if I ask him, and it'll be better coming from him.'

McLean recalled his strange meeting with the medium a few nights earlier. The more he thought about it, the more her secondary request – the almost afterthought that he might be able to give a home to her cats for a while – seemed to be the thing she really wanted from him. Chances were the attacks on her house were not something the police would have much luck looking into.

'Tomorrow's fine. Just returning a favour really. And I get the feeling Rose can look after herself anyway.'

22

'Got an address for that conspiracy nutter of yours, sir.'

McLean looked up from his desk to see the thin but smiling face of DS Ritchie peering around the door jamb. The bags under her eyes had faded a bit, her pale complexion perhaps a little more coloured than it had been a few days earlier.

'My what? Oh. Right.' His brain caught up with his mouth just too late. Poking out from underneath a series of reports that appeared to have been written by someone with English as very much a second language, he could just see a corner of the book taken from Ben Stevenson's study. McLean fished it out, staring once more at the cover.

'That's the chap.' Ritchie committed herself fully to the office as she saw the book. 'Douglas Ballantyne the third. He's been away in the US, apparently. Travelling since May, so I guess he's not a key suspect. Happy to see us any time we're passing. Soon as he's back.'

McLean flipped it over and scanned the blurb again. He'd been meaning to read the actual book, but there was never enough time. Or maybe it was just that he didn't want to have to wade through what would inevitably be a load of old rubbish dressed up as historical fact.

'You want to read it?' He held it up for Ritchie to take, but she backed away, hands raised to ward it off as if the words might somehow corrupt her soul.

'No thanks. My head's messed up enough as it is.'

McLean said nothing, although he may have raised a quizzical eyebrow. Ritchie took it as an invitation to shut the door, only then realising that there was no other chair for her to sit on. She leaned back against the wall opposite the desk, gathering her thoughts before she spoke.

'I know what happened to me, sir. Back . . .' Her words tailed off.

'You got sick. A nasty flu bug. People die of the flu you know.'

'Old people maybe. Babies, invalids. I'm thirty-two, fit. Well, I was fit.' She gave a little cough. 'Now I'm a fucking wreck. You saw what I was like after climbing three flights of stairs.'

'Give it time, Kirsty. You nearly died. Takes a while to come back from that.'

Ritchie wiped at a forehead suddenly damp with sweat. 'You make it sound like you've got experience.'

'In a way, I guess I have. Not like you, of course, but I've been there. Down so far you never think you'll make it back up again.'

'How did you? Make it back up again, that is?'

'Friends, mostly. And time.' McLean shifted in his seat, trying not to make it look like he was uncomfortable with the conversation. He was, of course. Just a little. But in a way it was his fault Ritchie was the way she was; he owed it to her to do his best to help her. Would have done even if it hadn't been.

'You have many friends out of the job?' It was an innocent question, he could see that, but it was also barbed.

'A few. Maybe not as many as I'd like.' And the closest,

the one who really helped him out through the bad days, was half a world away in California. McLean remembered the quick and unexpected call from Phil just the other evening, the memories it had sparked. He made a mental note to give his old flatmate a call back some time soon, filed it away with the large pile of mental notes he'd already made to the same effect.

'Didn't have many friends in Aberdeen anyway.' Ritchie continued as if she hadn't heard his answer. 'None of them have bothered coming to visit in the – what is it? Two years since I transferred down?'

'Christ, is it that long?'

It was a small thing, the slightest wince at the word. Unless he was being over-sensitive. Or maybe remembering the conversation he'd had with the minister.

'You'd think a city this size it'd be easy to make new friends, but when does a detective have the time, eh?'

'Well, policemen aren't all that bad.'

Ritchie laughed, which was a nice thing to see. 'You know what they say about doctor and nurse relationships, right?'

'There'll be all sorts at your evening meetings, though. Up at the church?'

Ritchie's face coloured slightly, the blush of a child caught doing something that wasn't strictly wrong, but might not be right either.

'You know about that?'

'Bumped into the minister the other night. She's been trying to get me to come along for months now. Might have let slip that I'd maybe see a familiar face there if I did.'

'You should come. It's – well, it's helped me come to

terms with what happened. I know who that woman really is now, what she did to me.'

McLean leaned back in his chair, said nothing. He didn't need to ask who 'that woman' was or what she had done to Ritchie. It was just hard to tally that knowledge with being a rational, logical person.

'Never really been one for sharing,' he said eventually. 'You know that. And I'm not that comfortable with belief, either. It's too lazy. Thanks for the invitation, but I'm fine with the friends I've got.'

'OK.' Ritchie nodded her acceptance. 'But I think you're ducking the issue. There are things that don't easily fit a rational explanation. Sometimes you have to believe something will work, otherwise it won't.'

'I prefer to look at it as thinking outside of the box. If I can't find a rational explanation, then I'm using the wrong definition of rational. And talking of work—' McLean peered at the book where he'd dropped it on to his desk. 'Douglas Ballantyne the third? Where's he live?'

'Down in the Borders. Near Peebles.' Ritchie stood up straight, once more the businesslike detective sergeant. She unpeeled a Post-it note from the top of the pad she'd been playing with throughout their conversation, stuck it down over the Santa Claus lookalike author image. McLean picked up the book and note together, glanced at the address. It sounded expensive, which suggested there was a ready market for idiot conspiracy theories.

'Give him a call, will you? Arrange a time. We're all one big happy Police Scotland now, so it's not as if Borders can complain if we spend an afternoon on their patch.'

'I'll get on it.' Ritchie pushed herself away from the wall, opened the door. 'And thanks.'

'For what?'

'For listening, I guess.'

'Any time.' McLean pulled the reports he'd been deciphering out from underneath the book. Held them up for Ritchie to see. 'It's got to be better than all this rubbish.'

Lunch in the station canteen was something of a novelty for McLean. He rarely had time for anything more sophisticated than a sandwich at his desk, and lately going into any place where a lot of junior officers congregated was uncomfortable. Probably more so for them than him; he didn't really care all that much what they thought about him as long as they did what they were told. Nevertheless, the speed with which any table he sat at emptied itself was at best impressive, at worst rude. It was true there were some officers who didn't mind sharing a coffee, muffin and blether, but then if McLean wanted to eat quickly it was best not to get caught in a conversation with DC Gregg.

Mercifully she was nowhere to be seen, and the few faces that looked up at him as he entered didn't immediately radiate hostility. Conversation continued its muted buzz unabated. Better yet, the canteen itself yielded a plate of ham sandwiches that looked like they might have been made sometime that week.

He'd barely sat down when the canteen doors burst open, and DC MacBride came rushing in. At almost the same moment, McLean's phone buzzed in his pocket, the harsh klaxon ring tone announcing that the control centre in Bilston Glen had need of his services. From the look on the detective constable's face as he scanned the room, it didn't take a genius to tell that the news was likely to be the same from both sources. McLean ignored the phone; they'd send him a text message anyway.

'I take it from your lack of breath that something important's happened?' He picked up his limp sandwich and eyed it ruefully. To bite, or not to bite?

'Call just came through, sir. They've found a dead body. A young woman. Out by Fairmilehead.'

McLean dropped the sandwich back on to the plate, pushed it away as he stood up. Probably for the best; he'd only end up with indigestion.

The lane had already been cordoned off by the time he arrived, which at least meant someone with half a brain was in charge. McLean had hoped DC MacBride would have commandeered a pool car, but the detective constable had been called away to another case. In the end, he had cadged a lift from the nearest squad car. The moment he'd clunked the passenger door shut the driver had executed a perfect reversing J-turn and sped off, which rather begged the question of how he was going to get back to the station once he was done. Not for the first time he realised he couldn't put off getting himself a new car much longer. If only people would stop dropping things on them.

'What are we looking at, Constable?' He showed his warrant card to the fresh-faced uniform who had been tasked with keeping the public on the right side of the blue-and-white tape. It wasn't a difficult job, really. Not this far out of town. Fairmilehead didn't exactly attract passers-by. Not on foot, anyway.

'Dead body, sir. That's all anyone's told me.' The constable lifted the tape to let him on to the site.

'Forensics here yet?'

'Over there.'

McLean headed in the direction he had been pointed, arriving at a cluster of white Transit vans and a couple of squad cars pulled up in a courtyard formed by three semi-derelict stone buildings: part of a farm that had long since succumbed to the ever-expanding housing estates that grew like cankers alongside the main roads branching out of the city. Through trees lining the lane, he could see a green field dotted with horses and then the seething mass of the city bypass. How long before the horses were evicted too, their grazing given over to yet more semi-detached boxes?

'Tony. You're here. Excellent.'

McLean didn't need to look to know who was speaking. He'd known Angus Cadwallader at least half his life. The city pathologist was already wearing a full-body forensic suit, the hood pulled down to reveal thinning grey hair. Judging by the gore smeared across the front of it, he'd examined the body, too.

'You've had a look, I see. Any thoughts?'

'Probably best if you see for yourself,' Cadwallader said. 'Wouldn't want to colour your judgement.'

McLean gave his friend a quizzical look, but the pathologist was obviously giving nothing away.

'I guess I'd better go and find myself a romper suit then.'

*

His initial impression was of something that had been thrown away because it had ceased to be useful. At first it was difficult even to tell that it was a body he was looking at, let alone a woman.

She had been dumped naked into a large metal bin, the sort of thing used to store horse feed and other items you didn't want the rats and mice to get at on a livery yard. Dumped was the word, too. This was no careful placing, so much as a body simply tipped in. She lay awkwardly, head staring sightlessly upwards from where it was squashed into the corner. She looked almost like a discarded mannequin, only one with real blood. And she was young. That much he could see despite the damage to her neck and the mess all over her face.

'Judging by the relative lack of bleeding, I'm going to guess she was killed elsewhere and brought here.' McLean dragged his eyes away from the grisly sight to Cadwallader standing beside him.

'Cause of death?'

'You have to ask, don't you Tony?' The pathologist ventured a grin, but it was a humourless effort. 'You'll be wanting a time too, I've no doubt.'

'When you can.' McLean gave his old friend a light slap on the arm. 'I'll go speak to the forensics team. See what they've got.'

He left Cadwallader with the body, and followed the marked-out pathway back to the forensics van where he'd borrowed his white overalls. They didn't fit, bunching up in his crotch and under his armpits in a manner that made walking difficult if you didn't want to look like a sumo wrestler. The scene of crime officers seemed to be able to move unhindered in theirs, which suggested they kept a special batch of ill-fitting ones just for detectives.

'Inspector McLean. We meet again.' The short, round figure of Jemima Cairns appeared around the corner of the nearest van. She wore the expression of a genius surrounded by fools, a near-permanent scowl on her face as she constantly scanned the scene for evidence of anyone doing things they shouldn't. Her quick up-down appraisal of his overalls suggested that he'd at least got that much right.

'Dr Cairns.' McLean nodded a greeting. 'How's the crime scene?'

'In a word, bloody impossible. No, that's two words.' Dr Cairns didn't seem to really mind. 'You couldn't have picked a worse place to leave forensic evidence if you'd tried. There's horses, goats, pigs, chickens, humans.' She said this last one as if she felt that was where humans should come in the pecking order. 'Christ only knows what else. The place is dusty as hell, and that wind isn't helping.'

McLean followed the forensic scientist's gaze across the small courtyard. A group of scene of crime officers were inching their way over towards the central building, studying the ground with commendable intensity, but every so often the wind dropping down off the nearby Pentland Hills would whip the dust up into eddies, covering up anything that might be a clue, or worse, moving it back to a place they'd already looked at.

'All we need now is some rain and we'll be buggered sideways till Tuesday.' Cairns looked up at the sky, pale blue and cloudless at the moment, but you never knew.

'So you don't hold out much hope of getting anything from here, then,' McLean said. 'Apart from the body, of course.'

'Chance'd be a find thing. This place is too contaminated by far. We might get something and never even realise. Or there might be nothing to find.'

'You think that's deliberate? Why the killer chose this place to dump the body?'

Something like worry flitted across Cairns' face at the idea. McLean could understand her concern. No one liked to be outsmarted. Not like this, with the stakes as high as they were.

'Nobody's that good,' she said eventually. 'We'll find something. You can trust me on that.'

23

'Subject is female, Caucasian, early twenties at a guess. In generally good health from her outward appearance.'

Another day, another visit to the city mortuary. McLean had hardly slept the night before, his dreams filled with the silent, pleading, nameless face of the dead woman. He'd risen with the dawn, then paced about the house drinking too much coffee until just before six. Even after walking to the city centre and stopping for yet more coffee, it had been a full hour after he'd arrived that the post-mortem was scheduled. Fortunately for him, Angus Cadwallader wasn't much of a sleeper either. They'd managed to find another insomniac pathologist to witness the examination and started early.

'What little blood was left in her has pooled around the shoulders and upper back, which is consistent with the way she was found. There was very little blood at the scene though, which would suggest she was killed elsewhere, then dumped.'

Cadwallader inched his way around the body, exposing the dead woman's most intimate secrets. A final indignity to add to the violence already done to her. McLean fought the urge to turn away. It was important he witness this, and not just so he could get the information he needed as quickly as possible.

'There's no obvious sign of her having been restrained. No bruising around the arms.'

'She knew her attacker, then.'

'That would be my best guess.' Cadwallader fell silent again whilst he studied the body some more. 'No sign of sexual intercourse, so she wasn't raped.'

'She was naked when we found her,' McLean said.

'Yes. Yes, she was. That doesn't necessarily mean any sexual motive though.'

'No. You're right. That would be too easy. Have you managed to narrow down time of death? I think we know what killed her.'

'Don't jump to conclusions, Tony. She could have been poisoned and her throat cut after she was dead.'

'Was she?'

'No. Well, I can't be sure until the tox screening's done. We've results for alcohol already, but the more esoteric poisons take time.'

'Alcohol? She'd been drinking?'

'Not a lot. Couple of glasses of wine maybe, but not long before she died.'

'Food?'

'I'm getting to that.' Cadwallader picked a scalpel off the tray of torture instruments his assistant Tracy had brought over. McLean turned away, like he always did at this point. The picture began to form in his mind. Young woman, finished work and off for a drink. Was she on her own or with friends? Where did she go, and who saw her? Actions for the investigation dropping into place. She meets someone she thinks she knows, but it turns out he's not the friend she thought he was. But why didn't she try to defend herself? Unless she didn't know what was about to happen. If so, it must have been quick, premeditated. And the method of disposal, so casual and yet at the same time so well thought out. It wasn't by chance that she'd been left somewhere so difficult to investigate forensically. Wasn't by chance she'd been stripped of all identification.

'Ah. Now that is interesting.'

McLean turned to see what Cadwallader was talking about, then wished he hadn't. The pathologist had opened up his patient and removed what was probably her liver. He turned it over and over in his blood-smeared hands, peering closely at it and prodding it. McLean was no expert, but even he could see it was diseased.

'Cirrhosis?'

'Quite advanced. Sad to say, but we're seeing it more and more, especially in young women. I'd guess this one's had a bottle of wine a day habit for quite some time. Probably binges on spirits at the weekends.' Cadwallader ploied the liver into a plastic specimen tub and Tracy took it off to weigh. 'Poor girl would probably have been showing clinical symptoms soon. Heading for complete liver failure in a year or two if this hadn't happened to her.'

'Some silver lining,' McLean said. 'But it's not really relevant to her death though, is it?'

'No, but it's interesting.' Cadwallader gave him a pained look. 'I suppose you want me to look at her throat now.'

He pulled the overhead light towards the young woman's head, illuminating the mess that had been made of her neck. 'The wound's deep, right through to the vertebrae. It's been done with a very sharp knife. Probably quite a large blade. I'd have to get a second opinion, but I'd hazard a guess he stood behind her, reached around with his right hand, swept from left to right.'

A chill formed in the pit of McLean's stomach, only partly at the horrible image of execution and the dead body splayed out on the examination table in front of him. 'You seen anything like it before?'

'If you're asking me was this done by the same person as did for your journalist, I really can't say.' Cadwallader prodded the fleshy mess around the dead woman's neck with the tip of his scalpel. 'If you're going to cut some-one's throat, there's only so many ways you can go about it. Same if you're cutting your own.'

'This wasn't a suicide, Angus. Even I can tell that.'

'Not saying it was. Just saying it's not enough to jump to conclusions. There's a few tests I'll run that can shed some light on it, but these things are coincidence, occasionally.'

McLean looked again at the dead woman's pale face, eyes closed, features relaxed in a manner that belied the violent nature of her ending. He shook his head gently, partly at the terrible waste of life, partly at his friend's words.

'You know me, Angus. I don't believe in coincidences.'

'Her name's Maureen Shenks. She's a paediatric nurse. Works at the Sick Kids.'

McLean looked up from his paperwork-strewn desk to see Detective Sergeant Ritchie standing in his open door-way clutching a sheet of paper that smelled as if it was fresh from the printer. A few days back at work and she was looking much better, seemed to have more energy. He wondered where she was getting it from and if there was any going spare.

'Maureen Shenks.' McLean repeated the name as if doing so might give any meaning to her death. 'We know anything about her?'

'Apart from this? No.' Ritchie flicked the sheet of paper with a finger, then stepped into the room and handed it over. The top half of the page was a photograph, quite obviously of the woman whose body they had found in the bin the day before. The rest was a brief summary of her life. Edinburgh born and raised. Twenty-three years old. Nothing on record with the police.

'Family?'

'Not sure. MacBride's working on it. She's young enough her parents could be still alive. This came from Missing Persons, though. She didn't turn up to work three days ago. Flatmate phoned it in.'

'I guess we'd better talk to the flatmate then.'

'I've given her a phone. She's on duty. Works at the Sick Kids too. Want me to bring her in when her shift's done?'

'I think this is probably serious enough to interrupt her shift, don't you?' McLean grabbed his jacket from the back of his chair. The wall directly opposite his window was painted bright with sunshine. 'And it's too nice an afternoon not to walk.'

'It's not like her to just up and leave like that. I mean, she loves the kids. Lives for them. Some of them get really upset if she doesn't see them every day.'

Maureen Shenks' flatmate was a mousy young woman called Adele. 'Pronounced like the penguin,' she'd said when they had first arrived at the hospital. She'd been hesitant about abandoning her duties, but as soon as McLean had identified himself as detective inspector her attitude had changed. Now they were huddled together in a small room at the back of the main building, which judging by its contents was a place old cardboard boxes went to die.

'I asked about. You know, just in case she'd gone off on a date and . . . well . . .'

'Did she do that often? Stay out overnight?'

The internal struggle in Adele's mind was writ large across her face, the conflict between telling the truth and protecting the reputation of her friend and flatmate. 'Not often.' The stress fell tellingly on the second word of her answer.

'Did she have a boyfriend, then? Someone she was seeing steady?' DS Ritchie asked the questions; they had decided it would be better that way on the walk over from the station. McLean's earlier idea that it was too nice a day not to walk had lasted almost ten minutes before the searing heat and his dark wool suit had persuaded him otherwise. It was refreshingly cool in their makeshift interview room, but his shirt was still clammy against his back.

'There was a bloke. Tommy something. But that was a year or so back. They went out for almost three months before she broke it off.' Adele paused in her flow long enough for Ritchie to start to ask another question, then added: 'Tommy Adshead. That was his name. Knew it would come to me eventually.'

'What about family?' Ritchie asked again.

Adele looked momentarily puzzled, as if she couldn't quite understand the link between ex-boyfriend and relatives.

'Her parents. Where are they?' McLean asked.

'Oh, right. Mo never knew her dad. All her mum would say was he was her worst mistake and Mo was her best. That's sweet, isn't it?'

'Have you spoken to her about Maureen? Her mother?' Ritchie had a pad in front of her and had scribbled 'boyfriend' and 'mother' so far. Nothing else. She'd already put a line through 'boyfriend'.

'Oh, no. Jane's away with the fairies. Half the time she doesn't even recognise her own daughter, let alone me.'

Ritchie ran a line through 'mother'. 'She's senile?'

'Early onset Alzheimer's. She's in a home in Corstorphine.'

'And there's no one else? Brother, sister?'

'Why do you . . . Oh.' Adele fell silent, her gaze going from Ritchie to McLean and back. The full implication of there being a detective inspector involved beginning to sink in.

'She's not . . . you've . . . I mean, she's OK isn't she? You've found her?'

'You reported her missing this morning.' Ritchie glossed over the questions with her own. 'How long had Maureen been gone by then?'

'I've been on days and she's been on nights, so we've not seen each other that much lately. But she usually lets me know if she's going out. I missed her completely yesterday, but I could tell she'd not been in when I got home last night. I got a call from here to see where she was. She never turned up to her shift, you see. Thought she might have been . . . I mean . . . I called you lot when I got in this morning and she'd missed another shift.'

'That was unusual, was it? For her to miss a shift?'

'Don't think Mo's ever . . .' Adele's voice tailed off as her eyes widened in realisation. 'You've found her, haven't you?'

'We think so, yes.' At McLean's words, Adele looked up from her nervous fingers. He held her gaze, waited until she had calmed down. 'Am I right in thinking Maureen had no immediate family other than her mother?'

'That's right,' the nurse nodded, seeming much younger than when they had first met.

'And how long have you known her?'

'Me? Since we were little. Six, maybe? Earlier?'

Damn, there was no easy way to do this. 'Well, I'm very sorry to have to tell you this, Adele, but Maureen's dead. We found her body yesterday afternoon.'

'Dead?' The nurse's voice had been squeaky to start with. Now it notched up another octave. 'How?'

'That's what we're trying to find out. All I can say at the moment is it wasn't natural, and it wasn't an accident.'

'She . . . she was killed?'

'I'm afraid so.' The nurse was fidgeting with her hands again, wringing them round and round each other. McLean reached out and took a hold of one, gently. 'Adele, I'm sorry. This must be a terrible shock, but it's very important I know as much about your friend as I can.'

She looked up at him, eyes wet with tears. When did adults start looking so young? Had he been like that, back when he first joined up? It seemed unlikely.

'Of course. Anything.'

'Thank you.' McLean patted the nurse's hand, then sat back. 'There is one thing. You're not family, so you can say no if you'd rather not. But we need someone to positively identify the body.'

Adele looked up sharply, the ghost of an idea flitting across her face. McLean had seen it all too often before, that tiny spark of hope. Maybe it wasn't her friend lying on the cold slab in the mortuary. Maybe it was someone else who just happened to look similar. Sometimes that spark flared, became a lifeline, and that made the crushing reality all the harder to accept. This time it died quickly; the rational, nurse's mind winning the battle. She wiped at her nose, sniffed.

'I've seen dead bodies before. Children, mostly. This place . . .' She trailed off.

'I'll have a word with your boss. See about getting you the rest of the day off. DS Ritchie will organise taking you to the mortuary.'

Adele's boss was a harassed-looking woman about McLean's age. He could see that she wasn't happy at losing yet another nurse for the day, but she took the news of Maureen Shenks' death in her stride. McLean had been going to ask her to come to the station; he'd have to interview her as part of the investigation. One look at the bustling busyness of the hospital, though, was enough to persuade him it would be better to set up something there instead; possibly the box-filled room at the back of the old building. Losing one of the nurses in such a terrible fashion was going to be disruptive enough without all the staff being dragged off across town at hourly intervals to talk to the police.

'We all done here?' He turned away from the reception desk to where DS Ritchie was standing, mobile phone in hand.

'For now, aye. Just sorting a car. I take it you want me to go with her?' She nodded in the direction of Adele, sitting on a chair in the waiting area and staring into the middle distance in the manner of someone trying to come to terms with news that's too big to comprehend.

'Please,' McLean said. 'I'll head back to the station and bring Dagwood up to speed. I've a horrible feeling this is another Category A, though.'

They were both walking across the reception hall, McLean for the door, Ritchie for the nurse, when she stopped in mid-stride, and turned so suddenly McLean felt her hand brush against him. He followed her gaze to where a white-coated doctor was disappearing through a door.

'You all right?' he asked.

Ritchie shook her head. 'Sorry. Just thought I recognised someone. Didn't expect to see him here.'

'Oh yes? Something I should know about?' McLean raised an eyebrow and grinned to let Ritchie know he was only kidding. He must have struck a nerve though, as her freckles darkened in embarrassment.

'No. It's nothing like . . . I mean . . . No. Just someone I met at a . . . meeting.'

'None of my business anyway, Sergeant.' McLean gave her a slap on the arm, as much to cover his own embarrassment as anything. He'd meant it as a joke, but it had clearly backfired. 'I'll see you back at the station, aye?'

He left her standing in the middle of the hall, resumed his walk to the door. He had an idea he knew what the meeting was that DS Ritchie meant, but couldn't quite work out why she was so uncomfortable talking about it.

24

'Jon's been coming here since he was six. Can you imagine that?'

I let him stew a fortnight, kept away from both hospitals, disappeared as if I'd been no more than a figment of his imagination. It was wise to keep away while the police were asking questions, too. She had to go, the nurse. She was too much of a temptation to him, and I couldn't risk him falling when he's so close to perfection.

It hasn't hurt to keep him waiting, though. If anything his righteous zeal has grown. When I appeared in the reception hall just after his shift end, he fell upon me like a starving man on a meal. No admonishment for missing our earlier engagement, no asking me where I'd been. He simply guided me through the building to an intensive care ward, pausing only to make sure we were both kitted out in sterile gowns and face masks, even though we will come no nearer to the object of his concern than a pane of glass away.

'What's the matter with him?'

It's fairly obvious, given the state of the boy. He lies sunken into plump white cushions, surrounded by machines, connected to them with wires and tubes. His face is mostly obscured by an oxygen mask, but what little I can see of it has a pallor associated more with the very old than the very young. His eyes are panda-like, dark and sunken as he dozes. He has no hair, not even eyelashes, just sweat-shiny skin the colour of rancid custard, splodged here and there with darker patches.

Jim reaches a slow hand up to the glass, splays fingers on the surface. 'What's right with him? Most of his organs are barely functional. Every time we think we've got it beaten, the cancer just comes back again. He's on chemo at the moment, but honestly, it's not going so well. It's a brutal way to treat a child, anyway.'

'What if we could try something different?'

'There is nothing different. Unless you mean prayer.' He looks at me. I can see the reflection of his head in the glass as he turns, but I keep my eyes on the boy. 'Trust me, if I thought that'd work I'd try it.'

'Actually I was thinking of something a little more . . . scientific? You'll be aware of cell line therapy. Individual cultures, DNA reprofiling?' I rattle off the words, all gleaned from the papers I found in his flat. Fascinating stuff, if you're into that sort of thing. His reflection drops its head, his hand coming away from the glass as his young patient continues to die a long, painful, drawn-out death.

'It's all too new. Too experimental. It takes too much time.' He rubs the grit from tired eyes. 'Jon doesn't have time. Not any more.'

'You know I work mainly on the research side these days, right?' I finally turn to meet his gaze. 'Can't remember the last time I actually treated a patient, if I'm being honest.'

'I did sort of wonder. See you about a lot, but never round the wards or in theatre.'

'Always think that by the time you've got there, it's

usually too late. I'd much rather have the body heal itself. Just maybe give it a little help.'

'You reckon you can help Jon?'

I make a show of studying the boy through the glass, even though I couldn't care less what happens to him. He is flawed. There is no point trying to save something as flawed as that. The silence feels right though, makes it look as if I am thinking.

'I don't know,' I say eventually. 'But I can try.'

25

'Why is it that of all the officers working out of this station, you are the only one who doesn't seem to understand the chain of command?'

Late afternoon, Detective Superintendent Duguid's office. Having cooled down at the hospital, McLean was once more hot and sweaty from his walk back. He could have gone straight to his nice cool office at the rear of the building where the sun never shone, but that would only have been a delaying tactic.

'I always find I get better results this way, sir. Every time I take something to DCI Brooks he sends me straight to you anyway. Thought I'd cut out the middleman, save us all some time.'

'With that attitude it's no wonder no one will take you seriously. You do realise they'll probably give Brooks my job when I leave, don't you? What're you going to do then?'

'I'll cope, sir. Same as always.'

Duguid made a sound halfway between a snort and a harrumph. 'So what's so important you had to bring it straight to me this time?'

'The young woman we found yesterday afternoon, out Fairmilehead way. We've got a name for her, a bit of background information. My first impression is this isn't going to be easy. There's no obvious suspect, no jealous boyfriend and no sign she was raped.' McLean summed up the facts of the case he'd uncovered so far.

'So what you're saying is we've got another major incident on our hands.' Duguid ran spidery fingers over his thinning scalp, slumped back into his seat. 'Fucking marvellous.'

'I'm sure Maureen Shenks is over the moon about it.'

That got him a sharp look. 'What are you on about? She's dead. She couldn't give a fuck. I'm more concerned about the sick bastard killed her. That's the difference between you and me, McLean. You're all about justice for the victims. I'm more interested in making sure the guilty are caught and locked up so they can't do it again.'

'Wasn't aware there was a difference, sir.'

'Course there's a bloody difference, man. You keep prattling on about ideals. I'm interested in results.'

McLean wasn't aware of any recent prattling, but he kept silent on the matter. 'You want me to lead on this one, sir? I've already got Grumpy Bob and MacBride organising the incident room.'

Duguid made a play of shuffling through the folders on his desk. Most of them were closed, some still tied up with string. McLean knew a fidget when he saw one.

'I want you to pass the case on to Spence,' the detective superintendent said eventually. McLean's first instinct was to complain, but then reason kicked in. He was already senior investigating officer on one major incident; the last thing he needed was another.

'Control assigned me the investigation, but I can see the sense in that. I'll get everything we've found so far drawn up into a report for him. Grumpy Bob can hand over to

DS Carter once he's done all the difficult stuff, and I've no doubt Spence will be pinching all the DCs anyway. Is Brooks going to be Gold on this one?'

Duguid gave him the sort of stare you got from a wary sheep. 'You don't mind?'

'How I feel about it's not really important, is it, sir? Just as long as we catch whoever did this, right?'

The tiny office, tucked away at the back of the station, was a small haven of coolness in the heat of mid-afternoon. McLean didn't much enjoy the mountains of paperwork that the job seemed to create on a daily basis, but when the temperature outside was hot enough to melt the tarmac, and the major incident room smelled of parboiled detective, it was nice to have somewhere he could escape to. Of course, it would be freezing in the winter, but that was a worry for another day.

Signing off overtime sheets was relatively mindless, and it wasn't too hard to justify the expenditure, not with two dead bodies on their hands. It gave him a chance to let the investigation percolate in the back of his mind, let the few facts settle and see what new connections might appear. The intervention of his telephone ruined whatever insight might have come. It took McLean a while to find the handset, buried under a spreading mound of folders. The flashing light told him the front desk was calling, but he knew from bitter experience not to believe it all the time.

'McLean.'

'Thought you might be there, sir. There's a bloke down here wants to see you about a car? You buying another one? Only after what happened to the last two . . .' Pete

Dundas was the duty sergeant that afternoon, it would seem.

'This one of your tiresome pranks, Pete? Only you can't pester me for the overtime sheets and send me off on wild goose chases.' It had been a while since anyone had tried to pull a fast one on him, but McLean was ever wary of the so-called humour of his fellow officers. Usually it involved costing him money and wasting the time of innocent bystanders.

'Honest as the day, sir.' Sergeant Dundas did a passable impression of a man offended at the very thought he might not be telling the truth.

'OK. Tell him I'm on my way.' McLean hung up, shuffled the papers into something resembling a child's idea of order and squeezed his way around the desk. He knew nothing about buying a car beyond that he'd been thinking about it. Unless he'd suddenly developed some kind of psychic ability, chances were this was some kind of prank. He just hoped it wasn't an expensive one.

It clicked when he saw the man waiting in reception. McLean had only met him a couple of times, the last being when he'd brought a flatbed truck to the garages of the forensic services and loaded the old Alfa Romeo on to it. McLean had thought the car beyond repair, its roof crushed under the weight of a falling body, but Alan Roberts had just looked at it, sucked his teeth and said it would be expensive. There had been a few telephone conversations since then, and McLean had written a couple of eye-watering cheques, quite probably more than it would have cost him to go out and buy an identical car. Lately it had been mostly silence, though now he thought about it, there might have been an email, buried quickly under a mountain of others.

'Inspector. Sorry to disturb you at work. Reckoned I had a better chance of catching you here, though.'

'Mr Roberts.' McLean shook the man by the hand, noticing his spotlessly clean brown overalls, like a mechanic from a bygone age. In many ways that was what he was. 'This about the Alfa?'

'It certainly is. Got her back from the body shop last week. We've just been finishing off the mechanical work. She's all done now. Good as new. Better really.'

McLean checked his watch. Too early to call it a day, and there was the small matter of a major incident investigation requiring his attention.

'That's great, thank you. But I don't think I'll be able to pick it up until the weekend. It's a little busy here.'

'Aye, that business in Gilmerton with the journalist. I heard.'

'You did?' Mr Roberts worked out of a busy little garage in Loanhead, which wasn't all that far from Gilmerton. Still, it surprised McLean that he'd take much of an interest in the case.

'Thought you'd be a bit too busy to come and collect, so I brought her over for you.'

Parked on the street by the front entrance to the station, Alan Roberts' flatbed truck had begun to attract quite a lot of attention from public and police alike. Partly this might have been to do with the double yellow line, but mostly it was the gleaming red classic sports car on the back.

McLean remembered his father's old car fondly. He'd

found it hidden away at the back of the garage after his gran had died, had it fixed up and driven it around for a year or so before Detective Sergeant Pete Buchanan had fallen several storeys on to its roof. Before that accident, the car had been tidy, but not exactly new. Its paint had been glossy and red, just a shame about the several different shades where individual panels had been resprayed down the years. Now it looked even better than it must have done in the showroom, sometime in the early 1970s.

It was still red, gleaming in the hot afternoon sun like something wet and dangerous. McLean didn't think he'd ever seen it so clean. Any car so clean, for that matter. Roberts set about undoing the straps holding it down to the flatbed, while yet more underemployed police officers wandered up to see what was going on.

'You got her fixed. That must have cost a bit.' McLean didn't need to turn to know it was DS Ritchie who had spoken.

'I couldn't see it scrapped,' he said as Roberts tilted the flatbed back hydraulically until it formed a long shallow ramp to the road. They both watched as the mechanic fished a key out of his pocket, unlocked the car and climbed in. The noise it made when he started it up was not what either of them were expecting.

'Didn't used to sound like that, did she?' McLean thought the question, but it was Ritchie who asked it.

'Not as far as I remember. They did say they were going to do a bit of mechanical work on it. Bring the brakes and cooling up to modern standards. Stuff like that.'

A bit more rasping exhaust noise and the little red Alfa Romeo inched backwards down the ramp, on to the road.

The cluster of police officers thickened around it, all peering in through the windows, so that McLean almost had to fight his way through them. Mr Roberts had turned off the engine and was climbing arthritically out of the low-down seat when he and Ritchie made it to the kerbside.

'Your keys.' Roberts handed them over. 'You'll want to take it easy for the first few hundred miles. Let the engine bed in a bit.'

'I thought you were just fixing up the bodywork and giving it a bit of a service,' McLean said. He ran a hand over the warm, smooth surface of the roof. The shine was so glossy it was almost painful to look at.

'That was the first cheque. We had that conversation about making a few improvements, remember?'

McLean thought he might have done, vaguely. Mostly it had been messages on his answering machine informing him of progress, or lack thereof. He'd not been too bothered, or rather he'd been too busy to worry about it. Roberts had a good reputation, the rest was just time and money.

'It's all in the folder there, Inspector.' Roberts reached in to the passenger seat with much popping of joints, and came back holding a large black ring-binder. Inside were many, many receipts, and photographs in neat plastic wallets. 'Oh, and there's this as well. Never did have much truck with technology, but there's a couple of thousand photographs on here.' He dug a hand into the pocket of his overalls, coming out with a small black memory stick.

'I . . . um . . . thank you.' McLean took it, dropped it into his own pocket.

'No. Thank you, sir. There's not many's prepared to

spend the money keeping these old girls alive. She's been a pleasure to work on. Just try not to break her again, eh?' Roberts gave him a grin, then walked away. McLean watched him as he started to pack up the flatbed, ready to leave. When he turned back to his car, DS Ritchie was on the other side, peering in through the window. She crouched down, ran a hand along the curve of the bonnet, then went to the front and looked back along the side.

'This must have cost you a fortune, sir. They've done a beautiful job.'

McLean looked at the gleaming chrome door handle and the trim around the window edges. They had been tarnished before, pitted by age and road salt. Now they were like new. The door itself had never quite sat right on its hinges, the gap at the front noticeably larger than that at the back. He couldn't see that now. It was almost as if they'd given him a different car.

'Hop in then, Sergeant.' He opened the door and smelled a heady mixture of leather cleaner and oil.

'What?' Ritchie stared at him over the roof.

'I said hop in. I think we should see what Mr Roberts has done, don't you?'

26

He had to wind the window down to keep cool; there was no air-conditioning in the little Alfa, of course. Even so McLean reckoned he must have had an idiot grin plastered all over his face as they drove south from the city centre. Traffic was mercifully light and they made good speed, the temperature gauge on the dashboard rising swiftly to the middle and then sticking there.

'Don't think I'll ever get tired of that noise,' DS Ritchie said, as they pulled out of a side turning and McLean put his foot down. The exhaust crackled and popped and the car surged forward like a terrier after a rat. Whatever Alan Roberts and his mechanics had done to the thing, it was a different beast indeed from the car he'd found tucked away in his grandmother's garage after her death.

A chuckle from the passenger seat brought him out of his musing. He glanced sideways to where DS Ritchie was sitting, a smile on her face as the breeze from her open window played with her short red hair. 'What?'

'I've not seen you look this happy in . . .' Ritchie paused a moment, her smile turning to a thoughtful frown. 'Can't really say I've ever seen you so happy, actually.'

'Thanks,' McLean said. 'I think.' He wrapped his fingers around the thin steering wheel, suddenly self-conscious. The moment's simple enjoyment had gone, the bubble

160

burst. It was still a damn fine day though, and a great way to be spending it driving a classic sports car.

'Where we going, anyway?'

'Nearly there.' McLean dropped a gear and sped forward to make it through a set of lights before they changed. The Alfa did exactly what he asked of it, chirping its rear wheels with a little spin. He had to admit he'd missed the thing. A couple of hundred yards further on and they slowed for another crossing.

'Gilmerton Cove?' Ritchie peered through the windscreen as the lights turned green. McLean indicated right, then dropped the clutch and spun the wheels trying to get across the turning before the car coming towards him. He didn't care about the blaring horn and rude hand gesture the manoeuvre got him. The car brought out the long-suppressed adolescent hooligan in him.

Parking in the lot behind the library at least meant they were off the street and largely out of sight. It still left him with a dilemma. Part of him wanted to make DS Ritchie stay and act as a guard. It would be too terrible to come back and find key marks in that lovely gloss-red paintwork. But that was just paranoia, and besides, she was a trained detective, not some junior uniform constable to be set menial tasks.

McLean still turned back and gave the car one last long look before he walked round the corner and out of sight.

'She'll be fine, sir. Don't worry.'

'You're right. I'm just being stupid.'

'Mind you, I don't think I'd dare leave something like that in a public place. Who knows what some little toerag'll do to her?'

'Not helping, you know.' McLean looked across at the detective sergeant, saw the smile on her face. She was recovering well from her brush with death, her cheek-bones less prominent, eyes less sunken, but she still had a way to go.

'We going to the crime scene then, sir? Only I thought forensics were all packed up and away now. Place is meant to be opening to the public again soon.'

McLean stopped at the edge of the road. Somewhere under his feet, give or take, Ben Stevenson had met his gruesome, violent end. He had gone willingly into the caverns, perhaps in search of higher truths, lured by some-one with motives he couldn't begin to understand. At least not yet. Going down there again himself would serve no purpose.

'There's only one way into those caves, right?'

'Pretty much. Well, there's two, but they both exit on to the road up there.' Ritchie pointed up towards the entrance to the visitor centre. 'There may be others, but they've been filled up with rocks for centuries. Stevenson and his killer had to have come past here at some point before he died.'

'And yet we got nothing off any cameras.' McLean pointed at the CCTV on a nearby pole. They'd already spoken to all the shops in the area, trawling the footage for the slightest glimpse of anyone who might have looked like the dead reporter. For a backwater suburb, Gilmerton was surprisingly well covered by cameras, but they'd found nothing.

'Half of them had been scrubbed by the time we got to them. Some weren't even working, just for show.' It was nothing McLean didn't know. That wasn't why he'd come out here.

'You can't always trust the cameras, anyway. But someone will have seen our man on his way here.' McLean turned away from the road, walked the short distance to the door to the betting shop on the corner. 'You just need to know how to ask.'

There were bookies and there were bookies. Some places you wouldn't go into without a stab vest and a fully armed back-up team. Some places you'd get a hard eye and a cold shoulder but certainly no answers to any questions, however civilly you put them. And then there were bookies that were simply businesses trying to keep afloat in the face of twenty-four-hour online poker, smartphone apps that made it even easier to lose your shirt, and a population increasingly too simple-minded to manage anything as difficult as studying form. McLean had noticed this one, part of a national chain, the first time he'd come to Gilmerton Cove. He had no doubt that some detective constable had been in, armed with his PDA and some questions, to quiz the owner about the night Ben Stevenson had died. There would be a transcription of the answers on file somewhere in the major incident room, and probably backed up to the cloud too, wherever that was. They weren't the sort of questions he was interested in now, and certainly not the right answers. It was always better to do these things yourself, anyway. And besides, he'd needed an excuse for taking the car out.

Inside, the bookies showed just as much promise as expected. The smoking ban had long since cleared the air, but a yellow nicotine stain still clung to the ceiling and walls. Burning tobacco would probably have been preferable to the medley of aromas that assailed his nose as McLean stood in the doorway and surveyed the scene. It wasn't exactly a hive of activity, just a couple of old men in opposite corners staring up at old-style bulky television screens screwed to the walls, a spotty-faced youth behind the counter. One other punter stood at a table in the middle of the room, tongue protruding from the side of his mouth as he concentrated on the tiny print in his *Racing Times*.

'What're we . . .?' Ritchie began to ask, but McLean quieted her with a wave of his arm as he stepped fully into the room. One of the old men looked at him with a distrustful glare, but the other one didn't take his eyes off the television. He walked up to the punter at the table.

'Got any tips?'

'Eh?' The man looked up, surprise widening his eyes.

'What's on this afternoon? Ayr?'

The man's eyes narrowed for a moment, then his gaze softened. 'Ayr, aye. Not much of a turnout, mind.' He folded up his paper so McLean couldn't see the horses he'd picked, then turned and walked away.

'Friendly,' Ritchie whispered.

'Doesn't want to chance his luck, does he?' McLean smiled at his own joke, headed for the counter and the spotty youth.

'The boss in?' he asked before the lad could speak. The youth looked up at him, startled, then saw the warrant card McLean had pulled out of his pocket.

'I . . . I'll just get him.'

He scurried off, disappearing through a door at the back just as McLean felt a presence by his side.

'He going to be long?' It was the punter with the *Racing Times*, now rolled up into a tight tube and clasped in a nervous hand. 'Only the race starts in five.'

McLean looked at his watch. 'Shouldn't be a problem. You got your runners all picked out then?'

'Yeah. Reckon.' The punter tapped his rolled up paper against his arm. He was short, wiry. A face like a shaven ferret. Malnourished might be the right word. It wasn't hard to see where most of his money went.

'Can I help you?' The manager had arrived, shadowed by the spotty youth. 'Only I already spoke to youse lot last week.'

'Take the man's bet first, aye?' McLean stood to one side, letting the punter in with his slip. Money changed hands, and then the man sidled off, the faintest nod of thanks as he went to find a stool from where he could see his luck run out on the racecourse. McLean watched him go, then turned back to the manager.

'Anywhere quiet I might have a word?'

27

The manager's office had the dubious honour of making the run-down betting shop beyond it look well kept. There was a desk, not large, and covered with a stack of paperwork that could give McLean's own one back at the station a run for its money. A couple of tall filing cabinets filled the back wall, a broken printer balanced precariously on top. Boxes cluttered most of the available space. There was certainly nowhere to sit other than the chair behind the desk, which the manager dropped himself into like a man whose legs have had enough. Given his size, McLean could only sympathise with them.

'Don't really know how I can help you, Inspector. It is Inspector, isn't it?'

'It is, yes. Mr . . .?'

'Ballard. Johnny Ballard.' The manager made the most minimal of efforts to get up, almost raised a hand to shake, then collapsed again into his chair.

'Well, Mr Ballard. I know you're a busy man, so I won't waste too much of your time. Like you said, you've already spoken to one of my constables.'

'Aye, young lad, scar on his forehead like that chap in the film.'

'You're not that busy today.'

'Today, every day.' Ballard rocked back in his chair,

making room for his gut behind the desk. 'Who needs a bookies when you've got the internet, eh?'

'People looking to be paid in cash, I'd guess.'

'Now look here . . .' Ballard would have sprung to his feet, McLean was sure of it. Had his belly not been in the way.

'Calm down, Mr Ballard. I'm not here to make life difficult for you. Quite the opposite. I imagine business has been even slower since our lot set up in the caves downstairs. Not much of a betting man myself, but I'd wager the two old blokes don't spend more than a fiver at a time, and the lad whose brew money you just took probably doesn't bring in any more.'

'Keith's all right. Even wins a bit now and then. Just enough to keep him going.' Ballard slumped back into his seat again. 'And you're right enough. Business isn't exactly booming here, but that stuff with the journalist? Well, let's just say it's not helping.'

'Sooner we're gone, the better?'

'Wouldn't hurt, aye.'

'So tell me then, Mr Ballard. In the month up to the body turning up in the caves. You notice any new people through the door?'

'What d'ye mean? We get new customers every day.'

'You sure of that? Every day?'

'Well, maybe not—'

'You have a core of regulars. Don't worry, I'm not interested in them. I'm looking for anyone who might've come in more than once over the last month or two. Maybe asking questions, maybe just looking around the place.'

Ballard furrowed his brow in a good impression of a man who found thinking hard. McLean knew it was an act, even if just a subconscious one. You didn't get to run a bookies in this part of town without having an above-average intelligence and a way with people.

'Kind've hard to remember it all. What, two months back? That'd be when they were working on the drains, digging up the road down the hill a bit. Had a few of the workmen come in. Not big spenders, and one of them cleaned up on a three-way accumulator if I remember right.'

'Roadworks down the hill?' McLean looked across at DS Ritchie, who was leaning against the wall by the door. 'Why've I not heard about this before?'

'No idea, sir. I'll find out.' She pulled her phone out of her pocket and started tapping at the screen.

'There was a bloke, now I think about it,' Ballard said, dragging McLean's attention back. 'Strange little fellow. Came in with the road crew sometimes. On his own others. Not sure he ever placed a bet though.'

'He speak to anyone? Meet anyone? Bookies is a good place to arrange to meet someone if you don't want to go to the pub.'

'Aye, could have been that, I guess. Bit bloody cheeky, mind.' Ballard furrowed his brow again, his eyes almost disappearing in the folds of skin around his face. 'No. Thought I could remember what he looked like, but it's gone. Just got an idea of a person, nothing more.'

'Well, it's better than nothing. We can speak to the road crew, see if any of them remember.' It wasn't much – probably wouldn't come to anything – but it was more than anyone else investigating the case had managed so far. 'I'll send an e-fit specialist up to see you too, if you can spare a half-hour from your busy schedule.'

'Never had you as a betting man, sir.'

'Can't remember the last time I put money on anything. And my knowledge of horse racing could be summarised neatly by the phrase "bugger all".'

'But . . .' Ritchie half-turned towards the now-closed door to the bookies.

'Bullshit with confidence, Sergeant. That's the trick.' McLean set off in the direction of the car park, anxious to get back to his precious Alfa before someone could drop something on it from a great height.

'No way that was bullshit. How'd you know all that stuff about Ayr racecourse? Not exactly your home turf, is it?'

McLean stopped mid-stride. Turned back to face Ritchie. 'I was three years on the beat, Sergeant. Not like some of you fast-track youngsters these days. Most of that time I spent with old Guthrie McManus. No one else had the time of day for him, but he was OK once you got to know him. Helped if you weren't completely useless at the job too, I guess.

'Thing is, Guthrie was fond of a flutter. I must have followed him into pretty much every betting shop in the city back then, watching while he placed his bets, claimed his occasional winnings. You don't do this job if you're no good at noticing things, so I picked up enough to get me by. Learned another useful thing, too. See Guthrie liked a bet now and then, but he also knew a good source of information. Wasn't a bookie out there he couldn't tap for answers if he needed. And he was good enough to more or less make it pay.'

Ritchie stared at him, jaw slightly slack, but McLean's attention was caught by the man exiting the bookmaker's, head down with the despondent weight of someone who's just lost the weekly food money on a horse that was a dead cert to win.

'Stay there a minute,' he said to the sergeant, then raised his voice to the ferrety little man. 'It's Keith, isn't it?'

At the sound of his voice, Keith stopped walking, looked up with that familiar guilty expression, mixed with confusion.

'It's OK. You don't owe me anything.' That seemed to relax the man, at least a little.

'What then? Only I'm—'

'Busy? Aye, I noticed that. So I'll not keep you long. You go in there a lot, I reckon. Make a bit, lose a bit?' McLean had positioned himself so it was difficult for the young man to move on without being obvious about it. Now he spoke more quickly than normal, giving him little room to get a word in.

'What's it to—?'

'Reckon you notice stuff, too.' McLean nodded at the tightly rolled-up *Racing Times* Keith was clutching as if it still held the secrets to all happiness. 'You look for the patterns, am I right?'

'I . . . yeah. Do my best.'

'And you like that. Noticing stuff, aye? Like when the road crews were in a few weeks back. When the police came round after they found that body in the caves.'

'Who are you?' Keith finally looked up at McLean's face,

took in his dark suit and began to reach a conclusion. Maybe not as observant as he thought he was.

'I'm Tony,' McLean said. 'And I'm trying to find out who killed that reporter.'

'You're polis.' It wasn't a question, and Keith finally seemed to understand something of his situation. As he moved to step past, McLean took a hold of his arm, as lightly as he dared.

'I'm not here to bother you, Keith. I'm looking for help, and if you can help me maybe I can help you in return.' He looked up, past the young man's head towards the door to the betting shop. Keith's head twitched involuntarily as his eyes started to follow, a haunted look on his face.

'What you want then?' he asked eventually.

McLean let go of the arm. 'Like I said, I reckon you notice things. See the patterns. You'll have noticed the road crews coming in and placing bets from time to time, and I reckon you'll have noticed someone else come in over the past couple of months. Someone who didn't quite fit in. Maybe didn't even place any bets.'

'Like someone casing the joint?'

'That's the one. Maybe even just hanging around to see who comes and goes and when.'

Keith shook his head. 'I dunno. Can't really think of anyone, right enough. I mean, there's always folk coming and going.'

'Well, give it some thought, OK?' McLean dug into his jacket pocket for a business card. There was a folded ten pound note in there too, another of Guthrie McManus's tips. He pulled both out together, hiding the money under the card as he handed it over like a magician. 'Give us a call if anything sparks a memory.'

'You think that was wise, giving him cash like that? He'll only lose it on the horses. Come back for more.'

They were making slow progress back towards the station, traffic backed up along Clerk Street by an accident, or just too many buses. McLean found it hard not to keep his eye on the temperature gauge, waiting for it to tip into the red like it always used to, but so far it had held perfectly steady in the centre of the dial.

'It's a risk, but you never know. If I were a betting man, I'd lay you a tenner he calls me in the next couple of days saying he thinks he remembers someone. I'll get him to do an e-fit, same as the manager. If we get two different people, we've just lost a bit of time and ten pounds. If they both come up with something similar . . .' It was thin, and McLean knew it. But then the whole investigation was thin. The harder they looked, the less evidence there was that anyone at all had killed Ben Stevenson. No forensics in the cave, nothing at his home but the all-too-obvious signs of his obsession, no motive, not even the slightest hint of a suspect.

'We're really clutching at straws, aren't we, sir?' Ritchie summed up the hopelessness in a simple cliché.

'Still one or two to go.'

'There are?'

'Oh yes. There's Douglas Ballantyne for one.'

'Douglas . . . oh, aye. I'd forgotten about him. The conspiracy theorist.'

'The same. He should be back from the US by now. Think we should pay him a wee visit tomorrow.'

'And you really think he'll be able to help us?'

'He was in contact with Stevenson. At the least he should be able to tell us what he was working on. Jo Dalgliesh has been looking into that, too. If we can piece together Stevenson's movements and motives leading up to his death, then maybe we can have a guess at why someone might want to kill him.'

The traffic started moving again, and McLean eased the car forward to keep with the flow.

'Straws,' Ritchie said as the acceleration pushed her gently back into her seat. 'Clutching.'

28

I gave the child a week. If it hadn't died by then I would have helped it along, but it only managed three days in the end. I'd have preferred five, if I'm being honest. That would have given me a little more time to prepare. But God's will cannot be gainsaid, and the child however flawed was one of His creations too. He has set me this task to perform. It is not for Him to make it easy.

People fall apart in surprisingly predictable ways. Jim, for all his years of medical training, had allowed himself to get too close, too emotionally attached to his patients. Losing them felt to him like failure, as if it were somehow his fault that the child had got cancer in the first place. This child was particularly special to him. I've no idea why. Maybe he had a friend who suffered a similar fate; that might explain his interest in medicine. The whys are unimportant, only the hows matter.

I find him where I expect him to be, at the glass wall where we had our little chat just a few days ago. He looks unwell, like a man who's not slept in days. He stares through at the empty bed as if he thinks that staring might make it unhappen.

'I'm so sorry. I just heard.' Not true, of course, but timing is everything. He turns at my voice and I can see the red around his eyes and nose, the tears threatening to come back at any moment. He wipes a sleeve against his face, sniffs hard. Says nothing.

'I tried,' I say. 'We might have been able to do something, if we'd had a little more time. There was a trial, but . . .' I let the words tail off, leave the next step to him.

'It always takes too long. Endless committees wringing their hands. If I could just bring them here. Show them this.' He slams an angry palm against the glass, making it wobble. A passing nurse starts to scowl, then realises who it is, bobs her head and hurries away.

'It doesn't have to.' I pitch my voice low and quiet, but he still hears. I can see the change in his posture. This is what he's been waiting for.

'You don't mean—'

'Not here.' I reach into my pocket, pull out the card I wrote earlier. An address, my assumed name. Nothing else. 'This evening at eight. There's some people I'd like you to meet. Some things you might like to see.'

I hold his gaze as he takes the card from me, slips it into his pocket. He nods once, just the slightest tip of the head, but it's enough. If he takes this step, he will be free. His redemption will be complete. Now only time can tell.

29

If his house was anything to go by, then making stuff up for a living was very lucrative. At least if you were as convincingly creative as Douglas Ballantyne. McLean had tried wading through the book that he'd taken from Ben Stevenson's flat, the mad ideas wrapped up in a plausible presentation of carefully selected facts. Like so many others, Ballantyne was obsessed with the Masons, the Knights Templar and all the associated nonsense that clung to them like body odour to a teenage boy. It was a rich market of paranoia to feed.

Nestling in a quiet glen about a half-hour's drive south of the city, Ballantyne House was surrounded by acres of parkland. Scraggy-looking sheep sheltered under ancient trees, doing their best to escape the withering summer sun. A small herd of deer peered nervously at the car as McLean navigated a narrow driveway that took him and DS Ritchie away from an already minor road and brought them finally to the house itself.

'Remind me to get started on that misery memoir when we get back to the city, sir.' Ritchie's gaze didn't shift from the building as she climbed out of the car and closed the door behind her. Even McLean had to admit it was impressive, as Scots Baronial piles went. Three storeys of red sandstone and harling radiating in the afternoon heat. It was almost picture perfect, although he reckoned it would be a bugger to keep warm in the winter.

'Any sign of our man? He knows we're coming.' McLean looked around, half-expecting to see a stout, bearded fellow with a couple of spaniels cavorting at his heels, striding across the fields to greet them. Instead, a low, menacing growl raised the hairs on the back of his neck.

'Oh bloody marvellous.' Ritchie reached very slowly for her car door, clicked it open again. 'I really don't like dogs.'

'You and Grumpy Bob both.' McLean tried to pinpoint the source of the growling, finally locating it as two Rhodesian Ridgebacks appeared from around the corner of the house. They didn't bark, didn't run snarling and slavering towards him. That was perhaps even more scary, in some ways; that someone had control over them even though they were clearly desperate to kill.

'Aubrey! Campion! Sit!' The voice was oddly high-pitched, and McLean thought for a moment that it must be a woman's. Whoever it was, the dogs obeyed with machine-like precision, settling on to their haunches in a manner that said quite clearly they were still ready for the chase. Bred for hunting lions in the African veldt, McLean recalled reading somewhere. He was no huge fan of dogs, having grown up in a house with few pets, and those mostly feline.

'Don't mind my boys. They won't bite unless I tell them to.' Again that high-pitched voice, but at about the same time as he saw who was speaking, McLean heard the masculine undertones in it. And sure enough, the man himself appeared, patting one of the two dogs on the head as he walked past them.

Douglas Ballantyne was a bit older than when he'd been photographed for his book, but it was undeniably the same man. His beard exploded from his chin and neck in a ruddy-grey mass that must surely be home to small nesting birds. He was dressed in loose-fitting jogging bottoms, with a dark velvet smoking jacket over a faded rock band tour T-shirt, making for a rather incongruous ensemble. The heavy-framed spectacles and ornate-topped walking cane didn't exactly help the image.

'What a lovely creature.' Ballantyne stared past McLean, then did a double-take as he noticed DS Ritchie. 'The car, I mean.'

'Of course you do. Mr Ballantyne, I presume.' McLean held out his hand, receiving an odd look from the writer.

'Yes, yes. And you're the policeman. McLean. Heard a lot about you.'

'You have? All good, I hope.'

'At least not bad.' Ballantyne relented and took McLean's hand, tried one of the Masonic holds. A test McLean must have passed by not acknowledging. 'Come on in. I'll make us some tea.'

The interior of the house was pleasantly cool after the fierce heat outside. Ballantyne had led them around the back; McLean suspected that the front entrance was probably locked and had been for years. A couple of small rooms opened on to a kitchen best described as lived in. There was no sign of a Mrs Ballantyne, and McLean doubted one existed. Nor was there any sign of staff. No PA, no cleaner, just the man himself and his two dogs. They'd calmed down once they realised neither he nor Ritchie was a threat, and slunk off to scruffy-looking beds in the far corner of the room as soon as they entered.

'Tea?' Ballantyne grabbed a heavy iron kettle, shook it

to see if it contained water, then clanged it down on the hotplate of the huge range cooker. He stared at it for about ten seconds, then took it off again. 'Idiot. I always forget it gets put out in the summer.'

He started again, this time with an electric kettle, then busied himself finding mugs and teabags. The kitchen was cluttered, busy, the large table strewn with papers, a laptop and piles of books, but it was by and large clean. Not unlike his own kitchen, McLean couldn't help noticing. Only bigger.

'You wanted to talk to me about Ben Stevenson, I understand. That's what the constable on the phone said, anyway.' Ballantyne spoke over his shoulder as he went from cupboard to cupboard, hopefully in search of biscuits.

'Detective Constable MacBride. Did he tell you why?'

Ballantyne gave up his search. 'Sit, Inspector, Sergeant. Please. Don't mind the mess.' He made a half-hearted attempt at clearing the table, mainly piling everything into a big heap in the middle, the laptop balanced precariously on top. 'He said something about him dying.'

'He was murdered, Mr Ballantyne. In the caves at Gilmerton Cove. You know the place?'

'Know it? I wrote a book about it. Fascinating place. All that talk about the Covenanters, Masons and God knows who else linked to it. All wrong, of course.'

'Oh? Who do you think built it, then?' DS Ritchie asked.

'Something far older than all of them.' Ballantyne was about to say more, but the kettle clicked off its noisy boil, distracting him while he poured water into mugs.

'Was that what Stevenson was looking into?' McLean asked once tea had been handed out and biscuits found.

'Ben?' Ballantyne laughed. 'No, Ben was still a novice. He was obsessed with the link between the Knights Templar and the modern Masonic movement. Textbook conspiracy theory stuff.'

McLean tried to remember the contents of the book he'd skim-read. It had seemed pretty much textbook conspiracy theory to him, but then maybe he, too, was a novice. 'So you don't think there's a link, then?'

'Oh, of course there's a link. It's as plain as the day when you know what you're looking for.' Ballantyne took a slurp of tea, leaning forwards over the kitchen table in his enthusiasm for the tale. 'But it's not what all the books say. Not what you'll find if you look it up on Wikipedia.'

'Let me guess. The Brotherhood?'

Ballantyne's eyes gleamed with excitement. 'So you have read my book. I'm impressed.'

'I read Stevenson's copy. The one you wrote the dedication in. It was well thumbed.'

'Was it? Was it indeed?' Ballantyne looked genuinely surprised. 'And I thought he just bought it to humour me.'

'I think he was rather more interested in your theories than you realise, Mr Ballantyne.'

'You do?'

'Yes. And I think he got too close to something. Maybe a true secret, or maybe someone who didn't want the world to know there was no secret.'

'And they killed him for it? I see where you're going, Inspector, but I very much doubt Ben would have uncovered anything worth killing for.' Ballantyne paused for a moment, as if a thought had interrupted his flow. 'You say he was killed in Gilmerton Cove? And you found his body, obviously, otherwise you wouldn't be here talking to me about it. Tell me, was there a ritualistic nature to his murder?'

'I'm not really at liberty to discuss that kind of detail,' McLean said. 'Why do you ask?'

'Well, it occurs to me that if poor old Ben really had uncovered something worth killing for, then you'd never have found him. You'd probably never have realised he'd gone missing in the first place.'

'Why do you say that?' McLean had a sinking feeling that he already knew the answer.

'The Brotherhood control the media, Inspector. Every aspect of it. The news, the television, films, books. Yes, even my efforts.' Ballantyne waved an arm in the direction of the precarious pile of papers. 'It may look like we're revealing long-hidden secrets, but it only happens because they let it. Much as it galls me to admit it, I am just an instrument in their greater plan.'

'And that is?'

'Oh, I've no idea. Well, that's not strictly true. I've an idea, but it's not something I'd dream of divulging. Not yet at least. Maybe there'll be a time I can write that book. If it serves the purpose of the Brotherhood to have it revealed.'

'So what if Stevenson had this same idea but wasn't prepared to wait?'

'That's the nub of it, Inspector. If he'd done that, then they'd have sent the Adrogenae after him. And if they had done, then he simply would never have existed.'

30

'The expression you're looking for is "stone bonker", I think.'

The road back to Edinburgh was relatively clear, just the occasional caravan to overtake with a satisfying surge of acceleration. It occurred to McLean after a couple of high-rev manoeuvres that Mr Roberts had told him to take it easy for the first few hundred miles. He backed off as they approached an articulated lorry, slowing to match its pace through the bends around Silverburn and Habbies Howe.

'Nut job does it for me. I was almost with him up until the point where he mentioned those weird supernatural assassins. What did he call them, Androgen-something?'

'The Adrogenae. Yes. I'd forgotten. He mentions them in the book. Apparently they're one of the reasons no one's ever heard about the Brotherhood until now.'

'I didn't really understand what it was they did, though. Do they go back in time and kill your grandfather or something?'

'Search me. I don't think making sense is high on Douglas Ballantyne's list of priorities.'

'So we wasted an afternoon then.'

'A bit, maybe.' McLean dragged his eyes away from the road briefly, looked across at the detective sergeant. Ritchie stared out of the window at the grubby back of the truck. Someone had written 'Danny takes it up the arse' in the grime, and then rather incongruously drawn a large pair of breasts. It didn't say much for the cleanliness of the logistics wing of a major supermarket chain.

'I'm not seeing any positive side to the whole thing. Apart from getting a ride in your car.'

'Well, the way I see it, Ballantyne's so full of shit you could plant flowers in him. But I've read his book. He has a way with words. His arguments are plausible because he's selective with the facts. It's an old trick, true, but he does it very well.'

'Every age has its snake-oil salesmen, I guess.'

'And willing idiots to buy it, too. Like Ben Stevenson.'

'You think he fell for that?' Ritchie hooked a thumb back over her shoulder in a vague approximation of the direction of Douglas Ballantyne's country estate.

'Hook, line and sinker. He was obsessed. You saw his secret room, the connections he was making.'

'But he was a journalist. Surely he'd have some kind of bullshit filter.'

'Recently divorced, missing his kids, not had a big story in almost five years?'

Ritchie didn't answer immediately, thinking things over. The road straightened out and McLean took the opportunity to overtake the lorry. For a gut-clenching moment he thought he'd overcooked it, the next corner arriving much more quickly than he'd anticipated. A dab of the brakes pushed him hard against the seatbelt, Ritchie's hand going out to the dashboard to steady herself. Mr Roberts had worked his magic on the braking system too, it seemed.

'You think that's enough to lose your mind?'

'I've seen people lose theirs over less.'

'Still doesn't get us any closer to finding out who killed him, though.'

'Maybe. Maybe not. It does tell us that he was very suggestible.'

'You think someone led him on? He wasn't on to anything at all?' Ritchie asked.

'I don't know.' McLean paused, drumming his fingers on the steering wheel as he tried to put into words the slippery thoughts he had about the case, the way it was beginning to feel to him. He needed a good long walk, really. That usually helped.

'It just doesn't stack up as some secret society trying to silence him before he could spill the beans. Ballantyne might be a loony, but he's right about one thing. If that were the case, if his Brotherhood or whatever he calls it really existed, really was all-powerful and really didn't want the cat let out of the bag, then Ben Stevenson would have just disappeared. Or he'd have committed suicide, had a tragic fatal accident. Anything but being slain in some mock-Masonic ritual and his blood smeared all over the walls of a cave where he was always going to be found.'

'So you think chasing the story he was working on is a waste of time?'

'Not quite. It was his obsession, and it was probably what led him to that cave. But I think we're asking the wrong questions.'

'So what are the right ones?'

'I wish I knew, Kirsty. I wish I knew.'

Traffic built up as they approached the city, as if cars were flies and Edinburgh a particularly ripe piece of rotting meat. McLean glanced at the clock on the dash, surprised at how late it was. Summer in the north meant long hours of daylight and with them the tendency to work well past the end of the shift. Not that he had shifts, but Ritchie did and technically she'd already put in an hour and a half's overtime.

'Think we need to have a recap at tomorrow's morning briefing. Get a better feel for where we are with this case. I'll have to speak to Dalgliesh, too. See if she's got any further on Stevenson's story.'

'Can't be easy, working with her.' Ritchie stared out the windscreen, one hand toying absentmindedly with her pendant, the little silver cross that she'd taken to wearing lately.

'Possibly the understatement of the year.' McLean slowed the car as they approached the junction with the bypass.

'She's not a bad journalist, when she puts her mind to it.' Ritchie looked away from McLean as she spoke, so he couldn't tell whether she was joking or not. He hoped she was.

'You heading back to the station?' she asked as he took the Burdiehouse turning.

'That was the plan. You can have the rest of the evening off, even after that last comment. I thought I'd head home, see how much damage the cats have done whilst I was away.'

'Cats? Plural? Thought you only had the one. She's not had kittens, has she?'

The thought of Mrs McCutcheon's cat giving birth to anything was so strange, McLean almost drove into the back of a car that had braked to turn into a side street. 'Christ, no. I'm looking after Madame Rose's cats for a while.'

'Oh, that's right. Grumpy Bob told me. Sounds horrible what's happening to her. Any idea who's behind it?'

'Haven't had time to look into it, to be honest.' McLean realised it was a while since he'd heard from the medium. Yet another thing to add to the to-do list.

'Well, if you're just going home you can drop me off at your church. I've got my bag, don't need to go back to the station.'

'The church? OK. I take it tonight's another one of Mary Currie's Bible classes.'

'Bible class?' Ritchie laughed. 'Hadn't really thought of it that way. No, we don't all sit around discussing the Gospels. It's more about tea and sympathy.'

'Still not selling it to me. Always been more of a beer and curry man.'

'Yeah, well sometimes there's beer. If Eric's remembered to bring any. He works in an off-licence in Morningside, gets all the bottles that are past their use-by dates. Sometimes he brings wine for us to taste. It's been very educational, even if Norman doesn't approve. Mind you, Norman doesn't approve of much. He'd be more for studying the Bible and maybe sharing a cup of water and a dry biscuit.'

McLean couldn't help but notice the change in Ritchie as she spoke. Her hands came up out of her lap as if they had a life of their own; her voice was more animated than he'd heard it in ages. Much more like the enthusiastic detective sergeant who'd transferred down from Aberdeen.

'Why'd you go in the first place?' he asked after a while. 'Never had you pegged as the religious type.'

'Didn't really think I was. Oh, I went to Sunday School when I was a kid, used to love singing hymns, carols at Christmas, all that stuff. But I grew out of it. Thought I'd grown out of it, anyway. I mean, it's hard to have faith when your mum goes senile. She was a genuinely good person, kind. Wouldn't hurt a fly, worked in a charity shop when she wasn't out earning enough to keep a roof over our heads. I kind of saw through the whole God thing then.'

'So what changed?' McLean asked the question even though he knew the answer. They'd had this conversation before.

'I nearly died is what.' Ritchie's hands dropped back down into her lap. McLean was concentrating on the road ahead, but he could see in the corner of his eye that she had turned to face him. 'And whatever the doctors say about that, all their talk of Spanish Flu and blood poisoning, none of them had a clue what was wrong with me.'

'And you do.' McLean knew he was pushing where he shouldn't, somehow couldn't stop himself.

'Too bloody right. You do too. Otherwise you wouldn't have come and visited me that night.'

'Which particular night? I visited as often as I could.'

'I had nightmares, you know? More like hallucinations, maybe. Visions of hell. People burning, screaming in agony. Their faces melting away. And sitting in the middle of it all, smiling, was that bloody woman.'

McLean realised he'd slowed down almost to a crawl, checked in the rearview mirror to make sure he wasn't causing an obstruction. They weren't far from his house and the church now, but he didn't want the journey to end until Ritchie had finished talking.

'Mrs Saifre?'

'Like you need to ask. And you know as well as me that's not her real name. Its real name.'

'I . . .'

'It's all right, sir. I know you see the world differently. Rational explanations and all that. Not going to ask you to name it, or anything. But you knew. You helped. Mary knows what you did, won't tell me, but I'm a detective so I'll find out sooner or later. Or maybe I won't. Doesn't really matter. All I know is I was ready to die and I was going to that place. She had me, plain and simple. Then you turned up in the dead of night, and the nightmare went away.'

They had reached the church now, for all McLean's attempts to drag the journey out just a little longer. He pulled in to the kerb, left the engine running.

'You had a high fever, Kirsty. Things can seem very strange when—'

'Don't.' Ritchie stopped him by reaching out and placing a single finger over his lips. He couldn't recall her having touched him before, apart from a handshake when they'd first met maybe. It was a strangely intimate gesture, for all that it was fleeting. Before he could protest, or say anything more, she had unclipped her seatbelt and stepped out of the car. She grabbed her bag from the footwell and slammed the door shut with just the necessary amount of force. McLean watched her as she crossed the pavement and half-jogged down the wide stone path, through the graveyard and into the open door of the church.

31

'Wasn't sure I'd got the right place. It's a bit off the beaten track, isn't it?'

I've been waiting for five minutes longer than I expected, was beginning to wonder if I'd made a mistake with this one. But no, here he is, and only a little late.

'It has to be. The work we do here is . . . close to the edge. We can't do it at the hospital, never get it past the ethics committee for one thing.'

The building is a faceless modern warehouse on the outskirts of town, part of a development of twenty or so identical units. Most house small start-ups, builders, storage units for internet shops. This one's been empty for several months now, all but forgotten by the letting agents. It's been a challenge to prepare, cleaned down and dressed as the set for the final act in this passion play. The effort will be rewarded, I am sure. He is so close to perfection, this one. Just needs to accept what God has ordained for him.

'I almost didn't come,' he says as I usher him in through the door. 'Jon's death, well, it hit me hard, you know. Then the police were round asking questions about Maureen. You know Maureen?'

'I'm not sure I do,' I say as I continue to walk down the corridor. He has to half run to keep up.

'Thought everyone knew her. She's a nurse at the hospital. Specialises in chemo.'

'So many hospitals, so many nurses. It's hard to keep track of them all.' I push open the door into the main room at the back of the building, moving to one side to let him pass by. He takes two steps in, then stops. I can't see his face from where I'm standing, but I'm sure his mouth is hanging open.

'What are you hoping to trial here?' He walks slowly into the centre of the room, runs a hand along the edge of one of the ICU beds, peers at the monitors, all switched off and silent for now. His eyes are everywhere, soaking up the detail. He is weighing the possibilities, considering the implications. I shudder at the thought of what is to come, drink in the tension as he turns back towards me. 'Is this even legal?'

'This isn't a licensed research facility, if that's what you mean. But then I think you already knew that.'

'I don't get it. Who do you work for? This isn't the university or the NHS. Big pharma?'

'Come. Let me show you something.' I head to the ante-room, confident he will follow. There are microscopes, centrifuges, machines that look like they might somehow read your DNA, though in truth they're nothing more than glorified ice-cream makers. The benches are spotlessly clean, the racks of glassware, pipettes and other paraphernalia shiny and new. Arranged along the back wall is a line of tall freezer units, humming gently to themselves. I sense him behind me as I stop at the first.

'In here are the cell lines that could revolutionise the treatment of at least a dozen different cancers. They've all worked well in animal studies, but they need trialling in humans.' I turn and face him, see the questions written large across his face. So very easy to read.

'Your young patient Jon might have benefited, had we been able to get him here. A therapy tailored to the specific DNA of his cancer. Pluck out the faulty genes and replace them with good copies. Self-replicating too. Our goal is a one-shot treatment that basically would've cured him.'

'You can do that? But I thought . . . I mean . . . That's years away, surely?'

'If you play by the rules, yes. But you and I, we know better, don't we?' I step to the side, feeling the moment build. 'You want to look?'

He hesitates, at the last. It's almost as if he knows that to open the door is to cross a line. As if coming here hasn't been. As if the endless nights of research, the furious quest for knowledge that will help him save those barely worth a second glance, wasn't a long slippery slope he'd been sliding down towards this point for years. But in the end he reaches for the handle, twists it, pulls the door open. Just as I knew he would when I first started to tug gently at his puppet strings. In that act he is committed. In that act he is pure.

'Wha——?' His last word is unfinished, the needle slides into his exposed neck, poisons pumping into his blood-stream and shutting him down like a child's toy with its batteries removed. I time it so my hand, shoved into the small of his back, tips him forward as his knees buckle. He kneels into the empty fridge like a man at prayer, weak hands struggling to slow himself as he plunges into the darkness within.

32

There were no cats to be seen anywhere when he drove the car into the old coach house that served as a garage. Nor could McLean see any lurking in the bushes or stalking across the lawn as he walked the short distance to the back door. The reason soon became apparent; they were all in the kitchen, clustered nervously around the figure of Madame Rose. Only Mrs McCutcheon's cat looked unperturbed, glancing up at him with an expression at once unreadable and obvious in its meaning.

'Rose—'

'Inspector. I'm so sorry. I didn't know where to turn.' The medium looked up from her seat at the table, and McLean almost didn't recognise her. The stubble he was just about prepared for, after their last encounter. What he hadn't expected was the heavy bags under the eyes, the tired creases dragging down the corners of her mouth, the lifeless greasy curls of greying hair and the general air of despondency. Even her clothes looked somehow as if she'd slept in them for a day or two.

'I gave you a key, remember? That kind of suggests it's OK for you to drop in when you want.' He went over to the Aga, heaved the kettle on to the hob. If ever there was a time he needed a beer, this was it, but tea would have to do.

'I thought that was just so I could look after the cats.'

Madame Rose stroked one particularly fluffy creature that had curled up in her lap.

'They don't need much looking after, really. Keep to themselves. Barely eat any food. I reckon most of the neighbours are getting through a lot more than usual, mind you.'

That brought the ghost of a smile to Madame Rose's face, but the effort of maintaining it for any length of time was clearly too much.

'You're too kind. You know that?'

'People mention it, from time to time.' McLean dropped teabags into mugs, poured boiling water over them. 'Tell me what's happened. We might as well start from the beginning.'

Madame Rose gathered herself together. She was tall, at least six foot two, maybe more, and sitting up straight she presented a formidable figure. Still, McLean couldn't help but notice the cracked nail varnish as she raised a hand to tidy her lank hair around her shoulder.

'They set fire to the fish and chip shop downstairs. Gianni's been there since the war, you know.'

McLean didn't, but he assumed Madame Rose meant the Second World War. Although knowing her, it could always have been the Boer War, or maybe even the aftermath of Bannockburn.

'Worse, they'd deliberately parked trucks all along the road so the firemen couldn't get easy access. It wouldn't have helped. By the time they arrived the place was going like a . . .'

'House on fire?'

Madame Rose scowled at him, but there was a spark in her eyes that hadn't been there before.

'I tried to get into my house, but they wouldn't let me. The street's cordoned off. It's chaos.'

'Hang on.' McLean tried to remember the last time he'd been to visit Madame Rose at her place in Leith Walk. The entrance was a single door opening on to stairs, sandwiched between a bookmaker's and a chip shop. He could see it now. 'If the chip shop's on fire?'

'My home is safe, Inspector. It will take more than a bully with a Molotov cocktail to burn me out.'

There was something in the way she said it that left McLean in no doubt as to the truth of her words. There were things about Madame Rose he didn't begin to understand; things he didn't want to understand, if he was being honest.

'What's going on here? What's really going on?'

'I don't know who's behind this, or why they're attacking me. And that's the worry, Tony. I really don't know.'

McLean resisted the urge to toot the horn outside the church, instead climbing out of the car and leaning on the roof in the vain hope that would make things happen more quickly. He'd phoned Ritchie, asked if she could help him with Madame Rose's problem. She'd asked for fifteen minutes and he was early, so technically she had another five before she needed to be out on the pavement waiting for him.

When she appeared it wasn't from the church itself, but from the gate further up the road that led to the rectory. That made sense, he supposed. The church only had half a roof at the moment, the rest covered by tarpaulin that snapped in the breeze like gunshots. Maybe tooting the horn wouldn't have been so bad after all.

She wasn't alone, that was the first thing McLean noticed. A young man, dressed in sober black, accompanied her to the gate. He looked like he was going to leave her there, but then saw McLean's car. The two of them came up together. McLean had been trained to be observant, but he didn't need that to notice they were arm in arm.

'You must be Inspector McLean.' The young man held out his free hand. 'Daniel Jones. Dan. Kirsty's told me a fair bit about you.'

'Has she indeed? All good, I'm sure.' McLean took in the dark-coloured shirt under a loose fitting jacket, white clerical collar just visible in the fading light of the evening.

'Daniel's working with Mary at the moment,' Ritchie said. 'He helps out with the discussion group.'

'Won't keep you. Just wanted to say hi.' Dan let go of Ritchie's hand. She nodded, then stepped off the pavement and went round to the passenger door.

'Nice to meet you,' McLean said, slightly confused as to what was going on.

Dan just smiled. 'I'll give you a call in the morning,' he said to Ritchie, then he turned and walked back towards the church.

'So that's why you've been looking so much chirpier lately,' McLean said as they both climbed into the car. He was rewarded by a flush of colour to her freckled cheeks.

'Sorry. None of my business.' He started the engine, pulled away from the kerb.

'It's OK. I don't mind.' Ritchie struggled with her seatbelt for a moment, head down so McLean couldn't see whether she was lying or not. By the time she'd sorted it out they were at the end of the road.

'Daniel's not long been ordained. He's working with Mary at the moment, looking for a parish of his own.'

'A minister?' McLean tried to hide the surprise in his voice.

'Is that a problem?' Ritchie didn't try to hide the defensiveness in hers.

'Not with me, no. None of my business, like I said.'

The evening streets were relatively clear of traffic as they drove back across town in the direction of Leith Walk. McLean told Ritchie about Madame Rose, the harassment she'd been receiving and now the fire. The detective sergeant listened, but didn't say much, and he began to wonder why he'd not come on his own. If it was serious there'd be plenty of police presence, and plain clothes would be called in once the fire was out. No real need to see what was going on just now.

He had to pull over to let a couple of fire engines pass, and when they hit North Bridge the extent of the chaos became apparent. It was mostly buses and taxis, but they still managed to block the northbound carriageway. At the end of the bridge, by the North British Hotel, he could see a cordon set up and a couple of traffic cops in hi-vis jackets trying to impose a semblance of order. No point driving to the scene, then. McLean made a quick U-turn and headed for the station.

'Think it'll be easier if we walk,' he said.

Alongside him Ritchie nodded her agreement. 'Not sure how much help we'll be, if it's that serious.'

It took half an hour to get the car parked and then walk

to Madame Rose's place. They needn't have rushed; there were still plenty of fire engines at the scene, and ominous black smoke billowing from windows to either side of the medium's terrace house.

'Who's in charge?' McLean flashed his warrant card at the first uniform he found, a dour-faced constable given the unenviable task of keeping the smartphone-waving gawkers at bay. No doubt the fire was being live-tweeted and posted to all manner of unsavoury websites.

'Sergeant Bain's senior officer at the moment, sir. But it's the fire service in charge for now.'

Service, of course. No brigades or forces any more. McLean thanked the constable and left him to his hopeless task.

'See if you can't find Bain. Find out what happened.'

DS Ritchie nodded her understanding and headed off into the melee. McLean turned up his collar as he picked a route past fire trucks. Night was falling in that half-hearted way it did in the city at this time of year, the street lights only really deepening the shadows. Half a dozen fire trucks were lined up on the street, blocked from the pavement by a number of badly parked cars and elderly Transit vans. They were a nuisance to the firemen rather than a difficult obstacle to overcome, but McLean could tell just from looking at them that the number plates would be clones, the vehicle identification numbers filed off. If they could be matched to any database, it would almost certainly be a list of stolen motors, all missing at least a couple of months.

'What's going on?' he asked the first fireman he found

who wasn't obviously busy. The young man looked at him as if he were mad, or perhaps a hallucination, until McLean showed his warrant card again.

'Two empty flats on fire. We're keeping it under control best we can, but it's not like any fire I've seen.'

'How so?' McLean looked past the trucks and abandoned vans to the shop fronts, cracked and blackened. There was nothing recognisable left of the chip shop, and the bookies on the other side of Madame Rose's door was a mess of billowing black smoke.

'It's spreading all wrong.' The fireman pointed to the tall houses set back from the shops that had been built in what would once have been front gardens. McLean could see what the fireman was on about. Hoses pumped water at the sandstone walls to either side of Madame Rose's place, beating back the smoke that poured from cracked windows, but the middle house had not caught fire at all.

'How's that even possible?' McLean asked.

'Beats me. Not complaining, mind.' The fireman rubbed at his face with a black-gloved hand, transferring soot to his chin and nose. 'Makes our job a bit easier.'

'You any idea how it started?'

'Best bet's the chip shop. Reeks of accelerant, so I doubt it was an accident. Let's put it out first, aye? Then you can go poking your nose in.'

McLean found Sergeant Bain at the back of one of the fire trucks, cradling a mug of tea and chatting to DS Ritchie. Alongside them was perhaps the last person he expected to see.

'Ms Dalgliesh? How did you get past the security barrier?'

'Nice to see you too, Tony.' Jo Dalgliesh scribbled something down in her notebook, closed it and slipped it into the large bag hung over her shoulder. 'Arson at the local chip shop. Just doing my job.'

'Didn't get the senior reporter's position then? Sorry to hear that.'

Dalgliesh pouted. 'Actually, I did. Doesn't mean I'm above a little local news. Besides, the mess you lot are making of the traffic, this'll probably be in all the nationals tomorrow. I'm surprised the telly crews aren't here already.'

'Oh, they are,' Sergeant Bain said. 'I managed to keep them to the other side of the street though.'

'Well, I guess that's something. And since you've obviously got everything under control, perhaps you can bring us all up to speed.' McLean remembered Bain from his early days as a beat constable. He'd be about the same age as Grumpy Bob, looking to his retirement and probably coasting a bit. He'd been a good copper, so maybe he deserved it. The sergeant looked somewhat sheepishly at his tea, searching for somewhere to put it down. He didn't quite have Grumpy Bob's nonchalance.

'Fire was reported a couple of hours ago, sir. Control sent me out to supervise the traffic and coordinate with the fire service. Didn't realise they'd assigned any plain clothes yet.'

'They haven't. I heard from one of the residents.'

'Madame Rose?' Dalgliesh asked.

'Who is none of your concern, Ms Dalgliesh.'

'Aye, but he lives there, don't he?' The reporter pointed

at the unburnt house, sandwiched between the two still merrily ablaze.

'Do we know what started the fire, Sergeant?' McLean wanted to tell Dalgliesh to piss off, but he needed her on his side, needed information from her about Ben Stevenson. So he decided the easiest thing for now was to pretend she wasn't there.

'Not sure yet, sir. Looks like it's probably arson though. These cars and vans . . .' Bain pointed at the abandoned vehicles. 'And there's a reek of petrol round the door now they've got that bit out. But who'd want to burn down a chippy?'

'That's assuming it was the target, of course,' Ritchie said. 'Madame Rose was getting harassment. Maybe this was meant for her.'

'Why'd anyone have it in for a barmy old transvestite fortune teller?' Dalgliesh asked. So much for ignoring her.

'I don't know. Maybe because the tabloids keep on drumming up hatred for people like her?'

Dalgliesh gave him an old-fashioned look, but didn't press the matter. No doubt she knew when she was outnumbered and could be marched off the scene at any moment. McLean turned his attention back to Sergeant Bain.

'Those two houses either side. We know if there was anyone in them when the fire started?'

'Both empty. No furnishings. Lots of building materials, piles of timber, paint pots, that kind of stuff.'

'All very flammable.' McLean watched as the firemen switched off the hose on the nearest building. Only steam was rising from its windows now. They'd have the other one out soon, by the look of things. 'I don't suppose for a moment that's a coincidence.'

He knew it wasn't, of course. Someone was trying to get Madame Rose to leave. Killing her cat hadn't worked. Pushing shit through her letterbox hadn't worked either. So now they were going to burn her out. Looking up at the house, it was clear that hadn't worked out quite the way they had intended. Which left the question hanging: what would they try next?

33

'Control decides who attends a crime scene. It's not up to officers to pick and choose where they go. You know that as well as I do.'

'With respect sir, control hadn't even worked out they needed to assign anyone from CID. I wasn't there as an investigating officer.'

'Well why the hell were you there then? And why did you have to drag DS Ritchie along with you? Her shift was over, for fuck's sake.'

Early morning, up in front of the beak again. McLean wondered whether DCI Brooks would move into this office, assuming he got the detective superintendent job once Duguid had finally taken his leave. The detective chief inspector's own office was only marginally smaller than this one, and had a better view from its window, facing out towards Salisbury Crags rather than over the rooftops towards the castle.

'Are you even listening to me, McLean?' Duguid's question cut across his musing.

'Sorry, sir. Just trying to work out the best way to explain it. I know the owner of the middle house. She came to me a while back complaining of harassment. Someone killed one of her cats.'

'She report this to the police?'

'Of course. It's Leith's patch, so they looked into it. Not much they could do, by all accounts.'

Duguid's permanent frown turned into a scowl. 'This wouldn't have anything to do with the nuisance Grumpy Bob was making of himself at Leith nick, would it?'

McLean said nothing, wondering who'd been telling tales and why. It was highly unlikely Grumpy Bob would have upset anyone enough to warrant a complaint.

'This isn't your own private police service you know, McLean. You can't go off investigating things just because you feel like it, or your friends ask you to. And you can't pull other detectives off their active cases just to look into things for you.'

McLean clenched his fists behind his back. Not because he was particularly angry, but to stop himself from making the obvious retort. He couldn't begin to count the number of times Duguid had abused his position in exactly that way.

'I'm sorry, sir. Didn't think asking Bob to have a word on his way home would bother anyone.'

'You never do, McLean. Think, that is. That's your problem. Always trying to be the white knight, rushing gallantly in to save the fair maiden.'

That brought an involuntary smile to McLean's face. Of all the ways Madame Rose might be described, fair maiden was not one.

'I'll leave it alone then, sir. Plenty for me to be getting on with on the Stevenson investigation anyway.'

Duguid's face creased even further and for a moment McLean thought he was going to cry. Then he realised that the detective superintendent was grinning. 'No. You won't leave it alone, McLean. I've squared it with control. You stuck your nose in, you can have the bloody case.'

It was probably for the best. McLean knew himself well enough to realise that he'd just pester whoever else was running the investigation. Duguid did as well, which was annoying. It meant that while he'd got what he wanted, the shine was rather spoiled by the knowledge that Duguid had too. And there was the small matter of the rest of his workload to cope with.

He cadged a lift in a squad car over to Leith Walk. Only one fire truck remained, a few firemen clearing up the last of the operation. It was a mess, but then fires always were. At least they'd managed to tow away the parked vehicles and get the traffic moving again.

'Fire investigator here?' McLean asked of the first fireman he could waylay. The startled young man said nothing, just pointed a heavy-gloved hand in the direction of Madame Rose's front door, where a tall, stout man was crouching down and staring at something. He wore a bright yellow hard hat that appeared about two sizes too small, perching on the top of his large head in a manner that suggested it wouldn't give much protection if anything should fall on it.

'Mr Burrows. We meet again.' McLean picked his way through debris pulled out of the shop fronts as the fire investigator stood and turned to meet him. Jim Burrows had investigated the fire out at Loanhead in which McLean had nearly died. That one had been put down to burning underground coal deposits and firedamp seeping up through cracks in the concrete. He was intrigued to hear what the investigator made of this unusual scene.

'Inspector.' He held out a hand the size of a dinner plate. McLean shook it, then pointed to where the fire investigator had been staring.

'Find something?'

'Yes and no. See here?' Burrows pointed at the door to Madame Rose's house. The street door, McLean corrected himself. There was presumably another door around the back somewhere. This was familiar from his previous visits, the rather faded sign above it still advertising the telling of fortunes and reading of tarots. The top half of the door had been glass, but someone had taken a brick to it fairly recently. The sheet of plywood in its place was spray-painted with the words 'faggot' and 'peedo'.

'What am I looking at?'

'All of it. Paint, wood, glass. Look here.' Burrows took a few steps down the hill to the remains of the empty betting shop. The window frame had been painted white some time in a previous millennium, and the heat of the fire had bubbled and browned it at the edges.

'It was hot enough here to partially melt this glass, see?' Burrows bent down and carefully scraped a few shards from the pavement. 'You wouldn't have been able to stand here while the blaze was going. Even if you could've breathed, the heat would've burned your skin right off.'

'And yet here.' Burrows took two admittedly long strides back to Madame Rose's door, then stopped. 'Here there's no sign of scorching at all. There's even some paper still stuck through the letterbox.'

McLean pulled latex gloves from his pocket, snapped them on, then plucked the paper out. It was a flyer for a local meeting. '!!!Stop the Developement!!!' misprinted in bold script across the top of the page, a badly reproduced photograph just below. There was no sign of singeing on it at all, but there was no way someone could have pushed it through the letterbox after the fire. He folded it carefully and slipped it into his pocket for later perusal.

'So what stopped it then?' he asked.

'Search me. Never seen anything like it before.' Burrows walked uphill while he spoke, coming to a halt in front of the charred remains of Gianni's Chip Shop. 'I mean, the wall's brick between the shops, so that might've stopped the fire spreading. And there's a gap between the back of the chippie and the front of the house. That'd go some way to explaining why the fire didn't spread back like it did with the other two.'

McLean studied the facade of Madame Rose's house, the stonework darkened only by a couple of centuries' exposure to Auld Reekie and more recent car exhausts. To either side the neighbouring houses were smeared with soot, black tears streaking upwards from every burnt-out window.

'You been inside yet?' he asked.

Burrows shook his head. 'Won't get inside those two. The roof's going to come down any minute, could take the front wall with it. Only safe way's to bring it down with machinery from the outside.'

'Won't that be a risk for the other houses?'

'Those ones, maybe.' Burrows pointed up the hill, then down. 'But they'll probably be OK. Engineers know how to shore them up. That one,' he pointed at Madame Rose's house. 'That'd probably stay standing if you dropped a bomb on it.'

34

'Got you working on this one too, have they?'

McLean had been looking for a squad car to give him a lift back to the station. It wasn't far, but the heat was oppressive. The city centre would be crowded with tourists come for the Festival and the Fringe, too, which always lessened the joy of walking. A quick search of the cordoned-off part of the street had revealed nothing but a short reporter, clad in a leather overcoat that must surely have been too warm to wear.

'Ms Dalgliesh. Back again, I see. I'd have thought you'd send a cub reporter to a job like this.'

'You're very stuck up, Tony. You know that? Some might even say repressed. Public school education, I guess.'

That stung. It was possible Dalgliesh was just guessing as she tried to wind him up, but it was just as possible that she had dug as deep into his background as she could and knew the names of both expensive and exclusive schools his grandmother had sent him to.

'I take it you're writing a piece about the fire.' It was feigned interest, but it seemed to do the trick of diverting her from talking about him.

'Just a puff piece, really. Apart from the traffic buggery last night, it's not much of a story. This part of town's been crying out for some regeneration for ages. Maybe this will kick-start something. Get the council off their arses.'

McLean's hand went unbidden to his jacket pocket, the 'stop the development' flyer he'd pulled from Madame Rose's letterbox. He stopped himself before Dalgliesh noticed, flexing his fingers into a fist and out again as if relieving an arthritic twinge.

'Actually, I was going to give you a call.'

'You were?' Genuine amazement spread across the journalist's face.

'Ben Stevenson. Could really do with an update. You found out what he was working on yet?'

'It's your lucky day then.' Dalgliesh gave him a broad grin that made her look like some kind of demented, wizened shark. 'But you'll have to buy the coffee.'

It came in a ridiculously large mug, more like a cereal bowl with handles than something designed for drinking from. On the plus side, the cafe they went to also sold large slices of very good chocolate cake. McLean had missed breakfast in his hurry to leave the house, so a mid-morning indulgence was, he thought, perfectly justified.

'First off, Ben Stevenson was a fine journalist.' Jo Dalgliesh brushed ginger biscuit from her moustache as she spoke, taking a mouthful of coffee as she chewed. Fortunately swallowing before she spoke again. McLean was too fascinated by her appalling manners and utter lack of self-consciousness to say anything himself.

'Oh, I know you lot think we're all vicious hacks churning out rubbish just to make life difficult, but actually it takes quite a bit of work sometimes.'

'Making life difficult? And here's me thinking it came naturally.'

'You know, for someone who wants my help you can be a right sarky bastard at times.'

McLean took a small bite of his cake to stop himself replying too quickly. Dalgliesh was right, of course. He needed her help. It was just difficult to put aside the loathing of years, harder still to sit across a table from this woman and not think about the hatchet job she'd done on him and the families of Donald Anderson's other victims.

'OK. Fair enough. Sorry.' He raised both hands in a mock admission of defeat. 'I'm not going to pretend I like you, Dalgliesh, but I'll try to be civil.'

'Aye, well.' Dalgliesh studied him as if trying to work out whether or not he was taking the piss. He must have passed the test, as she pulled out her notebook, laid it out on the table between them.

'Took a wee while to piece it all together, but I'm fairly sure I know what Ben was working on when he . . . you know.'

'The Brotherhood?'

Dalgliesh raised an eyebrow. 'Aye, that. Bunch of shadowy figures pulling the strings. The secret world government behind everything bad that's ever happened right through history. Fingers in all the pies. Even own the bloody pie factory. Make the illuminati look like amateurs.'

'And Stevenson was on to them?'

'Oh, he thought he was. Contacts here, secret meetings there. But it's all bollocks, aye?'

'It is?'

'Pure bollocks. You'll have talked to Dougie Ballantyne? Daft wee shite that he is.'

McLean nodded, remembering the trip down to the Borders. Tea and gibberish.

'What did you make of him?' Dalgliesh picked up her coffee, took a drink while she waited for McLean to reply.

'Delusion on a grand scale. But he's smart. Very good at seeing patterns, connections between things that you wouldn't think were connected. Most of the time that's because they aren't, but he makes a plausible argument.'

'If you only take his evidence, and only the way he presents it, sure. My job, yours too I guess, is to see all sides of an argument. Check the facts. Look for verification, a second source. You start doing that with Ballantyne's theories and they all fall apart soon enough.'

'But Stevenson believed him. I thought you rated him as a journalist.'

'Aye, I did. Ben was one of the best, when he put his mind to it.'

'So—?'

'You know what Ballantyne says about himself? How he justifies his rubbish?'

McLean thought back to the conversation. It had only been a couple of days, but rather more than he'd hoped for had happened in the intervening time. 'Something about being a messenger?'

'That's the one.' Dalgliesh slurped some more coffee, looked at her biscuitless plate with something akin to regret, rubbed a nicotine-stained finger in the crumbs and stuck it in her mouth. 'He reckons he can get away with revealing secrets because they're feeding them to him. All part of some strategy to come out from the shadows. He actually believes the Head talks to him and tells him what to write.'

'Ritchie's expression was "stone bonker". I think that just about sums up Douglas Ballantyne the third.'

'And yet, for all we can see him for the loony he is, Ben thought he was on to something.' Dalgliesh tapped the closed notebook lying on the table between them. 'He really believed there was a Brotherhood. Maybe even a dis-embodied talking head that ruled them all.'

'From what I've heard, Stevenson was under quite a lot of pressure. Workwise he'd not had a decent story in years. And his home life was hardly stable.'

'Ah. Youse lot have talked to Charlie then.' Dalgliesh's face was rarely a closed book, but even so McLean was surprised at the flash of anger that spread across it.

'Ex-wife of a murdered man? One of the first people we interviewed.'

'Aye, well. Did she tell you how she came off in the divorce? Did she tell you she was the one playing away from home?'

She hadn't, of course, but it didn't really change any-thing. 'All the more reason to suspect that Stevenson wasn't perhaps concentrating on the job as well as he should have been.'

Dalgliesh shook her head. 'You don't know Ben. That's not his way. If anything the pressure would have made him more careful, more – what's the word? Conscientious.'

McLean was surprised Dalgliesh even knew what it meant. 'You saw his secret room. That wall. Didn't look all that conscientious to me. Looked like the last stages of madness.'

'Actually, I'm glad you mentioned that.' Dalgliesh rummaged around in her shoulder bag, coming out with a handful of A4 colour prints. The first was a photograph of the room off Ben Stevenson's bedroom, the wall covered in photos, magazine cut-outs, Post-it notes. Everything linked together with endless lines of coloured string. At this scale it was almost impossible to make anything of it other than a bad piece of modern abstract art.

'Resolution's not too good on the printout.' Dalgliesh smoothed out the creases with a leathery hand, placed a couple more photographs alongside the first to make something of a montage. 'But I've got the whole thing on my computer and you can zoom in enough to see what's what. What's interesting is there's nothing here that's particularly Masonic. See, there's stuff about the Hellfire Club, Beggars Benison, all that nonsense. The Guild of Strangers gets a mention, there's some Templar writings. There's even some stuff about Police Scotland I'll have to look into at a later date. But there's no set-square and compass, no reference to any Grand Lodge or High Poobah. It's almost as if the Freemasons were deliberately excluded from what he was looking into.'

McLean pulled the first photograph across the table, swivelling it around so he could see it better. It didn't really help much, all the details too small to make out properly. The original was still in place, locked up after the forensics team had been through Stevenson's flat. He'd have to go over and have another look soon, but in the meantime he could take Dalgliesh's word for it.

'So he wasn't really looking at the Masons, then,' he said.

'Oh, he started there. Everyone does. But then he got

Ballantyne's book and went off in a different direction. See?' Dalgliesh prodded a yellowing finger at the photographs, sliding them over each other and obscuring half of the picture.

'Not really, no. I thought you said Ballantyne was nuts. Surely Stevenson saw that too?'

'Oh, aye. He saw that. But then something else caught his eye. Someone else.'

'Who?' McLean pulled one of the pictures closer, peered at the blurred lines as if they would magically clear just by squinting.

'That's what I'm trying to find out.' Dalgliesh flicked a final photo on to the table. This one was a close-up of the wall, a blurred image of a man standing underneath a street lamp in the dark. Impossible to make out any features, but Stevenson had scribbled over it in red marker. 'Who is he?'

35

The walk back to the station had, as predicted, left him clammy with sweat and bruised from the elbows and back-packs of the milling masses on the Royal Mile. It had also given McLean some time to think about Dalgliesh's research. It annoyed him that she had a detailed photograph of the wall in Ben Stevenson's flat, but since he'd not yet given it proper scrutiny himself, it was perhaps just as well someone had. The implications were clear. Stevenson had begun pursuing a conspiracy, and ended up finding something else entirely. Someone else entirely.

He needed to see the wall again, and not just a high-resolution photograph of it. He should have studied it more closely the moment they'd found it, obvious now that it was going to be crucial to unlocking the case. McLean couldn't quite understand why he hadn't done so, but then Dalgliesh had been with him, and Ritchie hadn't been well, and before he knew it they'd found the dead nurse, Maureen Shenks. Where the hell had all the time gone? And when had he become so distracted? Round about the time he'd stopped getting more than a few hours' sleep a night, perhaps. Or maybe when Duguid took over. He shook his head to dislodge the unhelpful thought, headed for the major incident room. DC MacBride was the first useful person he found.

'You busy, Constable?'

As questions went it was pretty stupid. MacBride was surrounded by a crowd of uniform constables and sergeants as well as several admin staff. He wasn't the most senior officer in the room by a comfortable margin, but he was quite clearly in charge.

'Just need to get this lot handed out, sir. Be with you in a moment.'

McLean left him to his task, heading over to the wall with its map, whiteboard and blown-up photographs. There were a few of Stevenson himself, sprawled on the ground in the damp cave. One of the room at his home that wasn't much clearer than Dalgliesh's. He stared at it unseeing as he tried to gather his thoughts.

Apart from the fact that Jo Dalgliesh knew a lot more about the details of the case than she should have done, the point she had raised was a valid one. Whoever had killed Stevenson had made it look Masonic, that much was clearly evident from the sigils daubed on the cavern wall in his blood. But the flavour of Freemasonry those clues pointed at was hardly secret knowledge, its exposure not really the sort of thing that would get you killed even if you were a Mason sworn to secrecy. And according to Duguid, Ben Stevenson wasn't and never had been a member of any Lodge. The more he thought about it, the more McLean convinced himself that the Masonic angle was a diversion, a feint to get them all looking in the wrong direction. The only problem was, there was no other direction to look in. No forensics, no CCTV, no clues at all.

'Just had to get rid of those actions. Sorry about that, sir.' DC MacBride appeared at McLean's side. He had a weary, hangdog look to him at odds with his usual unflappable cheeriness.

'Everything all right?' Yet another stupid question, but somebody had to ask them.

MacBride let out a long sigh. 'Could be better, sir. I thought Dagwood was meant to be Gold on this investigation, but I don't think I've seen him in here once. You're SIO, but apart from the morning briefings you're mostly out and about with DS Ritchie. Grumpy Bob seems to have disappeared completely and all the other CID officers are running around after Brooks in the hope he'll be nice to them when he gets the top job.'

'Meaning you've been left to run a major incident room on your own.'

'I wouldn't mind so much sir, only . . .'

'You're a detective constable and it's way above your pay grade?'

'That and the jokes.' The detective constable's hand went up to his forehead, unconsciously brushing at his fringe to spread it out over his scar.

'Still getting called Potter?'

'That would be fine, to be honest, sir. If that was as far as it went. But Christ, people can be dicks at times.'

McLean knew all too well what the constable meant. 'And policemen even more so, right?'

'There's times I wonder why I even bother. Plenty other lines of work I could be in.'

McLean gave MacBride what he hoped was a friendly slap on the shoulder. 'It's not that bad, Stuart. Believe me, they'll get bored and move on soon.'

'Really?' The look on MacBride's face suggested he'd take some convincing.

'Really. Now grab your coat and come with me. We've a crime scene to investigate.'

He knew as soon as he slid the key into the front door that something was wrong, paused before pushing open the door.

'Who secured the scene?'

'Er . . . Not sure, sir. You and DS Ritchie were the last ones here, I think.'

'Forensics haven't been?'

'Let me check.' MacBride tapped away at his tablet computer, holding it up close to the window, presumably to get a better signal. McLean wondered how the detective constable had managed to get his hold on it; uniforms had been using digital notebooks for a while now, but this was much more sophisticated.

'Scene was photographed and processed for fingerprints four days ago. Nothing else. Dr Cairns signed it off. Someone must have returned the keys to us.' MacBride nodded at McLean's hand, still hovering by the lock.

'That all?'

'That's all the computer says. You want me to call forensics and check?'

'No. I guess we didn't ask them to do any more than that. Something here doesn't feel right though. You got gloves?' McLean pulled out a pair of his own, squeezed his hands into the tight-fitting latex as MacBride did the same.

'Right. Stay close and don't touch anything if you don't

have to.' He didn't really need to say it, and the look on MacBride's face told him he'd struck a nerve. Well, there were times you just had to take it as it came.

The key caught slightly in the lock as he twisted it, as if it was reluctant to let anyone in. Beyond the doorway, the hall looked much like he remembered, bright and wide. McLean could imagine it being a warm family home, the sound of children playing in one of the other rooms, the smell of cooking from the kitchen to welcome the weary journalist on his return from work. That was the picture Stevenson's ex-wife had painted, but he knew now that it was a lie. And the odour that reached his nostrils was far from welcoming. Something rotting, overlaid with a smell he couldn't immediately place but which brought hazy images of childhood and grazed knees. Antiseptic, that was it. Only somehow different.

'Eww. What is that?' DC MacBride said.

'Not sure I really want to know.' McLean breathed through his mouth in the hope that it would help. It didn't really, but the gentlest of breezes from the landing outside made it just about bearable. He'd not wanted to spend very long in the flat, just enough time to look at Stevenson's wall, but now he was going to have to search the whole place. There'd be an awkward conversation with Jemima Cairns too, if she'd been the last person in.

The dreadful smell seemed to linger in the hallway. Through in the living room it was much easier to breathe, and in Stevenson's study there was nothing at all. It didn't look any different to how McLean remembered it from his first visit. Nothing on the main floor did. There was no obvious sign of where the stench was coming from, either.

'It's . . . I don't know. Almost like rotting apples or something?' DC MacBride was still pacing slowly around the hall when McLean emerged from the kitchen. The constable sniffed the air, took a few steps, sniffed again, his head tilted forward as he tried to pinpoint the source. Quite how he could do that without gagging, McLean didn't know.

'Well, you can let me know when you've found it. I'm going upstairs.'

The bedroom appeared no different to when he, Ritchie and Dalgliesh had been there a few days earlier. The smell diminished as he moved away from the top of the stairs, almost as if it were anchored to the front door. All thought of it vanished from his mind as he stepped into the small dressing room beyond the bedroom, though.

The wall was clear. No maps, no printouts, no photographs. For an instant, McLean wondered if the forensics team had taken it all down to recreate in their lab. That's what he should have asked them to do, but the tangle of coloured strings strewn over the dressing table gave the lie to that idea, as did the drawing pins spread lazily around in the carpet like so many traps for the unwary bare foot. There was no way a scene of crime officer would take down the photographs and leave the string. It was either all evidence or none of it was, which meant someone had been in here after Dr Cairns had sealed the place up.

'Think I've got it, sir.' DC MacBride's voice echoed up from the hallway below. McLean took one last look at the desecrated room before heading back down. He found the constable squatting by the front door, the Persian rug pulled back to reveal polished floorboards

underneath. Closer still, and McLean could see that Mac-
Bride had pulled up one of the boards, revealing a hidden
space beneath. The smell was overpowering, so much so
that he had to cover his mouth and nose with his jacket.
MacBride had done the same, his eyes watering slightly as
he looked up.

'Felt the floor move as I was pacing about.' His voice
was muffled by jacket and handkerchief. 'Found this. Not
quite sure what to make of it.'

McLean came closer still, peering down into the space
between the floor and the ceiling of the flat below. It had
been lined with tin foil, more of which had been stapled to
the underside of the floorboard, and inside lay something
he couldn't immediately identify. It was red and shiny, with
flecks of black and green. Tiny little white things wriggled
around in it, and as he focused on them, so realisation
began to dawn.

'Cover it up, Constable.' McLean took a step back, then
another, pulling his phone out of his pocket as he went.
The number was on speed dial, the call answered swiftly.
Even so he knew that the time he'd have to spend waiting
for the team to arrive would be far too long.

36

'Now there's something you don't see every day.'

Angus Cadwallader knelt in Ben Stevenson's hallway, leaning over the hole left by the removed floorboard. Returning scene of crime officers had set up spotlights that shone over the scene, leaving little doubt as to what someone had placed in this little hiding hole.

'It's a heart, isn't it?' McLean was unfortunate enough to have encountered one before. 'A human heart.'

'In the middle, yes. Not sure what all this greenery is around it. Not exactly my area of expertise. Some kind of nest I'd guess. Think that's where the worst of the smell's coming from, too.'

McLean stepped back from the edge and out on to the landing, breathing deep after too long of trying not to breathe at all. The smell was still strong in the hallway, even after the windows had been forced open. What he still couldn't quite work out was exactly what the smell was. Not rotting flesh; that, sadly, was another odour he'd encountered all too often in his career. No, DC MacBride was closer to the mark when he'd suggested rotting apples. There was a sweetness to the aroma, along with a harder, sharper edge, like vinegar maybe, or even—

'Embalming fluid.' Cadwallader joined him on the landing, pulling his long latex gloves off with a satisfying snap. 'Old-fashioned stuff. Not come across it in a long while.

We don't use it in the mortuary any more. I think it's reacted with the vegetation, or maybe the tin foil. It's not actually made of tin, you know.'

'Yes, I think I was aware of that, Angus. Anything else you can tell us about our somewhat macabre find?'

'Not a lot I can do here. Have to get it back to the mortuary and run some tests. It's a man's heart though. Adult.'

Lightning flashed and popped as the crime scene photographer recorded every moment while a couple of technicians tried to work out the best way of getting the heart, vegetation and foil out all in one piece. It reminded McLean of why he and MacBride had come to Stevenson's flat in the first place.

'Let me know what you find will you, Angus?' He gave his friend a gentle slap on the arm as he headed for the stairs.

'You not hanging around to watch them take it out?' Cadwallader asked.

'That's what underlings are for.' McLean pointed to the pale-faced form of DC MacBride, still stuck in the hallway with its fetid air. 'I need to find a crime scene manager.'

He found the woman he was looking for out in the street. Jemima Cairns was overseeing the return en masse of the forensics team, her normally dour face thunderous. It didn't improve when she saw him approaching, darkening even more if that were possible.

'Could you no' have left well alone?'

'It's not as if I put it there myself, you know.'

'Aye, well . . .' Dr Cairns muttered something under her

breath he didn't quite catch. McLean was all too aware that she could be caustic at times, which didn't make the next question he was going to ask any easier. Still, in with both feet at the deep end, that's what his grandmother had always said.

'You signed it off, right?'

The glare might have killed someone not ready for it. 'If you think—'

'That you missed something like that? Course I don't. I might be slow sometimes, but even I know better than that.'

Dr Cairns still glowered at him like a child whose favourite toy has been confiscated, but McLean could see a grudging acceptance in there too.

'So why d'you need to ask then?'

'Someone broke in after you'd left, but you were the last person to see the place before they did. That means I have to talk to you about what the place looked like. What you'd done. That wall display in the upstairs bedroom, for instance. You left it intact?'

'Aye, left it there right enough. Would've liked to have taken it down carefully. Find out what order everything got put up. You can tell as much from the way a thing's done as from what it is.'

'Why didn't you, then?'

Dr Cairns' scowl deepened again. 'That's your department, isn't it? Working out the puzzle from the clues left behind? I'm a forensic scientist, not a shrink. Besides, there wasn't the time or the budget. I asked, but was told no.' Realisation dawned on her face. 'It's gone, isn't it?'

'Yes.' McLean kicked at the ground with his foot,

reluctant to admit what had happened. As if not saying it would make it not so. Then the forensic scientist's words filtered through. 'Wait, what? You were told no? By who?'

'By whom, Inspector.' Dr Cairns couldn't resist the dig, obviously. It brought a brief smile to her face, which was better than the scowl. 'The request will be on file somewhere, I'm sure. And the response, although I think that was from a detective sergeant if I recall correctly. No idea who actually made the decision. I assumed it was you, since you're SIO on the case. Could've come from Detective Superintendent Duguid, of course. Or someone else higher up. Could've just been the DS who responded.'

McLean ground his foot harder into the pavement, trying his best to suppress his anger. The effort raised a slight twinge of pain in his hip, the last echoes of the broken bone reminding him that he'd never be quite as fit as before he'd fallen off that precariously balanced chair in his attic. Might have been better if he'd actually hanged himself. At least then he wouldn't have had to deal with incompetence on a grand scale.

'Judging by your face, this is the first you've heard of it?' Dr Cairns had lost her scowl now, showing not so much enjoyment at his discomfort as concern.

'Exactly so. If you'd asked me I'd have said yes. That wall is crucial to this case, I know it. And now someone's destroyed all the evidence tied up in it.'

Dr Cairns gave him a friendly pat on the arm, smiling at last. 'Just as well we took lots of photographs then, aye?'

The office was a haven of relative cool after the muggy heat of the walk back from Ben Stevenson's flat. McLean could have cadged a lift – there were enough squad cars milling around – but he needed time to think, a space where he wasn't being pulled this way and that by conflicting demands. And so he'd left the SOCOs to go over the flat, DCs MacBride and Gregg to interview the other residents of the tenement block, and set off back to the station on his own.

It hadn't helped. The pain that had flared up in his hip was a constant niggle, and he couldn't stop dwelling on the stupidity that had left a valuable piece of evidence open to tampering. As to what the hell was going on with the heart under the floorboards, he couldn't even begin to imagine. Had it been there all along? Not if Dr Cairns was to be believed, and she wasn't someone he'd have expected to miss something like that. Which meant that someone had gone back and taken down the evidence wall, then carefully placed a pickled human heart under the floorboards.

Whose heart was it? Where did you get a hold of a human heart? Why was it there? The questions kept whirling round and round in his head until he realised he was already back at the station, slumping into his office chair. No memory of the walk at all.

There was paperwork; when had there ever not been? But at that moment the idea of wading through something as dull as overtime sheets had a certain appeal. Perhaps if he immersed himself in something completely brainless then his subconscious could go to work on sorting out all the complicated stuff. As he flipped open the brown card folder, however, McLean saw that this wasn't the latest staff roster, but something else entirely.

Someone had cocked up on the filing and left him the

post-mortem report on the dead nurse, Maureen Shenks. McLean was about to get up, take it to the incident room where DI Spence was conducting that investigation. He'd not had a chance to find out how it was progressing, and it was always useful to know these things. A chat with his fellow detective inspector might be useful and enlightening. On the other hand, he'd witnessed the PM himself. There'd been similarities in the method of killing used on the nurse and Ben Stevenson. And if he asked Spence to see the report he'd get grief from Brooks, at best told to mind his own business, at worst a complaint to Duguid that he wasn't concentrating on his own cases. Perhaps this was a lucky chance to get ahead of the game.

And there was always that natural inquisitiveness, of course. He couldn't deny that. McLean rolled off the elastic band that had been holding the folder closed, leaned back in his seat and started to read.

37

He comes out of the coma slowly, exactly as it should be. It helps that he's connected up to all the machinery; means I can monitor him waking as the poisons are filtered out of his blood. I imagine he'll have the mother of all headaches right now, but that's a small price to pay for what awaits him on the other side.

'Wh . . . wha . . . where?' The question is barely a whisper, almost drowned out by the hum of the life-support systems. I hover out of sight, observing as he slowly comes to terms with his situation. The muscles around his eyes twitch, but they don't immediately open. As if the eyelids are stuck together with glue, the eyeballs dry inside. There is sweat on his skin, tiny beads forming around his temples and slicking his thin hair.

'Is . . . is anyone there?' And now he tries to move his head. He can't, of course. The bed is designed for epileptics, the restraints soft but very secure. His arms and legs are strapped down, too. In a minute or so he will realise just how helpless he is. As he should be when meeting his maker.

'You are blessed, Jim. You have a certainty about you few possess.'

I can almost see his ears twitching as he tries to pinpoint my voice. He opens his eyes now, but all he can see is the ceiling high overhead.

'Ben? Is that you?'

'Ben has gone on before you.' I reach out, stroke the side of his cheek with the back of my finger. 'Ben is already in heaven.'

'What's going on? Where am I? Why can't I move?' His voice is growing stronger, even as the panic rises. The machines tell me this, but I can read him without them. The same way I can see the readiness of his soul, free of the stains of life.

'I envy you. That's my downfall, you understand. You have found such a state of grace I can never hope to achieve. I can only pray that when it is my time to be judged He will look upon these works of mine favourably.'

'I . . . I don't understand. What are you—'

'Shhh.' I place my finger over his lips, silencing him. His eyes lock on to my face now, and I can feel the tremors that shake through his body, smell the fear rising from him. God is near, ready to take this perfect soul to his bosom. But this can't be a swift and violent end. Not like the journalist. I could feel him slipping back into sinful doubt almost from the moment he reached apotheosis. His end was always going to be quick or risk the loss of such a perfect prize. I knew that the moment I first met him, confirmed it over the weeks I fed his obsession, led him to the secret knowledge he so craved.

This one is different. He is scared, but he is also ever hopeful. I can taste it on him, see the colours of it playing in his aura. This one put his faith in medicine, science, technology. Only fitting then that his beloved machines hasten him toward his salvation.

'Go now, Jim. Do your great works. Heal the sick like our Lord Jesus healed them.'

He's ready, has been ready for hours now. Still, I want to savour this, feel the presence of the Lord when he comes to collect this soul. I reach over to the machine, flick the switch. The motors whirr and the ceremony begins.

'What's happening? What are you doing? Ben?'

'Don't panic. It will all be over soon.' I pick a careful path through the tubes and wires as the precious fluid drains slowly from his body. The litany is silent, the words flowing through my mind as I take up my perch on the stool by the door and watch.

38

'You got a minute, Spence?'

The detective inspector was holding court in the middle of his incident room, his thin, pointy head rising up over the gaggle of junior detectives surrounding him. McLean couldn't help noticing that there were more uniforms and admin in the incident room for the Maureen Shenks murder than he had working on the Ben Stevenson case. Indeed quite a few of the officers who were meant to be working with him seemed to have been poached. Some things never changed.

'Not got enough to do, you have to come sticking your nose in here, McLean?' Spence ambled across with all the urgency of a sloth. The look he gave McLean was one of a headmaster wearily dealing with an awkward boy, which given he was only two years McLean's senior seemed a bit much. Nothing he wasn't used to, though, and if Brooks got the promotion to detective superintendent that everyone expected, the chances were good that Spence would have his DCI job. That would be fun.

'Just thought you might have been looking for this.' McLean held up the PM report. 'Someone stuck it on my desk by mistake.'

'What is it?' Spence made no move to take the folder.

'Missing piece of your puzzle, if that board's anything to go by.' McLean gestured over to the whiteboard on the far side of the room. Several questions had been written on it in teacher's handwriting, but there were few answers as yet. How long had it been since Spence had taken over?

'What the hell are you doing here?' McLean turned in the doorway to see DCI Brooks lumbering up the corridor. Just once in a while, he thought, it would be nice if people could be civil.

'Afternoon, sir. I was just dropping off the PM report on Maureen Shenks. It got shoved in with my filing by mistake.'

'Maureen . . .?' For an instant Brooks looked like he was going to ask who, but he rallied with a noncommittal 'Oh'.

'You might want to read it sir. There's some alarming similarities in the method used on the nurse and on Ben Stevenson.'

That got McLean the full angry grimace, and at the same time he felt the folder being tugged from his grasp.

'You've read it?' DI Spence held the report at arm's length, as if it had been sullied. Either that or he needed his reading glasses.

'Of course I've read it. I attended the post-mortem, remember. Before you were assigned the case.'

'So you have nothing better to do than stick your nose in? Ben Stevenson's killer behind bars, is he?' DCI Brooks pushed past on his way into the incident room in a manner best described as brusque. The busy hum of activity that had filled the air when McLean arrived had dropped into a tense silence now.

'It's not a pissing contest, sir. I'm not trying to take over your investigation or steal your glory or whatever you think's going on. I'm just pointing out that there are similarities between two Cat A murders currently under investigation. If nothing else, it's a line of enquiry worth pursuing, don't you think?'

'I'll be the judge of that, McLean.' Brooks pulled the report from DI Spence's weak grasp, flipped it open and went straight to the back.

'Take your time,' McLean said. He fought back the urge to make a sarcastic comment, knowing full well how counterproductive it would be. 'You know where to find me if you need me.'

'Brooks tells me you've been sticking your nose into his investigation.'

As conversational openers went, it was much to be expected from Duguid. McLean was surprised at just how quickly the complaint had been made though, and how petty it was. It threw him, too. This wasn't the reason he'd come to see the chief superintendent.

'I was just giving them their PM report. Someone filed it in my office by mistake.'

'Oh, I know all that.' Duguid waved away the excuse as if it were a particularly annoying fly that wouldn't leave him alone. 'You didn't have to read it.'

'No, I didn't. True enough. I bet you're glad I did though.'

Duguid stopped swatting the fly, arched a fading ginger eyebrow at him. 'Glad?'

'You know as well as I do neither of these investigations is getting anywhere, sir. Forensics have found bugger all at either scene, background checks are coming up with nothing. There's no obvious motive for either killing. Category

A murders are rare as rocking horse shit. Makes sense to compare notes, at the very least.'

Duguid slumped back in his chair like a man defeated. 'Christ but I hate the complicated ones.'

'Couldn't agree more, sir.'

That got him a frown in return. 'Could've fooled me, McLean. What did you want to see me about anyway? I assume it wasn't to complain about Brooks telling you to piss off.'

'No, sir. It wasn't. I wanted to have a word with you about DC MacBride actually.'

'MacBride?' Duguid furrowed his brow in a fine impression of a man confused. 'What's Harry Potter moaning about now?'

Don't rise to the bait. Count to ten. 'Do you think that sets a good example, sir? Calling him names behind his back?'

'Thought it was quite clever, really. What with that scar of his. Wish I'd come up with it myself.'

'Really? You enjoy being called Dagwood behind your back do you, sir?'

Duguid's face reddened, a muscle ticking at his temple. 'It's just a name.'

'No, it's not. It's a sign of disrespect. It's officers thinking they know better than you and can go do what they please.'

'They do that anyway. Names never hurt anyone, McLean. Surely you learned that in the playground of your posh private school.'

And then some.

'You're missing the point, sir. It's not just name-calling.

MacBride's being systematically bullied by a small faction in this station. Under your command. He's trying to man up, as you might put it, trying to ignore them, but they're persistent buggers. It's affecting his work and if it doesn't stop soon I'm worried he'll quit. He's too good an officer to lose.'

Duguid stared up at McLean from his chair, mouth slightly agape at the outburst. All the redness had drained out of his skin, leaving him deathly pale.

'For God's sake, man. He's a detective. Dealing with nasty shit is almost his entire job description. If he can't take a little good-natured ribbing, maybe he'd be better off in a different job.'

McLean said nothing. He wasn't really sure there was anything he could say that wouldn't get him in even deeper shit than he usually was. He'd tried. Sometimes that was the best you could do.

39

The Good Lord moves in mysterious ways, His wonders to perform.

I've long since given up trying to second-guess my sight. His gift to me. Not everyone's soul is visible on the outside, and even fewer are close to pure. What is purity, anyway? A strict adherence to the teachings of a discredited church? I don't think so. Neither is it as simple as just being good. We all want to be good, after all. It's just that we almost always fall too far short. Some, and they are precious few, strive for one thing above all else. They approach purity simply because they let all the normal distractions fall away, the wants and needs, the lusts and the thousand thousand petty desires. They have found a focus, and in that focus lies their redemption.

But I don't know when I will see them, or where. Sometimes months go by, years before one crosses my path. And sometimes they appear in quick succession. Almost as if they are being sent my way. Which, of course, they are. For is this not the Lord's work that I do?

Which is why I shouldn't be surprised. But it's been a long time since my sight brought to my attention someone I already know.

I have watched him, of course. Studied him as he speaks and when he prays. Seen the people he associates with. They are lost causes, their souls dark almost to be invisible.

I had thought him the same, but now I can see I was wrong. Or maybe he has changed, found that purity of purpose so few ever find. It doesn't really matter. The sight has shown me; who am I to question it?

He has faith, this one. It has been tested, but he still clings to it. Despite all he has seen, all he has read about, he still holds to those discredited old teachings. He is searching for a higher truth though, and he is certain, so certain, that he is close to it. That is his focus, I see it now. That will be his undoing.

And his deliverance.

40

'Is that Detective Inspector McLean?'

Late evening, and he really should have gone home a long time ago. McLean had been wading his way through a particularly badly written report, not helped by a complete inability to stop his mind from wandering. The telephone was a welcome distraction.

'It is. Who's speaking?'

'Oh, yes. You won't remember me. I'm from the forensic services. Amanda Parsons. Dr Cairns said I should call you.'

McLean raised an eyebrow even though there was no one about to see it. 'She did? Why?'

'I've been running the DNA analysis on that . . . um . . . sample of yours. Not yours yours, obviously, but—'

'Sample?' McLean interrupted before the caller went off at a complete tangent. He couldn't recall sending any samples off for DNA analysis, but his brain was full of too many other things.

'The . . . the stool sample? Human excrement? From the bushes outside your house?' The voice on the other end of the phone sounded young, no doubt a junior technician given the task no one else wanted. At least McLean remembered now. The man in the bushes at the end of his drive. Of course. And the young forensic scientist who had come in the wee small hours to collect it.

238

'You've got a match?' he asked, knowing it was never as easy as that.

'Umm . . . no. Nothing on the database at all. A couple of close ones, but they didn't work out when I ran the full analysis.'

McLean stared sightlessly at the opposite wall of his office. It wasn't very far away. 'And you felt the need to call at this hour to let me know? Couldn't it have gone in an email?'

The technician didn't reply immediately, the static silence on the phone making McLean feel bad for his out-burst. If it had been an outburst.

'Sorry, it's been a long day,' he said. 'I take it there's more?'

'Yes, there is. See, there's no match on the database, but, well, I get given a lot of . . . that's to say—'

'You get all the shit jobs, is that it?' McLean couldn't help but smile as he said it.

'Exactly so. Shit, mucus, skin samples, semen. Christ, you wouldn't believe what people leave behind at a crime scene.'

'Trust me, Amanda. I would.'

'I . . . Yes, I suppose you would. Sorry. I get a little dis-tracted sometimes. But your sample. It wasn't on the database, like I said. Would have written it up and emailed you the results, but something bothered me about it and I couldn't work out what.'

'I take it you did work it out though, eventually?'

'Oh yes. Quite pleased with myself, really. You see, it wasn't on the database, but I recognised the profile. Ran a couple of close matches, no joy. But then I remembered we'd had another shit sample in recently. Hadn't got a match on that one either, and it hadn't made it on to the database either. Ran the two side by side and bingo. A perfect match. Well, as close to perfect as you'll get in this game. Whoever shat in your bushes did this one as well.'

McLean found he had leaned forward, hunched over his desk with the phone clamped to his ear, interest finally piqued. 'So where did this other sample come from, then?'

'Nasty one, that. It was shoved through a letterbox down Leith Walk about a month back.'

The drive home was quick, traffic light at what was really a very late hour to be still at work. McLean wondered what the young forensic scientist was doing at her lab, but it was always possible they had shifts to cope with the endless demands put on them. He'd have to thank Jemima Cairns the next time he saw her at a crime scene. Thank Amanda Parsons too.

He hadn't needed to ask any more details about the earlier sample. Leith Walk might be a mile long, but he couldn't imagine that many letterboxes along its length having excrement shoved through them in the past month. He should probably have brought it up as part of the fire investigation, but that had barely started, and if he was being honest with himself he'd forgotten. With the Stevenson case at an advanced stage of going nowhere, it was nice to have something he could get his teeth stuck into. A puzzle it might actually be possible to solve.

A couple of cats scurried off the drive and into the bushes as he arrived home. Light spilled out from the kitchen window, and as he pushed his way in through the back door he could smell something spicy cooking.

'I thought you were never coming home. It's not healthy, you know. Working such long hours.'

Madame Rose was back to her normal self. Face immaculately made up, hair arranged on top of her head in a greying bun, she had found an apron somewhere and was leaning over the Aga stirring a pot of something that bubbled and steamed. A couple of her cats were curled up at her feet, basking in the heat from the oven even though it wasn't exactly cold outside. Mrs McCutcheon's cat was nowhere to be seen.

'I find it easier to get stuff done at night. Not so many people distracting me. I can actually get some thinking done.'

'Well park your seat in a chair and get some eating done.' Madame Rose pulled a plate out of the warming oven. It was already heaped with rice, and she ladled a hefty portion of something that looked suspiciously like chilli con carne on top before sliding the heavy load on to the table. 'There's grated cheese in the bowl, sour cream in that wee jug.'

McLean noticed the two sitting in the middle of the scrubbed kitchen table, where Mrs McCutcheon's cat usually slept during the day.

'You don't need to do this for me,' he said, as the medium pushed the plate towards a place already laid out with cutlery.

'Nonsense, it's the least I can do. You helped me in my hour of need.'

He had done, McLean had to admit. But then she had helped him and Emma both. He pulled out the chair, slipped his jacket off to hang it over the back, then remembered what he'd been meaning to do all along.

'Well, it smells delicious but it'll have to wait two minutes.'

Madame Rose gave him something halfway between a scowl and a questioning look as he headed swiftly out of the kitchen. McLean had put on a clean jacket that morning, the previous one smelling rather too much of the Leith Walk fire. What he'd forgotten to do in the rush was transfer the contents of his pockets. It wasn't usually a problem; he had a few pairs of latex gloves and some small plastic evidence bags in all his jacket and coat pockets, except when they were fresh back from the cleaners.

This one hadn't made it that far yet, and he hauled it out of the growing pile in the corner of his bedroom, fishing in the pocket for what he wanted before returning to the kitchen and the unexpected meal. When he arrived, it was to find a glass of beer poured and waiting beside his plate, Madame Rose seated across the table with her back to the Aga.

'Not having any yourself?' McLean asked as he tucked in to one of the best chillis he had tasted since Phil had finally moved out of the flat in Newington.

'Had mine earlier.' Madame Rose glanced up at the clock on the kitchen wall, but said no more. There followed a silence while McLean ate for a while, then he unfolded the sheet of paper he had fetched, smoothing out the creases.

'What do you know about this?' He pushed the paper across the table. Madame Rose picked it up, read it through.

'First I've heard of it,' she said after a while. 'Where'd you get it from?'

'The door to your shop. It managed to survive the heat of the fire, too. Somehow I don't think that's on account of the paper.'

'I tried to get back in today but they wouldn't let me. Said it needed to be signed off by Health and Safety. It's my house and they won't let me in.'

'Standard procedure after a fire. I'm sorry.' McLean took back the flyer whilst spooning another mouthful of chilli into his face. It was cheaply produced, a line drawing of a shouting man with an exclamation mark in a speech bubble above him. Below it, the words '!!!Stop the Developement!!!'. Bad spelling apart, it was easy enough to see what it was about. Plans had been lodged to knock down the empty shops and redevelop some of the tenement blocks. Remembering the general air of run-down seediness about the place, McLean couldn't help thinking it would only be an improvement, but obviously enough of the locals disagreed.

'Your place on Leith Walk. You own that, right?'

Madame Rose nodded.

'And has anyone approached you about buying it?'

'Buying it?' The look of horror on the medium's face was enough of an answer.

'So you've not had any offers recently.'

'No. I don't think anyone's ever asked. And I wouldn't sell even if they did. It's my home. No, it's more than that.'

An image of the house, untouched by the fire and yet surrounded on all sides by destruction, swam unbidden into McLean's mind. Much more than a home, it would seem.

'Well, I've an idea I might know why you've been getting grief recently. Why they shoved shit through your letterbox and killed one of your cats.'

'You do?' Madame Rose clasped a large be-ringed hand to her ample chest.

'I don't know who. Not just yet. But I suspect the why is a rather crude attempt to soften you up. Someone's waiting for you to get the hint and put the place on the market. Then they'll swoop in and buy it at a knockdown price.'

'But who would do such a thing?'

McLean picked up the flyer again. At the bottom was a name, a contact email address and a mobile phone number. 'Right now I don't know. But I've a suspicion there's someone who might.'

The needle crackled quietly on the vinyl as it spiralled into the centre of the record. McLean sat in his favourite high-backed armchair, a glass of whisky on the table by his side, and let the repetitive hiss-thunk hiss-thunk wash over him. It wasn't often he had a chance to sit and think these days, even less so with a stomach pleasantly full of good food. A shame really that he had to go back to work the next day.

'Your grandmother had a keen eye.'

McLean opened his, only then aware that he'd closed them and was drifting off. Madame Rose had come in silently to peruse the bookshelves. She reached up and pulled out a hefty leather volume, one large finger caressing the spine like a lover.

'Can't be sure that wasn't one my grandfather bought. Might have been in the family for generations.'

'Yes, of course.' Madame Rose extracted a pair of half-moon spectacles from her ample bosom, where they were dangling on a fine silver chain. She slid them on before opening up the book. McLean reckoned it must have weighed at least a couple of kilos, and yet she held it as if it were no more substantial than a slim paperback collection of poetry.

'Did you ever get around to cataloguing them all?' he asked. He knew Madame Rose had begun the task, with Emma helping, but events had conspired to put a stop to that. And then Emma had left.

'I barely scratched the surface.' Madame Rose laughed as she closed the book and put it back where it had come from, lining it up perfectly with the others on the shelf. 'We made a start on this room, but there's plenty more in the old study, and boxes up in the attic that look like they've not been touched in a century. This whole house is a treasure trove.'

'It's too big and costs a fortune to heat in the winter. I really would be better off selling it and moving someplace smaller. Maybe more central.'

A look of horror spread across Madame Rose's face. 'Sell? Surely you can't mean . . .'

'Don't worry. I'm not serious. Selling and moving would be far more disruptive than staying here. And it's not as if I can't afford the bills.'

'It's more than that, though. Isn't it? This is your home,

same as it was your grandmother's before you. It would have been your father's too, had he not . . .' Madame Rose hesitated.

'Died? Abandoned me? It's OK. I don't mind talking about it. It was a long time ago.'

'And yet a part of you is still back there. Stuck in the past.'

'Isn't a part of all of us?' McLean took up his whisky, needing the fortification if this was going to turn philosophical. There wasn't much left in the glass, but pouring another one might not be wise.

'We are all defined by our past. That's not the same as living in it. You can move on if you want to. There's nothing holding you back.'

McLean downed the last of the whisky, hauled himself out of the chair and went to the record player. 'I'll take your word for it,' he said as he lifted the needle carefully back into its rest and switched everything off. 'But now I think I'd better get some sleep. I've a feeling it's going to be a busy one tomorrow.'

Madame Rose took another book from the shelf, caressing it as she had the first. 'They always are, Inspector. They always are.'

41

'I'm going to my dad's old school soon. It's gonnae be cool.'

We're sitting under the old cedar tree in his garden, Norman and me. I like his garden better than Gran's. It's smaller and the trees are older, like the house I suppose.

'You're not coming back to our school then? Next term?'

'Nah. Going down to some place in England. Near London, I think.'

'England? Wow.' Norman says it like it's someplace far, far away, and for the first time since Gran told me the news I realise that it is. It's further than I've ever been before. Further than I can really imagine.

'Come on. Let's go see if we can get to the top of the tree again.' Always easier to be doing things than thinking about them. And the view from the top's brilliant.

'Race you.' Norman scrambles to his feet, but I'm quicker. Stronger too, he's always been a bit weedy for his age. He goes for the lowest branch while I try to shimmy up the thick trunk. The trick to climbing the old cedar is getting to the first fork. Then it's easy. You can get there along a branch if you can jump up and pull one down far enough. Or you can shove your hands in the cracks and haul yourself up the trunk like those men Gran let me watch on the telly, climbing the Old Man of Hoy.

I'm almost at the fork when I hear a loud crack. Norman doesn't scream, but then maybe the solid thud of him hitting the ground has winded him. I'm not that high up, really. Looking round I can see a thick branch, a pale hand poking out from under a thick blanket of dark green needles. I jump down and hurry over, terrified that he might have broken his neck.

'Norman, you OK?' The branch is heavy, thick as my thigh where it's broken under his weight. It's a silly detail to notice, but I can see where something has attacked the wood, sticky sap oozing around a deep wound. That'll be why it's broken; Norman's not that heavy, after all.

He groans as I haul the branch off him, reaches up to his head. For a moment I think he's fine, and then I see the cut on his hand. It's deep, dark red blood flowing freely, smearing on his face as he pushes needles out of his hair.

'Shit. That looks bad.' He winces at the rude word, same as he always has. It gives me a thrill saying it though. Even if I know Gran would clip me round the ear if she heard me. I reach out and take his other hand, haul him to his feet. He sways, stunned by the fall or my cursing, it's hard to tell with Norman.

'Come on. Better get you back to the house. Get that cleaned up.'

'Mum's gonnae kill me.' Norman looks at his clothes, bloodstained and torn. His face is very pale, more so even than usual.

'No she won't.' I try to sound reassuring, even though I know how different Mr and Mrs Bale are to my Gran, to how I remember my own mum and dad. 'Well, maybe a little bit.'

42

'You know anything about common repairs, Bob?'

The tiny room they had commandeered for the fire investigation was a sharp contrast to the two major incident rooms a floor down. As was the manpower available for the job. Grumpy Bob made up the entire team at the moment, and he looked up from his desk at McLean's question like a man who had only just got comfortable enough for a quick nap.

'Tenements and stuff like that?'

'Aye. Used to be the council would serve a repair order. Not sure if they're doing it still. You know, when all the residents in one block couldn't agree what needed doing. Had it happen to my old place in Newington a good while back, but there's been nothing from them this time around. I wasn't sure if it still happened.'

'You'd be better off asking the lad. He'd have an answer for you in a couple of taps on that wee screen of his.'

'Didn't really want to load him up with any more work. He's already doing too much as it is.'

'Fair point. He's been looking a bit run-down lately.' Grumpy Bob scratched at his chin where the morning's razor had missed a bit. 'Doesn't help that he's so keen. Shows all the other constables up.'

'Christ, Bob. He uses his brain, shows some initiative,

and people think that's keen? It's the bloody job, isn't it? Least it was when I signed up.'

Grumpy Bob sat up straight, his face reddening slightly at the rebuke. 'Just telling it how it is, sir.'

'Sorry. Didn't mean to snap at you. It's just . . . this place, sometimes. People get an idea and run with it. Never seem to know when enough's enough. Like all those stupid pranks they played on me last year.'

'You got a nice car out of it. And a couple of suits.'

'Not helping, Bob. And you know that's not the point. I'm thrawn enough to weather it out, but MacBride's not coping so well.'

'Aye, I know. Been keeping an eye out. He'll get over it, mind. He's tougher than he looks.'

The door opening behind him put an end to the conversation. McLean spun around, expecting to see the object of their discussions. Instead it was DS Ritchie who shuffled into the room backwards, an awkward box under one arm, coffee in the other hand.

'Here, let me.' McLean thought of relieving her of the coffee, but took the box instead. 'Anything interesting?'

'Depends what you find interesting. It's mostly just photos from the scene.'

'Any news from the fire investigation team?'

'Report's in there, too.' Ritchie nodded at the box, then took a sip of her coffee. 'Sorry. Didn't think there'd be anyone in here yet.'

McLean put the box down on the nearest table and started leafing through the contents. The report was a thick sheaf of paper, densely packed type giving him a headache before he'd even started reading it. He flicked through, looking for the executive summary, gave up and turned to the photographs. These had been printed on glossy paper, which probably meant the budget for the investigation was blown already. The problem with digital cameras was a tendency of crime scene photographers to rattle off a dozen or more pictures of exactly the same thing. Fortunately someone had already been at this lot and only printed up a few duplicates of each.

'Definitely arson then?' Grumpy Bob had picked up the discarded report and begun flicking through.

'Double arson, if you're being technical,' Ritchie said. 'Someone shoved lighter fluid through the letterboxes for the betting shop and chippy both. They're not sure how the fire spread to the two houses either side of number twelve but left it untouched. Most of the report goes into technical details about stone wall thickness, safety gaps, stuff like that. To be honest, I think they're scratching their heads on this one.'

McLean took a series of wide-view photographs and pinned them to the wall. One taken from the far side of the street showed a line of vehicles parked in front of the burnt-out shop fronts and houses. 'We get anywhere with the vans?'

Ritchie guddled around in the box and came out with a handful of papers. 'Some of them are local. Had every right to be parked there. These three are untraceable as yet.' She handed the sheets to McLean, who scanned them for salient details. Two Ford Escort vans and a Fiat Doblo. Common enough that finding out who owned them without proper identification would be a pain.

'Let me guess. These were right outside the door to number twelve. Madame Rose's place.'

'That's the one. Forensics have got them all back at their labs. Might be able to get something useful from them. The plates are clones though, and they've all had their VINs removed. Might get lucky with the Fiat. Apparently some of the parts are individually numbered and they can cross-reference with the actual vehicle build number. They'll get the VIN from that and then we'll know who owned it.'

'Sounds technical,' McLean said.

'Well, you know me and cars, sir.' Ritchie smiled, took another sip of coffee.

'I presume this will take some time.'

'Could be a couple of weeks. Depends a lot on who we speak to at Fiat. Even then it'll probably turn out to have been stolen from down south a year ago.'

McLean fished the flyer out of his pocket, unfolded it and pinned it to the board next to the photographs. 'We'll have to try some other avenues of enquiry then.'

About five minutes into their questioning, McLean realised that Dudley Sanderson and Douglas Ballantyne had probably been separated at birth. They didn't look much alike, and Sanderson was a good ten years younger than the bearded conspiracy theorist, but the two of them shared a world-view with remarkable exactness.

He'd asked DS Ritchie to call the number on the flyer, hoping that she would take up that strand of the fire investigation and run with it. Mr Sanderson had volunteered to come in to the station immediately and answer all their questions. That should have set the alarm bells ringing; McLean was well experienced in nutters and could usually spot them before he had to interact. Perhaps he was more tired than he realised, tired enough to agree to sit in on the interview at least.

And so here they were, stuck in a hot and stuffy interview room three. It still smelled overpoweringly of fresh paint, and the hot sun shining through the small, high window was just enough to cook all the goodness out of the air.

'So what you're saying, Mr Sanderson, is that numbers ten and fourteen are owned by two different development companies. Number twelve is, of course, owned by the individual who lives there.'

Sanderson dragged his gaze away from Ritchie, or at least Ritchie's chest, at which he had been staring almost constantly for the whole interview. The expression on his face was almost as if he had forgotten McLean was there, which was perfectly possible given the rambling nature of his monologue. There was a hint of irritation in his eyes, too. Clearly not a man used to being interrupted, although that might have been because nobody ever listened to him at all.

'That is correct, Detective Inspector. Brightwing Holdings owns the freehold of number ten, and a company called Wendle Stevens owns number fourteen. They—'

'So if two different companies are involved, what makes you think there is any development in hand? These are big houses. Most of them have already been split into flats. I'm sure they're going to do the same to these, but that's not what you're claiming, is it?'

Sanderson left a short pause before answering, as if he were checking to make sure McLean wasn't going to say anything else.

'As I was trying to say before I was interrupted, Detective Inspector, the two companies are both registered with the same firm of solicitors. They both filed plans at the same time and they're using the same architects.'

'So you think they're actually the same organisation acting under two different names.' Foolishly, DS Ritchie asked the question. Sanderson's head snapped around, his attention once more fixed on her chest. McLean suspected that he was less fascinated with her breasts than embarrassed at looking into a woman's eyes. He could have been wrong though.

'I don't think it, Detective Sergeant, I know it.'

'You have proof? A paper trail?'

Sanderson's gaze dropped momentarily to the table. His hands were clasped together in front of him as if in prayer, and he fidgeted with them for a moment.

'It's not . . . They're very clever these people, you know. Companies within companies. Always hiding from view. I don't really know why they do it. Tax avoidance, probably.'

'So you don't have any proof.' McLean dragged the man's attention back to himself.

'Not as such, no.'

'Well what do you have then? What exactly is this development you so desperately want to stop?'

'It's there in the plans, Detective Inspector. If you just know how to look at them properly.' Sanderson's hands clasped together again as he warmed to his theme. 'Oh, they look like simple flats, splitting up the houses floor by floor, but you can see that's not what they want to do. Not really. It's just a ruse to keep the council happy.'

'And what is it they really want to do, Mr Sanderson?'

'Why, knock the whole terrace down and build a block of flats in its place, Detective Inspector. Somewhere they can fill with immigrants getting their rent paid by hard-working tax payers like you and I.'

With hindsight, McLean could see that the signs had been there all along. The more excited Mr Sanderson became, the redder his face grew. Little flecks of spittle arced from his mouth, spattering the table so that DS Ritchie had to lean back or suffer an involuntary shower.

'Where exactly do you live, Mr Sanderson?' It was a question he should have asked at the start of the interview, really.

'I'm not sure how—'

'Jock's Lodge? Restalrig maybe?'

'Newhaven, actually.'

'But not Leith Walk. Not, in fact, Leith at all.'

'Well, no.'

'Then why are you so concerned about what happens there?'

'They can't be allowed to get away with it. Knocking down all the best bits of the city and throwing up cheap boxes filled with foreigners stealing our jobs and prostitutes giving us their exotic diseases.' Sanderson lingered on the last two words as if the thought excited him somehow.

'Of course not. That would be terrible. But surely you should be looking out for your own patch? Let the people of Leith Walk decide what happens there.'

'Ah, but how can they do that if they don't know it's happening, Detective Inspector?' Sanderson dragged his gaze from Ritchie's bosom.

'And that's what you were doing with these leaflets, I take it.' McLean pushed the offending article across the table towards Sanderson, who picked it up and studied it closely, a triumphant smile spreading across his face as he did so.

'Exactly. Looks like it worked, too.'

43

McLean watched DS Ritchie escort Dudley Sanderson from the interview room and back towards the reception area at the front of the station. His head hurt from too little sleep and trying to get into the mindset of someone who saw evil intent in the most simple of things.

'Get anything useful from him?' Grumpy Bob sidled up with a mug of coffee in one hand, a newspaper rolled up and shoved under his arm.

'Rather too many nutters around these days, Bob.' McLean eyed the detective sergeant's spoils. 'You heading for an empty room and some quality time, then?'

'I don't know what you mean, sir.' Grumpy Bob gave his best deadpan face, then took a slurp of coffee, swallowing loudly before adding, 'Was just heading back up to the fire incident room, actually. Figured if you and Ritchie were interviewing, it'd be as quiet as anywhere else in the station.'

They set off for the stairs together, McLean filling in the details of the interview as they walked. It always helped to go over these things, but the more he spoke about it, the more he came to the conclusion that Dudley Sanderson was a deeply troubled man.

'So he's got no evidence. In fact he's got evidence to the contrary, and yet he still believes someone is trying to knock down an entire block of Leith Walk and redevelop it on the sly?'

'Exactly, and he doesn't even live there. Doesn't even live in Leith for that matter. I'm not sure I ever quite worked out what his interest in it was, if I'm being honest. Maybe Ritchie will have a better idea.'

'Still, it's a bit odd,' Grumpy Bob said. 'Even if your man isn't dealing from a full deck.'

McLean paused mid-step. 'What do you mean?'

'Well, the fire's been set deliberately. There's no doubt about that. Unlikely it's Gianni the chip shop owner, and the rest of the block was uninhabited. The two houses that burnt down were empty. Just Madame Rose's place there in the middle. And yet he was the one being targeted for abuse beforehand.'

'She, Bob.' McLean couldn't help himself correcting the detective sergeant. He wondered when it had become important to him. And why. Grumpy Bob raised a quizzical eyebrow, but said nothing else.

'We interviewed them all though? Gianni? The builders in numbers ten and fourteen?'

'Spoke to Gianni myself. He's either a bloody good actor or he genuinely has no idea how the fire started.'

'You ask him if anyone had offered to buy the place off him?'

'One of the first questions. He's a proud old bugger, make no mistake. Told me he'd been working there since his old man first set it up just after the war. Apparently he was a POW, Gianni's old man. Decided he liked Scotland so much he wanted to stay.'

'And he owned the shop outright?' McLean shook his head. 'No, I knew that already. Rose told me. What about the builders? Developers, whatever. The other two houses that burned down?'

'Still waiting for the lad to get back to me on that, sir.'

'MacBride? I thought he was busy with the Stevenson enquiry.'

'Aye, he is at that. But there's no one else here I'd trust to ferret out the information. Not in less than six weeks, anyway.'

'So we've not actually spoken to them yet.' They had reached the incident room and found it empty.

'Not as such, no.'

McLean rubbed at his forehead, found it didn't really do much to relieve the pressure. He could feel the case slipping away from him. Too many things to concentrate on and not enough time.

'OK. Speak to Ritchie when she gets back. Dudley Sanderson gave us the names of the developers. Should save us a bit of time searching them out. Set up some interviews, find out if they stand to gain anything from the fire.'

'Believe it or not, sir, I have done this before.' Grumpy Bob grinned as he spoke, and McLean realised just how annoying he was being.

'Sorry, Bob. Force of habit. I'll let you get on with it and keep well out of the way. Not as if I haven't got anything else to do, after all.'

'Stevenson?'

'For one thing, yes. Trying to coordinate with Spence on the Maureen Shenks case too, and you know how well he plays with others.'

Grumpy Bob placed his coffee mug carefully down on

the nearest desk, laid the paper alongside it. 'Don't much envy you that.'

'Aye, well it'll be even more fun when he gets made up to DCI. Think I might put in for a transfer then. I've heard Vice is nice and quiet these days.'

'The whole thing's a fucking mess if you ask me.'

DCI Brooks paced back and forth in the Ben Stevenson murder enquiry room, creating a small clear patch in an otherwise crowded space. All around, the uniforms, detectives and support staff were keeping themselves studiously busy, keen not to be drawn into the impromptu meeting. McLean could only sympathise with them; he too had better things to be doing than pointing out the obvious to people who should have known better.

'I'm not going to disagree with you there, sir. But that's not helped by everyone having to run up and down the stairs between two different incident rooms.' McLean didn't add that it wasn't helped by one enquiry constantly poaching staff from the other.

'Oh good Christ, you're not still suggesting these two are linked are you? They've absolutely nothing in common.' Brooks stopped his pacing for a moment, just long enough to give McLean his best 'you're an idiot' glare.

'Nothing? You mean apart from the fact that both had their throats cut from behind, left to right with a sharp, narrow-bladed knife? Apart from the complete lack of any forensic evidence? Apart from the fact that the likelihood of two Category A murders within weeks of one another not being connected is so vanishingly small it's hardly worth considering?'

McLean watched the detective chief inspector's reaction to his words, his fat face reddening with each new suggestion. It was easy to guess when Brooks was going to interject; he stopped pacing just an instant before opening his mouth.

'You—'

'Of course, I'm not jumping to conclusions.' McLean interrupted before Brooks could get his objection in. 'I think it's wise to treat the two as separate cases, even if they do end up being the same killer. I just think we can save a lot of time, and money, if we merge the admin and data processing of both enquiries. And if we're all working from the same incident room we're in a good place to spot any obvious connections should they appear.'

'If the press get hold of the idea we're linking the two cases . . .' Brooks left the obvious conclusion hanging. The idea of a serial killer would have the tabloids salivating, but it was unlikely they'd care much about the reputation of the police in pursuit of a juicy story.

'Quite frankly I'm more concerned with catching Ben Stevenson's murderer, and Maureen Shenks' too, than what the tabloids want to write about me,' McLean said.

'All right for some. You don't have to worry about getting sacked, do you?' DI Spence muttered the words under his breath, but it was easy enough to hear them.

'Neither would you, if you actually did your job, Mike.' McLean didn't bother to hide his scorn.

'What the fuck do you—'

'Enough.' Detective Superintendent Duguid had been silent up to this point. McLean wanted to think he was acting swiftly to avoid the demoralising effect on the investigation team of seeing two senior officers bicker in public, but it was more likely that he just wanted to get back to his comfortable, quiet office.

'McLean is right, difficult though that is to admit. There are too many similarities to ignore, and the cost of running two major incident enquiries side by side doesn't bear thinking about. Spence, I want you to bring your team in here. Any spillover can go into the smaller rooms across the corridor.'

'Would it not be easier to—'

'Up here, Spence. This enquiry has been going on longer. And it's less far for me to walk.'

McLean almost smiled at the joke, though it would have been funnier if Duguid had ever actually been in the incident room before. But the thunderous faces of DI Spence and DCI Brooks, Little and Large, were enough to kill any humour in the situation.

'Grumpy Bob's running the room at the moment, ably assisted by DC MacBride. They'll get you sorted for desk space and workstations.' McLean checked his watch, even though he knew exactly what time it was. 'I've got to run.'

'What?' Brooks rumbled the single word out in a low growl.

'Interviewing a possible witness. I'll let you know if anything comes of it.'

'How long have you been working on the Leith Walk site?'

If the offices of Wendle Stevens were anything to go by, the razing to the ground of their building by fire could only be a good thing. McLean sat in a room that was too small for the three desks squeezed into it. Too small for the three sweaty bodies too, judging by the smell. Still, it was a new company, with fresh hopes and making the best of what little it had. And anything was better than being stuck with Brooks and Spence.

'The building was auctioned in January. We probably paid a little more for it than we should, but that's the nature of the game, right?'

Jonathan Wendle was an infectiously enthusiastic man. Probably still in the first half of his twenties, he made McLean feel old and tired just by the energy bubbling off him. Stevens, the other half of the partnership, was out visiting another potential site, which was probably for the best. McLean didn't think he could have coped otherwise.

'And you'd started on the work a couple of months ago? What were you doing to the place?'

'Gutting it and starting again, Inspector. Not much else we could do, really. Place was a disaster. Some idiot had split it up into flats in the seventies, and we all know that's the decade taste forgot.'

McLean bit back the retort that he had fond childhood memories of the time. Wendle wouldn't even have been born much before the end of the eighties anyway.

'But things were going OK?' he asked. 'You were on schedule with the renovations, keeping to budget?'

Wendle waggled a large hand back and forth in an easily understood gesture. 'More or less. But it's the biggest project we've taken on so far, so we've got quite a lot of leeway built in.'

'What about the other buildings, number ten and number twelve?'

'What of them?'

'You weren't trying to buy them, then? Knock them all down and put up some cheap flats in their place?'

Wendle paused before answering, the thoughts writ clear across his young face as they knitted together. McLean had already decided the young man wasn't involved in the arson; his enthusiasm was still too great. Someone driven to burning their assets to claim the insurance money would have been far more desperate.

'A little bird's been tweeting at you, hasn't it, Inspector?' Wendle made little beak-closing motions with his fingers. 'I can't tell a lie, we've been approached about selling the site. But Bill and me bought it with our own money. We had a plan and we mean to stick to it. Of course, I'm not sure exactly what we're going to do now. Have to wait and see what the insurance assessor has to say. The engineers too.'

'But someone did try to buy the place off you? Before the fire?'

'Quite a few developers, actually. You'd be surprised how often sites change hands before someone rolls up their sleeves and actually does the work.'

'Anyone put pressure on you to sell? Get any threats?'

Wendle frowned as if the question surprised him. 'Not really, no. I mean, you get some unpleasant characters who don't like being told no, but . . . no, can't say as I have.'

44

'Gods. You wouldn't believe the number of people who've asked me that.'

Basil Temperly was perhaps the exact opposite of Jonathan Wendle, despite them both having chosen the same profession. Where Wendle was young and enthusiastic, Temperly stooped low as if the weight of the world was on him. What little hair he had left was grey and thin, the skin on the top of his head spotted here and there with brown. It looked like he'd spent too much time under the flight paths of Edinburgh's seagulls and forgotten to wear a hat.

'Has anyone been particularly insistent? Have you had any threats?'

'Threats?' Temperly scratched at his chin and leaned back in the rickety chair on the other side of the table in interview room one. McLean had thought to visit the man at his offices, the same as he'd done with Wendle, but Ritchie's phone call had found Temperly visiting one of his other sites, just around the corner from the station. Ten minutes was perhaps not ideal for preparing the interview, but you couldn't have everything.

'There's a rumour going around someone wanted to buy up that whole block, numbers ten, twelve and fourteen. Knock them down and build cheap flats in their place. I imagine you could probably double the accommodation if you did that?'

At her question, Temperly moved his head slowly in the direction of DS Ritchie. It wasn't that he hadn't noticed her already; she'd escorted him from the front desk on his arrival, after all. But there was no mistaking the look of distaste on his face. For a moment McLean thought that she might have hit on something, perhaps come close to some truth. Maybe he was the one who'd been trying to take over the whole block, and had torched it when he found himself thwarted. Then he realised it was just simple misogyny. A man like Temperly might agree to be shown around by a woman, but he certainly didn't expect her to ask him questions.

'Have you been talking to that dreadful man Sanderson?'

'We've been talking to everyone involved in the sites. This is a very serious case of arson, Mr Temperly.'

'Well Sanderson's a pain in the arse and nothing to do with my building site, or those upstart teenagers over the other side. You'll have spoken to that nonce at number twelve too, I expect. He'd not sell up even if everyone else would.' Temperly shifted his gaze back to McLean, where he was obviously more comfortable. 'And no, I wasn't about to sell up. Prime spot like that? Sure, I might make some easy money passing it on, but the real profit's in renting these days.'

'What about now? If someone were to offer you a good sum for the plot?'

'You mean soften me up first, then make an offer?' Temperly narrowed his eyes. 'Sneaky.'

'Very. But you didn't answer the question. What are you planning on doing with the site now it's just a burnt-out shell? There's a lot more work involved now. Might just be easier to cut and run. Take the insurance money, leave the heavy work to someone else?'

'I see where you're coming from, Inspector. And it's a tempting prospect. But no, I wouldn't sell up now. Who knows, the job might even be easier without planning making everything difficult.'

'Which, of course, would be a good motive for torching the place. That and the insurance money.'

'Oh come on!' This time Temperly rounded swiftly on Ritchie. 'I came in here of my own volition. Would I do that if I'd torched my own building? Am I a suspect? Because if that's the case I probably ought to call my lawyer.' He reached into his pocket and pulled out his phone, just in case they weren't sure how he was going to do that.

'You're not a suspect, Mr Temperly. No.' McLean cut in to defuse the sudden tension in the small room. Across the table, Temperly slowly pushed his phone back into his pocket. 'You're helping us with our enquiries. Nothing more. If I thought you had anything to do with the fires, you'd be under caution and you would, as you so rightly pointed out, be fully entitled to have your solicitor present during all questioning. I've a feeling neither your firm nor Wendle Stevens wanted this fire to happen. It was set by a third party, and I'm trying to find out why. Then I can hopefully find out who.'

'McLean. My office. Now.'

McLean was barely out of the interview room, watching as DS Ritchie escorted Basil Temperly from the station, when the all-too-familiar voice boomed out down the corridor. He turned slowly, knowing full well who it was had shouted at him.

'Is it urgent, sir? Only I was hoping to grab something from the canteen before they ran out of lunch.'

Duguid stared at him with puzzled, piggy eyes for a moment, as if the idea of someone not immediately jumping to attention at his command was inconceivable.

'Yes it is bloody urgent. Now get your arse up to my office. There's someone needs to talk to you and you really don't want to keep him waiting.'

Trying hard to keep his sigh inaudible, McLean closed the interview room door and headed in Duguid's direction.

'Who wants to see me, sir? Why?'

'Not here.' Duguid growled the words as they climbed the stairs. As far as McLean could tell, there wasn't a soul within earshot, but he'd long since given up trying to understand Duguid's moods. He'd find out soon enough.

Three flights up and they reached the door to Duguid's office. It was closed, the admin desk just outside it unmanned. Duguid reached for the door handle, grasping it before finally speaking. 'This had better be a huge misunderstanding, McLean. I'm not covering for you if it isn't.'

Bemused, McLean was going to ask what he was talking about, but without another word, Duguid opened the door and ushered him inside.

Two men were waiting for him, one in uniform and sitting in Duguid's expensive leather executive chair, the other in a dark suit and with his back to the door, staring out at the view. McLean had met the deputy chief constable a few times before, generally speaking when he'd done something wrong. The other man he didn't recognise, not from behind at least.

'Ah, Detective Inspector McLean.' The DCC leaned back in his purloined chair, swinging it gently from side to side. 'So good of you to join us.'

'Sir. Is there something I can help you with?'

'Very possible, Detective Inspector. Very possible.' The suited man turned from the window. McLean still didn't recognise him, but the English accent, cheap suit and general demeanour meant it wasn't hard to guess. He'd met enough detectives from Serious and Organised, or whatever they were calling themselves these days, to know one when he saw one.

'Tell me, how are your friends the McClymonts these days?'

'I'm sorry. Who are you?' McLean asked.

'Answer the question, McLean.' The DCC growled the words, irritation creasing his face.

'Happily, sir. When I know who I'm being interrogated by.'

The DCC's scowl deepened and he was about to speak when the other man butted in. 'Fair enough. Tim Chambers.' He held out a hand to be shaken. 'I head up the drug task force. NCA. We've been watching your friends the McClymonts for a while now.'

McLean took the proffered hand, stared Chambers in the face. He was perhaps early fifties if the lines were anything to go by, but fit, hair showing only the faintest of grey in among the dark brown. If he was National Crime Agency and accompanied by the deputy chief constable, then chances were he was a chief superintendent at the very least, which made the implicit accusation all the more serious.

'Sorry to be so defensive, sir. It's just that's twice you've referred to people I don't know as my friends. That kind of puts my back up.'

'Really? You're telling me you don't know Joe and Jock McClymont? But you had a meeting with them just a few weeks ago. You're listed as a partner in their latest development here in Edinburgh.'

'I . . . what?' McLean looked to the DCC and Duguid who was still standing by the door. He genuinely had no idea what Chambers was talking about. And then the penny dropped.

'The tenement block in Newington.'

'Ah, so now he remembers.'

'But that's mad. I'm not a partner in that. Well, apart from the fact I own a share of the site. And as for the McClymonts, well, yes I've met them. Just the once. I didn't like the plans they'd drawn up for the site, told them as much. Haven't heard anything back since, but then I've been a bit busy investigating a couple of rather unpleasant murders.'

Chambers raised a single eyebrow, Roger Moore style. He pulled a slim smartphone from his pocket, swiped it on and tapped the screen once, lifting it to his ear.

'The file on McLean. How many meetings?' A pause, during which his face darkened visibly. McLean had been on the receiving end of Duguid's anger before now, but he reckoned whoever had briefed Chambers was going to get it far worse when the man himself got back to HQ.

'One. That's it? And the documents lodged with planning. They're signed?' Another pause, then without another word, Chambers cut the call, slid the phone back into his pocket.

'I owe you all an apology, gentlemen. Particularly you, Detective Inspector. I was led to believe you had a long-standing relationship with the McClymonts. It would seem that's not the case.'

'You could have just asked.'

Chambers managed a thin smile. 'You know that's not how we do things.'

'Well, for the record, as I said, I've met them just once, didn't care for them or what they're trying to do to my old home. What've they done that's brought them to your attention?'

Chambers said nothing for a while. McLean knew he was supposed to think this was the senior officer deciding whether he could divulge operational secrets or not, but he also knew it was just for show. He stood and waited; some people couldn't help but fill a silence.

'We've had our eyes on them for a while now. Suspected they were bringing cocaine and other nasties into the country, using their development company to launder the proceeds. They were a canny pair though, almost like they knew what we were doing and when. That's why we got very interested when your name turned up on a planning application amendment document they submitted a couple of months back.'

'They what?' McLean found he'd clenched his fists, struggled to relax them. 'So that's how they got their planning permission. Christ, the cheek of it. When I get my hands on them . . .'

'That'll be difficult, I think,' Chambers said.

'You've arrested them, have you? I'll settle for that. For now.'

'No, we haven't arrested them. We won't be arresting them any time soon, sadly. Not ever. They're both dead.'

45

'Just why exactly do we have to do this?'

McLean stared out over the steering wheel at the road rumbling north towards Inverness. They'd left Perth long ago and were stuck behind a truck struggling to go faster than walking pace. Beside him in the passenger seat, Grumpy Bob had dispensed with his newspaper, finished the cup of half-decent coffee he'd managed to find at the last service station and was now fidgeting like a schoolboy needing to be excused.

'I have to do it, apparently, because I've dealt with the McClymonts before. And probably because the deputy chief constable was pissed off at being dragged away from his comfy office. Makes no bloody sense. Not when I'm meant to be heading up a murder investigation, but when the DCC says jump, it's a question of how high.' McLean gripped the steering wheel tight, his knuckles whitening in frustration. 'You're here because you weren't quick enough with an excuse and I didn't fancy making the trip on my own.'

The road opened up into dual carriageway and he dropped a gear, ready to overtake. Before he'd even checked his mirror the peace was shattered by a loud blaring of horn as the car behind squeezed through the narrow gap, one set of wheels on the dead zone where the central reservation began, the driver gesticulating wildly in his rush to get past, get on.

'Bloody hell. He's in a hurry to kill himself, isn't he?'
Grumpy Bob made a rude gesture as McLean looked over
his shoulder, checking there were no other idiots about
before overtaking the truck in a less hurried fashion, pulling back in just before the dual carriageway ended again.

'You want to go after him?' he asked. They were in an
unmarked squad car, complete with blue flashing lights
hidden in the grille and not-so-discreet siren under the
bonnet.

'Nah. It's not our patch, after all. Maybe just make a
note of his number and have a word with someone when
we get there.' Grumpy Bob fished his notebook out of a
pocket and scribbled something down. 'There'd be a weird
kind of justice if we passed that car upside down in a ditch
a bit further up the road, mind you.'

'Don't joke about it, Bob. This road's a bastard. Sooner
it's dualled the whole way, the better.'

Grumpy Bob said nothing in return, and McLean went
back to his musing. This whole trip was a complete waste
of time, a punishment detail if ever he'd seen one. He just
wasn't sure why he was getting it in the neck for a cock-up
on the National Crime Agency's part. They had been the
ones watching the McClymonts, the ones who'd not managed to actually pin anything on them in months of
investigation.

'Why aren't Serious and Organised doing it?' Grumpy
Bob voiced the question that hadn't been far from
McLean's mind all the way.

'And spend some of their own budget? Christ only
knows. Sooner we get there, the sooner we can get back to
some serious work.' He accelerated, safely overtaking the

next lorry, pushing the car up over the speed limit while the road was clear.

'Still seems a hell of a waste of time.'

'You won't find me arguing with you there, Bob. The whole thing's a complete fiasco.'

It took another hour to get to Raigmore Hospital, park and then find their way to the mortuary. Grumpy Bob moaned all the way, and McLean began to plot ways of leaving the curmudgeonly old sergeant behind. He would probably have preferred a train ride back to Edinburgh anyway.

'DI McLean and DS Laird. We're looking for a Dr Gilhooly?' McLean showed his warrant card to the receptionist, but before she could reply he was interrupted by the sound of someone clearing their throat behind him.

'Detective Inspector, eh? Your men in there must be important.'

McLean turned to see who had spoken, noticing for the first time a little waiting area tucked in behind the door he had just entered. A uniformed officer had been sitting there, and now he unfolded himself, standing so tall he almost had to stoop under the ceiling tiles.

'Sergeant Tanner, sir.' He held out a hand the size of a glutton's dinner plate. 'Was told you were coming. Anything you need, just ask.'

'Thank you, Sergeant. Seeing the bodies will probably be enough. Sooner I can get this done and stop wasting all of our time, the better.'

'Of course. Follow me.' Tanner raised his head a little

and spoke to the receptionist. 'Buzz us through will you, Janice.'

The mortuary was perhaps not as well equipped as Angus Cadwallader's den down in the Cowgate, but it was functional enough. Sergeant Tanner had to stoop through each doorway, but he moved with a slow gait that was at least easy enough to keep up with.

'Hear they're some kind of criminal masterminds, these two,' he said.

'Hardly,' McLean replied. 'All I know about them is they're a couple of property developers who've likely greased a palm or two over the years. NCA's had their eyes on them a while though, suspected drug-running, but they've not been able to pin anything on them.'

They had reached the examination theatre, a much smaller space than McLean had been expecting. The table in the middle of the room was already occupied, a body covered in a heavy white sheet.

'You'd be the Edinburgh police then?' A man in a white coat approached from the other side of the theatre, meeting them in the middle. He was slight, a fact made even more obvious by the looming presence of Sergeant Tanner. 'Was expecting you an hour ago.'

'Dr Gilhooly, I presume.' McLean didn't wait for an answer. 'This one of our crash victims?'

'Certainly is, and you're welcome to him.'

The doctor pulled back the sheet to reveal a man's head and shoulders. McLean had seen more than his fair share of car crashes, and they rarely left a body unscathed. The man he looked down upon had been badly cut across one cheek, almost losing an eye in the process. His nose had been flattened to one side and he was smeared in blood. His shoulders sat all wrong, suggesting worse to view under the rest of the sheet. The doctor was about to reveal more, but McLean reached out a hand and stopped him.

'That's OK. I've seen enough. It's Joe McClymont all right. This his dad?' McLean pointed to a gurney by the wall, another body covered in a white sheet.

'Reckon so.' The doctor pulled back the top, revealing the much less badly damaged face of Jock McClymont. He looked strangely peaceful in death.

'Yup, that's the old man.'

'Well I could've told you that. Saved you the trip.'

'I know. But there's a procedure has to be gone through. Talking of which, is the van here?'

'Ready and waiting,' the doctor said.

'Then we'll take these bodies off your hands. Get them back to Edinburgh where they belong.'

Dr Gilhooly walked back the way he had come, stuck his head through the open door and shouted something McLean couldn't quite make out to someone beyond. A moment later they were joined by two orderlies with a trolley. Joe McClymont was swiftly transferred from the examination table, then one of the orderlies fetched his father from his spot by the wall.

'Sign and they're yours.' The doctor produced an official-looking form attached to a clipboard, handed it over as the orderlies wheeled the bodies out of the examination theatre. McLean scribbled his signature, took the top copy.

'Now, if you don't mind, I've a ton of PMs to do this afternoon.' And with that Dr Gilhooly turned and left.

'He always like that?' McLean asked as they retraced

their steps back through the hospital, Sergeant Tanner leading the way.

'Pretty much. Can't be fun, dealing with dead bodies day in, day out.'

McLean was going to say that it didn't seem to have done his friend Angus Cadwallader any harm, then realised it would be lost on the sergeant. 'What happened to the car?' he asked instead.

'What's left of it's down the yard. Forensics are sending a covered truck up to fetch it back to their labs. Should be with them by the end of the day.'

'What's left of it? How bad was the crash?'

'As bad as a car hitting a rock at eighty miles an hour can be. Fire crew had to cut the roof off to get the bodies out. The younger one had most of the engine in his lap, poor bastard.'

McLean looked out across the car park to the pool car he had driven up in, remembering the idiot overtaking him and the long, monotonous hours stuck behind slow-moving lorries. Suddenly the train seemed like a much more sensible idea.

'You want to see it? The car?' Sergeant Tanner asked. 'It's not far to the lock-up from here.'

Grumpy Bob looked at McLean with a questioning expression, no doubt hoping it wouldn't be necessary. He wished it were so, but the one thing Detective Chief Superintendent Chambers of the NCA had asked was that he inspect the car and see that it wasn't tampered with before their forensics team could get a crack at it. For some unaccountable cloak-and-dagger reason, Chambers hadn't wanted anyone else to know that was what he was doing.

Almost as if he didn't quite trust the old Northern Constabulary. Rude, and a waste of time, but then a favour done was a favour owed by the NCA. That might come in handy some day.

'Better had. Since we came all this way.'

It was a struggle getting Sergeant Tanner into the back of the pool car, but he didn't complain. McLean drove, unable to see anything in the rearview mirror but face. At least the journey was short, ending up near the waterfront. Security fencing surrounded a compound filled mostly with half-wrecked cars, making it look more like a breaker's yard than anything.

'Your man's car's inside. Trying to keep it as clean as possible for the forensics boys.'

McLean didn't have the heart to tell him that most of them seemed to be women these days. He wasn't too keen on leaving the shiny new pool car parked so close to so many wrecks, either, but he locked it up and followed Sergeant Tanner into the large workshop anyway.

It wasn't exactly a hive of activity. Sound fizzed in and out of static from a radio, badly tuned into some pop station. There were half a dozen bays, each with a vehicle lift much like a well-stocked garage anywhere in the country. Two squad cars were undergoing repairs, various important-looking bits of machinery piled up around them. Three other bays were empty, and the last one held a large flatbed trailer with a tarpaulin hiding whatever it was that lay beneath.

'Aye, Boaby. How you doing?' A short man in greasy overalls appeared from the far end of the workshop, rubbing black-stained hands on an equally manky piece of rag.

'Got some detectives from the big city come to see that wreck, Tam.' Tanner gestured over to the tarpaulin as the mechanic eyed up McLean and Grumpy Bob. He must have found them worthy as he gave them a curt nod, then walked over to the trailer and began rolling back the cover.

'Bloody hell!' Grumpy Bob backed up the words with a low whistle of surprise. It wasn't hard to see why. McLean knew a bit about cars, and he was fairly certain this had been a 5 series BMW. It didn't look much like the manufacturer had intended though. There was no glass, for one thing, and the roof had been balanced precariously back in place, upside down, after being cut off to remove the bodies. The front end had folded in on itself so completely it was hard to tell where it had all gone.

'Do we know how it happened?' he asked, walking slowly around the wreck and trying not to imagine the horror of the crash. Had the McClymonts known they were going to die? Or had it all happened so quickly they'd not had time to consider it?

'Idiot was driving too fast, wasn't he.' Tanner's normally cheerful voice dropped to an angry growl. 'They all do it. Buy these stupid powerful cars and think they're Jim Clark or Stirling Moss. And we're the ones have to pick up the pieces. Least this bloke didn't take anyone else with him. Apart from his dad, of course.'

McLean crouched down and studied the back end of the car. It was new, not more than a few months going by the registration number. BMW M5, so very powerful indeed if he had his facts straight. DC MacBride would be able to find him the exact specifications, but it wasn't all that important.

'You think he just lost it going too fast, then? No evidence of foul play?'

'Nothing obvious at the scene, no.' Tanner turned back to the mechanic. 'You see anything obvious, Tam?'

'Not looked at it, have I. Told us not to. This one's for your big city forensics boys.' There was perhaps an edge of bitterness in the old mechanic's words, as if he felt the job of teasing out the car's secrets should have been left to him.

'I think they're more interested in the interior.' McLean studied the shut line, trying to work out if the boot had been opened. The rear end of the car was almost completely undamaged, but the release mechanism would be somewhere in the mangled remains of the front, so chances were that it hadn't been.

'Not much we can tell from here anyway.' He straightened up, feeling a twinge in his back that told him he would probably not enjoy the four-hour drive back to Edinburgh. 'Apart from the fact that he was driving too fast and met something that wasn't going anywhere. RIP Joe and Jock McClymont. Don't suppose you'll be much missed.'

'What were they doing up Inverness way?'

Cruising back down the road they had driven up that morning, McLean realised he'd been keeping his speed slow, not more than sixty even on the dual carriageway, slower when it dropped to single lane even though traffic was mercifully light. They'd dropped Sergeant Tanner off at his station, declined the offer of lunch in the canteen, and headed south as soon as was politely possible.

'What?' McLean risked a sideways glance, taking his eyes off the road for long enough to see that Grumpy Bob was searching his paper for anything he'd not already read.

'The McClymonts. They're Edinburgh property developers. Seems a bit odd the two of them heading up this way.'

'Maybe they were thinking of branching out. Property's expensive in Edinburgh these days. Might have thought it'd be easier to make money up here.'

'You don't believe that, do you sir.' Grumpy Bob didn't phrase it as a question.

'Nope. And neither do the NCA.'

'So what was young Joe doing hooning up the A9 then?'

'That's the big question. There's a lot of drugs come in through the west coast ports. All those old wee villages and hidden bays. Could be they were going to meet up with some of their suppliers. If they were running drugs at all, of course. No one's managed to pin anything on them so far.'

'That why you were so interested in the car boot then?'

'You noticed that?' McLean raised an eyebrow but kept his gaze on the road. 'Didn't think I was being so obvious.'

'That's my sharply honed detective skills at work.'

'Yes, well. That chief superintendent from the NCA, Chambers, wanted me to make sure the car was OK. It'll be interesting to see what forensics get from it. My guess is not much.'

'Should we have stayed with it until the truck turned up?'

McLean paused before answering, let another mile of road disappear under his wheels. 'Reckon that's what Chambers wanted me to do. Probably would have had me in the truck all the way back, just in case something went missing. Not sure where he gets his paranoia from.'

'How long have they been after the McClymonts, then?'

'No idea, but probably years. You know what they're like when they get an idea stuck in their little heads. Hadn't found anything enough to pin on either of them, though. That's why I didn't think there was any point staying with the car. Even if the suggestion that Inverness can't be trusted is a bit shitty.'

'Aye. Shitty. And a waste of time.'

McLean looked out at the scenery as they sped past Pitlochry and south towards Perth. Back at the station was a tiny office filled to bursting with paperwork, a major incident room going nowhere fast. A detective constable he couldn't afford to lose on the brink of quitting due to overwork. A boss who was getting demob happy. 'I don't know. There's worse ways to spend the day, Bob.'

46

The night air was warm and heavy as McLean climbed out of his car, then reached back in to fetch out the bag of takeaway curry he'd picked up on the way home. He ached from the long drive to Inverness and back, a wasted day. It wasn't until he reached the door, saw the light pouring from the kitchen window, that he remembered his house guest. Well, there was probably enough Rogan Josh to go around.

He needn't have worried. Madame Rose was leaning against the Aga when he came in, wearing the apron once again. He could tell just by the smell of the room that she'd been cooking.

'You don't need to feed me, you know,' he said by way of greeting. The medium merely nodded her head at the carrier bag.

'I can see that. You're quite the chef, it would seem.'

McLean put his carry-out on the table and went to the fridge for a beer. It took a while to find, hidden behind bags of vegetables and other unfamiliar produce. He was fairly certain it hadn't been that full the last time he'd looked.

'You went shopping.'

'Ah, the detective inspector's keen observation.' Madame Rose pulled a large saucepan out of the oven and put it on the hotplate. Steam billowed past her head as she pulled off the lid, letting it go with a clatter and a 'bugger' as the realisation dawned that its handle would be very hot. McLean suppressed a smirk, but obviously not well enough.

'It's not funny.' She blew on her fingers, flapping them past her lips in a fanning motion. 'I could have burnt myself.'

'Sorry.' He fetched a glass from the cupboard, poured the beer in, took a deep draught. 'But really, you don't need to go to all this effort. I'm used to looking after myself.'

Madame Rose fetched a plate from the warming oven, ladled what looked like a mountain of stew on to it, then juggled a baked potato bare-handed to the table.

'The least I can do, really.' She lifted the potato on to the plate with one final deft move, then slid the whole thing over to where a place had been set. The butter dish, salt and pepper were already waiting in the middle of the table.

'Well, thank you.' McLean sat down and contemplated a somewhat more substantial meal than the curry he'd thought would do him a couple of nights and maybe breakfast as well, if he had time for breakfast. 'This looks ... interesting.'

'It's a recipe I picked up on my travels in North Africa. Mutton stew. Of course the Berbers would have served it with couscous, but I couldn't find any in your cupboards.' Madame Rose gave him a look that suggested this was perhaps the most egregious of his many failings. As he looked at her, McLean realised that she was fully back to her old self now. Perfectly presented, even with the apron around her waist. The dark stubble and darker eyes were gone, her hair still grey, but recently washed and neatly arranged about her head. And she held herself upright, not stooped under some impossible weight like she had been directly after the fire. Clearly her fortunes had taken a turn for the better; he just hoped that his would follow suit.

He speared a piece of meat, smeared thick sauce over it with his knife and popped the whole thing in his mouth. The flavour was rich, with subtle hints of something flowery. Then he bit into the meat and tasted something that took him straight back to childhood.

'Where'd you get mutton from?'

A worried frown spread across Madame Rose's face. 'Do you not like it?'

'Actually, it's a lot better than I thought it would be. A lot better than I remember it being from my schooldays, anyway. I suspect this isn't scrag end of neck from a toothless old wether, though.'

'Everyone wants lamb these days, but you can't beat a good bit of mutton for flavour.' Madame Rose pulled out a chair and sat down opposite him. McLean took another forkful and shoved it in his face.

'Not having any yourself?' he asked perhaps a little too soon for politeness.

'I'm more of a six o'clock supper person.' Madame Rose glanced up at the clock and McLean couldn't help but follow her gaze. It was well past ten, even though the sky wasn't really dark outside.

'Can't remember the last time I had supper at six. Probably back when I was at school.' McLean cut open his potato and shoved a generous wedge of butter in it. He could, he realised, get used to having someone cook for him. But then it occurred to him that he always had someone cook for him; the chef at whichever takeaway he chose to dine from that evening.

'You hear anything from the building control people?' he asked.

'It's like dealing with children.' Madame Rose's frown deepened. 'The engineers won't go in until the frontage is secured, the scaffold crews won't do anything until they know who's going to pay them, and I can't go home until the others are secured. Round and round in circles. It's not even as if my house is unsafe.'

'I'm not even going to ask how you did that, by the way.'

'Did what?' Madame Rose's face was a mask of feigned innocence. Or it might just have been the heavy layers of foundation.

McLean shook his head, scooped up another forkful of stew. 'Well, you're welcome to stay here until it's sorted. Not as if I'm ever here myself.'

'Thank you, Tony. It's not everyone would be so kind. Quite the opposite, in fact.'

'About that. The hate campaign. You've still no idea who might be behind it?'

Madame Rose kept silent perhaps slightly longer than was wise when answering a policeman. She had a look on her face that suggested she thought the question double-edged. It hadn't been, not when he'd asked it. But it occurred to McLean in that slight hesitation that Madame Rose had always appeared in control of any situation when he'd met her in the past. She gave an impression of having hidden knowledge, perhaps even power. That was part of her act, of course, but he couldn't quite convince himself there wasn't more to it than that.

'It left me very puzzled,' she said eventually. 'And that in itself was a worry.'

'How so?'

'Can I be frank with you, Tony?'

McLean hesitated, another forkful of food halfway to his mouth. 'Have you ever not?'

That got him a pout that looked rather ridiculous on Madame Rose's face. 'There are forces at work in the world most people are not prepared to accept.' She paused.

'Go on.'

'Mostly that's fine. The sort of things I'm talking about rarely interact with the mundane lives of everyday people. They don't care if they're not believed in. But some of us are more sensitive to them. Some of us attract their attention, and some of us are charged with mediating. We keep the balance in check.'

McLean chewed and swallowed as Madame Rose fell silent once more. A part of him had been expecting this conversation for quite some time. Another, larger and more rational part of him had been wondering how he would react. A couple of years earlier and he would have scoffed, told the medium to stop trying to scare him with ghost stories. Now he'd met some of those ghosts, and they weren't all pranksters under white sheets.

'You're sceptical, and that's to be understood. You were raised by your grandmother to question everything. Don't stop on account of me. Just entertain the possibility that the answers to those questions won't always necessarily fit into her beloved science. There's far more to the world than that.'

'And what happened to you, the attacks, the fire, they're

all part of some . . .' McLean searched for a word that didn't sound silly. Failed.

'Call it a power grab, if that helps. A very subtle one at that or I'd have seen it coming a mile off.' Madame Rose considered her chubby hands for a minute, as if she too were searching for the right words. 'You and me. We try to maintain a balance. In our different ways. But there are others out there. Other sensitives who look to use that to their advantage. I believe such a one was behind what has been happening.'

'Do you have a name? I can get them brought in for questioning. If there's any possible evidence of a link to the fire—'

'Ah, Tony. Ever the White Knight.' Madame Rose leaned back in her chair, clasping a hand to her ample bust. 'There won't be any evidence. Not that your forensic scientists would be able to gather, anyway. But it doesn't matter. I am not without my own resources, and they have been brought to bear on the problem. I only needed time and a refuge to recover from the initial ambuscade. This house and your generosity have renewed me, given me the space to marshal my forces. The battle is already joined and my enemy is on the run.'

McLean looked down at his plate of mutton stew, half eaten and still delicious, and yet his appetite had deserted him. 'Sounds rather like you're taking the law into your own hands. Not sure how I feel about that. At least about being used to help it.'

Madame Rose let out a heavy, theatrical sigh. 'I am sorry you feel that way. It's not how I view it at all, and I wouldn't dream of so abusing your hospitality. Ours is a different law, an older law than the one you uphold as a policeman, but it respects society's rules. I won't be getting my collar felt any time soon.'

'Then why tell me at all?' McLean put his knife and fork down side by side at the edge of the plate, reached for his beer in the hope that it would help the sour taste that had appeared so suddenly in his mouth.

'Because it's only fair you know. Because things will happen soon that will seem to make no sense. Things may already have begun to happen. I feel a shift in the currents. The tide is turning once more in our favour.'

McLean looked again at the medium and saw that she was completely back to her old self now. In total control and weaving an aura of mysterious otherness around her like a fog. On balance, he thought he preferred the older, more vulnerable version.

47

'You ever get the feeling you're being pulled in too many different directions, Constable?'

DC MacBride looked sideways from the driving seat as he navigated through the endless rush hour traffic. 'You really want me to answer that, sir?'

'Stupid question, sorry,' McLean said. 'You probably do twice as much work as I do, and sometimes I wonder why I even bother having a home to go to.'

MacBride said nothing, but it wasn't an awkward silence. McLean let him concentrate on getting them to their destination, a fairly modern industrial estate in the arse end of Sighthill. McClymont Developments had its offices and stores in an identikit brick and steel warehouse, the same as eleven others clustered around a large tarmac parking area. Most of the units bore large, shiny signs, names of companies McLean had never heard of. A couple had estate agents' 'To let' boards nailed to their doors, the few front-facing windows boarded up, heavy iron roller doors closed with rusty padlocks.

'We know which one we're looking for?' McLean peered through the windscreen as MacBride drove slowly around the car park. 'Ah, there we are.'

It wasn't quite the most run-down of the units, but it wasn't far off. A small plaque screwed into the wall beside the main entrance read 'McClymont and Son' in flaking paint. MacBride parked right outside the large warehouse door, rolled down and padlocked like most of the others on the estate.

'Is there anyone here?' he asked, leaning forward, hands draped over the steering wheel as he stared at the building.

'Should be. Ritchie phoned ahead. The secretary should be here to let us in.' McLean popped open the door, heaved himself out of the car seat and into the heavy heat of the afternoon.

'What are we hoping to find?' MacBride slammed his door closed behind him, plipped the key-fob to lock the car.

'I'm not really sure. Was hoping we might know it when we saw it.'

If the outside of the building was unprepossessing, it was nothing compared to the inside. They were met by Ms Grainger. McLean remembered the time she'd approached him in the street, asked him to sell his flat, called him unkind. If she remembered it too, she didn't mention it. Her greying hair was swept up into a tight, conical bun and her pinched mouth gave her the look of someone who's run out of lemons to suck. She had a spinster's air and a Morningside twang to her accent, which made McLean suspect that a lifetime of not quite living up to expectations had worn her to this sharp point.

'It's a terrible business. Terrible.' Ms Grainger shook her head as if that might dislodge the fact of her employers' demise and so make it not have happened.

'It can be a treacherous road. I'm very sorry.' McLean

allowed himself to be led down a narrow passageway and into what must have been the nerve centre for McClymont Developments. A sizeable open-plan office, it had two large desks facing each other at one end, a smaller reception desk by the door. A couple of drawing tables stood side by side in the opposite corner, paper plans laid out on them, their corners curling slightly. Everything smelled of dust and mildew, the heat outside only just beginning to penetrate the walls. Ms Grainger crossed the room to a small kitchen area, filled a kettle and switched it on to boil.

'Do you know why they were going north?' McLean asked while she busied herself finding mugs and teabags.

'Old Mr McClymont liked to shoot the grouse. He had a gun at some place up on the west coast. Near Ullapool, I think it was.'

'And Joe was into that too, was he?'

'Young Mr McClymont didn't care for the shooting, no. He liked his deep-sea fishing. Used to take a boat out from Achiltibuie and catch the mackerel, out in the Summer Isles.'

'Business must have been slack, if they could spare the time.'

'There's never so busy you can't take a couple of weeks off in the summer. Old Mr McClymont never missed the start of the season, no matter what was happening. Besides, most of the workmen take their leave around now.'

'So it's booming, then?' McLean had wandered over to the drawing tables and was peering at the plans. He recognised some of them as the designs for redeveloping his old tenement block. They didn't appear to have been changed in the light of his objections.

Ms Grainger didn't reply immediately, occupied as she was with the preparation of tea.

'They'd be better if the Newington site wasn't held up.' She handed McLean a chipped and stained mug. The milk had curdled on the surface, forming an unpleasant scum. She hadn't at any point in the conversation asked whether he actually wanted tea, or what he took in it.

'Perhaps if they'd consulted me first, before starting work.' McLean put the mug down on the nearest available surface, making a brown ring mark on a yellowing building plan. 'Tell me, Ms Grainger. How many other projects are the . . . sorry, were the McClymonts working on?'

Ms Grainger gave him a cold look. 'They had a few things at early stages, but the East Preston Street site was the biggest thing they'd ever taken on. Put everything into it, they did.'

'Would it be all right if I had a quick look around the building?'

'There's nothing here. A couple of vans, some machinery, scaffolding. Most of the plant gets hired in these days.' Ms Grainger sat down at her desk, and that was when it hit McLean. She had a small old-fashioned computer monitor, keyboard and mouse, but there was nothing at any of the other desks. Most places nowadays did everything using CAD software. Even the scruffy offices of Wendle Stevens had been dominated by large flat-screen monitors. McClymont Developments, in contrast, looked like it belonged in the 1970s.

'It won't take long. Then we'll leave you in peace.'

Ms Grainger's face soured even more at the word, but she didn't move from her desk. 'Suit yourselves. I've got to get all the accounts in order for the bank and the lawyers. Just as soon as youse lot release the bodies we can start winding up the company.' She gave a heavy sigh, the veneer of respectability falling away.

'How long have you worked for Mr McClymont?' McLean asked. Ms Grainger looked up at him in surprise.

'Since I left school. When I was sixteen. Used to run messages for old Jock Senior. There was a character. He taught me how to do the books. I was always good with numbers, just couldn't do the sums in the exams.'

'There's no Mrs McClymont, I take it. Joe's mother?'

'She died what, twenty years ago now. Broke old Mr McClymont's heart at the time. Cancer, it was. Probably something to do with the forty-a-day habit she had. Catriona. Och. Haven't thought about her in years.'

'Any other family?'

Ms Grainger didn't answer straight away. McLean supposed that she'd not really had time to come to terms with the news. Sudden death had a habit of doing that to people. They rationalised, of course. They told themselves everything had changed, their loved one, colleague, parent, whatever, was gone now and never coming back. But then they just carried on doing the things they'd always done, not realising that there was a hole that wouldn't be filled. Not until they stumbled into it.

'Young Mr McClymont had a girlfriend, but I wouldn't have called her family. They were always breaking it off, getting back together, breaking it off again. I don't know if she even knows he's dead.'

'Do you have contact details? I'll send a liaison officer round to break it to her gently.'

Something akin to relief spread across Ms Grainger's face at the thought she wouldn't have to perform that particular duty herself. She opened a drawer and pulled out a black leather address book, flicking through the pages until she found what she was looking for. She wrote something down in meticulous script on a yellow Post-it and handed it over. McLean read the name and couldn't help but raise an eyebrow.

'Thank you, Ms Grainger. You've been very helpful.'

'We looking for anything in particular, sir, or just being nosy?'

They had left Ms Grainger in the office, going about her business. Not for the first time McLean wondered why Serious and Organised, or the NCA as they liked to think of themselves nowadays, hadn't closed the place down for a full forensic investigation. But then there was nothing to suggest the car crash that had done for the McClymonts was anything other than a tragic accident, and despite their suspicions, they'd never managed to find anything that could link the builders directly to the drug trade. Even the car had been clean, at least after preliminary analysis. It was still in the yard at HQ undergoing a more thorough examination, but if it had been used to transport any kind of narcotic, they would have found it by now.

'Nothing wrong with being nosy, Constable.' McLean found a panel of light switches by the door into the main warehouse, flicked them on to a hammering of fluorescent tubes. Light flooded the large room, augmenting the meagre illumination that had penetrated the grubby roof windows high overhead.

As Ms Grainger had said, there were a couple of panel vans parked in the middle of the warehouse, side by side. White, and getting on for ten years old if their registration plates were to be believed, they were exactly the sort of thing builders all over the country used. One of them had 'McClymont and Son' stencilled on the front in fading red paint, but the other was unadorned by anything other than rust spots. The front wall was taken up by the roller doors; the other three were clad with industrial-strength shelving, except where a set of steps led up to the space above the office. The higher shelves were filled with cardboard boxes, piled randomly. McLean walked around the room, taking in heaps of scaffolding, rusty and unused, cement mixers crusted around their edges, piles of hand tools, pretty much everything you might expect to find in a builder's yard. Only a builder's yard stuck in the previous century.

'Something up here you might find interesting, sir.' McLean looked around, then up to the top of the narrow stairs where DC MacBride now stood.

'What is it?' He threaded his way between the two panel vans and climbed the rickety steps. The space was cluttered with yet more junk, empty boxes, black bin bags bulging with the heavy cloth sheets decorators used. Everything was caked in a thick layer of dust, untouched in many a year. A narrow walkway snaked through the detritus towards the back of the building, where a skylight cast mottled light on something much newer.

'Couldn't help noticing there weren't any computers down in the office. Well, apart from that old thing the secretary was using. They even had a fax machine that's probably as old as I am.' MacBride reached into the nearest pile and pulled out a shiny white box, shook it to show that it was empty. McLean recognised the brand; it was the same logo on the back of his phone.

'This is all new stuff?' he asked.

'Looks like it, sir. We've got at least a dozen tablets and phones, four top-spec laptops, a couple of high-end desktops.' MacBride stepped further into the pile of boxes, lifting and shaking to check none still had their contents in them. 'The McClymonts surely liked their Apple products.'

'And yet none of it's downstairs in the office. Interesting.'

'Could just be that they had it delivered here to run it through the business. Get the VAT back, that sort of thing.'

'A dozen phones though? There's only the two McClymonts and Ms Grainger on the payroll full time. I met them, Constable. They didn't strike me as the type to hand out top-of-the-range phones to contract staff.'

'I guess we'll have to search their houses, then.' MacBride ended his sentence with a heavy sigh, reminding McLean of just how much pressure the constable was under. Taking him out of the station on this trip was supposed to be a break from the endless admin of coordinating the multiple major incident enquiries, but now he thought about it, the work would still be there when they got back.

'Actually, it'll probably remain a mystery. Unless the NCA boys want to look into it. Come on. We've wasted enough time here as it is.'

McLean handed the box to the constable, turned back to the stairs, then stopped in his tracks. 'Those boxes, they've got serial numbers on them, right? Same as on the computers and phones and stuff that was in them?'

'That's how it usually works, aye.'

McLean pulled his phone out of his pocket, thumbed around the screen until he remembered how to work the camera function.

'Let's just take a note of them all then, shall we? I've a suspicion there's more to this than meets the eye.'

'You want me to run these through the database, I take it, sir?' MacBride tried to hide his weary resignation, but it wasn't a very good effort.

'I think you'd probably do it better than me, Stuart. It's not high priority though.' McLean peeled the Post-it note off from where it had stuck itself to his phone's camera lens, looked once more at the name he'd been given. 'Besides, there's someone I should probably talk to first.'

48

'Ah, the prodigal son returns. And about bloody time.'

McLean had left DC MacBride to park the car. He'd been intending to head up to the major incident room, catch up on the day's lack of progress and hopefully find DS Ritchie. Instead he was barely through the back door to the station when the familiar, irritating tones of Detective Chief Inspector Brooks rang out across the hallway.

'Were you looking for me, sir? Only I've been out on a case.' McLean pulled out his phone, held it up for Brooks to see. 'You should have called.'

'Don't get cocky with me, McLean. I know what you're like.'

'Was there anything in particular? Only I'm quite busy.'

'Aye, I heard that. So busy you've time to go poking your nose into NCA business. Thought you were meant to be heading up a murder investigation. Isn't that a bit more important than some idiot killed himself in a car accident?'

'I agree. It would be nice only to have one case to work on, sir. And much as I'd like to, saying no to a detective chief superintendent isn't really wise. Not when he's got the DCC's ear too. I'm sure you've had cases where you felt the same?'

Brooks' eyes narrowed, the folds on his face deepening as his anger rose. 'Two people are dead, McLean. They had their fucking throats cut. One of them was dumped in a bin like so much trash and whoever did it is still out there. I'd say that was a good bit more important than your developer friends.'

'I've been out less than two hours. And for your information they weren't my friends. I hardly knew them. If I thought the investigation into Ben Stevenson and Maureen Shenks' deaths could be helped by my pacing back and forth in the incident room, rest assured that's what I'd be doing. I don't recall it having all that high a rate of success when you've tried it though.'

He shouldn't have said it. McLean knew that as the words were coming out. Brooks wasn't Duguid, for all that he was likely to have the top job in a few months. McLean could cope with Duguid's bluster; his temper was quick to ignite and just as swift to blow over. Brooks was a different prospect altogether, needed much more careful handling. The detective chief inspector's scowl relaxed rather than deepened, as if he knew he'd scored a point in some arcane competition to which only he knew the rules.

'Perhaps if you were paying attention, you'd know that we've new forensic results on the nurse. Results that could crack the whole thing open. Need I remind you that time is critical in any murder investigation, McLean? You should have been here directing operations, not gallivanting off across the city. You delegate that shit to the sergeants.'

And they fuck it up, so you have to go and do it all anyway, wasting yet more time. McLean shook his head slightly, more at himself falling into the same old trap than anything Brooks had said. The DCI was right, up to a point, but that didn't make him any less of an arse.

'Thank you for the reminder, sir. And thanks for letting me know about the forensic update. I'll be interested to see what that's all about. There's just one small thing.'

'Aye? What?' The scowl was back, a hint of worry in those narrow eyes.

'DI Spence is SIO on the Maureen Shenks case. Not me.'

Brooks' face darkened, building up to a righteous anger.

'You're the one wants both cases investigated together, dammit. You need to be here to coordinate that. If you can't manage that then I'll have to suggest to control they assign a more experienced detective.'

The late afternoon sun baked the streets, tarmac shimmering as it melted in the heat. McLean watched the temperature gauge in his Alfa nervously as they sat in traffic heading south from the city centre. Brooks' important piece of new forensic evidence had turned out to be nothing of the sort, just an excuse for the DCI to give him a hard time. McLean couldn't see any point in pacing the incident room, getting in the way of the admin and constables who were doing all the real work, so he'd found DS Ritchie, and persuaded her to come and help him break the bad news to Joe McClymont's on-again off-again girlfriend. She was currently fanning herself with a notebook.

'What I wouldn't give for a bit of a breeze right now.'

Both windows were open, but without any noticeable forward progress, all that meant was they had the pleasure of breathing exhaust fumes.

'I probably should have kept the pool car. Shame Mac-Bride only signed it out for the morning.' McLean inched forward as the traffic freed up, then slowed to a halt again a few yards on. 'This old girl's fun to drive down country lanes, but not exactly appropriate for this kind of work.'

'Old girl?' Ritchie raised a slim eyebrow. They'd never really grown back properly after she'd pulled him out of a burning factory a couple of years earlier. Her hair had, though, and it was longer now than he thought he'd ever seen it, cut shoulder length. Was it his imagination, or was it a deeper red than he remembered? Shinier and healthier-looking, too.

'I know. Very sexist of me. What can I say, I'm a throwback to an earlier era.'

'No, it's kind of appropriate.' Ritchie patted the dashboard with her free hand. 'But you're right. You shouldn't be using her for this kind of work. Get yourself something new.'

'And keep this for my days off?'

'Aye, well there is that.' Ritchie smiled at the joke. 'It'd be a shame if something got dropped on her again, mind. You have something of a reputation now.'

The traffic eased a little, and McLean concentrated on driving smoothly past the blockage, a delivery truck far too wide for the narrow road. He glanced nervously upwards at scaffolding clinging to the side of a modern office block as he passed, searching for any heavy objects that might be descending from on high. It was foolish, really, but then given how much it had cost to fix the Alfa, maybe something cheap and dispensable was a good idea.

'Not sure I'd know where to start. With a new car. Seems like there's always more important things to do than flicking through magazines and cross-referencing specifications.'

'You could get Stuart to do it. He loves that sort of thing.'

'I rather think he's got enough on his plate right now.'

'True. Oh well, I might have a look-see. Always fun spending other people's money.'

'Is it? I wouldn't know.' McLean turned down a side street, looking for the right number. This was an expensive part of town, decent-sized detached houses set back from the road. Almost all the front gardens had been paved over, with top-end motors parked up or spaces where they would soon be returning from work. They put him in mind of Joe McClymont's flash BMW, and sure enough there were plenty of similar models to be seen. Conspicuous affluence, or more likely just barely managing to make the payments each month.

The house he was looking for had a Range Rover outside the same year and specification as Duguid's. McLean parked in the street in a welcome bit of cool shade under a large tree. He had to wait for Ritchie to wind up her window and get out so that he could lock her door, yet one more reason why a car from the early seventies wasn't perhaps ideal as an everyday runabout and workhorse.

'You ready for this?' he asked, more for his own reassurance than hers. He wasn't entirely sure he knew why he needed to come here. The news could have been broken by a trained family liaison officer, after all.

Ritchie gave him a funny look. 'Reckon so. Just have to hope she's in.'

The look on Charlie Stevenson's face when she answered the door was enough to tell McLean that she had already heard the news. That and the smell of alcohol. Afternoon was progressing towards evening, but it was still a little early to be hitting the sauce.

'Oh, it's you.' She opened the door wide, then turned and walked away, expecting him to follow. McLean did so, Ritchie making sure the door was closed behind them. They walked through an elegantly decorated hallway, shoes clacking on polished wooden floorboards, and into a large open-plan kitchen-diner.

'The girls not at home?' McLean asked. There was plenty of evidence of them. Childish pictures pinned to the fridge door with magnets, the dining table given over to colouring books, a box in the corner heaped with Barbie dolls and plastic horses. Piles of clothes, neatly folded and waiting to be put away.

'Why? You here to interrogate them?' Stevenson slumped in a high seat, leaning against the breakfast bar that separated the cooking part of the kitchen from the dining area. A bottle of wine stood erect on the counter alongside a large wine glass that was half full.

'Sorry, bad joke. They're at their gran's. Hard enough explaining to them why they can't see daddy any more without having to tell them Uncle Joe's not coming to visit any time soon either.'

'I'm sorry.' McLean pulled out a stool and sat on it, across the breakfast bar from Stevenson. No, not Stevenson, he reminded himself. She'd reverted to her maiden name, Christie.

'Why are you here, Inspector?' Christie picked up the wine glass and swirled around the clear liquid within.

'Firstly, I came to tell you about Joe McClymont. I'll

admit, I was surprised when Ms Grainger gave me your name.'

'Bitch. She phoned me about an hour ago. Never heard her sound so happy in her life.'

'Happy?' Ritchie asked.

'Who're you then? Inspector's squeeze? Better-looking than the last one at least.'

McLean saw Ritchie stifle a smile. They both knew that Grumpy Bob had sat in on the previous interview.

'Detective Sergeant Ritchie.' She produced her warrant card, holding it up even though Christie showed no interest in it whatsoever. 'I'm sorry for your loss.'

'Really?' Christie swirled her glass, then took a long swig. Coughed as it burned its way down.

'Really. I don't know you, never met Joe McClymont, but I've had the bottom fall out of my world before. It's not nice and I'd not wish it on anyone.'

'Yeah? Well you could wish it on whoever it was ran Joe off the road. You could wish it on Ms Violet fucking Grainger.'

'I take it the two of you didn't get along.' McLean decided not to point out that the accident had not involved any other cars.

'Can see why they made you a detective.' Christie put her wine glass down with surprising dexterity. Perhaps not as drunk as she was acting. Either that or just lucky.

'How long have you and Joe McClymont been seeing each other?'

'Seeing each other. How very polite of you. Joe and me were at school together. Grew up in the same street. I'd probably have married him if I'd done the same as everyone else. Left after my O grades and got a job in Tesco. But I was cursed with a brain, Inspector. I went to university. Got ideas. Met Ben.'

'But you kept in touch with Joe, I take it.' McLean began to understand why the marriage had failed. Built on sand and hope. A childhood sweetheart just around the corner to offer a sympathetic ear, a shoulder to cry on and temptation when things got rocky.

'Joe was a good listener. Ben only liked the sound of his own voice. When it got bad, I'd go round to his place and just talk. It didn't get physical until much later.'

'But before you and Ben split?'

Christie stared at him a long while before answering. 'Yes.'

'Do you know what Joe was doing up Inverness way?'

'This time of year, probably going deep-sea fishing. He's got a cottage in Achiltibuie, and a share in a boat up there. Jock liked his shooting, but Joe just loved to be out on the water.'

'Did you ever go up there with him?'

A look of horror shuddered across Christie's face. 'Once. God it was awful. Never stopped raining, and the midges. The girls were bored out of their tiny minds, kicking up a fuss you wouldn't believe. Don't think Joe really wanted me there, either. He seemed tense a lot of the time. Only really happy once he'd been out on the boat.'

'You go fishing with him?'

'Christ, no. I'm hopeless on boats. Just spend the whole time throwing up.'

'So you only went the one time.'

'Yeah.' Christie stared into the middle distance as if the

thought had only just occurred to her. Her hand reached out for the glass and she took another long gulp before focusing once more on McLean. 'Lucky, really.'

'Ms Grainger suggested that you and Joe weren't seeing each other any more.'

'My, you are full of questions today, Inspector. Sure you only dropped round to give me the bad news?'

McLean shrugged. 'Thought you'd rather hear it from a familiar face. And I wanted to know more about the McClymonts. They were redeveloping the tenement block I used to live in, after all.'

Something like understanding dawned. 'Oh, you're that policeman,' Christie said. 'Makes sense, I guess. And yes, we were in one of our off periods, but they never lasted long. You might have had something to do with it, now I come to think of it.'

'Me? How?'

'You wouldn't sell your flat. Joe was baffled by that. The amount of money they were offering. Old Jock and that bloody harpie of a Grainger woman couldn't believe it either. Heard them talking about it one time I was round the old man's place. She kept on going on about how it was impossible you could refuse them.' Christie shook her head. 'No idea what that was about, but it fair buggered up their plans.'

She took another swig from her glass, refilled it from the bottle. Stared at it as if she were contemplating just necking the wine instead.

'Was he a violent man, Ms Christie?' DS Ritchie filled the awkward silence.

'Joe? Not really. Never hit me, anyway. Quite the

opposite. He could be very generous if he wanted to be. He gave me my car, for one thing.'

'Really?' Ritchie arched an eyebrow in surprise. 'I wish my boyfriend could afford something like that.'

Christie picked up her wine glass, drained it in one. This time when she put it down it wobbled drunkenly on the counter.

'Yeah. Me too.'

49

He didn't notice her as he drove into the car park at the back of the station, but DS Ritchie must have done. It wasn't until McLean had locked the passenger door and looked up that he saw what had caught Ritchie's attention. A short, wiry figure was leaning against the stone gatepost, cigarette dangling from her mouth and leather overcoat wrapped tight despite the lingering late afternoon heat.

'Think someone wants a word, sir.'

McLean let his shoulders slump. He'd not really been looking forward to the incident room, but a session with Jo Dalgliesh was probably worse.

'I'll be back as soon as I can.' He glanced at his watch. 'But don't hang around for me if I'm not back by shift end.'

Ritchie nodded her understanding, headed to the station while McLean walked back across the car park towards the waiting reporter.

'You've been hiding from me, Tony.'

Jo Dalgliesh looked tired, that was the first thing McLean noticed. She was more slumped than usual, leaning against the gatepost like she needed the support. She didn't stand up as he neared. The smoke from her cigarette spiralled lazily from the tip, and she spoke around it, as if the effort of taking it out of her mouth was too much.

'Ms Dalgliesh, what a surprise.' McLean hadn't meant it,

but as he got a better look at her wizened face, he found that he did. Her eyes were sunken, lines crinkling around them far deeper than he remembered. 'Everything OK?'

A thin smile spread across her face at that. 'Aww, I didn't ken you cared.'

'I don't. Just trying to be polite. Was there something you wanted, or is this a social visit?'

Dalgliesh finally pushed herself away from the wall, letting out a low 'oof' as she did so. 'No' as young as I used to be,' she said. McLean couldn't help but notice the limp. 'You gonnae buy us a coffee then?'

McLean considered the options. He could tell her to piss off, but then she'd just write something nasty about him, or worse, write something nasty about one of his colleagues and attribute it to him. He'd been out of the station pretty much all day, which meant there'd be a mountain of questions awaiting his immediate answer, none of them remotely interesting or useful. He needed to get back up to speed on the Stevenson and Shenks murder investigations in time for tomorrow's morning briefing, and there was no doubt a sea of paperwork waiting for him in his office. On the other hand, she'd come looking for him, which meant she probably had some information. Not that difficult a decision to make, really.

'Come on then.'

It took longer to get to the cafe than it should have, Dalgliesh clearly in some pain as she limped up the road just a little behind him.

'Someone give you a kicking?' McLean asked. 'Only, if you let me know who it was, I'll send flowers.'

'You're all heart, you know that, Inspector?' Dalgliesh hobbled in through the cafe door as he held it open, heading straight for an empty chair. McLean went to the counter and placed his order, trying to remember what the reporter had drunk the last time. It must have been right, or she just didn't care, as she greedily slurped at the latte he brought over to the table a few minutes later, eyeing up the pair of chocolate brownies he'd added for good measure.

'And cake as well? I must have been a good girl.'

'Thought you looked a bit peaky. And sorry, by the way. That dig about the flowers was uncalled for.'

Dalgliesh raised an eyebrow, chocolate brownie paused halfway between plate and open mouth. 'Is that Tony McLean in there, or has there been some invasion of the body snatchers thing going on and I never got the memo?'

'Old habits die hard. I'll never like you much, Dalgliesh. You've caused me enough pain as it is. But I've seen people beaten up badly and whoever did you over knew how to cause pain. Not sure you didn't do something to deserve it, mind.'

Closer up, and in the unflattering light of the cafe, McLean could see the make-up inexpertly plastered on Dalgliesh's face, not quite hiding the bruises. Her nose had always been crooked, no doubt a relic from run-ins with the subjects of her more lurid stories in the past, but now it was swollen around the bridge and spidery veins bloodshot her eyes. The hand holding the cake shook gently.

'Aye, well. That is part of what I wanted to talk to you about.'

'Last time we spoke you were looking into Ben Stevenson's story. The one that took him off to Gilmerton Cove.'

'You bought me cake then, too. Must be love.'

'Seriously, Dalgliesh. I thought you'd decided Stevenson was barking up a non-existent tree. Seeing Masonic symbolism in everything?' In truth, McLean was having a hard time remembering exactly what it was Dalgliesh had told him.

'Aye, I did. But I don't think Ben was barking up the wrong tree so much as being led up the garden path. Since you're so fond of your metaphors.'

'How do you mean?'

'Well, he'd hooked up wi' Dougie Ballantyne, aye? We all ken what a nutter he is. Ben thought there might've been something in it, but his later notes show he was beginning to suspect old Dougie was a sandwich or two short of the full picnic.'

'Wait . . . what? His later notes?' McLean struggled to remember whether he'd seen any notes at all. There'd been the single notebook they'd recovered from the murder scene, but that hadn't yielded anything other than the doodled Masonic symbol on the cover, and Dalgliesh hadn't seen it. Hadn't even been told about it.

'Aye, did you no' get the message? He'd backed up everything to the Cloud. Just took me a day or two to work out what his password was.'

'And you didn't think to tell us?'

'Aye, I told youse. Sent an email to your man MacBride about it.'

Had he mentioned it? McLean supposed it was possible, though he really didn't remember. 'OK, so what you're saying is Stevenson had decided Ballantyne was talking bollocks about the Brotherhood and all his other nonsense. There was no story there?'

'Other than a piece about how gullible folk are, no. And nobody likes to read a piece about how stupid they are.'

'So how did he end up in the cave with his throat cut?'

'That, aye.' Dalgliesh paused for another swig of coffee, her eyes falling on the second of the two chocolate brownies. McLean nudged the plate in her direction; it was a small price to pay for information.

'Ben knew Dougie was as mad as a Scottish Tory,' Dalgliesh continued through a mouthful, 'but he reckoned he knew why, too. Someone really was feeding Ballantyne information, and it really did point to something that looks a lot like his Brotherhood, only without the talking head and the supernatural assassins. Just a good old-fashioned secret society pulling a lot of the strings in the background. There's stuff in there about devolution and the referendum, like a road map as if it was all planned from the start. Scary stuff if you take it seriously. A load of old pish if you don't.'

McLean took a sip of his own coffee, trying to get the flow of ideas straight in his head before seeing where they led. It wasn't easy.

'You don't, I take it.'

'Top marks to the inspector.' Dalgliesh gave him a cheeky nod that turned into a painful wince.

'So what you're telling me is that Stevenson started off investigating Ballantyne's claims, discovered they were built on paranoia and too much late-night cheese?'

Dalgliesh nodded, her mouth full of the last bite of chocolate brownie.

'But he then found out that there was actually some basis for that paranoia in reality, and decided to look into that instead?'

'Aye, and that's when he started to get a wee bit obsessed. That's what all the stuff on his wall was about.'

The wall. He'd been hoping for a chance to speak to forensics about that. Go through their photographs and see what he could find. Better still if he'd been able to analyse the real thing, but someone had put paid to that. Someone who didn't want them knowing what Stevenson had been working on right at the time of his death.

'You think you know what was going on? You think someone was leading him on deliberately?'

'You're no' as stupid as you sometimes seem, Inspector.' Dalgliesh relaxed back into her chair a little, wincing as her shoulders sagged. 'Aye, I think someone was leading Ben on. Stringing him along, more like. The way his notes read, it's as if whoever was doing it knew exactly how to press all the right buttons.'

'Any idea who this person might be?'

Dalgliesh shook her head. 'That's where I hit a brick wall. Thought I was getting somewhere, but every lead just dissolved away to nothing. Ben was being played, Inspector, but whoever was playing him left no trace. Well, apart from a dead body in a cave. And that's no' the question you should be asking, anyways.'

McLean thought for a while before saying 'Why?'

'Exactly. Why? There is no secret society, just someone pretending there was, and doing it well enough to fool a seasoned hack like Ben. But if it was all just a wind-up, then why did he end up dead? That's no' a very funny punch line, eh?'

50

McLean expected Dalgliesh to get a taxi, or wander off
back into town once they'd finished their coffee, but she
walked with him back to the station, or at least limped
along as fast as she could manage.

'So who beat you up, then? Thought you might have got
too close to Stevenson's secret society, but if it doesn't
exist I doubt it would have worked you over like that.'

Dalgliesh grimaced. 'Different story altogether. Something I've been working on a while that's none of your
business. Least not for now, anyway. About a week ago I
got a call, one of my sources saying they'd some info for
me. Only when I got there the wee scrote was nowhere to
be seen. On the way home I got jumped by two scallies up
Calton Hill way. Felt like I was being mugged for my phone
and money, but I know a punishment beating when I get
one. Too many questions, aye? Getting too close to someone as don't want to be seen.'

'You want someone's collar felt, you only need to ask.'

Dalgliesh let out a short sharp snort of laughter,
stopped and leaned against a nearby wall. Whether that was
because she was tired and needed a rest, McLean couldn't
be sure. He suspected it was down to what he'd said.

'That's priceless, you know. "Collar felt." Jesus, I've not
heard that expression in a decade or two.' Dalgliesh wheezed
a bit, then guddled around in her bag for a cigarette. It was

a new bag, McLean noticed, and wondered why he'd not done before.

'You know what I meant. You've been helpful. I'm grateful for that and I'll return the favour if I can. If you don't piss me off again first, that is.'

'Aye, you're all heart, Inspector. I know.' Dalgliesh sparked up, inhaled deeply and let out a long plume of smoke through her broken nose. 'I can look after myself fine, but don't you worry. I find out who those boys were jumped me, you'll be the first to know.'

'You needing a lift anywhere?' They were just across the road from the station, and even though he really didn't want to offer, McLean couldn't help himself from doing so.

'Nah, you're all right.' Dalgliesh waved him off with the hand holding her cigarette, ash fluttering around in the still air and spiralling to the pavement below. 'Just needing a wee minute for my ribs to settle doon, then I'll head off back to the office. Don't you worry about me, Inspector. I'll be fine.'

The station was quiet, afternoon having almost turned to evening now and most of the day shift gone home. McLean went in the back way to avoid being caught by the duty sergeant and buried under the inevitable pile of messages that would have come from being out of the station for more than five minutes. He really wanted to go straight to his office and try to batter into submission all the disparate pieces of information that were flying around in his head. There was one person he needed to talk to before he forgot though, and at this time of the day there was only one place he could possibly be.

The major incident room was suffused with that air of desperation an investigation achieves after a week or more with no progress. A line of uniforms sat at desks, manning the phones though there seemed to be very few calls. Over in one corner, a printer spat out endless sheets of paper; actions to be checked, allocated, worked, rejected. Someone had stuck a couple of pins in the map of the city that adorned one wall, alongside a whiteboard mostly empty of ideas. McLean scanned the room, noticing a distinct lack of senior officers. He found Detective Constable MacBride leaning over the shoulder of one of the admin staff and pecking out commands one-fingered on the keyboard of her computer. He looked up, alerted by some well-honed sixth sense to the presence of his boss.

'Ah, sir. I was hoping I'd see you before shift change.'

McLean glanced up at the clock on the wall above the door. 'Sorry to disappoint. I got waylaid by a certain journalist. Says she sent you an email a while back.'

A look of puzzlement flitted briefly across MacBride's young round face, then realisation dawned. 'Oh, Jo Dalgliesh. Yes. She sent me all of Ben Stevenson's research. Well, links to where it's stored online, to be fair. That's what I wanted to see you about.'

'Any particular reason why you didn't share this with me earlier?'

'Erm . . . you weren't here, sir? It came in while you and Grumpy . . . DS Laird were up in Inverness. I read through it all, but there wasn't much to begin with, and the further you read the less sense it makes.'

'Pretty much what Dalgliesh told me. I'd still like to have a look myself.'

'There's a printed copy on your desk, sir.'

'Thanks. I think.' McLean turned back to the door, then remembered something. 'You get anywhere with those serial numbers we found? You know, the phones and computers at McClymont Developments?'

'All clean. Least, not reported stolen or anything. The phones were all SIM free, which is a bit unusual, and it's top-spec kit. The only thing that's really weird is that none of it was around. I asked the mortuary and put a call up to Inverness. Both McClymonts had iPhones, but previous generation. Whoever's got these new ones, it wasn't them. Neither of them had so much as a laptop with them.'

'A puzzle for the NCA, I expect. But thanks for chasing it up.' An image swam unbidden into McLean's mind then; a pair of Portakabins squeezed into what had been the back garden of his old tenement block in Newington. Plans strewn around a temporary site office. Had there been computer equipment there?

'Get back to Ms Grainger if you've a spare moment. Tomorrow morning's early enough. Find out what's going on with the tenement development and see if you can arrange a site visit, will you? We'd look a bit silly if they'd got all the kit there.'

MacBride nodded, picked up his tablet computer and started swiping at the screen. 'I'll see if we can't do a location trace on the phones. If any of them are switched on, it might be helpful to know where they are.'

McLean glanced up at the clock again, realising just how far past shift end it was. He didn't begrudge the detective constable the overtime, but the lad needed to find some work–life balance too.

'OK. Thanks. But it's low priority. Not our case, really. And do it tomorrow. Time you went and reminded yourself what home looked like.'

True to his word, MacBride had left the printout of Ben Stevenson's working notes on the top of the stack of paperwork adorning McLean's desk. It was a slimmer file than he had been expecting, and the words were printed double-spaced, often no more than short single-word bullet-point lists that made little sense. Unless you looked at it from the point of view of a mind slowly unravelling. He wondered what Matt Hilton would make of it, but the psychologist had left not long after the incident at the disused mental hospital, suddenly announcing that he'd been offered a lecturing post in Brisbane. McLean suspected that the two things were not unrelated.

There were other specialists who could be called on to give their learned opinions about the notes. It would probably be a good idea to get someone to do just that, then at least it would look as if they'd been thorough in their investigation. McLean could see after a casual flick through that they weren't going to find any clues as to the identity of the murderer, though.

He was just about to put the whole thing back in its envelope with a scribbled note to that effect, when his phone rang. He glanced up at the clock, wondering how it was already half-past seven in the evening, before grabbing the receiver.

'McLean.'

'Ah, Detective Inspector. I was hoping I might catch you in.'

He recognised the voice, but took a couple of seconds to put the name to it. The forensic scientist who got all the shit jobs, and seemed to work late shifts. 'Miss Parsons. What can I do for you?'

'I think it's more what I can do for you. I've been doing the analysis on that car you had sent down from Inverness. Nice motor, apart from the whole being written off in an accident thing. You know that engine develops more than five hundred brake horsepower?'

McLean did, as it happened, but it surprised him that Miss Parsons did too. Then it annoyed him that he was surprised. Why shouldn't she know about cars?

'I thought your speciality was interesting effluvia?'

That brought a peal of nasal laughter down the phone line so loud he had to pull the handset away from his ear. When he put it back, Miss Parsons was halfway through her explanation.

'. . . Jack of all trades, really. You've no idea what people leave behind in their cars. Saliva on the dashboard and steering wheel, nasal pickings in the upholstery, urine in the carpets, even faeces sometimes. And you wouldn't believe how much semen and vaginal secretions people spray about. You might want to think about that next time you buy a used car.'

McLean had only met Amanda Parsons once, in the early morning at the end of his driveway when she'd fetched a stool sample out of his bushes. He couldn't really remember what she looked like, but he was warming to her as a person.

'So what's so special about McClymont's BMW?'

'It's complicated.' Miss Parsons paused before adding,

'Any chance you could drop by the lab? Easier if I show you, really.'

McLean glanced up at the clock, even though he knew what time it was. 'Now?'

'Well, I'm still here and you're still there. It can wait till the morning though, if you'd rather.'

There was a pile of paperwork stretching back a couple of weeks to deal with, and technically the results of the forensic examination of Joe McClymont's car was an NCA matter, nothing to do with him. On the other hand, the paperwork wasn't going anywhere, the two murder investigations were stalled, and this intrigued him. McLean scribbled a message on a Post-it and slapped it on the envelope containing Ben Stevenson's deranged notes, then threw it into his out tray.

'I'll be with you in half an hour.'

51

The forensic services technical and engineering labs were on the outskirts of the city, beyond the airport. Evening traffic was light, and McLean made the journey in almost exactly half an hour. A bored-looking security guard raised an eyebrow at his car, but let him through as soon as he saw the warrant card, barely uttering a word during the whole exchange.

Miss Parsons was waiting in reception. 'Got to sign you in myself. Janine goes home at five and we've no cover for the late shift.'

She busied herself writing down details in the visitor book and finding a name badge, handing it over before finally remembering to introduce herself. 'I'm Amanda, by the way. We never had much of a chance to talk when I came to your house.' She stuck out a hand and McLean shook it, somewhat overwhelmed by her restless energy.

'It was . . . early.'

'Very. We met before that. Rosskettle Hospital? You probably wouldn't recognise us SOCOs, all dressed up in our overalls and face masks.'

'You were on that forensics team?'

'Everyone was on that forensics team.' She rolled her eyes like an eight-year-old. They were large eyes, set in a face just as young as McLean had been expecting. Her straw-blonde hair was held back with an Alice band, which didn't help to make her look any more mature. Neither did the loose-fitting tour T-shirt for a rock group McLean had heard of but which had probably split up before she was born. Cargo pants and heavy black DMs were maybe fashionable, or they could just have been the most suitable apparel for her line of work. To McLean they just suggested that she'd nicked all her clothes from her big brother. Or maybe her dad.

'The BMW's out in the workshop. Probably quickest if we go this way.' Amanda pushed open the front door, bustling through almost before McLean could catch it and follow. He'd not got far before she stopped.

'This is yours? This must be yours. Oh, I'd heard . . . but she's beautiful.' She stood just a few paces away from his Alfa, staring for a moment. Then as if it had taken that long to summon up the courage, she ran a hand lightly over the bonnet, roof and boot, walking slowly around the car.

'You just have to take me for a spin sometime. I love, love, love old Alfas.'

'Perhaps,' McLean said. 'But we were here to see Joe McClymont's BMW?'

Amanda gave the Alfa one last longing pat on the rump. 'Of course. Sorry. Tend to get a bit carried away. Here.' She strode off in the direction of what turned out to be the workshops.

Much like any modern garage, it was a line of roller doors set into the front of a tall, utilitarian building. Most were closed, but one was rolled all the way up, spilling artificial light out into the warm evening. Just inside, McLean could make out a heap of bent and twisted scrap metal that might once have been a BMW M5. Pieces had been removed, placed to either side as if it were no more than a plastic toy belonging to a child with insatiable curiosity and a pair of pinking shears. The roof lay upside down at the back of the workshop, all four doors stacked alongside it. The wheels were in a neat tube, one on top of another, beside the far pillar of the four-post lift holding the rest of the chassis just high enough off the ground to enable work on it without stooping.

'It's amazing how much damage hitting a rock at eighty can do. If the rock's big enough.'

'Wasn't this bad the last time I saw it.' McLean noticed that the engine had been removed, and looked around to see where it might be. He found it in the next bay, bolted to a wheeled engine stand and surrounded by the cream leather seats. The front two, he couldn't help noticing, were splattered with dark brown bloodstains.

'Forensic science can be a bit messy.' Amanda fetched a heavy pair of rigger's gloves from a workbench at the back of the room and handed them to McLean. 'Sharp edges,' she said by way of explanation.

'So, what is it you found for me? And you know this is technically an NCA investigation, don't you?'

'They're only interested in drugs, and we didn't find any traces anywhere. Nothing in the boot, no hidden compartments, not even some residue in the carpets, and you'd be surprised how much of that there is about.' She flicked at a stray curl of hair, unable to get it under control with a gloved hand. 'No I called you rather than them because this is more relevant to you.'

'Still not sure how. Are you going to explain it, or do I have to guess?'

Amanda's face reddened at the rebuke. McLean hadn't really meant it as such, but his words might have been a bit harsh. It had been a long day.

'Sorry. I do tend to go on a bit. See, here.' Amanda stepped closer to the vehicle, pointing to the spot on the twisted chassis where the manufacturer had etched the vehicle identification number. McLean peered at it, but could find nothing amiss. Not that he was an expert.

'The VIN, yes.'

'Now see this.' Amanda stalked off to the engine, hunkering down so that she could point to a similar series of numbers etched in the casting of the block.

'Engine number. I take it they don't match up then?'

'Would that it were so easy.' Amanda pulled off her heavy gloves as she crossed to the spotless workbench at the back of the garage. A computer screen, keyboard and mouse looked rather out of place among the heavy spanners and other tools.

'They match perfectly, and they're up here on the DVLA database. Same car, same colour.'

'What's the problem then?'

Amanda clicked a couple of icons on the screen, coming up with a list of incomprehensible numbers and text, the familiar BMW logo at the top the only thing McLean could easily identify.

'Put simply, it's the wrong red.'

'How so?'

'Here.' Amanda turned to the back of the car, lifting the boot lid open and pointing at a sticker with a colour code on it. 'This is the correct code for the colour on the car. I've checked. But this,' she turned back to the screen. 'This is a different shade.'

'Mix up when they entered the data?'

'This is a German car, Inspector. Not Italian.' A gentle smile spread across Amanda's face as she clicked a couple more times, bringing up a different page of equally incomprehensible data. Sooner or later she was going to get to the point, but McLean could wait. Her enthusiasm was infectious and far preferable to the oppressive misery of the station.

'The colour mismatch was just a little niggle, really, but it got me thinking and I really don't like mysteries. So I did a bit more digging. This car, electronically speaking, should be a Category C insurance write-off. Records have it as being badly damaged in an argument with a bus last October. That's before it should even have come into the country, by the way.'

'It's a ringer, then?'

Amanda treated him to another one of her coy smiles. 'Oh, it's so much more clever than that. Until your man McClymont hit that rock, this car had never seen so much as a scratch, but it's been given the identity of a write-off. And it's been done so well I couldn't tell at first. Those VIN and engine numbers are the best fakes I've ever seen. Add that to the clever fooling of the documentation, and this car's almost completely untraceable. It could certainly be bought and sold throughout its entire life without anyone ever knowing anything was amiss.'

'So where did it come from?' McLean cast his eye over the mangled wreckage. It was difficult to imagine someone going to so much effort over a car, but then new it was probably worth eighty grand or more.

'That's where it gets interesting. Waiting on confirmation from BMW, but as far as I can tell, this car was stolen from the private garage of an exclusive apartment development not twenty minutes' drive from here, about four months ago.'

'Four months.' McLean cast his mind back. He wasn't aware of any great spate of vehicle thefts in the city, but there were cars being stolen every day. Even Duguid's Range Rover had been nicked not that long ago.

'That's not important. The thing is, it's been done so well. If this car hadn't crashed . . . no, if it hadn't crashed and then been brought to this forensic lab, it would never have been discovered.'

52

He probably should have gone straight home from the forensic services garage and lab, but there were too many implications arising from the discovery that McClymont's car was stolen. McLean knew he wouldn't be able to sleep until he'd at least begun piecing together that puzzle. He drove back to the station slowly, mind working over the few facts he had without any satisfactory explanation presenting itself to him.

He needed to talk it over with other people who knew the case, but DC MacBride had finally gone home, and Grumpy Bob was nowhere to be seen. Out of desperation, he went in search of Duguid, but the detective superintendent wasn't in. Hardly surprising, given the hour. Only DS Ritchie was still about, peering myopically at her computer in the CID office.

'Evening Sergeant. Anyone else about?'

Ritchie looked up at him, pale skin washed out by the light from the screen. She rubbed a weary hand over her face before answering.

'Carter's around somewhere, and DC Gregg's keeping an eye on the incident room. It's a quiet one though. Why?'

'Just got some interesting information about the McClymonts. Wanted to run it past someone before I called Serious and Organised.'

As he explained the case to Ritchie, a few of the pieces started to come together, but it was still a bugger's muddle.

'Sounds like you need a list of all the sites they were working on; pay each one a visit and see what you find.' Ritchie turned her attention back to her screen just long enough to turn it off, whatever she'd been working on no longer important. 'Or, you know, leave it for the NCA to deal with.'

'You're right. It's their case, not mine. I've done them enough favours already.' McLean looked around the rest of the empty CID room, imagined the pile of paperwork waiting for him in his office, the running commentary on her home life he'd get from DC Gregg if he went up to the incident room.

'Heading home any time soon, sir?' Ritchie had gathered up her bag, slung it over her shoulder.

'Reckon so. Nothing much to be gained hanging around here. Why?'

'I was wondering if I could cadge a lift. Mary's having another one of her little get-togethers this evening. I'm already late, and waiting on a taxi will only make me later.'

The light spilling out over Ritchie's face as she opened the door to the rectory and stepped inside made McLean realise that it was starting to get dark. Summer nights in the city were so brief it was often much later than he thought, but the clock on the dashboard said half-past nine. The days were slowly getting shorter. Soon it would be winter again, the endless cycle repeating once more.

He sat in the car parked outside the church, and stared at nothing in particular in the street. Home was no more than a minute's drive, and yet he couldn't bring himself to go there. Madame Rose would be waiting for him in the kitchen, a hearty meal prepared, and right now he couldn't quite face dealing with her. It wasn't that she was bad company, really. Just that he'd grown used to being alone. Just him, the cat and the occasional postcard from Emma to remind him why he did what he did. Why he put up with the shit, the antisocial work hours and even more anti-social colleagues, the daily bath in the dregs of humanity.

He looked at the clock again. Twenty-five to ten. A quiet time of the evening away from the city centre. Later there'd be people coming home from the pub, or whatever Edinburgh Festival show they'd been to. Earlier it would have been the office and factory crowds heading home. Now was a lull in the night-time activity that suited him just fine.

Switching on the engine, he executed a perfect U-turn in the wide, empty road, and headed back the way he had come.

Scaffolding still clung to the front facade of the building, ungainly metal rods sticking out at all angles. Broken bones in the darkening sky. The first level of planks was too high up to jump and catch on to, deliberately so to deter drunken revellers. The uprights – standards, if he remembered the arcane builders' jargon – were smooth, and wrapped in shiny tape to make them smoother still. Even so, there were always idiots who tried, egged on by alcohol and friends who didn't know better. As a beat constable, McLean had seen more than his fair share of broken arms, legs, backs and necks from people who got building sites and playgrounds confused.

It wasn't a problem for him, though. The front door to his old tenement block was closed and locked, but he still had the key he'd used when he'd lived there hanging on his key ring. More surprisingly, it still worked. He looked up and down the street, but shadowed by the scaffolding no one would have been able to see him even if there'd been anyone about.

Stepping through the familiar front door sent a shiver down his spine. As he closed the door behind him it cut off the low roar of the city for a moment. He stood in the darkness and almost imagined that the past two years had never happened. Or the last twelve. He would climb those stairs like he'd done uncounted times before. Kirsty would be waiting for him. His Kirsty, with her long black hair and infuriating way of seeing right through him. They would share a bottle of wine, chat over whatever music he put on, fall into bed together.

A siren on Clerk Street cut through his musings. McLean shook his head, though only half-heartedly. He didn't really want to lose that tiny, happy moment, even if he knew it was madness to dwell on such things. But he'd come here for a reason. Best get on with it.

There wasn't much sign of progress on the building front. Hardly surprising, given his objections to the plans and unwillingness to sell up. What would happen to the site now that McClymont Developments was effectively no longer trading? One for the lawyers to fight out, he had no doubt. McLean stepped quietly through the front door to Mrs McCutcheon's flat, then followed the new concrete steps down to the communal garden.

It was an oasis of dark calm. To either side the lights

from the neighbouring tenements illuminated washing lines, garden furniture and unkempt vegetation, but here in the middle there was nothing. Off to the rear, the bulk of the Portakabin offices squatted like some alien spaceship. A mini digger parked alongside it looked strangely awkward in the half-light. The rest of the garden had been dug down, backfilled, the drainage points jutting out of freshly laid concrete like mafia victims struggling to break free. He clambered carefully down to basement level, testing the surface with the tip of his foot. It looked like it might be still liquid, but that was just a trick of the light. The floor was firm, the concrete set rock-solid, the tiny outlines of the planned basement flats etched in narrow blockwork.

McLean approached the Portakabins quietly. As far as he could tell, there was no one about, and it wasn't as if Joe and Jock McClymont were going to suddenly appear for a late-night site inspection, but still he knew that he shouldn't really be here. So far he'd not broken any rules. He had a key and a legitimate right to be in this place. The cabins were a bit of a grey area though, legally speaking. No, who was he kidding? This was breaking and entering, fair and simple.

Like much of the kit in the McClymonts' warehouse, the Portakabins had seen better days. The front door was locked, but the windows weren't, and a little jiggling of one had it swinging open. Clambering in was more difficult than it should have been, but McLean made it without knocking too much off the nearest desk. At least he'd remembered to put on gloves.

He was in the same room where he'd first seen the plans

for the redevelopment. They'd been pinned up on the far wall, and were barely legible in the reflected glow of the street lamps. The desks between him and them were old, basic Formica tops on metal frame legs. There were no phones, no computers, nothing more sophisticated than an elderly microwave oven sitting on top of a fridge, a grubby kettle alongside it. Nothing in here to raise any suspicions.

The door led out into a narrow corridor running the length of the two cabins. Hard hats and hi-vis jackets hung from hooks along one side. The other sported a motley collection of Health and Safety Executive warning posters, reminding the workforce what a lethal place a building site could be. Opposite where he stood, a second door should have opened into the next Portakabin, but when McLean tried it, he found it was locked. He went back into the first room, rummaged around in drawers until he found a bunch of keys. Not too hopeful that any of them would be the right one, but it was worth a try.

The darkness in the corridor was almost total now. He didn't want to turn on his torch though, worried he might be spotted by someone in the flats that looked on to the garden. He worked his way through the bunch largely by feel, sliding each key into the lock, twisting, meeting solid resistance. On to the next, then the next. And then finally it clicked. The door swung open and he peered inside.

A high window let what little light was left into the room. His eyes accustomed to the gloom, it was still as much as McLean could manage just to see the vague shapes of desks and tables. This place smelled different from the rest of the Portakabin though. Electric, charged. Over in the corner LEDs flickered on and off, green and red on the front of some kind of computer equipment. Screens lined up along one wall. McLean was about to step fully into the room, but common sense finally kicked in. This wasn't his case, just a mystery he couldn't leave alone. And if a crime had been committed, the two perpetrators were beyond the law now.

He pulled the door closed, locked it after him and returned the keys to the drawer where he'd found them. Then he cleared up all the papers he'd knocked to the floor when he came in. He considered the window, but decided it was too risky going back out that way. The front door was a Yale lock, so he could get out without it being obvious anyone had been in at all.

Back in his car, convinced he'd been watched the whole time, McLean pulled out his phone and thumbed at the screen until the number he'd been given came up. He hovered over the dial icon for long moments, knowing it was none of his business. Except that they'd made it his business, hadn't they? When they'd put his name on the planning documents. When the NCA had hauled him over the coals for something he'd not done. Sorting this mess out might not be his job, but with the McClymonts dead, the worry was nobody else would do it.

A quick glance at the clock. Late, but not so late you couldn't phone a policeman. Especially a detective chief superintendent.

53

Traffic was light on the drive back home, which was just as well as McLean's mind wasn't really on what he was doing. The conversation with DCS Chambers had gone better than he might have expected, but it had also made yet more work for him and his overstretched team. He drove slowly past the church, still shrouded in scaffolding, the rectory alongside with light shining from the front porch. Pulling over a hundred yards from his own drive, he took out his phone, jabbed at the screen until he found the number.

'. . . Can't answer the phone right now . . .' DS Ritchie's voice sounded strangely unconvincing on the tinny line, but he really needed to talk to someone. He tried Grumpy Bob's number, let it ring and ring. He was about to hang up when it was finally answered, the noise of a busy pub easily identifiable in the background.

'Evening sir. Anything I can do to help?'

Grumpy Bob wasn't a heavy drinker, not by old-school police standards, but there was a point in any pub evening beyond which he'd be unable to pull it back and be an effective member of the team. Judging by the slur in his voice, that point had long since been passed.

'Going to be a busy one tomorrow, Bob. Early start if you can be in.'

'Right you are, sir.' There was a noise much like a man rapidly downing a pint of beer, followed by a muffled belch. 'I'll head home and get some kip then. Was getting a bit bored of the company in here anyway if I'm being honest. What's up? Anything interesting?'

'McClymonts senior and junior. Seems they were up to no good after all. Briefing at seven sharp. I'll fill everyone in then.'

McLean hung up before Grumpy Bob could complain. He hovered his hand over MacBride's number, then sent a text instead. Stared at the screen in surprise when there was no instant reply.

A change in the light dragged his attention around to the rectory. The front door had opened and someone was stepping out. Another person, then another, they clustered around the doorway in that manner people have. Suddenly remembering all the things they want to say now that it's time to go. Before he'd really considered the implications, he'd snatched the keys out of the ignition, climbed out of the car and headed across the road. When he got to the gate and the short path leading up to the door, the conversation was still in full flow.

'You got a minute, Kirsty?'

DS Ritchie looked around as she heard her name. Finally saw him at the gate.

'Sir? I thought you'd gone home.'

'Almost. Just had to check something out first.'

Everyone was looking at him now, so he had no choice but to open the gate and approach them. Mary Currie, the minister, stood in the doorway, flanked by a young man also wearing the black shirt and dog collar that suggested he too was a minister, or maybe a curate. Either that or he'd come to a fancy dress party woefully ill prepared.

'You went back to your old flat, didn't you?' Ritchie met him a few steps up the path. 'Find anything interesting?'

'If you need a lift home, I can fill you in on the way.'

Ritchie looked back to the group, standing just a few paces away. 'Actually, Daniel already offered to drive me.'

McLean followed Ritchie's gaze back to the front door as the young minister stepped forward into the light.

'Tony. Good to see you again.' He held out a hand to be shaken. McLean took the proffered hand, expecting a limp wrist. He was surprised by a firm, dry shake.

'You'll know Mary.' Daniel assumed the task of making introductions as if it were the most natural thing in the world. He gestured with an open hand towards a couple who had been standing to one side looking awkward. 'This is Eric and Wanda.'

'Are we all going to stand around on my front doorstep all night?' Mary Currie cut in to the conversation. 'Only it's getting a bit chill and I wouldn't want to have to put the heating on.'

'Sorry, Mary. I'll just run Kirsty home. Won't be long.'

'You stay out as long as you want, Daniel. I'm not your mother.'

Even in the poor light, McLean saw the embarrassment blush the young curate's face. He pulled a set of car keys out of his pocket to cover it, turned to the couple. 'You two want a lift too?'

'Gotta go, sir. Unless it's really important?' The question in Ritchie's voice was unmistakeable, as was the hope his answer would be no. Seeing all these people with their life outside of work did put things in perspective.

'No, you go home. But we've an early start tomorrow. Briefing at seven, OK?'

Ritchie nodded her agreement and she, Daniel, Eric and Wanda headed off into the night.

'Should I be worried about those two?' McLean turned as he asked the question, the light spilling from the hallway giving the minister a pale yellow halo.

'Young love will ever run its course.' Mary Currie smiled at him like an indulgent parent. 'You want a cup of tea? The kettle's not long on.'

McLean had never been inside the rectory before, and was surprised to find it not unlike any other home. It smelled old, much like his grandmother's house, but it was warm and bright and welcoming. There were occasional reminders that this was a place where someone religious lived – a discreet cross hanging by the coat rack in the front hall, a couple of pictures that might have looked more fitting in a seminary – but by and large it was just homely.

He followed the minister through to the back of the house and a large kitchen. Judging by the mismatch of chairs arranged around an old table, this was where the evening's Bible class had taken place. Except it wasn't really a Bible class, he could see that now. Just a bunch of people looking for answers. Or maybe some company.

'Roof should be finished by the end of the month. Then we can get shot of that scaffolding. Start holding services again.'

'I didn't realise it was that bad.'

'Oh it is. There's probably more steel inside than out. Still, thanks to your generosity it'll all be done soon.'

McLean wasn't sure why he felt uncomfortable about that. He'd given them money because he liked the building, not what it represented. 'DS Rit . . . Kirsty's doing very well these days,' he said by way of a change of subject. 'Not sure what you get up to in your sessions, but it seems to be working for her.'

'I think that probably has more to do with Daniel than me.'

'Daniel. Of course.' McLean accepted a mug of tea, noticing it had milk in it already.

'Oh to be young and in love. It's sweet, really.'

'He's all right, I take it?'

'Is that paternal concern I hear in your voice, Inspector?' Mary Currie gave him a wicked grin. 'Just teasing. And yes, since you ask, Daniel's all right. Earnest, but then I was too when I was his age. He's not long finished his training, looking for a parish to go and do good things in. The bishop already offered him a rural one, but he says he wants to work in the city.'

'Very earnest, then. I look forward to meeting him when he's in less of a rush sometime.'

'Do I detect the sign of a challenge being laid down?'

'I don't share your faith.' McLean shook his head. 'If I'm being honest it's the whole notion of faith I have a problem with. Doesn't really square with being a detective. I gave up accepting things at face value a long time ago.'

'So like your grandmother.' There was that wry smile again, as if the minister could see right through his facade. It wouldn't have surprised him.

'How's your house guest settling in?' she asked. The change of subject took him by surprise.

'Rose? Fine, I guess. Don't see much of her except in passing.'

'That's a very generous thing you did, letting her stay.'

'Not as if I haven't got the space. And she helped me when Emma was at her worst. I owe her that much. She's a good cook, too. If she stays much longer I might start getting fat.' McLean patted at his stomach. 'There'll be something wholesome and hearty waiting for me when I get in, I've no doubt. Told her she doesn't need to, but I can't exactly stop her.'

'And it beats a takeaway curry, I expect.'

McLean nodded his agreement, envying Grumpy Bob his pint or two down the pub. 'I should probably be getting home anyway. Early start tomorrow.' He stood up, the un-drunk mug of tea still sitting on the table in front of him.

'Yes, I heard you tell Kirsty. Dawn raid, is it?' The minister stood as well, accepting that their all-too-brief conversation was over.

'Nothing so glamorous, I'm afraid. Just a long day of stuff I can't really talk about.'

'Police secrets. Kirsty's just the same. You're very lucky to have her.'

'Trust me. I know. Don't think I don't appreciate it.'

'I'm sure you do, Tony. But don't forget to tell her from time to time. It's nice to have your efforts recognised.'

McLean smiled, nodded, unsure he could really say anything to that. It was true, and he was as guilty as the next man of taking his team for granted. Compliments from higher up the greasy pole were so rare these days, he'd all but forgotten how much good a little well-earned praise could do.

The first thing he noticed when he opened the back door was the absence of cats. It wasn't even as if not seeing any immediately in front of him on entering was all that strange, and yet somehow as he walked through the short passageway from the door to the kitchen, McLean knew that they weren't there. Or rather, just one was there.

Mrs McCutcheon's cat looked up at him from a spot in front of the Aga she hadn't been able to occupy for a few weeks now. McLean scanned the rest of the room, but Madame Rose's familiars were nowhere to be seen. Neither was the medium herself. The smell in the kitchen suggested she had left something edible behind, however. A quick look in the plate-warming oven revealed enough cassoulet to feed an army, and a half-dozen baked potatoes. Not exactly classic fare for a warm August night, but very welcome all the same.

'Surprised you didn't go with them,' McLean said to Mrs McCutcheon's cat, as he searched around for oven gloves. Only when he dumped the casserole dish on the kitchen table did he notice the post piled up against the pepper grinder in the middle. A couple of letters bore the ominous mark of his solicitors; someone was still trying to persuade his grandmother to take out a credit card at an eye-wateringly usurious rate of interest even though she'd been dead two years and more; and the electricity bill needed paying soon, judging by the red-printed 'final reminder' on the envelope. There were two others in the stack: a plain white letter with no stamp or postmark, just the word 'Tony' in neat block capitals; and a postcard, its edges battered and corners folded. The image on the front was of a Japanese temple and the handwriting on the back brought a gentle leap to his heart even before he read the words.

Not many with us now, and those last few are often reluctant to go. It's getting easier though. Spent some months in a monastery here. You should visit it some day. Can't get much further away, so I must start coming home soon.

It was signed with that familiar looping E, so stylised it could almost be a K. McLean propped it up against the other, unopened mail and set about spooning some food on to a plate. Mrs McCutcheon's cat looked up as the smell of sausage casserole filled the room, but she didn't leap on to the table to help herself. No doubt confident there would be plenty going spare later.

The fridge yielded a cold beer and as he poured it, McLean felt a little twinge of guilt at the mug of tea he'd left behind in the rectory. He pushed it aside, instead savouring the bitter flavour of the ale. Butter melting in his baked potato, a couple of mouthfuls of delicious stew, and then he reached for the plain white envelope.

Inside, a single sheet of paper was almost covered in dense, neatly written script. It didn't surprise him to find that Madame Rose was a fountain pen and ink person, or possibly even a freshly cut quill and ink one.

My Dear Tony, it began.

It is with a sense of deep shame that I feel I must confess to having abused your most generous hospitality. It is true that I turned to you when I felt there was no one else to whom I could turn, and it is true that I was recently attacked in a most grievous and personal manner. The danger to myself was, however, never quite so severe as I might have intimated, certainly not physically. My familiars were threatened, this is true. One poor soul was lost, as you know. My gratitude to you for giving the others safe haven knows no bounds.

But I myself was never in great danger. The fire was of course an inconvenience, a difficulty that took a little time to overcome. And that is all I really needed, time to bring my own resources to bear on the problem. It has been many years since I have been challenged in the manner I have recently been challenged — I will not name it directly as I know you yet have difficulty admitting to the existence of such things; our conversation the other night reminded me of that. Suffice to say I am not without my own resources and these have now been brought to bear. I am confident both that the threat has been neutralised, and that your generosity has been rewarded in the process.

The physical face of my troubles was a development company, run by a father and son with whom I believe you are acquainted. You will know too the fate that has befallen them. In the grand scheme of things, they were but petty criminals dabbling in affairs far greater than they could possibly have comprehended. The unravelling of their little empire will reflect well on you should you so desire, though knowing the boy your grandmother raised, I suspect you will pass any glory on to those around you.

There is one more player in this sorry tale, the one who

engineered this situation in a bid to oust me from my position in
this great and ancient city. I have taken steps to neutralise this
usurper and life will soon return to normal.

I thank you for my time under your roof and your protection.
You do not know it, but you have powerful friends. Should you ever
require my assistance, you need only ask and it will be freely given.

Yours in gratitude,
Rose

McLean stared at the letter, trying to make sense of it. One
fact kept coming back as he stirred his half-forgotten cassoulet around the plate. It was the McClymonts who had
been trying to get Madame Rose out of her house, develop
the whole block into cheap flats. They'd killed the cat, set
fire to the chippy and betting shop. Probably even shoved
the shit through her letterbox, and then later his.

And now they were dead.

He pulled out his phone, tapped away at the screen until
he found what he was looking for. Keyed in a message and
sent it off to all the officers on his team. He'd told them the
morning briefing would be at seven sharp. He hoped
Grumpy Bob's head wasn't too sore to make it in for six.

54

'Doesn't look like there's anyone in, sir.'

DC MacBride stood on tiptoe, peering in through the grubby window of the offices of McClymont Developments. At seven in the morning it was hardly surprising, though there were signs of life at some of the other businesses on the industrial estate. The car park that had been more than half full when last they had come here had barely any cars in it at the moment, and most of those were police.

'Break down the door.'

'Umm . . . we don't have a warrant, sir.' Worry painted itself clearly over MacBride's face.

'I can smell fire. Sure of it. Can't you?'

The worry didn't go away, but the detective constable nodded, scurrying off to instruct a couple of uniforms. It was only a moment's work to smash the lock and force their way in.

The first thing McLean noticed was the smell. Not burning, but something rotten and mouldering. It hadn't been there the last time, he was sure of that, but now the air tasted as if it had been trapped in a bin.

'What is that?' Beside him, MacBride covered his mouth with the back of his hand, squinting as if the fetid stench was attacking his eyes.

'No idea, but it's not good. Come on.'

They went through to the offices, and McLean stopped at Ms Grainger's desk. The elderly computer was still there, and the fax machine. When he pulled open the drawers though, they were all empty. Glancing around the room he couldn't see much different, but then it had never struck him as a place actually used to conduct business. Not building development, at least.

'Go check those computer boxes, Constable.' McLean watched as MacBride scurried out of the room, then went over to the table where the plans for his tenement had been laid out. They were still there and he leafed through them, wondering again how the planning department had ever passed them. Another puzzle to add to the mix, though proving that any bribe had either been offered or accepted would be tricky. Something for Serious and Organised to worry about, not him.

Running a hand over the printed paper moved it slightly, revealing other plans underneath. He rolled away the fate that would now no longer befall his old home and peered at what the McClymonts had been planning for some-where else. Except that it wasn't a building plan. The sheet pinned to the drawing board was a city street map, black and white, showing an area centred on Waverley station and spreading out to Leith Docks in the north-east, Cra-mond Brig in the north-west, Sighthill and Craigmillar in the south-west and south-east. Points on the map marked his tenement block in Newington, Madame Rose's terrace house on Leith Walk, but they weren't the only sites. Others dotted the map, and peering close McLean saw his grand-mother's house among them. Faint lines traced from one point to another, scarcely visible in the poor light filtering into the office through the grubby window. He ran a finger along them, trying to make some sense out of the pattern. There was something circular about it, but jagged too. One point stood out, ringed in pencil. To the west of the city, but just inside the bypass. McLean was peering at it, trying to remember what was there, when MacBride returned.

'The boxes are still there, sir. One of the vans has gone, though.'

'Have we got an address for Ms Grainger?' McLean asked the question even though he knew that she wouldn't be there. Before the detective constable could answer, his phone rang. A glance at the screen showed a number only recently added to his address book. He took the call knowing what it would be about even before he was told. The conversation was mercifully short.

'That was DCS Chambers. I've got to go and meet him in Newington.'

MacBride didn't question, just nodded his acceptance. 'I'll get this processed, sir. Don't imagine we'll find anything, mind you.'

'I don't suppose we will. But get some of those uniforms to go door to door round the other businesses, OK? See if anyone saw the van leaving. Better yet if they've got any security cameras.'

MacBride nodded, tapping notes into his tablet computer. McLean was about to leave, when he remembered the map. He pulled it off the drawing board, spread it out between them and tapped on the point that had caught his attention before. 'One other thing. Get someone to go and have a look here. Might be nothing, but it was important to someone.'

'You really know how to complicate things, don't you McLean.'

Detective Chief Superintendent Tim Chambers of the National Crime Agency was less friendly at eight in the morning than he had been the first time McLean had met him. Perhaps being dragged along to a six o'clock briefing wasn't how he'd intended starting his day, but he'd seemed interested in the information both about Joe McClymont's stolen car and the computers. They'd agreed to hit the offices and the building site at the same time. Unlike the offices across town, the building site appeared not to have been touched since McLean had visited it the evening before.

'Not sure what's complicated about it, sir. I told you there were computers here, and here they are.'

They were standing in the middle of the Portakabin, perhaps a little closer together than was comfortable for two men who didn't know each other well. There wasn't much choice in the matter, as the rest of the room was filled with large flat-screen monitors, sleek modern computer boxes and mile upon mile of cabling. The lights McLean had seen flashing the night before were dead now, but the rack of servers that had been producing them looked very expensive. More the kind of thing you'd find in the basement of a multinational technology firm than a building site lock-up in Newington.

'You any idea what these are all for?' McLean watched as an NCA technician inspected the nearest computer.

Another was going through a pile of mobile phones, all plugged in to the server array and forming some kind of wireless network link, if he understood these things correctly. Maybe he should have stayed at the company offices and sent MacBride over here. It seemed more suited to the detective constable's expertise, somehow.

'We won't know until we've got them powered up. Whole thing's dead as a doornail at the moment.' The nearest technician turned in his seat to answer the question.

'Everything? Even that server thingy over there?' McLean nodded in its direction.

'Yup. There's power to the sockets, but nothing's plugged in.'

'There was last night. There were lights flickering.'

'How did you even know they were in here?' Chambers shook his head before McLean could answer. 'No, don't tell me. I can guess.'

'I have a key to the front door, sir. I'm probably the only person alive who owns a share of this site. I've every right to come in here.'

'Not in here, you don't.' Chambers nodded in the general direction of the Portakabin wall. 'We'll gloss over that for now. We've enough from the stolen car to get a backdated search warrant. Just need to find out what's on these computers now.'

'Umm . . . that might not be easy, sir.' The technician sitting at the monitor had turned his attention to the computer itself, pulled something out of the tiny metal box that looked more like it should have come out of a catering academy stove at the end of the first lesson. A faint whiff of singeing filled the air.

'I take it they're not meant to be like that,' McLean said.

'Nope. It's fried. Someone's got to these, and recently judging by the smell. They're all solid-state memory too. Don't expect we'll get anything off them.'

'Shit. And you didn't find anything at the offices?' Chambers turned to McLean, his anger low and threatening.

'There wasn't much there to start with. One of the vans and the company secretary's cleaned out her desk. I'm sorry, sir. This wasn't exactly high priority. If you'd wanted us to secure these places when the McClymonts died, you should have said.'

Chambers kicked his foot hard against a stained carpet tile. 'I know. That's why I'm so pissed off, really. It's not your fault, it's ours. We've been treating Joe and old Jock like a couple of country bumpkins, when they were much more sophisticated than that.'

McLean recalled Madame Rose's letter, still lying on his kitchen table. The more he considered its contents, the more he wished he'd paid more attention to the acerbic Ms Grainger. Jock and Joe McClymont were perhaps not quite country bumpkins, but they weren't as sophisticated as their operation might have suggested. Something, or perhaps someone, had been protecting them, maybe directing them, and just possibly using them to an end the NCA and Police Scotland would neither understand nor believe. He wasn't sure he believed it himself, and certainly didn't understand.

'What have you got on the company secretary, Ms Grainger?'

'Grainger?' Chambers stopped destroying the carpet tile with his foot for a moment. 'She's not a part of this.

We profiled her at the start of the investigation. Pegged her as just an employee on the legitimate side of the business.'

'Do you know where she is now?'

Chambers pulled out his phone and tapped the screen a couple of times, lifted it to his ear. It looked very impressive; McLean had a hard enough time trying to find the number pad on his so he could dial out at all. On the other hand, there was probably only one number Chambers ever had to call. He had minions to do everything else for him.

'Grainger. Where is she now?' That he didn't introduce himself or ask who had answered reinforced the idea. Chambers was a man used to being obeyed without question, and if the frown wrinkling across his forehead was anything to go by, a man not used to having things go awry.

'You're sure of that?' A short pause. 'Empty? Nothing at all?' He tapped the screen to end the call and slipped the phone back into his pocket.

'Let me guess. She's disappeared.'

'Without a trace.' Chambers scratched his head like a cartoon character baffled by the sudden appearance of a wall. 'And I mean without a trace. It's like she never existed. Computer records, surveillance photos, tax records. I've got my IT guys double-checking it's not a glitch, but . . .'

The detective chief superintendent fell silent. McLean suppressed the urge to clap him on the back and say 'welcome to my world'. He had a suspicion it wouldn't have helped.

His own phone broke the slightly awkward silence. McLean pulled it out, peered at the screen. DC MacBride calling.

'Constable?'

'Can you spare a moment, sir? It's about that site on the map you asked me to look into.'

McLean glanced around the Portakabin. 'Reckon we're about done here. Why?'

'I'm there at the moment. Think you might want to see what we found.'

He'd seen the building site many times before. You could hardly miss it, sitting behind a rotting security fence just off the city bypass. Weeds had begun to reclaim the parking area, pushing up through the tarmac like triffids. The main building itself was an unfinished mess of concrete pillars and boarded-up windows, reinforcement bars poking out at odd angles like rusty broken bones through grey-green skin. The only sign advertised a security firm, the image below the logo suggesting both cameras and dogs, although McLean could see no evidence of either as they pulled up at the gates. A uniform constable approached, peered uncertainly at DCS Chambers in the driving seat, then nodded as he saw McLean.

'I'll get the gate, sir. You want to go round the back, where the deliveries would've been made.'

The rough ground and horrible crunching noises as unidentified objects hit the underside made McLean glad they'd come in Chambers' car and not his little Alfa. They parked up in the shade of the vast building, alongside a couple of squad cars and what appeared to be a newly arrived forensic services van.

'What's going on?' McLean asked as soon as he tracked down DC MacBride. The constable was standing by a small service door let into one of the much larger roller doors that lined the loading area.

'Worked out what the mark on the map was, sir. This place was supposed to be the biggest shopping mall in Scotland, but the developers went bust in the crash and it's been like this ever since.'

'You got a warrant to search this building, Detective Constable?' Chambers asked.

'Would you believe it wasn't locked, sir? Not even the gates back there.' MacBride nodded in the direction of the perimeter fence. 'There was a chain looped round, but no padlock. And this door opened when I tried it.'

Chambers looked unconvinced, but McLean could well believe it. If this was something to do with the McClymonts' operation, then chances were it had been hidden away by something much more effective than locks and chains.

'What exactly have we got here?' he asked.

'Best look for yourselves. Just don't touch anything, aye? Dr Cairns is on her way.' MacBride stood aside to let them in. Chambers led the way, ducking his head to avoid braining himself on the low doorway. McLean followed and almost walked into the back of the detective chief superintendent, who had stopped still just a pace inside. Half-skipping to one side, McLean's eyes focused on the room, and he understood why.

It was a vast area, designed so that articulated lorries could drive in, reverse up to loading bays, unload and then drive straight out again. The roof high overhead was a lattice of beams, with clear windows in the steel roofing sheets the only source of illumination. It was enough light to see a collection of cars that wouldn't have looked out of place in the most expensive garage forecourts in the city.

'Bloody hell.' Chambers took a couple more steps until he was standing alongside a sleek-looking Bentley. He reached out to touch it, then stopped at the last minute, shoved his hands in his pockets.

McLean did a quick count, made it to twenty-four before he was distracted. All the cars were new, though some were beginning to attract dust. They were all expensive, mostly German or high-end British as far as he could tell. Their number plates were gone, and over in the far corner a couple of two-post lifts and some heavy-duty mechanic's tool trolleys suggested some kind of workshop.

'How the fuck did we not know about this?' Chambers asked the question to the open space. McLean knew better than to offer an explanation. Let the NCA puzzle that one out for themselves. A few things were beginning to come together in his mind though, and the sight of a high-spec Range Rover at the end of one of the rows of cars left him with a particularly unpleasant suspicion.

'Think we should leave this to forensics, sir.'

Chambers turned to face him. 'What? Oh. Yes. You're right. Don't want to contaminate this any more than we have already.'

'Best not to,' McLean said. 'And besides, there's someone I need to talk to. Think you should meet her too.'

55

Charlie Christie had obviously found solace in the bottle of wine McLean and Ritchie had left her with the afternoon before, but now it looked like it was getting its revenge. Her face had a pallid green shade to it, with dark bags under her eyes and no make-up to hide them. She wore a full-length towelling dressing gown, squinting as if she'd only just recently crawled out of bed. Glancing at his watch, McLean realised it was just gone ten, so chances were she had.

'You again?' Christie looked at McLean, then shifted her glance across to where Chambers stood beside him. 'Who's your boyfriend?'

'Detective Chief Superintendent Chambers. National Crime Agency.' Chambers showed his warrant card, eliciting the sort of response he no doubt had been hoping for. Christie pulled her dressing gown tight, even though it hadn't exactly been revealing anything.

'Please, come in. I've got some coffee on.'

McLean trod the familiar path to the kitchen at the back, this time with Chambers rather than Ritchie in tow. Christie busied herself with mugs and milk, pouring fine-smelling coffee from a jug that would have been enough to supply half of CID. How a lone, single mother thought she was going to drink it all he had no idea. Her hangover must have been of epic proportions.

'You're not overly fond of Ms Grainger, the company secretary,' he said after they'd all settled at the breakfast bar.

'Company secretary? That what she's calling herself these days? Witch wouldn't know shorthand if it bit her on her scaly arse.'

'Are you saying she wasn't the secretary, Miss Christie?' Chambers cradled his mug of coffee like a small kitten. 'What was she then?'

'Joe always introduced her as a partner. She turned up round about the time his mum died. Sort of inveigled herself into the business.'

'Inveigled?' McLean asked the question, but he could see by Chambers' one raised eyebrow that he'd been thinking it too.

'Mind, this was a good few years back, when me and Ben were at uni. I only saw Joe from time to time then. I remember the funeral though.'

'She was there? Ms Grainger?'

'Oh, aye. She was there. Holding up old Jock like she'd been a family friend all his life. Poor man took Cat's death hard. I didn't see either of them for maybe a year after that, and when I did, Ms Grainger was in there with her feet under the table, just about running the place.'

'You think she and Mr McClymont senior . . .?' McLean let the question tail off as a look of horror spread across Christie's face.

'Good God no. Jock would never so much as look at another woman after Cat died. Doted on his son, mind you.'

McLean was about to press further. The story Christie

was painting was quite at odds with what Grainger had told him herself. But Chambers cut in, changing the subject with no subtlety whatsoever and even less sensitivity.

'The car McClymont was driving. Had it long, had he?'

For a moment Christie was taken aback. McLean imagined it couldn't be easy thinking swiftly with the mother of all headaches.

'His car? What's that got to do with anything?' she asked.

'It's part of an ongoing investigation,' Chambers said. 'We're fairly sure it was stolen.'

'Oh.' Christie swallowed a mouthful of coffee, holding the mug up to her neck like a shield. 'Well, no. He'd not had it long. Joe never did keep his cars long. Always trading them in for the latest model.'

'Do you know where he got them from?'

A short pause before answering, as if she were trying to work out where this was going. McLean almost pitied her. 'Never occurred to me to ask. He gave me my Range Rover what, four months ago? I just assumed it came from the local dealership.'

'You've got all the documents. Registration and so forth?' McLean asked.

'Of course. Why?'

McLean looked sideways at Chambers. He didn't know the man, had never worked with him before. Wasn't really sure if this counted as working with him now. On the other hand, he was a chief superintendent, so could make life awkward if he wanted. Even more so than Duguid and Brooks.

'I'd like one of my forensic specialists to have a look at

it, if that's OK?' He decided on the less confrontational route. After all, sometimes his hunches didn't play out. Just not often.

'Umm. OK. I guess. Will they need to take it away? Only I've not got anything else to take the girls to school in.'

Or go to Waitrose for smoked salmon and organic fair-trade chocolate bars. 'She should be able to look at it here. I'll get someone to phone and arrange a time.'

Chambers had been silent through the exchange, but the expression on his face suggested he didn't like not knowing what was going on. He was about to say something, but Christie beat him to it.

'There was one thing I thought a bit odd.' She left the thread dangling. Perhaps the coffee was working its magic.

'Go on,' McLean said.

'Well, you see, Joe used to take his dad up north a lot. Every couple of months, at least that I know of. And he'd always drive those flash cars of his. I went with them once. Me and the girls. I told you about it, remember?'

McLean nodded, unwilling to break her flow now that she was talking.

'Well, we all went up in a Mercedes estate that time. I remember it was like a barn inside, and all plush leather and stuff. The girls loved it. Only, we came home on the train after a week. It was all getting too much, and I thought Joe needed his time alone.'

'So what was the odd thing?' McLean asked, sensing Chambers about to jump in.

'Well, it's . . . I don't know. I never saw that car again, and far as I can tell Joe came home by train too. Not the first time, either. I picked him up from the station a couple of times, off the Inverness train, when I was sure he'd driven north.'

They let themselves out not long afterwards, leaving Christie to her coffee and hangover. She seemed to have hit the numb stage of grief; dealing with the deaths of two people who had been close to her couldn't have been easy. McLean made a note to make sure a family liaison officer accompanied Amanda Parsons when she went round to check over the Range Rover. Quite what having her one solid link to Joe McClymont taken away would do to her didn't bear thinking about.

'What was that all about, McLean? Duguid told me you were prone to flights of fancy, but I don't think I've ever seen—'

'Do you know the story about the wheelbarrow thief, sir?'

'I . . . what?'

'I don't remember the full details, but it was something along these lines. Bloke works in a factory, and every evening when his shift's over he wheels a barrow full of straw out through the gate. The security guards knew him, and every day they'd check the barrow, making sure he wasn't stealing stuff from the factory and hiding it in the straw. He never was, so they'd let him through.

'Come his retirement, the bloke finishes his shift and leaves. On his way out, one of the guards stops him and asks: "Five years you came and went. We were sure you were stealing something, but we never found out how."

'The old man looked at the guard and smiled. "You

always raked through the straw, every evening as I was going home. The thing is, I wasn't smuggling anything in the wheelbarrow. It was the barrow itself, see?"'

'Not sure I see your point. McClymont was a drug dealer, not a wheelbarrow salesman.'

'It's just a story, sir. The idea is the old boy was hiding something in plain sight. We've been looking at McClymont the wrong way, treating him like a drug smuggler. What if he was just a car thief?'

'A car thief? That not a bit low rent?'

'Not when you're nicking stuff worth fifty grand or more. Give it a new identity, ship it overseas. I've heard there's a big market for high-end motors in the Far East. Africa's quite keen on them too. The job they did on McClymont's own motor, they could've sold it here and nobody would have known better.'

'Why take them north? Why not ship them out of Rosyth or Leith? Or drive them down to London and stick them through the Channel Tunnel?'

'I think that's something for your lot to figure out, don't you? The point is he was taking cars north but coming home by train. If our forensic expert's right, and I'm inclined to trust her, then the cars were ringers. That car,' he pointed at the all-too-familiar-looking Range Rover parked on the driveway in front of the house, 'is a ringer too. I'm fairly certain it really belongs to Detective Superintendent Duguid, as it happens. Or at least his insurance company.'

Chambers stared at the car as if he'd never seen one in his life before. 'This? But surely there's thousands like it out there.'

'Maybe. But they don't all have a dent in the back door there. I saw Duguid reverse into one of the Transit vans back at the station, six months ago? Something like that. Dent in exactly the same spot.'

Chambers said nothing for a while, just kept looking at the back of the Range Rover and stroking his chin.

'OK. Since you seem to have all the answers. Where does Ms Grainger fit into all this, then?'

'Brains of the outfit?' McLean offered, getting a sceptical look in response.

'Look, did you ever meet the McClymonts? Speak to them?'

Chambers shook his head.

'Well I did. Just the once, but it was probably enough. I didn't get the impression they were the types to think out of the box much. The plans they had for my place were unimaginative, just trying to cram as many flats into the space as possible. Probably as cheaply as possible too. For all I know, they might have been dealing drugs, might have been doing anything they could to get money. Laundering it through the development company. But the moment they died, Grainger does a runner? Sounds like she knew what they were up to at the very least.'

'And now she's disappeared completely. Fucking marvellous.'

'Ah, so you've decided to show up for work after all. You do know you're supposed to be conducting a murder investigation, right?'

McLean had barely stepped through the back door to the station before the words rang out across the hallway.

Detective Superintendent Duguid stood by the stairs, his face dark and threatening. A couple of uniforms chatting nearby looked around nervously before scurrying off, not wanting to get caught in the crossfire. McLean glanced at his watch, already knowing that it was approaching noon.

'Actually I was in at half-five this morning, sir, preparing a briefing for six. I'd have invited you along, but it was all a bit last-minute. Didn't think you'd appreciate a call that early.'

Duguid's scowl deepened, the tic of a vein on his forehead a sure indicator that someone was going to get a tongue-lashing or worse.

'What's so bloody important it takes precedence over two dead bodies?'

'My "friends" the McClymonts, sir.' McLean made bunny ears with his fingers. 'Seems there was more to their business than even the NCA suspected.'

'What are you going on about? Since when were you working on that case anyway?'

'Since you and the DCC sent me up to Inverness to ID the bodies, sir. Since I got a call from forensics and found out the car was stolen.'

'Stolen? How?' Duguid's rage bled away, replaced by bewilderment. 'When?'

'I don't have the full details, sir. As you can see, I've just got back in. I'm hoping there's a full forensic report waiting for me in my office. Once I've had a chance to look at it I can bring everyone up to speed. Oh, and I might have found your old Range Rover, by the way.'

Duguid's mouth had dropped open, giving McLean an unenviable view of the detective superintendent's chipped and yellowing teeth. He looked like he was struggling to process all the information that had barged its way into a brain fully prepared for tearing off a strip from whomever he could find.

'Wh—' Duguid began, but before he could say anything more, the back door to the station banged open. McLean turned to see a worried-looking DC MacBride tapping wildly at his tablet. At the same moment as the constable looked up, McLean's phone pinged a message. Duguid's did the same a second later.

'Sir. Ah, sirs.' MacBride looked momentarily confused, then rallied. 'I've just messaged you. Sorry. Need to get back to Sighthill. We've found another body.'

56

The building looked nothing special from the outside, much the same as McClymont Developments across the car park. Tucked into the far corner, close to the railway line, its windows were boarded up and a faded 'To let' sign hung at a drunken angle from the frontage. The only way in was through a solid metal door set into a much larger roller shutter concealing a loading bay beyond. DS Ritchie must have seen him coming, as she met him out past the edge of the police tape boundary.

'How did anyone even know to look in here?' McLean asked. He'd parked a good distance away from the squad cars and forensic vans. The car park might have been large, but the individual bays were narrow.

'Stuart had some of the uniforms go door to door round the other businesses, like you asked, sir. Overzealous constable knocked on this one even though it's obviously empty. Found it wasn't locked and thought he'd check it out before calling the letting agent. He found . . . well, I'm not really sure how to describe it. A body, for certain.' DS Ritchie had more of a spring in her step than McLean could remember seeing in a while, no doubt at the prospect of getting her teeth into a particularly interesting case. Either that or Daniel hadn't made it home to the rectory as early as might be expected of a man of the cloth.

Shaking the idea from his head, he followed her across

the car park and ducked under the crime-scene tape, almost immediately receiving a complaining cough from the nearest scene of crime officer.

'You'll be wanting to put on some overalls if you're going in there.' The SOCO herself was dressed in a full white boiler suit, hood pulled up tight over her hair. McLean could only tell it was a she because her face mask hung around her neck on its elastic string. She was sitting in the back of one of the Transit vans, munching on a sandwich, but put it carefully back in its Tupperware box before reaching around and pulling out white paper overalls and something that looked a bit like a cross between a shower cap and the bag you brought your curry home in.

'Grubby in there, is it?' he asked as he passed a pair of overboots to Ritchie.

'Quite the opposite. Place is cleaner than a Labrador's dinner dish. Doubt we'll find anything in there unless you lot traipse it in. Could do without the hassle of working out what's what.' The SOCO picked up her sandwich and took another bite, conversation over.

McLean waited until they had reached the door before climbing into the paper suit and slipping the overshoes on. He snapped on a pair of latex gloves for good measure before ducking into the darkness beyond. It was a large loading area, as might be expected for such a place. Looking around, however, he started to see what the SOCO had meant. In marked contrast to the dust and grime of McClymont Developments, it was spotlessly clean. More like the sort of laboratory where they build satellites than a storage room for a firm of electricians. Arc lights overhead reflected off a smooth floor that squeaked under his feet as he walked to the far side and an open doorway. A bunny-suited SOCO was kneeling by the door, brushing at the frame with a fingerprint kit. She looked up as his shadow passed over her, and McLean recognised the face of Amanda Parsons.

'Didn't expect to see you here. Thought you were doing the cars across town.'

Parsons grinned. 'They're no' going anywhere. And we're a bit short-staffed right now, with all these bodies you keep finding. I've got fingerprint training. Overtime's always handy.'

'Well I don't think there'll be a problem with that. The pathologist here?' McLean asked.

'In there.' Parsons cocked a head towards the entrance. 'You been in?'

'No. Not sure I want to, from what I've been hearing.'

'I'd best see for myself then,' McLean said, and stepped through.

'Good Christ. What is this place?'

McLean stood just inside the open door, staring upon a scene that might have been from a modern horror movie. Half a dozen intensive care beds were arranged in a semi-circle, each attended by their own motley collection of life-support machinery. Much of the kit seemed last generation, or perhaps older, but the effect was chilling regardless, especially given the setting. This was a disused warehouse in a bad part of town, after all. Not exactly the Western General Hospital.

Of the six beds, five were obviously unoccupied, the machinery pushed neatly to the walls at the head of each.

The last bed was obscured by the city pathologist and his assistant deep in discussion about the body they were examining. McLean was about to head over and see what all the fuss was about when a voice distracted him.

'It gets better. Come have a look at this.' He turned to see Jemima Cairns, dressed in the full bunny suit so beloved of the forensic services. It never ceased to amaze him how they could recognise each other in that get-up, but somehow they managed. She led him through another door into a smaller room, fitted out like a research laboratory.

'Some of this stuff's better than the kit we've got back at HQ.' Dr Cairns picked up a microscope and peered at the manufacturer's logo on the base.

'Expensive?'

'Very. Well, some of it.' She put the microscope back, moved down the bench to where a smooth-sided box with a smoked Perspex cover sat. Clicking open the cover revealed an empty shell. 'Most of it's mock-ups, though. The sort of thing they bring along to medical research conferences.'

'So this is all a sham then?' McLean walked across to the wall freezers, reached out to open one then stopped. 'Can I?'

'Knock yourself out. They're all empty. We've dusted the place for prints, too. Only one set so far and they look like they belong to the victim.' Dr Cairns nodded at the tall freezer. 'He opened that. Doesn't seem to have touched anything else.'

'Nothing at all?'

'Not a thing. This place is as clean as I've ever seen. Surgically clean.'

'What about through there?' McLean pointed back to the larger room, where the beds were, and the body.

'Much the same. Oh, we'll keep looking, but we've not found anything yet. Got to hand it to whoever did this. They know how to sterilise a crime scene.'

'So people keep telling me, but I've not even seen the body yet.'

Dr Cairns raised an eyebrow. 'You've not?'

'Only just arrived. I was going to have a look when you dragged me in here.'

'Sorry. I didn't realise.'

'No worries. Never hurts to look at the whole scene anyway. Sometimes better to do that first, before you even look at the body.'

Cairns said nothing as McLean pulled open the freezer door. As she'd told him, it was empty. It didn't appear to be switched on, either. He walked slowly down the narrow aisle between the spotlessly clean work benches. Stuck out a finger and ran it over the nearest flat surface, then inspected his fingertip for dust. There was none.

'What do you make of it?' he asked.

'This? If I didn't know better I'd say someone was making a movie.'

McLean paused in picking up a pipette. Could it be that simple? Had they stumbled upon some film set that nobody knew about?

'It's not though,' Dr Cairns said. 'A movie set, that is. There's nowhere to put the cameras, for one thing. And then there's the body, of course. That's real enough, not a prop.'

'It's still a set though, a sham. Not a real medical lab?'

'Not one I'd want to work in. Like I say, most of this kit's fake.'

'But why would someone go to all that effort?'

'That's your department, Inspector. Not mine.' Dr Cairns scratched at her forehead where the tight-fitting hood of her overalls pressed against her skin, then gave up and pushed the whole thing back off her head. 'But if I was to hazard a guess, I'd say someone was playing some kind of con. Wouldn't be at all surprised if there wasn't big money involved. This lot must have cost a packet, even if most of it's not real.'

McLean was about to reply, but a familiar face appeared at the door. DS Ritchie's eyes widened in surprise as she saw the set-up.

'They're ready to move the body, sir. Thought you'd want to see it before they do.'

The large room was no less impressive for his having seen the laboratory next door to it. McLean wondered how anyone had managed to get all that machinery in without being noticed, wondered too where it had all come from. These and a dozen other immediate questions fled his mind as he approached the bed and the body lying on it.

He was naked, skinny like a man who hasn't eaten in months, and impossibly pale. Sightless eyes stared up at the ceiling, slightly filmed as if the eyeballs had begun to ossify. His face was cadaverous, mouth hanging open to reveal yellowing teeth. Thinning hair, lank and in need of a cut, hung from his skull and splayed out on the pillow. McLean's first impression was of someone in the first stages of mummification.

'Tony. Good of you to join us.' Angus Cadwallader stood on the far side of the bed, his assistant Tracy at his side. Two technicians hovered behind him with a gurney, ready to take the body away. It seemed a bit unnecessary; they could have just wheeled out the bed he was lying on.

'What have we got here, Angus?' McLean asked. Looking at the face he found it almost impossible to decide if the man had been young or old. His skin had an odd pallor to it, and he looked shrunken, almost as if the bed had begun to swallow him.

'Something very nasty indeed. And I say that as someone who thought he'd seen it all.' Cadwallader reached forward and gently lifted the dead man's arm. As he did so, McLean noticed that it had a cannula inserted into it, a long tube leading away to a machine at the head of the bed.

'See this?' McLean nodded, following Cadwallader's hand as he traced the tube back. It was clear plastic, but there were occasional clots of almost black material in it.

'This is a dialysis machine,' the pathologist continued. 'You'll be familiar with how it works.'

'I thought they usually had two tubes. One out, one back in again.' McLean had a terrible feeling he knew where the conversation was going. He looked back at the man's face again. Not old, quite young, really. Just drained.

'You always were quick on the uptake, Tony. You're quite right. Normally the blood would flow through the machine, which filters out all the unpleasant by-products of metabolism. Then the freshened blood is returned to the body. This . . .' Cadwallader paused for a moment, something McLean couldn't recall his old friend ever doing at a crime scene before. Normally it was a job to get him to stop talking, such was his enthusiasm at hunting down clues from the recently deceased.

'This machine's been modified. Not sure exactly how, that's something for the technicians to puzzle out. It's taken his blood and . . . well, I'm not entirely sure what it's done with it.'

'So what you're saying is he bled to death.'

'No, what I'm saying, Tony, is he was bled to death. There's a difference. This man has had almost all of the blood drained from him. And slowly, too.'

'Slowly? How so?'

'If it had been quick, if he'd had his throat cut or something, his blood pressure would have dropped fast and his heart would have stopped. Doing it slowly like this dragged it out. He's been placed on the bed very carefully, too. Everything slopes down to this point. It's impossible to drain all the blood out of a body without pumping something in to replace it, but this comes pretty damned close.'

'How long would it take, do you reckon? An hour? Longer?'

'Much longer. This could have taken half a day.'

McLean shuddered, though that might have been because of the chill in the room. 'It'd be painless though, wouldn't it? And he'd have passed out soon enough?'

'That really depends on how slowly the machine was working, but he'd have known what was happening. Jesus, what a horrible thing to do to a person.'

McLean looked from the shrunken, shrivelled body to the snaking tube, the corrupted dialysis machine and then back to the man's face. Clouded eyes stared straight up, as if pleading to heaven for salvation. He followed that gaze to the ceiling, white paint bright in the glare from the arc lights. The shadows of the metal roof beams painted a dark cross directly overhead.

57

'You realise we're going to have to draft in officers from Strathclyde to help make up the numbers? You've no idea what a mess that's going to make of the staffing rosters.'

McLean stood in his usual spot in Duguid's office on the top floor, trying hard to focus on the detective super-intendent and not let his thoughts wander out the window. This meeting was a formality, a chore that had to be done before he could get on with the job. As usual there was nowhere for him to sit, and frankly he was happier stand-ing. The same couldn't be said for DCI Brooks, whose hulking presence made the large room seem somehow inadequate.

'Hang the bloody rosters, Charles. We've got a third murder in as many weeks. Nothing simple about any of them. What the fuck's happening to the city that every-one's hacking each other to bits?'

Brooks prowled back and forth as he ranted, his shoes making odd 'chuff chuff chuff' noises on the carpet tiles. It was hot in the office, and sweat sheened the detective chief inspector's shaven head, dripping down into his eyebrows. Occasionally a bead would make it to one of his chins and then break free.

'We should pool our efforts again.'

Brooks stopped mid-turn, his anger focused on McLean.

'You're not really suggesting they're linked are you, McLean? You know how rare serial killers are?'

'It wouldn't surprise me if they were connected, actually. Like you said, three murders in as many weeks, all Category A. That's more than a statistical outlier; it'd be stupid of us not to consider a possible link between them.'

He regretted using the S-word almost as soon as it slipped out of his mouth, but he was tired and it was hot and he was finding it hard to think straight with Brooks moving around like a caged bear. McLean felt the atmosphere in the room chill, though not enough to bring any comfort.

'Both Detective Chief Inspector Brooks and I know how to run a major incident enquiry, McLean.' Duguid's voice was a low rumble like the threat of thunder.

'I'm sorry, sir. I didn't mean to suggest you . . . I only meant there are aspects of all three investigations that can be combined to save time. Like we did before. No point going over the same actions over and over again. It was true when we combined efforts with the Stevenson and Shenks cases. It's even more true now.'

'And you're volunteering to coordinate this, are you?' Brooks asked. McLean resisted the urge to suggest that both senior officers knew how to run a major incident enquiry. The irony would likely have been lost on them.

'If you think a detective inspector is sufficiently senior to be heading up such a thing, then I guess so. I'd have thought the press would expect someone a bit higher up the food chain though.'

'Oh yes. The press. Tell me, how is Jo Dalgliesh these days? I hear you two are getting quite pally.'

It was his weak spot and Brooks knew it. McLean rounded on the DCI, struggling to control the anger that flared up in him. 'If you had any fucking idea—'

'That's enough, McLean.' Duguid's barked words surprised him into silence more effectively than McLean would have thought possible. He looked back at the detective superintendent leaning forward in his chair, elbows on the desk and long-fingered hands pressed together tightly.

'John, you know as well as I do that Dalgliesh is helping us with the Stevenson case. She was the first to notice him missing, she got us access to all his research and she knows more about what he was working on than anyone.'

'She's a bloody menace is what,' Brooks muttered under his breath, but loud enough to be heard.

'I don't think any of us disagree with you there. But she's useful and at the moment she's on our side. I'd quite like to keep things that way for as long as possible.'

Brooks glowered, but said nothing. Duguid must have taken that as a tacit agreement. McLean hoped so, otherwise the DCI really was as stupid as he so often looked.

'OK. I'll front up all three investigations. John, you'll be in overall command of operations. McLean, you and Spence can coordinate. Get a team on to analysing the similarities between each murder.' Duguid slumped back in his seat as if the effort of making such a momentous decision had exhausted him. 'And let's just pray we don't get more bodies turning up any time soon.'

*

'His name's James Whitely. Friends all called him Jim. He was a consultant at the Western General, specialising in paediatric oncology. Worked at the Sick Kids too.'

Running out of room at the station, they'd taken over a corner of the Ben Stevenson major incident room to make a start on the new investigation. DC MacBride had somehow managed to find space for more computers, and a small army of uniforms and admin staff were beginning the process of kicking the investigation into life. Compared to the quiet of the rest of the room, it was a veritable maelstrom of activity.

'Who ID'd him?' McLean asked.

MacBride consulted his tablet. 'One of the pathologists recognised him. Dr MacPhail?'

'And we've had that confirmed? Next of kin?'

'No next of kin, no. But his boss confirmed it, and he's been missing from work over a week.'

McLean stared at the clean whiteboard as a uniform constable pinned a large photograph of Jim Whitely's pale dead face to it with magnets.

'He worked at the Sick Kids, you say. Same as Muriel Shenks?'

'Maureen Shenks, yes.' MacBride swiped at his little screen. 'You think there might be a connection?'

'Two people murdered? No obvious motive or killer for either? Both work at the same place and probably knew each other? I'd be astonished if there weren't.'

'What if he killed her?'

McLean paused before responding, not quite allowing himself to hope it would be that easy. 'Go on,' he said after a while.

'Well, Whitely's body, the way it was found. It's creepy as . . .' MacBride struggled for words.

'Creepy as fuck?' McLean suggested.

'Aye, that. But it could be suicide, couldn't it? I mean, he could've plugged himself into that machine and, I don't know, just let it drain all his blood away?'

McLean tried not to shudder. 'Interesting theory, Constable, and given how improbable his means of death was, it's just possible he did it himself. It had to be someone with a great deal of medical knowledge, after all.' He walked over to the whiteboard, searched around until he found a marker pen and wrote 'suicide?' close to the newly pinned death-mask photograph. All around him there was sudden silence as heads turned to look at what he'd written.

'Is that even possible?' He looked around to see that Detective Sergeant Ritchie had just entered the room and was, like everyone else, staring at the whiteboard.

'To be honest, I've no idea. But it's as good a place as any to start.' McLean addressed the collected police and admin staff, now that he had their undivided attention. 'Assume nothing, but I want this line of enquiry pursued as far as it will go. We need to trace Dr Whitely's movements over the last month. Interview all his work colleagues; I want to know about his state of mind. And talk to everyone who works in that industrial unit too. We need to know who's been in and out of there recently. If there's CCTV, so much the better.'

'You want me to get started on organising all that?' Ritchie asked. McLean could see she wasn't all that keen. Beside him, DC MacBride had already started breaking the problem down and assigning tasks to various members of the team. Most of whom were more senior than him, but seemed happy to defer to his assumed authority.

'Have we got a home address for Whitely?' he asked in a moment when the detective constable paused for breath.

'Here, sir.' MacBride tapped a couple of times on his screen. 'I've sent it to your phone.' Sure enough, the handset vibrated and chimed in his jacket pocket. McLean pulled it out, stared at the address on the screen until it blanked out again. Sciennes. Not far. Just a matter of getting hold of some keys.

'OK, you man the fort here. Get cracking on the suicide angle.' He turned back to DS Ritchie. 'You can come with me. See what kind of a person this Jim Whitely was.'

58

'I thought they paid doctors well these days.'

DS Ritchie stood in the dank hallway of an unremarkable tenement block in the back end of Sciennes, and sniffed. Getting in had been far easier than McLean had hoped; the cheap entry-phone system had long since broken, and the front door had opened to a gentle shove.

'Way the housing market's going, it's probably all he could afford.' He peered at the tarnished brass nameplate on one of the two downstairs flat doors, trying to make out the name in the half-light. It didn't spell 'Whitely', that was for sure.

'I guess it's handy for the Sick Kids.' Ritchie bent to inspect the other door, straightening up quickly when it opened.

'You want summat?' A fat, balding man stood in the open doorway, scratching at a flabby belly that strained to escape from a pair of stained pyjama bottoms. He had a threadbare dressing gown on, but it hung open to reveal rather more than anyone would want to see.

'Detective Sergeant Ritchie.' She produced her warrant card, holding it up for the man to see. 'We're looking for James Whitely's flat.'

'Jim? Top floor. Left-hand side. The blue door.' The fat man twitched his head upwards in the general direction, his jowls wobbling in time with the motion. 'What's he done?'

'You know him well, Mr . . .?' McLean stepped forward from the shadows. The fat man's eyes widened in surprise.

'Here, I ain't done nuthin.'

'I never suggested you had. I was looking for Mr Whitely's flat, but I'm also going to want to talk to everyone who knows him. Seems like you're pretty high up on that list, Mr . . .?'

'Durran. Hunter Durran. And who're you?'

'Detective Inspector McLean.' He showed his own warrant card. Mr Durran pulled his dressing gown closed and belted it up. An improvement, but still rather more of him was on show than was strictly necessary.

'How long has Whitely lived here?' Ritchie asked. Durran's eyes flicked away from McLean and back to her again.

'I dunno. Three, mebbe four years?'

'And you knew him well?'

'Wouldn't say well. Keeps to hisself mostly. Pays his rent on time. Quiet. Can't ask for much more.' Durran paused a moment, then added. 'You said knew him well. He's no' dead is he?'

'Pays his rent?' McLean ignored the fat man's question. 'You're his landlord?'

Durran rubbed a finger over his top lip, sniffed so loudly that for a moment McLean thought he was going to spit on the floor. 'Aye.'

'You'll have a key to his flat then.'

'You got a warrant?'

'I can get a warrant, if you insist.' McLean made a big show of pulling his phone out of his pocket, tapping at the screen. 'It'll take a while though, and I'll have to station a couple of uniform officers here while we wait. No one in or out until we're done. Not you, not any of the other people living in this block.'

'You can't do that. I—'

'I can do that, Mr Durran. If I have to. You're right, Mr Whitely is dead, and under very suspicious circumstances. You can't begin to understand the powers that gives me.' He stared at the fat man, locking eyes with him until he backed down.

'I'll just get the keys then.'

The smell was the first thing he noticed. It reminded McLean of his university days, those times when the pile of clothes in the corner of the bedroom was twice as big as the pile spilling out of the chest of drawers, and a trip to the laundry couldn't really be put off any longer. Unlike his student flat though, Dr Jim Whitely's tiny top-floor apartment was relatively tidy. It just hadn't been aired recently, and the clothes spilling from the top of the laundry basket in the corner of the shower room had been accumulating for a long while. Either that or they'd been breeding.

'You think he ever opened a window?' Ritchie peered through an open doorway, swiftly stepping back into the hall and shaking her head as if to get rid of some particularly unpleasant odour.

'Probably not.' McLean looked around the shower room. It was small, like so many of its kind in these blocks. Being top floor, it had a skylight over the shower. Most of the remaining space was taken up by the overflowing laundry bin, a tiny basin and a toilet you'd not be able to stand at and close the door. There was enough floor to turn around in if you had a child's feet, but only if you didn't mind trampling over all the papers strewn about the place.

Bending down, he picked one up between latex-gloved fingers. It was a scientific paper from a medical journal, that much McLean could tell. Most of the words in the title he could only hazard a guess at, though. He crouched down, shuffling the rest of them towards him. All scientific papers, all well thumbed, all about as easy to understand as the offside rule.

'You might want to come and look at this, sir.'

McLean stood up, locating DS Ritchie by the one open door off the hallway. It led into a sitting room that overlooked the street, mostly giving a fine view of the living rooms opposite. The floor in this room was strewn with more papers, expensive-looking textbooks and several lined A4 pads with scrawly handwritten notes all over them. A sofa had been pushed into the bay window, but it was covered in books. Only a single armchair offered anywhere to sit, and this was obviously Whitely's preferred place of repose, judging by the coffee mugs, empty plates and surrounding circle of yet more papers. Some of these appeared to have been organised into separate piles, though by what filing criteria he couldn't begin to guess.

'Seems Dr Whitely had a bit of a bee in his bonnet.' McLean stepped carefully over one pile of papers, finding a space of carpet just about big enough to stand in. Ritchie must have used it to stepping-stone her way to the middle of the room. She nodded at the wall beside the door through which he had just come.

'That remind you of anything?'

McLean turned carefully, aware that a misstep would

result in a cascade of paperwork that might bury them, and would certainly annoy the forensics team who would surely have to go over the place. A cheap desk had been shoved in behind the door, an elderly laptop computer and printer taking up what area of its surface wasn't heaped with yet more papers. But it was the wall that was of most interest.

It looked a little like an incident room for a particularly complicated and unusual crime. A half-dozen photographs were pinned up in a line, about a foot apart. Each showed a child or young man, each quite clearly taken whilst the subject was in hospital undergoing some kind of treatment. A couple were smiling despite their bald heads and nasal tubes. One was giving a thumbs-up to the camera, though the hope in the gesture didn't spread as far as his eyes. Around each photograph were pinned front pages and abstracts from more medical journals, Post-it notes with question marks scribbled on them, the occasional barely legible word. And running over it all and the glimpse of clear wallpaper behind, thick black lines were drawn with a heavy marker pen linking seemingly disparate ideas together.

McLean stared at it all a long time before realising that he'd been holding his breath. He let it out in a long sigh.

'I think it's fair to say Jim Whitely was a troubled man.'

'Troubled enough to kill that nurse then stage his own suicide?' Ritchie asked.

It was an interesting idea, but life was never that easy.

'No, I don't think so.' McLean took a step closer to the desk, brushing a pile of papers with his leg as he went. It slid sideways, fanning out on the floor. He ignored it, leaning over the desk until he could begin to decipher the scrawled words. He followed a line from a paper that appeared to be about cell-line therapy, whatever that was, through a single word 'blastocysts?', across to another paper about transfusions and then on up to the photograph of the young man with his thumbs up. He stepped back again, more carefully this time, shoved his hand in his pocket and pulled out his phone. 'No, this isn't the work of someone thinking of killing themselves any time soon. Quite the opposite.'

'How do you mean?'

'He's been trying to save these kids. Looking for any way possible. He's obsessed with this. It's what drives him. He couldn't give this up even if he wanted to.'

59

'Well look at you, all grown up and smart.'

Gran stands behind me, hands on my shoulders as we both look in the mirror. It's the first time I've tried on my new school uniform and it feels very grown-up. The jacket was my father's; it smells of mothballs and it's too long in the arms. But it was his. He wore it just like me, years ago when he was a young boy. I can't quite get my head around that, but I feel very proud to be following in his footsteps.

'Take it off now. I'll show you how to fold it properly.'

Gran takes my jacket from me, checks the pockets even though I've only been wearing it for five minutes. Then she does something I can't quite follow, turning it inside out, folding and tucking until it's a neat little square of shiny fabric. She puts it down on my bed alongside all the other clothes, some old, some new, that I'll be taking with me to school tomorrow. The old leather travelling trunk lies open on the floor. It has my grandfather's initials stencilled on the lid and paper tags tied to the handles, foreign-sounding destinations inked on to them in fading, ancient script.

We spend most of the afternoon packing, or at least that's what it feels like. Outside the summer is fading to autumn, but it's still warm and sunny. Ideal weather for climbing trees. Instead I learn the art of fitting things into a tiny space, as shirts, socks, underpants, trousers, jackets, towels, flannels, ties, handkerchiefs and a dozen other things I never thought I'd need are all neatly stowed away. Everything has been labelled with my name, red letters on little cloth tags. I've never needed my name on things before. It makes me feel important, but also a little scared. Is everyone else going to have exactly the same clothes?

'There. That's perfect.' Gran closes the lid of the trunk, only having to kneel on it slightly to get the clasps to fit. I try to lift one end, but it's far too heavy.

'Don't worry about that.' She laughs, and tousles my hair the way I really don't like. 'I'll get Jenkins to take it to the station. It'll go on ahead of you.'

Finished with the packing, I sense my opportunity. 'Can I go see Norman? Won't have a chance to again. Not till Christmas.'

I've not seen Norman since he fell out of the tree and cut himself. It seems a lifetime ago even though it's probably only a couple of days. His mum was so angry that time, I didn't dare go back. Not until now, at least.

'Norman's not well, Tony. He had to go to the hospital.' I can see the worry in Gran's face, but she hides it with a smile. 'Don't worry though. He'll be fine in a week or two. You can write to him from school, tell him all about it. And you'll see him in a few months.'

I never do write to him, of course. Never see him again at all.

60

'Sorry I'm late, Angus. I take it you started without me.'

'Nearly done, actually. Take a pew and I'll give you the potted history in a minute.'

McLean had left DS Ritchie in charge of sorting out forensics at Whitely's flat and questioning the neighbours about his movements over the previous weeks. He'd set out across the Meadows, past the university and down into the Cowgate where the city mortuary carried out its grisly unseen business, hoping that the walk would give him a chance to think things through. He needed headspace to try and rationalise the alarming similarities between Ben Stevenson and Jim Whitely. Not in their deaths, but in their lives, their single-minded obsession. But the heat had made it difficult to breathe, and the noise was far worse than he remembered from his days in uniform. His thoughts had been stuck in a loop, missing some crucial piece that would unlock the puzzle. The cool interior of the mortuary had come as a welcome relief, the distraction of Dr Whitely's post-mortem doubly so. Now he sat in a hard plastic chair with his back to the wall of the examination theatre, watching silently as Angus Cadwallader examined the dead man.

'Not a nice case, this one.'

McLean looked around to see Dr MacPhail, no doubt

here as witness to the proceedings should corroboration be required at any inquest into the death.

'Shouldn't you be . . .?' McLean nodded his head in the direction of the examination table. 'You know, witnessing?'

'I probably shouldn't be here at all, actually. Since I was the one identified him.'

McLean remembered then, the conversation with DC MacBride earlier that morning. 'Of course. You knew him. I'm sorry.'

'Oh, he wasn't a friend or anything. Just so happens we both went through med school at the same time. I'd see him around from time to time if I was up at the hospital. We'd nod, say hello. Nothing more than that.'

'Med school? I thought Whitely was older than that.'

'I'll take that as a compliment, Inspector.' Dr MacPhail gave him a lopsided grin and slumped into the next chair along. He smelled of dead people, with an underlying sharp scent that was familiar from somewhere McLean couldn't quite place. 'I'm older than I look, really. And what happened to Jim there. Well . . .'

'Do you remember much about him? When he was a student?'

'Now you're asking.' MacPhail puffed out his cheeks and scratched at his head. 'He was always quite intense, I guess. Bright. He never seemed to struggle with exams. Didn't talk to him much. We moved in different circles, had different friends. He went into paediatrics, too, which is kind of the opposite of my speciality. At least most of the time.'

'If you two lovebirds have got a moment to spare.'

Angus Cadwallader's loud voice echoed across the examination theatre. McLean looked up to see him staring in their direction.

'You all finished?' He stood up, feeling the sweat on his back where it had soaked his shirt and then cooled down.

'As much as I can do here. The lab results will take a little longer, but I think I can comfortably say Dr Whitely didn't take his own life.'

'Didn't?' McLean felt that familiar cold sensation in the pit of his stomach. He'd not been overly keen on the murder/suicide hypothesis, but it at least had the merit of being simple. And it would have solved two cases at the same time. 'What killed him, then?'

'Oh, that bit's easy. His heart gave out when his blood pressure dropped too low. He'd have been unconscious by then, which I guess is a blessing.'

'And you're sure he couldn't have done it to himself?' McLean crossed the room and stared at the violated, naked body.

'He could have done it to himself. Technically. It's a bit of a gruesome way to die though, and far too elaborate. So many things could have gone wrong, and then there's all that kit to lug into that warehouse. In my experience people wanting to kill themselves don't go in for that kind of spectacle.'

'No. You're right. Would just have been neater.'

'Death is never neat, Tony.' Cadwallader's scolding was friendly, but there nevertheless.

'I know, Angus. This one even less than most.'

'Yes, well. There's other reasons why I can say with a fair degree of certainty that it wasn't suicide. This, for instance. Cadwallader moved away from the head, down one arm, then picked up a hand, showing the thin, pale wrist to McLean. 'There's ligature marks here. There were straps on the table where we found him, but they were undone. He lost so much blood it was hard to see at the scene, but here it's fairly obvious he was tied down to start with.'

'He was strapped down until after he fell unconscious?'

'Or at least until he was too weak to do anything about it, yes.'

'So whoever did this would have watched him die.'

'That or gone away and then come back. But given the method of killing, the lengths he went to, I'd have to say he most probably watched.'

McLean shuddered at the thought of it, but before he could comment, Cadwallader had moved around the table to the dead man's neck.

'Oh, and there's this of course.' He pointed to a tiny mark just below the ear.

'Injection site?'

'See, you do learn things occasionally. Yes, indeed, it's an injection site. He didn't have much blood left in him, poor fellow, but we've sent some off for screening. I suspect a fast-acting sedative, something to knock him out so that whoever did this to him could get him hooked up to that infernal machine.'

McLean took a step back, staring once more at the whole body laid out on its back. After the cruel incisions of the post-mortem, and Dr Sharp's expert stitching to put him back together again, he couldn't really think of Whitely as a person any more. Or maybe it was just that he hadn't had time to build a picture of the man yet, could only think of him as this bloodless corpse.

'There's one question I notice you haven't asked me yet,' Cadwallader said.

'Time of death. I know. I was getting there.'

'Me too. The blood thing makes it difficult to be accurate, so I've sent off some samples for testing. My best estimate though is that he was in that place no more than a week.'

'That fits with when he was last seen at the hospital. Gives us something to work on.' McLean touched Cadwallader gently on the arm. 'Thanks, Angus. I'll see myself out.'

He was halfway to the door when he remembered something, turned back. 'Actually, there was one other thing.'

Cadwallader raised a quizzical eyebrow. 'Just one?'

'Well, yes. That heart, you know, the one we found at Ben Stevenson's place. Did you get round to examining that yet?'

'The heart? I think that was one of Tom's.' Cadwallader turned his attention to his fellow pathologist. 'That right, wasn't it?'

'Yes. Did it a couple of days back. You should have had the report by now.'

McLean pictured his office, tucked away at the back of the station. The image swam easily to his mind, a stack of paperwork covering his desk, more spilled out over the floor. What he couldn't remember was if he'd actually been in it any time in the past week.

'You couldn't give me the executive summary, could you?'

*

'It's human. Quite healthy, really. Belonged to someone in their late thirties, early forties. Male, given the size.'

Dr MacPhail bent over a bench in a small laboratory off the main examination theatre. McLean stood behind him and just enough to the side to be able to see the object laid out on a metal tray. The heart had been cleaned up, the strange green foliage removed from it and sent away for analysis. Now it looked unpleasantly like the kind of thing you might find in one of the more esoteric butchers' shops. The kind where you could buy all the parts of the animal never intended for eating unless they'd been finely minced, mixed with oatmeal and spices, shoved in a sheep's stomach and boiled first.

'Any idea whose it is?'

'Not a hundred per cent sure. Still waiting for the DNA match to come back. But I've narrowed it down.' MacPhail consulted the top sheet of the report he'd printed out before leading McLean into the lab. 'Judging by its condition, and the place we found it, I'd estimate it's been out of its owner's body a month.'

'Forcibly removed?' McLean stared at the organ, looking for signs of violence. It just looked like a piece of meat, the veins and arteries neatly cut a decent length from the bulb of the four chambers. He really didn't need another murder to add to the growing list.

'Depends what you mean by forcibly.' MacPhail picked up the heart as if it were nothing of great importance, turned it this way and that as he pointed out markings only he could see. 'It's been cut out, of course, but whoever it belonged to was dead before that happened.'

'How do you mean?'

'This is a donor heart. Or it was meant to be. You can see from the way it's been cut. Here, and here.'

'A donor? But surely there'd be records. We'd know if one had gone missing before . . . before it could be used. Wouldn't we?'

'We should, yes. Though sadly not every organ harvested ends up in a new body. Things go wrong.'

McLean didn't want to ask what. It wasn't all that relevant anyway. 'So do we know whose it is? Where it came from?'

'Not yet. Still waiting for confirmation. I've asked around the hospitals about recent transplants too. We should have a name and a place soon enough. Thing is though, this has been preserved.'

'That unusual?'

'Very. Especially the way it's been done. Far as I can tell this is embalming fluid. The stuff undertakers used to use. That's what's giving it this odd smell, and why it's only partially rotted.'

61

'Right then. You all know what's happened. We've got three dead bodies all killed in the last six weeks. The chances of them not being connected are hardly worth thinking about, so we're combining all three investigations as of now.'

McLean stood to one side, listening as Detective Superintendent Duguid addressed the troops. To give him some small credit, this was the sort of job Dagwood was quite good at. Actually coordinating an investigation not so much, but being a figurehead and acting important he had down pat.

'Now I know we haven't got very far with the investigation into Ben Stevenson's murder, and the enquiry into the dead nurse isn't much better. But there's a good chance now that we can begin to analyse the patterns emerging. Start to put together some kind of profile. Paint a picture of our killer and work out his motivations.'

Straight out of a textbook, and one a couple of decades out of date if McLean was any judge. He glanced sideways at DS Ritchie, who rolled her eyes conspiratorially as she saw him looking. Most of the station was assembled in the large incident room, filling it in a manner that would give Health and Safety palpitations. Young uniform constables stood to attention near the front, some taking notes. Older, wiser heads slouched at the back, knowing a pep talk when they heard one.

'Detective Chief Inspector Brooks will be keeping an eye on all three investigations,' Duguid continued, blithely unaware of the crowd's general lack of interest. They were waiting for the assignments, the only thing that really mattered. Get a nice cushy desk job, manning the phones or even better punching actions into the computer, and all would be well. The poor saps who were going to be sent out on door to door would have a harder time of it.

'Detective Inspector McLean is in charge of the Stevenson case.' Duguid scanned the crowd until he saw McLean, motioned him to the front as if no one in the station knew what he looked like.

'Detective Inspector Spence is running the enquiry into the dead nurse.' The thin man joined them at the front, a nervous scowl on his pinched face. McLean wanted to whisper in Duguid's ear that the nurse had a name, Maureen Shenks, but he knew it would be a waste of time. The DS's unthinking misogyny was a thing of legend.

'We're a bit short of senior officers at the moment, so we've poached one back from uniform. Detective Inspector McIntyre will be looking into the latest discovery. You there, Jayne?'

There was a pause, and then a familiar figure pushed her way to the front. She was thinner than McLean remembered her, and of course no longer a detective superintendent destined for yet higher office. It seemed a cruel reversal, having not so long ago been Duguid's boss, to find herself working under him. On the other hand, she'd managed to keep her job despite the best efforts of the press. Yet another reason not to trust them.

'You've all got your teams. Assignments will be handed

out shortly.' Duguid waited until the susurrus died down, clearing his throat noisily when he realised it wasn't going to. The arrival of the old boss was probably the most exciting thing to happen in the station in days. 'I shouldn't need to say this, gentlemen, but I will anyway. Three murders is exceptional. Three possibly connected murders and you can all guess where the press are going to run with this.'

More murmuring in the ranks at the suggestion any of them would do anything so reckless as talking to a journalist off the record.

'The last thing we need is a panic. Especially at this time of year. City's bad enough as it is, full of bloody tourists and mime artists. Nothing, and I mean nothing, gets leaked to the press that hasn't been through me or one of the senior detectives first. Got that?'

There were a few noncommittal mumbles from the gathered officers. It was the same at every briefing for every investigation, big or small. Press contact was meant to be controlled, and just occasionally that worked. Rather unpleasantly, the thought of Jo Dalgliesh swam into McLean's mind. She'd played fair so far, trading the sensational story for something with a bit more depth. And possibly to help out her dead friend as well, though that would have implied she had some kind of heart hidden under that horrible leather coat. She wasn't the only player in the game though, and it was only a matter of time before the other tabloid hacks smelled blood.

'Right then. I don't need to tell you all how important this is. Go to it, teams, and let's get this sick bastard caught before he kills anyone else.'

*

'Good to see you back, Ma'am.' McLean forced his way through the throng of uniforms, admin staff and detectives milling about the major incident room to where Jayne McIntyre was staring at one of the whiteboards.

'Jayne I think, Tony. We're both inspectors now.'

'I know. I heard. Sorry.'

'Don't be. It was my own stupid fault after all. Could have done without Mr Stevenson here telling the whole world about it, of course.'

McLean looked at the whiteboard, seeing Ben Stevenson's dead face taped to the top. Most of the questions and actions written beneath it had been there since the start, testament to just how much progress they had failed to make.

'Why is this so difficult to solve?' McIntyre tapped at her teeth with a short, cracked fingernail as she scanned the board. 'Haven't forensics come up with anything?'

'Nothing that wasn't his. The other caves were too contaminated by the public to get anything useful.'

'Hmm. How did he get in there?'

'Must have had a key. The cave he was found in wasn't part of the tour, but the only way in's from the tour centre.'

'And we've no CCTV, no strange people seen loitering around?'

'Plenty. All of it useless. We've had teams running all the number plates we could identify, tracking down the people walking past the bookies and the local chip shop. They both have cameras that take in the street. Problem is, it's not a small number of people. Except around the time we think Stevenson must have gone into the caves. Then there's nothing at all.'

'What about the locals? They see anything odd?'

McLean remembered his trip to the bookies with DS Ritchie. Had anything come of that? He'd given the punter his card, so any contact would have been direct. Someone was meant to be getting the manager to do an e-fit, though.

'Should be something here somewhere.'

'No matter. I'll get a chance to catch up soon enough. I take it you reckon all three are linked?'

'I wasn't sure to start with, but I've seen a bit of how both men lived. Their characters are very similar, which might suggest a theme. Not sure how Maureen Shenks fits in, except that she worked at the Sick Kids, same as Whitely. Thought for a while he might have killed her then topped himself in remorse, but the PM doesn't support that theory.'

'What if she was unlucky and just got in the way?'

McLean stared at McIntyre as the words filtered through his brain, the horrible possibilities behind the idea.

'Go on,' he said.

'Well my old chum Stevenson was obsessed with his latest story. A nasty little character trait of his. Seems our man Whitely was a bit driven, too.' McIntyre pointed over at the far side of the room where that investigation was just starting to come together.

'Both of them were chasing a lie though. Something designed to hook them. Tuned to their particular obsession. With Stevenson it was a secret society controlling everything. Whitely . . . well, you said his flat was full of medical texts, case notes, that sort of thing?'

McLean nodded. 'If we're treating all three murders as

linked, then we're looking at one murderer. Two of these fit a pattern, the nurse doesn't.'

'But she might have been a distraction, if she were coming on to Whitely while our killer was trying to lure him in.' McIntyre shook her head as if dismissing the whole thing as nonsense. 'Of course, the nurse might be nothing to do with the other two. They might all be unconnected.'

'There's nothing to lose from exploring the similarities.'

'Such as?'

'Lack of forensics, for a start. Whoever's done this knows their way around a crime scene. Stevenson and Shenks were both left somewhere that would be impossible to process. Whitely's scene was so clean you could eat your lunch off the floor. Never seen anything like it. Jemima Cairns hadn't either.'

'Jemima?' McIntyre raised an eyebrow. 'You've been putting yourself around a bit since I left, Tony.'

'Stop it. You're as bad as bloody Dagwood.'

'Sorry. I'd missed that too.'

McLean saw the smile spreading from McIntyre's eyes, betraying her normal poker face.

'It's good to have you back, really. Even in reduced circumstances. Not sure I'll ever get used to it though.'

'Actually I don't really mind. Being knocked back to inspector, that is. Being a superintendent meant never getting outside, always sitting behind a desk, attending meetings, managing idiots and dealing with the fallout when they cocked up. It's nice to be back at the sharp end.'

As if on cue, McLean's phone chirped a particularly jaunty tune; this one was reserved for the worst of his contacts. A quick check of the screen confirmed his suspicions. Jo Dalgliesh wanted a word.

'You might want to hold that thought . . . Jayne.' He still couldn't get used to that. 'I think our friends in the press might be on to us again.'

'You're meant to be keeping me in the loop, Inspector. That was the deal, wasn't it?'

The first thing McLean noticed was that Dalgliesh hadn't called him Tony. He hated it when she did, but it didn't take a genius to realise that 'Inspector' was reserved for those times when she was particularly annoyed with him.

'I take it you're talking about the body we found in Sighthill.'

'Too bloody right I am. You any idea how many juicy stories I've had to pass up on just to keep onside with youse lot?'

For a moment McLean almost believed her. Working with Dalgliesh on a semi-regular basis had almost inured him to her presence, a bit like the way spending more than half an hour in a small space with DS Carter inured you to his overpowering body odour. At least until you went outside the room and were reminded of what fresh air was supposed to be like. Meeting Jayne McIntyre again had reminded him just what a bunch of self-serving shits the gutter press could be; a handy inoculation before he became too used to the reporter's presence and dropped his guard.

'We only found the body yesterday. We're still processing the scene, interviewing colleagues.'

'So you've identified it. Him, I should say.'

'Yes.'

'And?'

'I can't tell you, Ms Dalgliesh. Not until we've assessed whether releasing that information to the general public would hinder our investigation or not.'

'God you can sound stuck up sometimes. Posh bloody education I guess.' Dalgliesh's voice muffled at the other end of the line, overlaid with the sound of a clicking lighter as she sparked up a cigarette. Not at her desk then.

'Look. We're going to be having a press conference later on today. I'll know what we can and can't say before then, and I'll make sure you get that ahead of everyone else. I can't do any more than that.'

'You reckon it's the same bloke as killed Ben?'

'I don't even know if Stevenson's killer was a man. You know as well as I do how little we've got on that.'

'Aye, true enough.' Dalgliesh paused. 'What about that nurse? Shenks?'

'What about her?'

'Ha ha. You're very funny, Inspector. She worked at the same place as your new body, aye?'

'Why do you bother calling me, Dalgliesh? You think you know all the answers anyway.'

'Got to check my sources though. Can't go printing any old rumour and supposition.'

It never stopped you before. 'If Duguid finds out which officer has been speaking to the press without sanction, he'll be off the force without a pension. Are you going to press with this story tonight?'

'Maybe. Depends what I get that's better.'

McLean sighed, pinched the bridge of his nose in the hope that it would make all the annoying things go away. It didn't, and he knew all too well that hanging up on them wouldn't work either.

'Look, I can't confirm the identity of the body, but I don't think I need to really. You've got your sources and if you don't trust them, don't pay them. I can confirm that we're looking at similarities between all three murders. That doesn't mean we think there's a serial killer running loose any more than we think all three committed suicide. All options are on the table and we're working as fast as we can to solve this. If you stir up some moral outrage or get a bunch of halfwit politicians breathing down our necks then that'll just make our job more difficult. So ask yourself what's in the public interest: selling a few more papers, or finding the person who killed your colleague before they kill someone else?'

A stunned silence echoed over the airwaves and out through the earpiece of McLean's phone. For a moment he thought the line might have gone dead; reception was pretty rubbish in the dark corner at the end of the corridor outside the major incident room where he'd scurried off to take the call in the first place. A quick glance at the screen showed him he was still connected.

'Jeez. You really haven't got anything on this guy, have you.' Dalgliesh's tone was her normal mix of sarcasm and disdain. McLean wondered whether the silence had been her muting her phone so she could have a lung-loosening cough. It would certainly take more than impassioned words to get through to her. A pickaxe, maybe.

'Like I said. We don't even know if it's a guy. Don't even know if the three killings are by the same person.'

'Don't know shit?'

It was meant to be a joke, albeit in poor taste. McLean couldn't bring himself to laugh, though. It was too close to the truth for that.

62

If McLean thought the hospital had been depressed after the death of Maureen Shenks, it was nothing compared to the shock running through the place following Dr Whitely's demise. It was true that people seldom spoke ill of the dead, and especially not of those who had died young and violently. Even so, it was hard to square the universal sorrow and expressions of admiration with the image he had built in his head from visiting the doctor's flat.

They had commandeered the same small room at the back of the old building, and were working through interviews with all of Dr Whitely's colleagues and associates. One of the first jobs had been to draw up a list of names, but as they worked through it, so it grew.

'I never realised quite how many doctors and nurses passed through this place.' DS Ritchie flipped through her printed list, now much amended with scribbled names. 'And that's before we even get to the admin staff, cleaners, porters. Christ, it's never-ending.'

'Just as well he didn't have much of a social life then.' McLean slumped back in his seat, not quite sure why he'd decided to come and help out with the interviews. Jayne McIntyre was meant to be heading up the investigation, after all. And this kind of background stuff was sergeant work, really. On the other hand, the thought of going back to the station filled him with gloom; the Ben Stevenson investigation had gone cold and things didn't look much better for Maureen Shenks. This at least had the benefit of being a new case, even if it was beginning to look rather too much like the other two. Random, brutal, and with a disturbing lack of forensic evidence to work with. He'd leapt at the chance to take it on while McIntyre got back up to speed.

'Who's next?' he asked.

'Dr Stephanie Clark. Another specialist in paediatric oncology, apparently.' Ritchie ran a finger over the relevant line in her list. 'Sounds fun.'

'Laugh a minute, I'm sure. OK. Let's get her in.'

Dr Clark was younger than McLean had been expecting. He wasn't sure why, but for some reason he'd pictured a serious woman in her mid-fifties, greying hair cut short or tied in a workmanlike bun. But the woman who presented herself at the door to the makeshift interview room at her appointed hour was probably the same age as DS Ritchie. She was tiny, too. Not much over five foot, and proportioned like many of the children she treated. You wouldn't have mistaken her for a child, though. Her eyes gave the game away. That and the air of weariness that seeped out of her.

'Would you say Dr Whitely was under a lot of pressure?' DS Ritchie asked the question. They had established something of a routine now, with the sergeant doing most of the work. McLean would sit back and watch, only occasionally adding something. He really didn't need to be there at all.

'Show me a doctor here who isn't.' That was the other thing that gave Dr Clark away. Her voice was deeper and more mature than the teenager she might be mistaken for. She paused as if expecting some sympathy before carrying on. 'But no. I wouldn't have said Jim was any more stressed than any of us. Last time I spoke to him he didn't seem much different from every other time.'

'What about his work? Had he lost any patients recently?'

That brought a frown. 'That's a harsh way of putting it.'

'I'm sorry. I didn't mean it to be.' DS Ritchie fidgeted with her list. 'I'm just trying to get a picture of his mental state. Find out if there was anything that might have tipped him over the edge.'

'You think he committed suicide?' Dr Clark gave her a look that mothers give children who have done something particularly stupid. 'Well you can scratch that one off your list. Jim would no more take his own life than he'd take one of his patients'.'

'So we've heard, but it's always good to have it confirmed from multiple sources. Did you know he was very interested in cutting-edge research?'

Dr Clark nodded. 'That was Jim. Always had his head in a paper. He was fascinated by all the new therapies coming through. If there was one thing that got him down it was the difficulty he had persuading the board to let him trial some of them.'

Something clicked in McLean's mind. 'Not easy then, I take it.'

'Christ no. I mean, fair enough, some of the stuff he was on about has only just been trialled in the lab. You can't go using that kind of stuff on sick kids, however desperate they are.'

'Did you think he might try, though? Maybe as a last resort for someone terminal?'

'And risk losing his job? Being struck off the medical register? Going to jail? I don't think so. That wasn't Jim at all.' Dr Clark shook her head again, the faintest of smiles crinkling the corners of her eyes at some memory. Then a frown washed it away. 'Mind you, he was talking to that research chap.'

'Research chap?' DS Ritchie asked. She leafed through her ever-growing list of names.

'Yes. Last few weeks, I think it was. I saw them together at the Royal Infirmary too. Here a couple of times. Some researcher from the university, probably.'

'And does this researcher have a name?'

'I guess he probably does. Can't say I know it though. Never talked to him myself.'

'As far as I know Jim wasn't working on any research programmes. Don't think he'd have had the time, to be honest, what with his work here and at the Royal.'

The last interview of the day, or at least McLean sincerely hoped it was the last interview of the day. Whitely's boss lounged in the chair on the other side of the table from him and DS Ritchie. He was a fat man, that was perhaps the kindest way of putting it. An administrator rather than a physician, though McLean had met plenty of large doctors in his time. He burst from his ill-fitting suit as if he had been smaller that morning and mysteriously swelled with the day. Perhaps he would go home soon and explode.

'So he wasn't running any clinical trials? New therapies that could only be tried out on terminal patients?'

'Good lord, no. Where did you get such an idea? We can't do stuff like that.'

'But he was talking to a research scientist. There's at least half a dozen doctors and nurses here saw him.'

'News to me.'

'So you've no idea who this fellow is, then?' DS Ritchie pitched in with the question. She had her list of names, most neatly ticked off, and was poised to add yet one more to the collection of handwritten additions at the bottom.

'Absolutely none. It's the first I've heard of it, to be honest.'

McLean leaned forward, resting his arms on the table. 'Do you do much research here?'

'Sure, we run trials with the major drug companies, universities. It's all above board though. We've ethics committees coming out of our ears and nothing gets tried out until it's been thoroughly lab tested.'

'So it's very unlikely Dr Whitely would have been involved in some unofficial work. Maybe keeping it under the radar until it could be shown to be effective. Doing stuff off site?'

'You really don't understand how this all works, do you Inspector?' The fat man squeezed himself forward, risking the buttons on his jacket. 'You can't just set up a trial, draft in a few terminally ill kids and start pumping them full of experimental drugs in the hope they might magically get better. There are procedures. Consent needs to be given. Risk assessments. Cost–benefit analyses. And meetings – God, you wouldn't believe the amount of time I spend in meetings. Even getting agreement between two doctors working with the same patient can be a struggle sometimes. The idea that Jim might have been doing anything without approval is laughable, really.'

63

He is undecided now. I can see the change in him as clearly as if he'd painted his face. The sweet brightness of his certainty is being dulled by some terrible indecision. Have I left him too long, taken my eye off the prize?

He goes about the daily business of the church, unaware that he is watched. And perhaps that is another sign. Here, in the house of the Lord, how can one not always be aware of being watched? He is all around us, in us, even though the lines of wooden pews have been moved to the walls, the central nave filled with ungainly rods of steel.

This has always been a place of awe. Its builders understood the grandeur they were trying to capture. The vaulted ceilings echo His ineffable silence; the stained glass casts everything in hellish hues as if to remind us of the perils of sin. Yet now the windows are obscured, the arches lost in a forest of rusting steel. The echoes are muffled by heavy wooden scaffold boards.

And he is humming.

I came here to pray, as I have done every day of my life. As my mother and father did before me, my grandparents before them. We have kept this parish alive, kept faith with God in this place. It is sacred ground no matter the signs outside declaring it dangerous to enter. No harm can come to any in here save that the Lord ordain it.

At first I think it is a hymn he is humming as he attends

to the altar, but the notes distort and mutate into something that might have been playing on the hospital radio the last time I was there. This man who I had thought godly has become corrupted. So quickly, so thoroughly, it is hardly surprising I did not notice it before. And yet as I study him from my place in the shadows, I can see still that glimmer of purity, the spark that first alerted me to him as sure as the flame attracts the moth. It is not too late to save him, but I must act swiftly now. Decisively.

I study him, watch him go through the same ritual I have seen a thousand times before. No, ten thousand times. I know when he will kneel, when he will bow his head and begin to pray.

Silently I move through the shadows until I am standing just behind him. Head down, his neck is exposed, the starched white of his collar showing clearly under the black fabric of his shirt. He has a smile on his face as he prays, and I understand what has happened. His body has been corrupted, but his soul is still pure. It can still be saved.

He turns at the last minute, perhaps sensing my presence and wondering if God has come down to bless him in person. Surprise widens his eyes, but it is short-lived. Needle slips effortlessly into exposed flesh and he tumbles gently forward to the floor.

64

The ringing phone stirred McLean from a fitful doze. He'd nodded off at his desk, an all-too-frequent occurrence these days, it seemed. He wondered idly if it was just a symptom of getting old. More likely the fact that he averaged around four hours' sleep a night. And broken, troubled sleep at that.

A glance at the number on the screen meant nothing, but at least it wasn't any of the journalists he'd put in the address book for the purposes of avoiding their calls. He thumbed the answer button and held the phone up to his ear.

'Yes?'

'Is that McLean? The polis man?' Thick Edinburgh accent he couldn't immediately place. Those last words definitely pronounced separately, as if that's how the speaker would spell them.

'This is Detective Inspector McLean, yes. Can I help you?' No point asking a name if it wasn't immediately offered. The caller had his number from somewhere; might as well try to find out what he wanted first, then get to the bottom of who exactly he was.

'You lookin' for a man. Hanging around the bookies up Gilmerton way.'

The pieces dropped into place. The gambler studying the form, addicted, and not very successful by the look of him. McLean had given him a tenner and his card. No doubt the one was long gone, the other kept a hold of until it might be useful. Or he was desperate enough.

'That's right. Have you seen him?'

'Not sure. Might've done. Up at the hospital.'

'Hospital?'

'Aye, y'ken the new one over at Little France.'

'The Royal Infirmary. I know it.'

'Well, I was up there yesterday getting my scrip, ken? An' I was sure I saw that same chappie youse was asking about? Only he was all togged up in the white coat an' stuff.'

'It's Keith, isn't it? I remember now.' McLean had been racking his brain for the man's name, sure he knew it as soon as he'd placed him. The silence at the end of the phone was ominous.

'Look, you've been a great help, really.' McLean decided to go for broke. If nothing else, at least he had the man's phone number now. 'But it's possible you could be even more useful.'

'I'm no' coming anywhere near a polis station.'

'I wasn't going to suggest anything of the sort.' McLean had been, but it was obvious that wasn't going to work. 'I can meet you somewhere, but I'd really like you to sit down with an e-fit specialist. Get us a better description of this man you saw.'

Another long pause, then Keith spoke again. 'I don't know. I'm that busy, y'ken.'

Unemployed, disability benefit going on the horses. Very busy. 'We could meet up at the bookies, if that'd be easiest?' McLean didn't explicitly say there'd be another ten-pound note in it, but the offer was there.

'Aye, OK. When?'

He looked up at the clock on the wall. Half-past two. Twenty minutes to find someone trained in the software, half an hour to get out to Gilmerton if the traffic wasn't too bad. 'Say half-three?'

'No, his eyes were wider apart than that. Aye, about there no?'

The bookies was busier than it had been the last time he'd been here, maybe because the police had finally packed up and gone from the caves around the corner. McLean had tried to find DS Ritchie, then DC MacBride, but both were away on errands for DCI Brooks. Casting around for someone else with e-fit training had produced the unlikely figure of DC Sandra Gregg, which meant he'd had his ear bent about her new house and how they were struggling to persuade the insurers to cover the cost of replacement goldfish, all the way from the station to Gilmerton Cove. He felt a certain responsibility for the accident that had seen her old terrace house destroyed in a gas mains explosion at the start of the year, so listened as attentively as he could manage. Fortunately Keith had been waiting for them, no doubt hoping to get the job over and done with so he could continue his pursuit of the perfect six-way accumulator.

'He was clean-shaven. Mebbe just a hint of stubble.'

To give her her due, Gregg was quick and efficient with the software, pulling up menus and swapping facial features around with a practised ease. It was just a shame that Keith wasn't the most reliable of witnesses. He changed his mind considerably more often than his underpants if the vaguely unwholesome aroma coming off him was anything to go by.

'That him?' Gregg tapped at a couple of keys and the screen on her laptop filled with a mugshot.

'Aye, that's pretty close. Mebbe didn't look so much like a crook, mind.'

'We can tidy him up, put him in a suit. You saw him at the hospital, right?'

'Aye. Looked like a doctor wi' one of them white coats and ear thingies.'

'Stethoscope?'

'Aye.'

McLean tapped the man gently on the shoulder, dragging his gaze away from the screen. 'You've been a great help, Keith. Thank you.' As he got up from the cheap plastic chair in the corner of the bookies, McLean held out a hand to shake. He'd palmed the twenty-pound note earlier and was unsurprised when Keith took it with just the barest of nods, headed straight to the counter to get his unsatisfying fix.

'We done here, sir?' Gregg asked, starting to pack up the laptop. McLean looked past the cashier to the door leading to the manager's office. Someone was supposed to have come out here and gone through the whole e-fit process with him too, but if it had been done he'd not seen the result.

'Not quite, Constable. Someone else we need to speak to.'

*

'You sure these are the same person?'

It had taken a lot less time to run through the e-fit procedure with the betting shop manager than it had with Keith, but the results hadn't been all that promising. If you squinted at the two images painted side by side on the small laptop computer screen, and maybe smeared grease over your scratched spectacles, then there was a passing similarity between the two. Looked at more analytically though, it was hard to accept that they were even related.

'I guess DS Ritchie was right when she said this was a straw-clutching exercise.' McLean put the key in the ignition and fired up the engine. Frowned as he looked out the windscreen to find a large white splat of bird shit on the once-shiny bonnet.

'Pretty much everything to do with this case is clutching at straws, you ask me.' DC Gregg sat in the passenger seat in much the same way as DC MacBride, trying hard not to actually come into contact with any surface in case she somehow damaged it. McLean was going to have to do something about that soon.

'You know anything about cars?'

Gregg looked at him askance, thrown by the non sequitur. 'Cars?'

'You know, four wheels, engine, makes vroom-vroom noises.' McLean pulled away from their parking space at the kerbside perhaps a little too enthusiastically, underlining the point.

'Not much. That's more Ritchie's thing.'

'You've got a car, though?'

'Aye. Barry has one with the work. No' as nice as this, but it's comfy enough. Why you asking?'

'Just looking for suggestions. I can't really drive this around all the time. It's been smashed up once already and I don't want that happening again. Been a while since I last read a car magazine. There's never time to go to a garage, and frankly I could do without the sales patter.'

Gregg didn't answer, and they fell into an uneasy silence as McLean drove across town in the direction of the Royal Infirmary. He didn't know the hospital as well as the Western General at the other end of the city, neither was he recognised by any of the staff, which made tracking down someone helpful more difficult than it should have been. Eventually they were directed towards the admin offices and HR department, where a harassed-looking young woman peered at McLean's warrant card before letting out a heavy sigh.

'Aye? What is it now?'

'Wondering if you knew which member of staff this was.' McLean nudged DC Gregg, who opened up the laptop computer and showed the mugshot they'd teased out of Keith the punter.

'Have you any idea how many people work in this place?'

'He was wearing a doctor's white coat, had a stethoscope round his neck. I reckon that probably rules out most of the support staff.'

'Still leaves several hundred medical staff. Assuming it wasn't someone in fancy dress. Or a student.'

'Well could you at least look at it?' McLean could put up with only so much whining, even if he knew that antagonising human resources was never a good idea.

'OK.' The young woman sighed again and made a show of studying the image. 'Not very realistic, is it?'

'I appreciate that, and I wouldn't bother you if it wasn't important. So it doesn't ring any bells?'

'No. Sorry.'

'Right. Well. Thanks for looking. If I email it over, could you send it around everyone in the hospital? If anyone recognises him it could be crucial to solving a particularly unpleasant murder.'

That finally seemed to get the young woman's attention. The yawn she had been hiding badly disappeared in an instant, her eyes widening in surprise. 'Murder?'

'Yes, murder. So I'd quite like to get access to your CCTV footage as well.'

65

'Getting kind of frustrated with these. Is this really the best anyone can do?'

McLean held up a colour printout of the man Keith the gambler reckoned he'd seen at the Royal Infirmary. White, male, black hair and staring eyes. It could have been anyone, or no one. A half-dozen people working out of the industrial estate in Sighthill had claimed to have seen someone going in and out of the building where they'd found Whitely's body and each of them had produced an e-fit image too. Add in the one from the betting shop manager and they had eight images. Hard to imagine eight more different variations on the same basic theme.

'It happens sometimes. There's people out there with just average faces. No outstanding features. And if someone's deliberately trying not to draw attention to themselves . . .' DC MacBride sidled up from the far corner of the major incident room. McLean couldn't help noticing that the constable's hair was getting very long at the front now, like some throwback to the early-eighties New Romantic bands. Given that MacBride hadn't been born before most of them had broken up, it seemed more likely he was still getting grief about his scar.

'Don't suppose there's anything we can do about it?'

'Well, we could composite all the different e-fits together. See if that comes up with anything. But that's assuming they're all of the same person. If not, then we'll have a picture of nobody.'

'At the moment we've half a dozen pictures of nobody. More. Might as well give it a go, eh?' McLean noticed the slight slump in the constable's shoulders at the thought of yet another task. 'Or get someone in admin to do it?'

'No, I'll run it myself, sir. Quicker that way.' MacBride didn't even try to hide the sigh in his voice.

'Sooner or later you'll have to learn to delegate if you want to make sergeant.'

MacBride made no reply, but neither did he turn and walk away. McLean was put in mind of an awkward teenager, not quite sure how to broach a tricky subject with an adult.

'Everything all right, Constable?'

That brought a wry smile. 'That depends on what you mean by all right, sir. Thing is, I've been offered a job, outside the force that is. Pay's about four times what I'm earning here, hours are long but fairly predictable.'

'Why are you still here then?'

'Could ask you the same thing. And I didn't join up because I wanted to get rich. Never really fancied a nine-to-five desk job, either. It's just . . .'

'The more you hang around this madhouse the more appealing it seems?'

'Something like that, aye. I get so sick of the joke. The same joke. Over and over again as if repetition makes it more funny each time.'

'I had a word with Duguid already, for all the good it did. I'll see what else I can do, but honestly Stuart, this isn't a job for idealists. Trust me on that.'

'Thanks. I thought that's what you'd say. Problem is, people don't really listen to you, do they sir?'

'Not all the time, no. And I don't suppose Brooks will be any better than Dagwood. But McIntyre's a different matter altogether.'

MacBride raised a disbelieving eyebrow, almost missed under his floppy fringe. 'You reckon? After what she did?'

'Last I heard leaving your cheating husband for another woman wasn't a crime.'

'No' just any woman. And she broke that reporter's nose.'

McLean tried not to smile. 'You think there's anyone here hasn't wanted to do that? They only threw the book at her because he pressed charges. Sheriff ruled there was no case to answer and now Jayne's back as a DI. In charge of an important case too. Don't underestimate her. I'd bet Brooks doesn't.'

MacBride said nothing for a while, but he did look across the room to where the newly reinstated detective inspector was holding court surrounded by a gaggle of detective constables and sergeants. Probably the same detective constables and sergeants who found it so amusing to point out the similarities between MacBride's scar and that of a famous fictional wizard. Something of a smile played across his face.

'I'll get that composite image run through the program, sir,' he said.

'You do that,' McLean said. 'And remember, sergeants get to order constables around.'

'Situation report, gentlemen. Lady. Just where exactly the fuck are we with all these investigations?'

Mid-afternoon, pre-briefing meeting and McLean found himself in the unusual position of sitting down in Duguid's office. The man himself took the head of the conference table that occupied one end of the room. Beside him DCI Brooks and DI Spence formed their own little huddle. There was a noticeable divide between those three and himself. Jayne McIntyre sat directly opposite him, her gaze wandering around the room that not so long ago had been hers. She let it fall finally on him, raising both eyebrows in weary resignation before starting to speak.

'Forensics are going to be on site for a while yet, but early indications are the whole place was deep-cleaned. Whoever did it knows how we process a crime scene, which ought to be a starting point for our investigations were that information not readily available on the internet.'

'Still something worth pursuing, I'd have thought.' DI Spence's skin stretched over his cadaverous cheekbones as he spoke, his Adam's apple bobbing nervously. He'd not reacted well to the return of the old boss.

'Oh, of course Michael. Don't you worry. We'll be pursuing it most assiduously. But there are other avenues that might be more productive in the meantime.'

'Such as?' DCI Brooks asked.

'There's a lot of large machinery in that warehouse. It has to have come from somewhere, and it has to have been brought in by someone. Assuming for the moment we're looking at a lone killer, then he would have had to get help with most of the larger items.'

'Find the source, trace the person who delivered it, who signed for it, that kind of thing.'

'Exactly. Grumpy Bob's been coordinating door-to-door

around the industrial estate. We've already got some e-fits of someone seen loitering around there. Checking through CCTV to see if we can get anything from that. I've got a couple of constables collating manufacturer names, models and serial numbers, and there's teams going round the hospitals and universities looking to see if kit is missing.'

Duguid nodded his approval. Not much more they could do at such an early stage.

'MacBride's running some analysis on the e-fits. The ones we've got from the Stevenson case too,' McLean said. 'It's a long shot, but it might throw up something.'

'You still think these are linked?' DCI Brooks asked.

'You still think they're not?'

'Gentlemen, let's not get started.' Duguid leaned forward, steepling his long fingers together and jamming them under his chin. 'There's no harm in looking at the possible connections. God knows we've got nothing even remotely useful like a motive for any of these.' He turned his attention to DI Spence. 'What's the situation with the nurse?'

'We've tracked down her last two boyfriends, but they've solid alibis. Not much in the way of motive either. Current hypothesis is that she was picked up by her killer the same night she was killed. Probably a one-night stand that went wrong. Forensics haven't been able to get anything useful from the dump scene, but that's not where she was killed. We're still looking for that, and her clothes.'

Duguid said nothing, but his face was as easy to read as the front cover of a tabloid newspaper. A week on from taking over the investigation, and Spence had progressed it exactly nowhere. McLean almost felt sorry for him. It wasn't as if there was anything easy about the case.

'Where are you with the heart we found in Stevenson's flat, McLean?' Duguid asked.

'It's a donated organ. Intended for use in a transplant, but the recipient died before it could be used. They can only keep these things alive for so long, sadly, so it was scheduled for cremation. The hospital's not sure how it was lost from the paper trail, but it must have been about a month ago. Whoever took it used embalming fluid to stop it rotting.'

'All good and well, but what the bloody hell was it doing there?'

'If I had to guess, sir, I'd say it was to distract us from our investigation. Lead us up a blind alley and give whatever clues there might have been more time to go cold. To be honest, I don't think why it was there is important. It's how it got there and where it came from we should be asking. We really need to be looking at the hospitals angle.'

'Hospitals?' Duguid gave him a puzzled stare that made it look as if the detective superintendent were trying to stifle a fart.

'It's a recurring theme, sir. Maureen Shenks worked at the Sick Kids, where she would have known Jim Whitely. The bulk of the material coming out of that warehouse is old stuff, machinery that's probably been replaced in a recent revamp of some of the ICU wards. Chances are it's been dumped in an outbuilding somewhere and forgotten about. You know what these organisations are like. There's twenty years' worth of outdated IT kit down in our basements that no one's ever got around to throwing out. The heart has to have been intercepted on its way to disposal, which would have been at the Royal Infirmary most likely, and lastly whoever killed Dr Whitely must have had some detailed medical knowledge.'

'It's all a bit thin though, isn't it?' Brooks said.

'Everything is thin. We're having rings run around us by this guy. He somehow persuades people to follow him into places where they won't be found. Places he's prepared well in advance. He kills them without any obvious sign of struggle using methods that are as precise as they're bizarre. He has to have had medical training. A doctor himself, or a skilled nurse.'

'But why? Why's he doing this, and why's he picking these victims? If you're so sure we've got a serial killer on our hands, what's the link?' This last question came from McIntyre, and for a moment McLean bridled at the thought that everyone was ranged against him. Then he saw the look on her face and realised she was trying to push him into stating his case better.

'I'll leave the why till we've caught him. Let's find out how he's doing this without leaving a trace. There can't be many people with the skill and resources to do what he's done. That's where we need to be concentrating our efforts.'

'You not going to your Bible class this evening?'

McLean had wandered into the combined incident room in search of DC MacBride, hoping for an update. Instead he had found DS Ritchie sitting at one of the desks set aside for the information hotlines, tapping away at a small laptop computer.

'It's not a Bible class, sir. You'd know that if you ever came along.'

'Sorry, that was uncalled for.' McLean pulled out a chair and sat down. The whole room was quiet, far quieter than an incident room for a triple murder had any right to be.

'Don't worry, I'm not easily offended.' Ritchie's smile showed she meant it.

'But you are still here.' McLean looked at his watch. 'And normally this time on a Tuesday you're not.'

'True. We're down on numbers this week though. Eric and Wanda are off on holiday, and Daniel's gone up to St Andrews to see the bishop.'

'The bishop? Anything I should know about?'

Ritchie's ears reddened at the question, but she didn't answer. McLean knew better than to push it, and despite his discomfort at the whole religion angle, he'd rather liked the earnest young minister who seemed to have caught his sergeant's eye. There were worse choices she could have made. Far worse.

'What're you up to then?' he asked.

'Just collating some of the new information Jay— DI McIntyre's got from the Whitely scene.'

'Anything promising?' McLean peered at the screen, but it was a meaningless screed as far as he could see.

'Not especially. Unless you take the view that a singular lack of evidence for all three crimes suggests they were committed by the same person. It's all rather tenuous though, isn't it?'

'Tell me about it. And while you're at it, perhaps you can explain how someone can fill a warehouse with medical equipment without anyone noticing.'

'Maybe he was seen. Stuart should have finished running the e-fit program by now. Might throw something up.'

'Did I hear my name?' DC MacBride appeared at the door, his tablet computer clutched in one hand. The constable's fringe was pulled down low again, almost covering his eyes. Sooner or later someone senior was going to tell him to get it cut.

'You got those e-fits?' Ritchie asked. MacBride nodded, tapped the screen a couple of times and handed the tablet to her.

'Just added in the ones from the Whitely crime scene. Composite image is at the end. Not sure it's any good, mind you.'

McLean peered over Ritchie's shoulder as she swiped through the images on the tablet. They were all vaguely similar and all vaguely familiar, but that was most likely a result of the e-fit system rather than anything concrete. There were too many differences for them to be the same man. Then Ritchie got to the last image and let out a little gasp.

'Dear God. It can't be.'

'What is it?' McLean reached for the tablet, staring at the final, composite image. It looked like no one he'd ever met.

'I . . . I think I know this man. Don't you recognise him?'

'Me?' McLean peered closer at the image, getting no spark from it. 'No. Should I?'

'It's Norman. Your neighbour. Well, a couple of houses down. Could swear it's him.'

'Norman?' McLean's puzzlement was obviously written large across his face. Ritchie took the tablet back and zoomed in on the e-fit eyes and nose.

'Norman Bale. You must know him, surely?'

A cold feeling seeped into the pit of McLean's stomach, that all-too-familiar sensation of things spiralling out of control.

'How do you know Norman?'

'Thought everybody knew him. He comes to the meetings. Never misses one. He's been a regular at the church since he was a boy, too. His folks with him, until they died.'

McLean was only half listening, his mind going back to the past, that long hot summer so many years ago.

'That isn't Norman Bale.'

'But it looks just like him. The more I see it, the more I wonder how I didn't recognise him before.'

'You misunderstand me.' McLean looked into those e-fit eyes, searching for any suggestion that he was wrong. Finding none. 'I don't doubt you when you say this is the man who attends your meetings, but it can't be Norman Bale. I knew Norman Bale, we grew up together for a while. And yes, he lived with his folks in the big house at the end of my street. But Norman Bale had leukaemia. He died when he was six years old.'

66

The house looks the same as it always has, but it feels different. I walk from room to room, places I used to play, places I used to hide, trying to work out what is wrong. And then it hits me; the house is just the same as ever it was. It's me who has changed. One term at that terrible boarding school, twelve weeks of struggling to understand why the other boys found my accent so amusing, of trying to fit in. Three months of wondering how I'd been so misled, why I'd been abandoned in such a horrible, unpredictable place. I wasn't the same six-year-old boy who'd travelled down all alone on the train. For one thing, I was seven now.

'You want something to eat, Tony?'

Gran came to meet me at the station and we went to Jenners for tea. It felt very grown-up, surrounded by old ladies in their finery, me in my school blazer and short trousers even in December. But I couldn't help remembering the dark wood-panelled dining hall with its lines of tables and benches. Over-boiled vegetables and something that might once have been meat, slathered in gelatinous brown gravy that tasted of salt and little else. If I had one abiding memory of that school beyond the random beatings, the interminable dull Latin lessons and the overwhelming sense of bewilderment, it was the nagging, constant hunger. I polished off two pieces of cake with my tea, a rare luxury, but now just a few hours later I am ravenous again.

'Yes please, Gran.' I take one last look at the drawing room, somewhere I never really spent much time anyway, then follow her to the warmth and welcome of the kitchen. Old Mrs Johnson's cooked a hearty stew, filled with dumplings and carrots and meat that tastes right. There's mashed potato that hasn't got bits in it and bright green peas I can mush up into it to make peaple pie. And best, there's gravy that runs around the plate and smells so wonderful I finally feel like I'm home.

'There's a choc-ice in the freezer for afters.' Gran pours a glass of orange squash from the jug in the middle of the table and pushes it over towards me. Sometimes she eats with me, but not tonight. I don't mind, too fixated on the food even to make conversation. I know I need to finish it if I'm going to have ice cream, and it's been a long, long time since I had ice cream.

It's only as I'm chasing the last of the mash around the plate, soaking up the last of the gravy, that I realise Gran has been sitting watching me the whole time. She hasn't said a word, just watched me eat.

'What is it?' I ask, pausing before the final mouthful.

'You've changed, Tony. Grown. Shot up like a beanpole.' Gran smiles at me, but there's something not right. I remember that smile all too well. It's the same smile she had when she told me mum and dad weren't coming home after all. Despite what they'd promised.

'Is something wrong?' I ask, and her shoulders slump.

'Oh, Tony. You've had so much to deal with already. It hardly seems fair to add yet more.' She says nothing for a while, and neither do I.

'It's about your little friend up the road. Norman.'

The rest of it is lost as Gran describes to me something that can't have happened. He got ill, started bleeding and wouldn't stop. The doctors did everything they could, but he had a disease. Something that sounds foreign and horrid, and all I can think of is the sight of his cut hand, the deep red blood oozing out, mixing with the dry dusty earth under the cedar tree. Was that the last time I saw him? I can't remember. All I know is that he's dead. Like mum and dad. Gone for ever. And he bled to death from a cut that wouldn't heal. A cut that was all my fault.

67

'Where're we going, sir?' Glancing in the rearview mirror, McLean could see DC MacBride slumped across the rear seat, the air from the open window ruffling his fringe and making him look even more like a teenager than usual. Had he not been wearing a dark suit, he might easily have passed for an undergraduate arrived in the city early for the start of his studies. Or maybe one of the countless hopefuls come to try his luck at the Festival.

'The church?' DS Ritchie peered out through the windscreen as they turned into the street. The evening sun was low in the sky, casting the spiky steeple in dark relief. Fingers of scaffolding surrounded it like barbed wire around a concentration camp. Keeping the faithful out, or maybe keeping something else in.

'Nothing in there, if Mary's to be believed.' McLean brought the car to a halt outside the rectory. 'Go see if she's in. Find out more about this man claiming to be Norman.'

Ritchie unclipped her seatbelt, opened the door. 'What about you?'

'I'm going to have a quick look at the old Bale house. See if anyone's been there recently. We'll meet back here in twenty minutes or so.'

Ritchie nodded, clambered out and shut the door. McLean watched her through the gate, then pulled away from the kerb. It wasn't far to his own driveway, but he carried on past, looking for the right entrance, wondering how best to play this. How many times had he been to this house? It had all been so long ago, that last lazy summer before his grandmother had packed him off to boarding school in England. He remembered it as dark, quiet, not all that much unlike his own place. At six, he'd not understood the dynamics of the family that lived there; all he'd known was that there was a boy the same age as him he could go and play with. And then that boy had died from a disease he couldn't even spell, let alone pronounce.

'On foot, I think.' He pulled over to the kerb, just past a gateway into a garden so choked with mature trees that it was impossible to see the house that lay beyond. They both climbed out, feeling the heat of yet another long sunny day reflect off the street and the stone walls to either side. That was when McLean noticed the smell.

'Well, well, well. What on earth brings you here?'

He turned to see an unwelcome figure climb out of a nondescript car parked just a few tens of yards further on. Jo Dalgliesh had a lit cigarette dangling from her mouth and breathed out the words in a cloud of her own smoke.

'I'm tempted to say the same for you, Ms Dalgliesh.'

'Suspect we're both interested in the same thing.' The reporter nodded in the direction of the house. 'Norman Bale?'

'What do you know about him?' McLean tried not to make the question sound too urgent, but he could see from Dalgliesh's stance that she knew something and was playing with him.

'He's no' in. That's one thing.'

'You've been up to the house?'

'Aye, creepy place it is.' Dalgliesh took a long drag on her cigarette, stared at it for a while as if unable to comprehend why it had finished, then flicked it on to the pavement and ground it out under her foot. It was obvious she wasn't in a sharing mood.

'Look. You know how important this investigation is. Are you going to tell me why you're here, or do I need to get Constable MacBride to arrest you for littering?'

Dalgliesh let out her lungful of smoke in a long slow breath, then started to search for something in her bag. 'All right, all right. You were much more fun when we were working together, you know.'

'Thought we were supposed to be still.'

'Aye, well. If you'd been a bit freer with the sharing, maybe I'd have given you this a bit quicker.' Dalgliesh handed over a thin sheaf of papers, mostly photographs of the research wall in Ben Stevenson's flat. McLean leafed through them, but it was hard to make out details in the failing light.

'Always thought it was a bit strange, Ben falling for some conspiracy nutter.' Dalgliesh produced a cigarette packet from the depths of her bag and proceeded to light up again. 'He could be a bit stupid at times, but no' like that. When you told me someone had broken in and taken down all that stuff he'd got, I reckoned it had to be important.'

'And it led you here?' McLean asked.

'Aye. Took a while to find it, but it was there. He worked out his contact was following him, so he followed him back. Reckon he probably thought there might be more to the story than he was being told. Guess he found out the hard way how true that was. So tell me, Inspector. Why do you want to talk to Norman Bale?'

'He's not here, sir.'

McLean and Dalgliesh both started at the voice. DC MacBride appeared from the gloom, his feet barely making any noise on the gravel.

'Jesus, Constable. You're a creepy sod sometimes.' Dalgliesh gave a low chuckle.

'No one home at all?' McLean asked.

'Doesn't look like it. Door's locked. Most of the downstairs windows are shuttered.'

McLean looked up the driveway into the gloom. His eyes were adjusting to the falling darkness now, better able to make out the house. It didn't look at all changed from how he remembered it, but it felt very different. Very wrong.

'Let's just go have a closer look, eh?'

The house was dark, surrounded by trees that cut off even the minimal light from the street lamps and the darkening gloaming sky. McLean stood outside the front door and was transported back decades. He remembered that one final summer as if it had been a whole lifetime; a clarity of memory associated only with childhood. Growing up brought so many distractions.

'Are we looking for anything in particular, sir?' DC MacBride stood perhaps a little too close, and McLean could tell from his body language that he wasn't all that happy to be there. Over by the large window that opened on to the morning room, Jo Dalgliesh was poking around in the gloom like an inept cat burglar.

'Small pot. It used to live by the boot scraper in the porch. Probably a bit less obvious now.' McLean fetched his pen torch from a pocket, then shone it around the area. Sure enough, an upside-down terracotta pot in the flowerbed a few feet off yielded a rusted key. So much for security.

'Touch nothing.' He handed a pair of latex gloves to Dalgliesh, pulled a pair on himself. There were so many reasons why he shouldn't have been doing this, and yet he needed to know what secrets the house revealed. In the blackness the nods of understanding he received from his companions were minimal. He directed the torch at the keyhole, slid the key in and turned.

Inside was a smell that he couldn't place. Not mouldering or rot, but something older and darker. It put him on edge, and did the same to Dalgliesh and MacBride if the way they drew closer in was anything to go by. McLean reached out and found the light switch, lower down the wall perhaps than he remembered, but exactly where his six-year-old self would have expected it to be. He flicked it up and bathed the hallway in light.

'Warn me before you do that again.' Dalgliesh stepped away from him, her hand reflexively going to her side. McLean wondered whether she had been about to hold his, and found he couldn't blame her. There was nothing obviously unusual about the room they were standing in, but it raised the hairs on the back of his neck all the same.

'Kitchen's that way, if I remember right.' He pointed across to a door beside the stairs. 'That's where the family spent most of their time.'

'You know this nutter then?' Dalgliesh asked.

'One summer. A long time ago, Norman Bale was my

friend. Whoever we're looking for, whatever he says, he's not Norman Bale.' McLean led the way, retracing childhood steps along a corridor far shorter than he remembered, through a much smaller door still strangely covered in green baize, and into the kitchen.

'Looks like a kitchen to me.' MacBride walked slowly around the table in the middle of the room, ran a gloved hand over the spotless wooden surface. McLean remembered a room full of life, a place where things happened, food was prepared, plans made, prayers said. This wasn't the heart of the house any more. He crossed to the stove, placed a hand on the cover over the hotplate, lifted it and felt the flat metal underneath. Cold, or at least as cold as the summer heat would let it be. Certainly not lit.

'Not in here,' he said. 'Maybe this way.'

They followed him out into the hallway again, then through another door into the drawing room. This was no more alive than the kitchen, the air stale, the dust heavy on every surface. If the man claiming to be Norman Bale had been in the house, he hadn't spent any time in here.

Neither had he spent time in old Mr Bale's study, the morning room or the library. With each new door opened, each light switched on, McLean found himself transported back in time. And with each new door he also began to see how the house had been frozen in time, how nothing had changed since that long-ago summer.

And then they reached the dining room.

Perhaps he had been expecting it and given off subliminal signals. Or maybe there really was something about the place that put people's backs up. Either way, as he pushed open the final door downstairs and reached for the light switch, McLean could feel Dalgliesh and MacBride press in close behind him. The smell that had bothered him when he'd opened the front door was stronger in here, a wrongness he couldn't quite place. Until he switched on the light.

As a young, innocent wee boy, McLean had eaten lunch at that table. Guzzled down plates of jelly, Angel Delight and all those terrible things people had thought were food in the 1970s. He remembered a polished surface you weren't allowed to put your glass of squash down on, a slightly scary room where adults talked to you as if you might one day be an adult too.

'Oh my God.' Dalgliesh took his hand this time, clutching it hard and drawing herself closer to him than was perhaps comfortable. Behind him, McLean heard DC MacBride take a sharp breath, and he could hardly blame the constable. Neither he nor the reporter had ever met Colin and Ina Bale, after all.

They sat as they always had done, much older than he remembered them, but still easy to recognise. Mr Bale was at the head of the table, his wife to his right and at the side. In the artificial light it was difficult to tell how long they had been dead, but it had been a while. They looked like wax dummies, hair turned thin and straggly, faces fixed in rictus grins, eyes dried and white with cataracts. Places had been laid at the table in front of them both, empty plates awaiting food that would never come. And to the other side was a third place where someone had quite recently sat and eaten a meal.

68

'The Christian cross is a misrepresentation, of course. It looks impressive, but from a carpentry point of view it's inefficient. Most Roman crucifixes were just two bits of wood roped together in the middle and splayed to form an X.'

He is woozy from the anaesthetic, but I can see the spark in him as he awakens. Arms splayed, legs akimbo, I imagine he must be struggling to work out where he is. The drugs will dull most of the pain, but soon he will feel the nails through his palms and feet. I imagine he'll start to panic then.

'It's no matter, of course. Christian symbol, Roman torture. It's all a means to an end. Your end, as it happens. And your beginning.'

Eyes flutter under lids taped down. It will be dark where he is. His breathing is growing rapid, snot spiralling down from his nose to form a little puddle on the floor. He can't breathe through his mouth, of course. That's taped up too. We are closer here to any passers-by. I can't take the risk of being interrupted before this ceremony is over.

'You don't know just how blessed you are. How lucky. God has singled you out to be with him in heaven. Your soul is pure.'

Naked, his body is thin, ribs straining through pale skin turned orange by the light of the setting sun outside.

Greens and reds and blues mottle the flesh on his arms, low light filtering through the smaller north windows. East–west the church lies, catching the rising and setting sun through stained glass at either end of the aisle. Except that this far north, at this time of year, the sun rises far north of east and sets far north of west. It doesn't matter, truly. The perfect moment will be here soon enough.

I stand before him, watching as the light shifts and swirls over his body. Outside, the city roar has faded away to nothing. It does not exist any more. We are alone, he and I. And God.

'Our father, which art in heaven, hallowed be thy name.'

He shakes his head from side to side, cheeks puffing in and out as he tries to breathe. His arms tense, hands sliding over their slippery nails, but I've bent the ends over. He won't escape them. Blood drips from his stigmata, runs down his arms and drips from his elbows. It mingles in the dust on the floor with the blood from the wounds in his feet.

'Thy kingdom come, thy will be done on earth, as it is in heaven.'

I can feel the moment building, the tension stretching the air as if it were made of foam. I too find it difficult to breathe, awed in the presence of God.

'Give us this day, our daily bread. And forgive us our debts, as we forgive out debtors.'

I am heavy now like a sack of bones. Their weight drags me to the floor, knees settling into the dirt and the blood. And still I am ground down by that awesome presence, squeezed until my face is pushed into the mess.

'And lead us not into temptation, but deliver us from evil.'

His breathing is ragged now, the weight of his body making it almost impossible for him to suck in air, the panic crushing him even as the weight evaporates from my shoulders. He won't hang upon the cross for long, agonising hours. Death will take him swiftly, God's mercy as He gathers up this saved soul to Him.

'For thine is the kingdom, the power and the glory.'

I look up and see the golden light of the sun, piercing through the coloured glass to limn his head like a halo. For a moment I see the crown of thorns, the blood running down his cheeks, then it blurs as my eyes fill with tears, my whole body suffused with joy.

'For ever and ever.'

He is close now, and I know the perfect ecstasy of being in the presence of the divine. And yet even in that moment there is the exquisite sadness. Knowing that it is not my soul that will be gathered up. Knowing that it is not yet my time, that I must struggle still longer in this mundane, sinful world. And as I gaze up at this perfect, dying man, I feel the serpent of jealousy squirm in my guts and know why it is that I am not yet worthy.

The tears come freely now and I drop my head in supplication. Kneel before Christ on the cross and pray.

'Amen.'

69

The gloom outside the Bale house was only slightly less menacing than that within as McLean pulled the front door closed. He considered asking Dalgliesh to stay in her car, or better yet to go home and wait for him to call her, but he knew that wasn't going to happen. She was too much of a reporter to resist following him around as this juicy story unfolded.

'Get on to control will you, Constable. We need to secure the scene as soon as possible. Wait here until back-up arrives, then come and find me at the rectory.'

MacBride nodded his understanding, pulled out his air-wave set and started to make the call.

'And Stuart? Don't do anything stupid. This man's very dangerous.'

'I'll keep out of sight, sir. And don't worry, I'll not try and tackle him on my own if he shows up.'

'Right. Dalgliesh, you're with me. And keep your eyes peeled. Last thing I want is to bump into this man unawares. Whoever he is.' McLean set off down the drive at a rapid pace, partly to avoid any of the inevitable questions the reporter would throw at him, but mostly because his stomach was telling him something bad was going down.

'Whoever he is . . .? You mean he's no' real?' Dalgliesh wheezed as she struggled to keep up. McLean ignored her. They reached the rectory in minutes, and he rang the doorbell. A light shone in the porch even though it wasn't yet dark, the evening sun still painting the side of the stone steeple in autumn orange. Some of the scaffolding had begun to come down, he noticed. Piles lying beside the graves. It still surrounded the old building like a canker. Engulfed it.

DS Ritchie opened the door a few moments later. Her expression was one of alarm, her free hand unconsciously reaching for her throat and the slim silver band that hung around her neck and tucked into her blouse.

'You've not found him, I take it?'

'No. Is Mary in?'

'Kitchen.' Ritchie stood aside and let them pass.

'Norman's not here, Inspector.' Mary Currie appeared from the hallway, her face pale in the shadows.

'Norman's not Norman.'

'That's what Kirsty said, but it can't be true. I've known Norman for years.'

Could he be wrong? McLean pulled the e-fit photo out of his pocket, unfolded it and stared at it again. Impossible to tell whether the badly constructed image was the same person as the weedy six-year-old boy he'd known. The boy whose parents were so religious. The boy who his grand-mother had told him was dead.

'Daniel's missing too,' Ritchie said.

McLean's train of thought derailed. A horrible cold sensation forming in the pit of his stomach. 'I thought he'd gone to St Andrews to meet the bishop?'

'So did I, but he never showed up. They phoned about an hour ago, apparently. Wondering where he was.'

McLean could hear the panic rising in the detective

sergeant's voice. Controlled for now, but betraying her thoughts all too clearly. They weren't that far from his own.

'Look, why don't we all go through to the kitchen?' Mary Currie was the voice of reason. 'The kettle's on. We'll have a cup of tea and get to the bottom of this.'

'Dan's still not answering his phone. Just keeps going to message.' Ritchie paced back and forth in the rectory kitchen, doing a good impression of DCI Brooks despite her lack of bulk. She'd called the number three times since McLean and Dalgliesh had followed her into the kitchen.

'We'll find him. Find both of them.' McLean tried to reassure the detective sergeant, only realising what he'd said as the words came out.

'You think they're together? Why would they be together?'

'No. That's not what I meant.' McLean tried to convince himself, couldn't quite manage. He turned his attention to the minister, even now pouring teaspoons of sugar into everyone's milky tea.

'Mary, I'm right in thinking Daniel's living here? In the rectory?'

'Yes, of course. It's a big old house to rattle around in on my own. I'm forever picking up waifs and strays. Much like you, really.'

'I couldn't have a quick look at his room, could I?'

The minister frowned. 'Why would you want to do that?'

'Just to see if he left any clue as to where he was going.' It wasn't a good lie, but the minister shrugged.

'Well, I suppose if I can't trust a policeman, who can I?'

She picked up two mugs, handing one to Dalgliesh, who took it with a little start of surprise.

'I'll show you, sir.' Ritchie stuck her phone back into her pocket, call number four having been as unsuccessful as all the rest.

'Stay here with the minister, we won't be long.' McLean said to Dalgliesh, then realised that he'd not yet introduced them to each other. 'Sorry. Mary, this is Jo Dalgliesh. She's a reporter. You might get Detective Constable MacBride knocking on your door in a moment, too. I'm sure he'd be very grateful for a cup of tea, if you didn't mind.'

'For someone who gave so generously to the church roof repair fund? Not in the least.'

McLean nodded his thanks, then turned to follow Ritchie out of the kitchen, but not before he noticed Dalgliesh's eyebrow shoot up in surprise.

'So, you know where the curate sleeps. Should I be worried for the state of his soul?'

DS Ritchie stopped halfway up the stairs, looked around over her shoulder and gave McLean a very old-fashioned stare.

'Sorry, that was uncalled for. Especially given the circumstances.'

'It's OK, sir. I know you're just trying to ease the tension a bit.' Ritchie started climbing again, speaking to the dark landing above. 'To be honest, I've never seen Daniel's room. I only know where it is because it's next to the bathroom. Here.'

McLean followed her across the landing, stopped outside a plain wooden door indistinguishable from a half-dozen others. The gloom was only alleviated by the light spilling up the stairwell, and a faint orange glow through a pair of recessed skylight windows overhead. Silence filled the air like cotton wool as he reached out and rapped a knuckle on the panel.

'Daniel? Are you in there?' If only it were that easy.

'OK. Let's have a look then.' McLean dropped his hand to the doorknob, twisted it and pushed.

It was a large room, high-ceilinged and dominated by two tall windows in the far wall. Heavy, dark furniture looked like it must have been craned in before the roof went on, but had presumably been hefted up the stairs by stout Victorian workmen a century or so ago. By the light filtering in from outside, McLean made out a narrow single bed, a washstand in the far corner, floorboards covered by an old Persian rug. A desk sat between the two windows, but it was hard to see any great detail. Then DS Ritchie flicked on the light.

'Oh my God.'

The room was mostly tidy, that was perhaps the best way to describe it. The bed was made and everything was lined up square, the gaps between each individual item of furniture arranged so that they looked in proportion. In amongst the order, the desk stuck out like a nun at a rugby club stag night. It was piled with books, all of a jumble as if Daniel had been going through them in a rush, looking for snippets of information first from one then another, tossing them aside when they didn't yield what he searched for. Others lay on the floor in a circle around the chair, wagons drawn together against the Indian attack. On the desktop, ground zero, an A4 spiral-bound notebook lay in the middle of it all, splayed open to reveal a page of scribblings. McLean approached it carefully, not wanting to disturb anything, and peered at the words. He couldn't make anything out, and he was used to deciphering Grumpy Bob's impossible scrawl. It didn't matter; the stacks of newspaper cuttings, Post-it notes and half-read books told the story quite clearly enough.

'I never knew.' Ritchie stood by McLean's side, peering down at the evidence of an interest verging on the brink of obsession.

McLean picked up the nearest book, turned it over to reveal the title. *Urban Deprivation: Causes and Cures*. Other books followed a similar theme. No light bedtime reading here.

'We need to find him.' He put the book back down on the pile. Hoped to hell no one else had found him already.

Mary Currie and Jo Dalgliesh were chatting like old friends when McLean and Ritchie came back into the kitchen. The minister broke off, her face asking the question before she voiced it.

'Find anything?'

'Not what we were hoping for.' McLean wondered how best to broach the subject, then realised there wasn't really time for niceties. 'Tell me, would you have said Daniel was obsessive about things?'

Mary frowned. 'Obsessive? Not really. He's earnest, keen. His faith is very strong. But I wouldn't have called him obsessive.'

'He has a thing about social deprivation though.'

'Oh, that. Yes, there is that. But I wouldn't call it an obsession, really. More of a fixation. If there's a difference.'

'When was the last time you saw him?' McLean asked. 'When was the last time you saw this chap who claims to be Norman, for that matter?'

'I've not seen Norman since Sunday. We had a service at Saint Michael's across town. Can't use our own church at the moment. It's full of scaffolding and building stuff.' Mary Currie frowned as she tried to gather her thoughts. 'Dan was here for breakfast. He was meant to be getting the half-ten train to Leuchars, to have lunch with the bishop and be home in time for Evensong. He was thinking about taking him up on his offer, wanted to discuss it face to face. That's Daniel for you. Likes to be hands-on.'

Ritchie looked up from her phone at the words. 'The bishop's offer? He was going to take it up?'

'I'm not sure, but I got the feeling he was considering it. He's been torn about it for weeks now. Sometimes he prays for guidance, but it's been weighing heavy on him.'

McLean watched the exchange, not quite understanding it but sure somehow that it was important. 'I'm missing something here. The bishop's offer?'

'There's a parish in Perthshire that's looking for a new minister. Daniel was offered the post, but he always saw himself as more of a missionary. Never seen someone with such zeal before, but I think he might have been starting to reconsider.' Mary glanced at DS Ritchie standing in the doorway, clasping her phone as if it were the most precious thing in the world. 'Can't think why.'

The doorbell ringing broke the silence that followed.

Ritchie stood bolt upright at the sound, as if someone had wired her into the same circuit as the tinny electronic bell. Without a word she darted out of the kitchen and down the hall. Moments later she returned, less energetically, with DC MacBride in tow.

'Squad car's arrived and parked outside the gate, sir. Keeping an eye on things until the forensics people arrive. Bale's e-fit's gone out to all officers in Scotland. Should be hitting the news later. Oh, and Dagwood wants to know what's going on.'

'Did you tell him?'

'Thought it best coming from you, sir. He sounds hopping mad you ran off without updating him on Bale.'

'Well, he'll just have to wait. We've a missing curate to find.' McLean tried to remember what the minister had been saying before they were interrupted. 'He was praying for guidance? Where would he do that?'

'Where? What do you mean?'

'Well, if the church is off limits, where would he go to pray?'

'Oh, I see what you mean. No. We can't hold services in the church; Health and Safety won't let us open it to the public. Nothing stopping Daniel or me from going in there though. If he was looking for a little peace and quiet he might well have gone in there. But he wouldn't have spent all day there, let alone into the evening.'

'What about this man . . . Norman? Would he go there to pray too? Even if the signs said keep out?'

McLean didn't wait for an answer. He could see it dawning on the minister's face. He checked his watch, counted the hours. Too many, surely.

He put a hand on Dalgliesh's shoulder, pushing her back into her chair as she tried to get up. 'You stay here, keep Mary company.' He turned to MacBride. 'Stay with them. And get more uniforms over here as soon as you can.' And finally to Ritchie, already putting her phone away. 'You're with me.'

70

Darkness filled the inside of the church like peat water, shadows casting weird shapes in the open space. Scaffold poles marched down the aisles and criss-crossed in a tangle of metal; the untidy nest of some improbably large bird. The echo of the closing door took less time to fall to nothing than McLean had expected, muffled by heavy wooden boards overhead. He held his hand up for silence before Ritchie could say a word, then strained to hear anything unusual in the quiet.

Nothing. Not even the muted, distant hum of the city outside. The church was unnaturally still, as if something somewhere held its breath in anticipation. Treading softly, McLean stepped into the body of the kirk, all the while listening out for something louder than the thunder of blood in his veins, the racket of his heart beating.

The ancient, carved stone font squatted in its familiar place, where he had seen it scant months ago, but the rest of the church interior was unrecognisable. Piles of unused scaffold boards stacked up against the pews, themselves dragged to the walls. Looking down, he saw scuffed flagstones, some inscribed with words in memory of the mouldering bones lying beneath them, barely visible in the final gloaming of the dying day. Beside him, Ritchie was turning slowly on one heel, searching for signs of life, when she let out a low moan of horror.

'What is it?' McLean spoke the words in a low whisper, but she was already moving away from him at a run. And he could see for himself what had set her off.

At the far end of the nave, just as the low stone steps climbed up to the altar, someone had constructed a makeshift crucifix from scaffolding poles and what looked like roof beams. The first thing that struck McLean was its size, so much bigger than the crosses he was used to seeing on the few, uncomfortable occasions he had found himself in a church. The second thing he noticed was that this cross, unlike the usual Christian affairs, was a crude X. The sort of thing he remembered from school and lessons in ancient history.

The third thing he saw was the naked man, arms and legs splayed, dark marks where he had been nailed in place.

'Wait!' McLean tried to shout, but his voice caught in his throat. It was a wasted effort anyway. Ritchie was almost at the body now, reaching out for it. As she did so he recognised the man nailed there as the young minister, Daniel, and the pieces started to fall uncomfortably into place.

He took a step further into the church, straining his ears to hear anything over the low 'no, no, no,' of DS Ritchie as she tried to get to the cross and the man spreadeagled upon it. He had thought the church empty, but it was hard to tell. Too many shadows, dark upon dark in shapes that could simply be benches stacked in a corner, or a murderer lurking with evil intent. He reached the aisle, turning slowly, letting his eyes adjust as he fumbled out his mobile phone. The screen blazed light at his touch, almost painful to look at. Still he thumbed at it until the speed dial for the incident room came up, clamped the phone to his ear as he approached the crucifix.

'McLean,' he said as soon as the call was answered. 'Who speaks?'

'It's me, sir. Sandy . . . that is, Detective Constable Gregg, sir.' Well it could have been worse.

'Constable, I need a full tactical team out here as soon as possible.' McLean gave her the address as he approached the body. The cross was surrounded by a jumble of scaffold poles, precariously balanced one upon another so as to make getting within touching distance almost impossible. Instead of clearing them, Ritchie was trying to climb over, but every time she put a foot down the pile shifted under her and she had to step back again.

'I can't reach him. We need to move this.' She bent down and pulled at a scaffold pole, then let out a shriek as it rolled over, trapping her hand. McLean managed to find the end of the pole, lift it enough for her to free herself, then they both had to scramble backwards as the pile collapsed.

'What's going on, sir? Sounds like a car crash.' DC Gregg's voice sounded thin with the clattering of steel pipes still ringing in his ears, but McLean was more concerned by the crucified priest. The noise had stirred him, his head shifting so slightly it might even have been a trick of the light. Except that there was barely any light in the place now to trick them.

'I need an ambulance and a fire team. Five minutes, Constable.'

'I'm on it, sir. Only Superintendent Duguid . . .'

Whatever it was Duguid wanted, McLean never found out. Ritchie had managed to pick a path through the tangle of scaffold poles now. She reached the cross and began climbing it, looking for a way to cut her boyfriend down. The instant she touched him, the church filled with a screech like some terrible, fantastical monster roused from its slumbers.

'You must not interfere. This is God's work!'

McLean barely had time to react before a figure came flying through the air at him. He ducked out of the reach of a hand he thought was going for his throat, tripped on a coil of rope left behind by the builders and fell backwards. Sharp steel glinted in the half-light, whistling through the air where his neck had been, then his head smacked against something hard. Stars crazed the darkness, a roaring in his ears like standing in a tunnel as the train comes. He fought to stay conscious, vision narrowing to a dark-circled point that focused on the crucified priest and Ritchie's frantic attempts to cut him down.

'His soul is pure. You cannot stop the Lord from taking him.' The words were oddly distorted, like a radio dropped into the bath. McLean struggled to pick himself up off the floor, hands finding everything slippery. He lifted one up, seeing it smeared in something dark, and only then did the pain register, a cut across his palm, another at the back of his head where it had hit.

Everything was in slow motion except the man moving through the shadows. He was everywhere, flicking in and out of existence like some child's nightmare monster. The jumble of poles was no more of an obstacle to him than chalk lines on a pavement. Closer and closer to the cross, the crucified priest and DS Ritchie, that wicked shining blade blazing with fire as it caught a stray beam of light from the stained glass windows. McLean knew in that instant exactly what had happened to Maureen Shenks. And why.

'No!' The word sounded dull in his muffled ears, but there was an urgency in it that must have carried. As he scrambled to woozy feet, so Ritchie finally turned her attention away from the cross, saw her attacker at the last possible moment. She ducked away from him as he lunged, her training kicking in as she positioned herself best to deal with the blade. McLean stumbled towards her, the room still spinning in his head, aware somewhere in the back of his mind that he was unarmed, concussed and approaching a man with a knife. The nave seemed to draw away from him as he struggled towards the altar and he watched in horror as Ritchie fell backwards over one arm of the makeshift cross. The man who claimed to be Norman leapt around it, his movements more like those of an ape as he pressed his advantage. She was on her back, arms up to protect herself from the stabbing knife and still McLean was too far away.

'Norman, stop.'

Whether it was the pitch of his voice or something more fundamental, the use of that name stopped the man in his tracks. At his feet, DS Ritchie was curled in on herself, arms covering her head, the sleeves of her jacket shredded and bloody. Bale straightened, turned to meet his accuser, and McLean realised he was much closer to the cross than he'd thought. He looked up briefly at Daniel's pale face, wincing in pain as his head protested at the movement.

'Do you like what I've done, Tony?'

The voice was at once alien and hauntingly familiar. Older, true, but also just the same. Could it really be him? Had his grandmother lied to him about Norman's death? Had he really survived? Grown up to become this monster?

Norman stepped lightly away from Ritchie, the knife still sharp in his grasp. As he walked around the cross, he ran his free hand down Daniel's naked thigh, smearing the blood that had dribbled from the crucified man's hand down his arm, dripped from his armpit like thick, red sweat. A low noise stirred from the body, bubbles of spittle and blood leaking from his nose. Still alive. There was still hope. And help was surely on its way now. He just needed a little time.

'I thought you died. All those years ago. Leukaemia. That's what they told me.'

'Oh, I died, Tony. I had a disease that your precious science couldn't cure. Of course it couldn't. It was God's will that I die. He took me into his arms and told me I was chosen.'

McLean couldn't be sure whether his head was clearing or not, but he felt a little steadier on his feet. He edged slowly backwards, up the aisle in the direction of the font. The man who might have been Norman followed him, still holding that wicked sharp knife.

'Why, Norman? What were you chosen for? What was Daniel to you? What were the others?'

'You don't know? You can't see it?' Norman took a step closer and McLean could see the madness in his eyes, glinting in the last of the light. They flicked around like a bird's. Darting here and there, trying to take in everything but seeing something very different to the mundane.

'Tell me what I should be seeing.' McLean edged back another step, hoping Ritchie wasn't badly injured. Any minute now the cavalry would arrive. Surely.

'Of course you can't see it. None of them could. But I can. I can see it in them. In Daniel here, in Ben and Jim and all the others. And I can see it in you.'

Norman lunged forward, knife hand outstretched. McLean moved slowly, too slowly, his head still filled with sawdust and fireworks. A ripping sound, and he felt a tug on his jacket, a sharp pain in his side as the knife slid across his ribs. He pirouetted around, trying to get out of the way as Norman danced in the darkness, coming in for a killing strike. Something blocked him, the ancient carved stone font. He was trapped, helpless.

'Such glory in his work. Two perfect souls will go to heaven this day.' Norman stepped up close, knife held high as he made to strike. McLean raised his hands in defence, knowing it was useless, remembering the mess that had been made of Ben Stevenson and Maureen Shenks.

And then confusion. A dull thud echoed briefly in the hall. Bale's eyes shot upwards even as his knees gave way. He dropped the knife, crumpled to the silent floor. Behind him a grinning Devil's face loomed out of the shadows. Jo Dalgliesh held a short length of scaffold pole in her hand, an evil glint in her eye.

'You already killed one of my friends. Got few enough of them as it is. Damned if I'm going to lose another.'

71

He sat on the edge of a stone sarcophagus, unsure if that was even the right word for it, as a paramedic wound a pure white bandage around his hand. McLean wasn't quite sure if he was in shock or just working his way through the latter stages of mild concussion. Either way, the world had a surreal tinge to it that made some things indistinct whilst bringing others into sharp relief. It was fully dark now, the street lamps surrounded by their individual insect tribes. The trees rustled in a warm breeze and the night air brought sharp smells.

'Here, drink this.' A smiling, worried face hoved into view, bearing a mug of steaming tea. McLean took it, nodding gratefully before realising that it had been given to him by Mary Currie.

'How's DS . . . Kirsty?' he asked.

'She'll be fine once the cuts heal. They're only superficial. Going to need a new jacket, mind you.' The minister sunk down on to the stone beside him. She smelled of old classrooms, he realised. Not those where he'd been humiliated in front of his peers by inadequate teachers, but the warm, dusty, sun-filled classrooms where he'd semi-dozed and listened to wonderful stories of Roman history, Celtic warriors and adventurous ancient Greeks. The classrooms where he'd discovered poetry and realised that God was a lie. The thought brought an ironic smile to his lips.

'Norman. How terrible. And Daniel.' Mary Currie sounded like she was in shock herself. She probably was, and yet she'd still made tea for the ever-growing number of police descending on her church. The crime scene.

'He's not Norman. Norman died when he was six years old.'

Mary's face wrinkled in puzzlement. 'But he lives in the house. His parents . . .'

McLean shook his head, winced in pain. 'I don't know. Smacked my head on a pew in there. Things will probably make more sense in the morning.'

The minister said nothing more for a while. Then nodded towards the church door, wide open and with a young uniform constable standing guard outside.

'Is he . . . Daniel?'

As if to answer his question, a commotion from the church door spilled several paramedics and a couple of uniform officers out into the night, wheeling a gurney. One of the paramedics was holding a saline bag up high as they bustled past. Not something you did for a dead man.

'He was alive when we found him. Poor bastard. Going to take some healing. Mental as well as physical.'

'I'd better go with him. To the hospital.' Mary Currie stood up again, too swiftly. She swayed slightly, putting a hand on McLean's shoulder to steady herself. The contact was a reassurance, and it eased away the last of the fog from his brain.

'I'll make sure there's a constable on the rectory door.' He looked around at the bustle. 'Not that I think anyone's going to try and break in with this lot here.'

'Thank you, Tony. You're a good man.' She gave him a weak smile and trotted off after the paramedics.

'So everyone tells me,' he said, but no one heard him.

Detective Superintendent Duguid arrived long after the commotion had died down. His thinning hair was awry, and he had the look about him of a man on the edge of a nervous breakdown. McLean spotted him climbing out of his car and going to speak to DCI Brooks, which meant he could duck out of sight behind an ornate carved headstone before he was seen.

'Going somewhere, Inspector?'

Jo Dalgliesh was leaning against the headstone, an unlit cigarette in her mouth. As press, she should technically have been ushered back past the crime-scene tape that surrounded the church and graveyard. DC MacBride must have said something, as all the policemen milling around were studiously ignoring her.

'Keeping away from the boss, if I'm being honest. Not sure I can cope with a debriefing right now.'

'Know how you feel. Going to be interesting breaking this one to the office.'

'There'll be a prize or two in it for you, I'd have thought.'

'Aye. Mebbe. Ben died chasing this though. Feels a bit . . . I dunno.'

'Is that a conscience I see growing?'

'Fuck off, aye?'

McLean risked a glance around the headstone, saw Duguid and Brooks in deep discussion, DI Spence hanging around them like a needy spaniel. They didn't appear to be looking for him, which was all the encouragement he needed.

'Come with me,' he said to the reporter, then strode off towards the church and the shadows. She took a moment to catch up, taken by surprise. 'Where we going?'

'To find MacBride, maybe Ritchie if she's not gone off to the hospital with her boyfriend.'

That raised an eyebrow. 'Thought there was something more going on there than just devotion to duty. Why'd you need my help? Thought you couldn't stand the sight of me.'

'My house is just over the road.' McLean nodded in the general direction, then winced as the lump on the back of his head throbbed its disapproval. 'Don't know about anyone else, but I reckon I could do with a large dram. Figure I owe you one too. You probably saved my life back there, even if I did ask you to stay in the house with the minister.'

'Probably?' Dalgliesh pulled the cigarette out of her mouth, stopped walking for a moment as if insulted. Then she shook her head. 'Aye, probably's right enough. Probably.'

72

'He still claiming to be Norman Bale?'

McLean stood in the observation room looking into interview room one. Through the one-way glass, the man who might be Norman Bale sat silently at the table, staring into the middle distance. Detective Superintendent Duguid held a long-fingered hand up to the glass as if he wanted to reach out and pluck the man's head off.

'That's his story and he's sticking to it. We couldn't find any ID on him, but forensics put him all over the Bales' house. He's been living there a while now. Mary . . . the minister's known him as Norman for at least five years. He's a regular at the church, every Sunday without fail.'

'So it could be him,' Duguid said.

McLean squinted through the glass at that thin, pale face. Tried to square it with the boy he'd known all those years ago. It was possible, he supposed. But how was it possible?

'We've checked the hospital records. Norman Bale was admitted to the Sick Kids with leukaemia when he was six years old. He died shortly afterwards, according to the death certificate.'

'And yet here he is.' Duguid leaned against the glass, then backed off when the man at the interview table looked up at him.

'His folks packed up and went to Africa not long after

he died. Norman, that is. The real Norman. Left that old house empty for a good few years. Some kind of missionary work. My gran was very sceptical about it.'

'She was sceptical about pretty much everything, if I remember right. Religion more than most.'

McLean looked at Duguid in surprise. Of course the detective superintendent would have known his grandmother; she'd been a consultant pathologist at the city mortuary long into her retirement. Called in to comment on the more bizarre cases the city occasionally threw up. He just couldn't remember Duguid ever having mentioned her before.

'Strange, now you mention her. She never said anything about Norman to me. Or his parents, but she'd have known when they came back to Edinburgh.'

'Well, it doesn't really matter. Norman Bale or someone else. Odds on he killed them, creepy wee fuck that he is. The other three as well.'

'I've a nasty feeling that's just the start of it.'

'What?' Duguid's face drained of colour.

'Bale's parents have been dead at least five years. That's when they were supposed to have been buried. Ben Stevenson was killed just over eight weeks ago. You honestly think he's been doing nothing all that time? I'd be digging up the unsolved case files, missing persons, that sort of thing.'

If anything, Duguid went even paler. 'Don't fucking complicate things, McLean. Leave that to the cold case boys. Just get a confession out of him.'

McLean looked away from the detective superintendent, back to the interview room through the glass. Norman, or not Norman, was staring straight at him now, a slight frown on his face that sent a shiver down McLean's spine.

'Somehow I don't think that's going to be a problem, sir.'

There was something unnerving about his calmness. That was the thing that struck McLean most as he took his seat in the interview room. A duty solicitor sat beside the man claiming to be Norman Bale, his chair a little further away from the accused than was perhaps polite. Another chair was still tucked under the table, Grumpy Bob having decided that he preferred to stand by the door. No one had complained so far.

'You say your name is Norman Bale. That you're the only child of Colin and Ina Bale. And yet our records show the real Norman Bale died when he was six years old.'

'Records. You know as well as I do how easy it is to fake those, Tony.'

McLean met that staring gaze, still trying to reconcile it with the boy he'd known all those years ago. Norman had called him Tony just that way, but he still couldn't accept that this was indeed his old friend. If it was, then his grandmother had lied to him. That opened up an even nastier can of worms.

'So you're telling me your death was faked.'

'Oh no. I died. God took me to his bosom. Medical science failed. But the Lord had plans for me, and so I was reborn.'

'Straight away? Or did you spend some time in heaven before returning to this mortal plane?'

'Time has no meaning there. It is just one endless

moment of perfect bliss. You'd know that, Tony. If you just believed.'

Bale, or not Bale, flicked his eyes to the right, looking briefly up as Grumpy Bob pulled the chair out from under the table and sat down. McLean paid the detective sergeant no heed, taking the time to study the man sitting opposite. For a moment he'd been uncertain, but in that one look he'd finally accepted that this wasn't Norman Bale. Who he was would be a question for another investigation, another detective and maybe a team of psychologists. He was probably someone the Bales had taken in, a lodger or just a charity case. They had always been good people that way. Whoever this person was, he had insinuated himself into their lives, and maybe they had encouraged him. Maybe they, too, had seen something of their dead son in his eyes. Fooled themselves that he had returned.

'OK. Let's accept you are who you say you are. For now, at least. So tell me. Did you kill your parents, Norman?'

Grumpy Bob flipped open his notebook and pretended to take notes, even though the whole interview was being recorded. DS Ritchie had wanted to attend, but she wasn't long out of hospital, still on antibiotics for her cuts. And her relationship with Daniel meant she had been taken off the case. McLean wished he could beg the same favour.

'I would advise you not to answer that, Norman.' The duty solicitor's enthusiasm was almost too feeble to measure. He appeared to have written this one off as an insanity plea already.

'They were the first. The first time God showed me

what my purpose in life was to be. After he sent me back to them.' Norman's voice was calm, matter of fact. As if he understood perfectly the situation he was in, accepted it as just another day.

'Why did you kill them?'

'They were such good people. You met them, you must have known. They prayed every day, went to church on Sunday, gave money to the poor, time to charities. Their whole lives were dedicated to His service. It was only a matter of time before their souls became pure. When they did, I knew at once what had to be done. A pure soul cannot survive long in this world without becoming corrupted, after all.'

'So you killed them to save their souls?' McLean didn't try to hide the element of doubt in his voice.

'It's funny, really.' Norman smiled like a shark, turning to the duty solicitor. 'You have no hope. Your soul is a dirty thing. It will burn in eternal hellfire. You,' he nodded at Grumpy Bob, 'you'll be judged at the end. Saint Peter will have his scales ready for you. I truly hope you won't be found wanting. But you,' and now he turned his gaze back to McLean, 'you are so close, even though you don't know it, won't admit that you even have a soul at all. You are like Ben and Jim, Daniel and all the others, just needing that little push. You were to be my next project.'

'Were to be?' McLean suppressed the shudder that wanted to run through him. The way Bale spoke, the way he acted, suggested he thought of his current situation as nothing more than a minor inconvenience.

'God has other plans for me.' He shrugged. 'And for you.'

*

467

The electronic warbling of his phone was a welcome distraction from the enormous pile of paperwork threatening to bury him. They might have caught Bale, or whoever he really was, but three major incident enquiries still had to be wound up, overtime accounted for, staff rosters reorganised. The clean-up was always messy.

'McLean.' He cradled the phone in the crook of his shoulder, needing both hands to shore up a particularly precarious stack of report folders.

'Seems I owe you an apology, Inspector.'

'Who is this ... ah, Chief Superintendent.' McLean took a moment to recognise the voice of Tim Chambers. 'Is there something I can help you with?'

'Oh, you have already. Ms Violet Grainger, to be precise.'

'You found her?'

'In London, yes. Holed up in the Savoy, of all places. I wanted to let you know. And to thank you for putting us on to her. All those months and years wasted chasing up the two McClymonts and we never got anywhere. Soon as we started looking at the secretary though, the whole thing fell apart.'

'The whole thing? I'm afraid I don't know what you're talking about, sir.'

'Really?' Chambers sounded sceptical. 'Oh well. It'll all come out at the trial. Good a piece of misdirection as I've ever seen. No wonder we couldn't pin anything on father and son. I wouldn't be all that surprised if they didn't know half of what was going on themselves. Except that young Joe was the wizard with the cars. His old man probably didn't have a clue what they were doing though.'

'So what were they doing?' McLean steadied the folders,

picked up a pen and scribbled on a notepad to check whether it worked or not.

'Stealing top-end motors. Giving them a new identity. Shipping some of them overseas. That was one half of it. The other half was a very slick drugs operation. All the proceeds went through the development company. Our forensic accountants are salivating over the details right now, and trust me it takes a lot to get them excited.'

McLean didn't doubt it. The very idea of forensic accountancy made him feel thirsty.

'Just wanted to thank you, really,' Chambers continued. 'If you hadn't put us on to the secretary, we'd have had to tuck this one away as unsolved. Hate having to do that.'

'Well, I'm glad I was a help.' McLean wasn't sure that he had been, but he'd take the compliment anyway.

'Yes, well. If you ever get bored of Edinburgh, give us a shout. Could use a few more detectives who can think outside the box.'

'Umm . . . thanks. I'll bear it in mind,' McLean said, but Chambers had already hung up.

Scaffolding clung to the building facades like metal ivy, yellow and black safety tape wound around it in a parody of flowers. The remains of the burnt-out shops had been bulldozed, leaving just the street door and staircase up to Madame Rose's house. It looked strangely out of place, a gimcrack addition to the building now that the structures to either side were gone.

A month on since she had left his house, taking her cats with her, and McLean had seen and heard nothing from his guest. He still had her letter with its strangely cryptic ending, and he couldn't stop dwelling on the improbable set of coincidences that had led to the discovery of Jim Whitely's body and the capture of the man claiming to be Norman Bale. If they hadn't been investigating the McClymonts, they would still be struggling to make any headway in the Ben Stevenson case, digging deep into the unhappy life of Maureen Shenks. They were all tragic deaths, but hers was the most depressing. Killed simply because she was in the way. Dumped like garbage.

He was with the psychologists now, Norman. Or not Norman. Happy to talk to anyone, it seemed. Some of the senior detectives were worried he was going to get away with an insanity plea, but McLean wasn't much bothered. It was enough that he'd been caught. There wasn't really any doubt that the man was insane, whoever he was. Perhaps spending the rest of his life in a secure psychiatric home was the best thing for him.

Shaking his head at the thought, McLean tried the door. It was locked, and a sign in the window said *'Closed during building works. Regular customers please call.'* He pulled his phone out to make a note of the number, but movement in the corner of his eye dragged his attention away for a moment. He couldn't see what it was at first, then noticed a single cat standing in one of the upper floor windows. It stared at him, blinked lazily, then jumped down from its perch, disappearing into the dark room beyond. McLean stood for a while, waiting to see if it would come back.

'Load of old rubbish that is, fortune telling. Don't waste your money on it, dear.'

He turned to see a little old lady wheeling a tartan shopping trolley down the pavement. She nodded at him as she passed, and before he could say anything she was gone. He still had his phone in his hand, ready to take down the number. There was no need though, he realised. And nothing to be gained from asking the questions he really didn't want to ask. He clicked off the phone and slipped it back into his pocket, began the long walk back to the station.

Acknowledgements

The arcane process of writing is a solitary thing, but every finished book is a team effort. I am very lucky to have a great crew behind me, polishing my grubby little words until they shine. A huge thanks to Alex and all the team at Michael Joseph for making these books as good as they can be. Thanks, too, to Katya and the publicity team who do such a brilliant job of telling the world all about me.

I am forever indebted to my agent, the inimitable Juliet Mushens. There aren't enough thanks in the world for her, but I'll keep sending the pink bubbly as a poor substitute.

I must thank Stuart MacBride too, for my continued misappropriation of his name. What started as a joke between friends all those years ago has rather grown out of control.

Thanks as ever to Barbara for keeping me just about sane. I still do some of the heavy lifting on the farm, but she pretty much runs it day to day now. Without her, this book would have taken a lot longer to write.

David Erskine provided me with much of the information about procedure and technology I have used in the book. If it's right, then that's down to him. Wrong is all me. Many others have helped me along the way. Too many to name here, but you know who you are. Thank you everyone. I owe you at least a drink or two.

And finally my thanks to the good folks at Gilmerton

Cove, who showed me round on a wet Saturday in January 2014. Yes, it's a real place, although I may have embellished it a little. Away from the beaten track of Edinburgh tourist attractions, it's something of a hidden gem, fascinating and eerie. If you find yourself in the capital looking for something to do, I thoroughly recommend a visit. You can find details at www.gilmertoncove.org.uk. Hopefully there won't be any murdered journalists down there when you go.

ALSO AVAILABLE IN THE BESTSELLING INSPECTOR MCLEAN SERIES

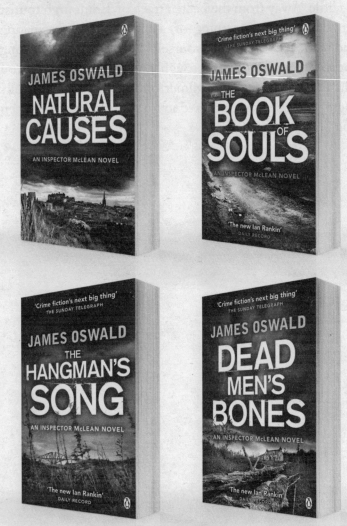

'Oswald's writing is in a class above most in this genre'
Daily Express

BY *SUNDAY TIMES* TOP TEN BESTSELLING AUTHOR JAMES OSWALD